HISTORY OF A DYING PLANET

ALSO BY JAMES SWEARINGEN

Fiction

Black Sheep (2011)

The Prodigals (2013)

In the Hollow of Time, Galatea Saga, I (2021)

Starship Galatea: A Sacred and Profane Time Machine, Galatea Saga, II (2021)

7 Maladies of the Soul (forthcoming)

Nonfiction

Reflexivity in Tristram Shandy (Yale, 1977)

HISTORY OF A DYING PLANET

THE GALATEA SAGA, III

By Yori Kashimoto

Cover layout and Interior Design: Creative Publishing Book Design
Cover designs inspired by Michael Rooks and Jeffrey Cassens

ISBN Paperback: 978-1-7373376-4-5
ISBN eBook: 978-1-7373376-5-2

Printed in the United States of America

"Something festers in the heart of Middle Earth."
—Tolkien, *The Return of the King*

"For although thy people be as the sands of the
sea, yet a remnant of them shall be saved."
—Isaiah 10:22

PART ONE
A Pilgrim's Regress

CHAPTER 1

A YOUNG MAN WANDERED, absentminded and discouraged, down Central Park West toward Midtown Manhattan. Immune to the grumble of traffic a few feet away, to the deafening noise of jackhammers on a nearby construction site, and to the whop-whop of a police helicopter rebounding from the sides of buildings, oblivious even to the pedestrians at his elbow, rushing feverishly to work—none of this affected his concentration until at 66th Street where he turned north again toward the university.

At the corner of Broadway and 66th a chorus of car horns forced his attention to a classic instance of twenty-first-century Ulro rumpus. In his distraction he brushed accidentally against the arm of another pedestrian moving in the opposite direction, and an artist's portfolio fell to the pavement scattering drawings underfoot. Three in particular: the first a royal face of dignity incised in copper, vertically scarified. The second, a figure with deformed cranium and face misshapen by disease, yet as serene and beautiful as the first. And third, a richly carved diviner's tray—all Nigerian drawings instantly recognized as his own forgotten heritage.

When not scrambling about the sidewalks of city streets, he was an imposing man. Descendant of Yoruba chiefs, every inch a prince, tall, quiet, regal. What once was called "a man of parts." Opeyemi Adawale by name, scholarly by temperament; well-spoken in three languages and comfortable in others; new doctorate in hand, recipient of a research fellowship at Columbia where he gave the time of his life to revising a promising, if discouraging, thesis on the cultural origins of global conflict. On all fronts, an uncommon man in an all-too-common world.

As the sea of pedestrians flowed by on all sides, Adawale quickly restored the drawings to the portfolio and looked up at the person they belonged to. A young woman stood over him in traditional Yoruba dress, the *iborun,* with a tie-dyed cotton wrap called the *kuba,* and a colored tie or *gele* folded in circles crowning a line of black hair.

Climbing to his feet, he encountered a glowing face not in the least flustered by the event. Her eyes were laughing at the sight of such a man flailing about on the ground chasing sheets of paper. He responded to the laughter with a shy smile. As he returned the drawings, their eyes met again—but differently. The laughter stopped and the commotion of the city died away as, face to face, each was arrested by a total stranger. Wherever these two had been going a moment before, they weren't going any longer. Before reflecting, they had advanced too far down a new path to turn back.

In Yoruba, Opeyemi apologized. "I'm sorry."

She answered in the same language: "I wouldn't have missed that performance for the world."

He roused himself enough to say, "Have dinner with me."

The laughing eyes turned solemn and she nodded.

"Here." He pointed to the little island of sidewalk under their feet. "At seven."

If this story of Ulro belongs to anyone, it belongs to Opeyemi Adawale, the young Nigerian scholar, divided from himself at birth by the baffling multiplicity of his native land and its five hundred languages. Divided again by transplantation to the Western Hemisphere. Caught between the ancient strains of tribal sensibility and keen critical intelligence, seeking tirelessly for harmony in himself and in his world. His Nigeria had not been a country at all until European colonialism forced it. Then complexity grew with Christianity in the north, Islam in the south, and a Western-style government grafted onto ancestral stock. If Nigeria didn't add up to one world, neither did New York, unless it's one as a soup pot is one.

Even the *uni*-versity was not *one* either. There the outsider appeared as a brilliant, bookish person, alone in a circle of cosmopolitan colleagues. When he needed a rest from dark reflections on a public world that had lost its way, he closed his books and walked to one or another of the parks: west to Riverside, east to Morningside, south to Central Park or, occasionally, into the bustling city where it was easier to escape low spirits than in the tranquility of nature.

The dinner foretold took place that same evening at the appointed hour, the marriage to come was celebrated back in Nigeria, and the couple returned to New York, where Opeyemi spent his days struggling to make sense of global politics while Yetunde studied African tribal art.

In a climate where nothing is forbidden, the story of how a love affair leads to marriage is hardly a story worth telling.

But how love grows between two people absorbed in different lines of work, whose exchanges are more intellectual warfare than tender sentiments—that *is* a story worth telling. These lover-warriors bumped into each other, body and mind, night after night, on the narrow battlefield of a galley kitchen, where each kept a sharp eye out for the illusions of the other.

As when Yetunde, knowing full well what new vitality she had brought into Ope's life, nonetheless mocked his frustration with the messy currents of history. She was likely to say things like this: "You haven't understood your own work. If political life is rooted in old habits and ancient stories, as you say, why do you expect—or even want—things to be tidy?"

Nor were the criticisms less keen from his side. As when, writing an essay for an exhibit catalogue, she became exasperated with the task of conveying Yoruba myths as a coherent system of belief.

Ope replied mischievously, "Nothing so easy. Just tell them that your name means 'Mother has returned,' and that you are a reincarnation of your grandmother, then confirm the point by explaining that the earth was created when Oduduwa's bird scattered dirt on the primordial sea and it became the holy island city of Ile-Ife. Once they've got that bit, they'll understand the Yoruba as beings from the beyond and belonging to a world that is 'a river that is never at rest.' Where's the problem?"

She met the satire with the same wide-eyed disbelief he gave her when she exposed his worship of historical continuity. And she had the credentials.

For generations Yetunde's Yoruba family, the historical Ransome-Kuri family line, had been famous for syncretizing native religions with the religions of the book. Descended from that lively background, she was fascinated by the different names people give to the darkness beyond the present world. Adwale's passionate Western belief that rationality had to defend against such superstitions inspired him to say—more often than he should—"Your stories turn reality into a sea of primordial liquids. It's madness. Real and unreal, truth and error, nature and super-nature, politics and religion all turn to mud. Either the world is composed of discrete objects and intelligible relations or all is chaos and action is impossible."

Where she dreamed of a single key to all mythologies, he dreamed of people who can sit down and reason together. Where she argued that ancient traditions survive unconsciously in symbolic forms, he answered with empirical criticism of mystery-mongering. Each, repelled by the voice of the same axiom in the other, wanted to improve the world by making it consistent. And yet under the influence of Yetunde's sensibilities, Ope's research gradually moved beyond the historical facts of his doctoral thesis toward the narrative or "spiritual" roots of political conflict. Later he would understand—it was to be her legacy—that inventive life requires even violent differences, rooted in deep memory, as between this man and this woman.

Their relationship was prefigured in its beginning, as was much of the unwritten biography of his future. To look back on the life-altering event of little more than two minutes on that New York sidewalk, is to see that they knew each other even before he raised his head and met the glowing face and amused eyes.

In a single leap, she had grasped a predisposition to melancholy in the man at her feet trying to order the fragments of an atomistic world. And the same moment and the very gesture that rescued her scattered images disrupted his fragile harmony as three images of cultural cohesion roused memories that had been laid aside and neglected.

Instantly Adawale knew these images of forgotten kindred rediscovered on a busy street halfway around the world and the effects would become a benchmark in his search for a sound political structure in a doomed world.

As for story of love-at-first-sight, what is worth discovering is how a kaleidoscope of world relations anticipated a love destined to reach maturity only across an uncrossable distance.

Another person in New York also had a beneficial, and wrenching, influence Opeyemi Adawale. Boris Razumovski was a Russian physicist on a research fellowship at Columbia who lived in an adjacent apartment. The two men spent many nights debating the future of the nation-state in a world bent on suicide. On one occasion when they had talked into the early hours of the morning, Ope went home, deep enough in vodka to write a single paragraph that would become the theme of his influential study of planetary culture wars, ancient and modern.

Marriage often weakens the bonds of friendships like his with Razumovski, but this one didn't. Instead, the quiet vigor of Yetunde's intelligence added further dimensions to their long debating sessions until she, who drank less and ranted less than the men, went off to bed or fell asleep on a threadbare sofa in Boris' cluttered sitting room. She regularly reminded both that "an abstract conceptual map of the world is not useful when it leaves out the world it professes to describe." By giving abstraction its proper name, she slowly altered the intellectual climate of these discussions. Yet none of them recognized at the time how the peculiar mix of interests among the three might broaden their perspectives, for the effects on what followed were to be immense.

A year after the marriage, Adawale took his degree and stayed on at Columbia on fellowship, turning his thesis into the book that would attract much attention. He was offered a teaching post at one of the venerable liberal arts colleges that lined the northeast coast of the States. It was an icon of American history set in a pastoral landscape far—or so he thought—from the noisy world of commerce and *realpolitique.* There for the next five years he taught political theory and observed firsthand as higher education in America approached the terminal stages of decline.

Soon enough he discovered that education and the contemplative life, having been found unprofitable for the marketplace, had become dispensable. The ancient passion for understanding had dwindled to administration in service of convention, utility, and, ultimately, pleasure.

So great was his disenchantment that in one afternoon he and Yetunde talked the matter through once more and wrote his letter of resignation in one short paragraph. Almost immediately he accepted a diplomatic post at the UN, and they returned to the city. But at a price. The sudden change meant that Opeyemi was often dispatched to the ends of the earth on confidential missions where he was out of touch with home, and, in one such period, life changed utterly when Yetunde was struck by a truck in the streets of New York and killed.

Before the news reached him somewhere in the depths of eastern Russia, her body was claimed by her family and taken back to Nigeria, and her death stamped "vanity" across the face of all his hopes: *Vanitas vanitatum, omnia vanitas!* In an instant she, who had shielded him from dejection and enriched a life of thought, vanished, and left his world as empty as "a ring that has lost its gem."

But such love is not extinguished in an instant. It remains and *did* remain his one defense against losing faith. Afterwards, he filled the vacancy by searching out cures for the maladies of global civilization. For fifteen years he scarcely looked up from the task or noticed the cumulative effects on his own spirit. That recognition would begin to dawn only when, back in Nigeria visiting family and Yetunde's grave, he was awakened early one morning by an urgent knock on the door and a security officer with an envelope from New York. It contained the following urgent message:

> This officer will drive you to the airport for an imme-
> diate flight to Vienna. On arrival, you are to report
> directly to the UNOV Office for Outer Space Affairs.

CHAPTER 2

EURO FLIGHT 642 FROM Lagos descended from bright sunlight through a blanket of clouds onto a rain-swept runway at Schwechat airport. The passengers were conveyed by bus to International Concourse D, where a disembodied voice announced arrivals and departures:

"Arriving passengers are advised of a local security alert. For surface transportation and security restrictions please check with your airline or with Tourist Information." The anodyne voice sent a wave of uneasiness through the noisy terminal, reducing it to a low grumble. "Passenger Prof. Dr. Opeyemi Adawle, please meet your party in the secure baggage claim area."

A young woman, armed and in uniform, approached from the direction of the main terminal. Officer Beverly Georghiu of the United Nations Security Section in street dress, was an attractive Romanian brunette, but in uniform she was all business, and her business was security. As she held up her badge, the stern unsmiling edge of the official persona was neither personal nor appealing.

"Professor Adawale? Officer Georghiu from United Nations Organization. I'm your driver."

Adawale bowed slightly and offered what passed for a smile on a solemn face. "I heard the alert. No need for your trouble. I could as easily take the U-Bahn."

"Nothing for you to worry about, sir. The trouble is contained inside the city and above ground, but we prefer to avoid the streets and the underground stations."

His annoyance with the whole situation included her, but he didn't think to resist her authority as she took charge of one of his bags and guided him across the terminal to an official car in waiting. Officer Georghiu stowed his luggage, then guided him by the elbow into the back seat of a vehicle that was less car than armored personnel carrier. Inside, a driver with an automatic weapon on the seat beside him was surrounded by detection technology as dense as an armed bunker, with enough firepower to win—or lose—a war. But Adawale was no stranger to heavy security.

With professional detachment Officer Georghiu ignored these details, leaned back into the seat, and addressed the situation with a casual question. "You've been to Vienna before?"

He answered grudgingly. "Not in years. And only as a tourist. Never to the international zone."

She was ready with explanations. "Tensions in the camps have spread to the streets. It happens from time to time. No threat to you, of course. You probably know that the underground city, *Unterstadt*, is extraterritorial and completely secure."

"I am aware of the general conditions," he replied curtly. "It's the year 2070. Human progress has gotten as far as a planetary war zone."

"In Nigeria too?" She kept the talk going against the drag of his uncommunicative disposition as though it was in the line of duty.

Against his will, something in her invited him out of his somber mood. "Not so much in Lagos, but I live in New York. It's the same everywhere. Above ground the teeming masses. Below ground the few who control the wealth of the planet."

"For safety, of course."

"Also environments degraded by decades of recklessness and the homeless masses left to survive as they can. We have become citizens of the underworld."

Georghiu kept the chatter going as they joined the A4 north toward the city. "There are still rural areas in Austria, as in America, where nature is relatively unspoiled. Secure reservations in remote places like the gated communities of the past where city-dwellers can visit on holiday. But people rarely live there."

The bulletproof vehicle passed along a route paralleling the Danube. As it crossed a bridge to the right, Adawale caught a first brief glimpse of the parallel ribbons of water and the grassy banks below. Then the inviting sight vanished.

UNO City was located on an island between old and new channels of the river northeast of the once imperial circle. Across the bridge, the vehicle entered the *Kaisermühlen Tunnel* and passed through security into a garage closed to the public. From the garage, Officer Georghiu guided Adawale an indeterminate distance below ground until the moving sidewalk ended in the light of *Unterstadt,* the underground city where, despite his world-weary melancholy, Adawale was capable of being surprised by several things. One was the extent of the security perimeter. That prompted further explanation.

"Except for the public transportation corridors, we left Austria when we crossed the river. We are now under the jurisdiction of international law."

The second surprise was the apparent extent of the underground. It reminded him of a story about the original architectural competition for the UN office towers somewhere above their present location.

"I remember there was a major engineering problem in building the towers on the river. Something to do with floating tall structures on a bed of sand. How did they solve that problem?"

On this his guide was less well-informed, but she answered, "I've heard something about giant concrete slabs for supporting the towers. I suppose if they could do that, they could do more."

"Does the city extend under the waterways as the tunnels do?"

"I don't know. The maps don't show the dimensions or exactly how the city lies in relation to the terrain. For security reasons, I suppose, but it's a sprawling area that certainly extends under *Donaupark* [Danube Park] to the north of the International Center. Though that would hardly solve the construction problem since there's still water all around."

A brief walk along another concourse led them to an expansive pentagon-shaped atrium. A lobby and lounge area with casual "sidewalk" cafes like a city square including "garden rooms" planted with flowers, hedges, and even shade trees as though for protection from an invisible sun. On each of the five sides of the atrium, banks of elevators stood ready to hurl people skyward through residential towers or into mysterious depths below. The contemporary design of everything in sight offered a stark contrast to the baroque exhibitionism of old Vienna that tourists once came to enjoy.

Pointing in another direction, Officer Georghiu announced the next point on their agenda. "Now I'm to take you to UN security for clearance." As Adawale cringed irritably at the officiousness, her voice brightened momentarily with some amusing, uncensored thought. "Until we can prove who and what you are *not*, we can't be sure who you really *are*. Here identity is a negative reality."

The remark startled him, as though there might be a mind somewhere in that official persona. It brightened his mood just enough for a tired reply. "An unreal real. The same in New York. As puzzling as it is necessary." Then actually looking at her, he added in a marginally personal tone, "Where do you get such odd ideas?"

"I'm a philosophy student at the university, but don't tell. If they knew what goes on in my head, they'd drop me from the program . . . or worse. You know what happens to people with ideas in a template world."

When Adawale said nothing she, perhaps regretting having spoken so openly, pointed upward into the atrium and in a more restrained voice changed the subject. "Your guest apartment is up there."

Looking up through and beyond the glass dome, he observed five towers like glass spears splitting the sky at just the angles to reflect each other endlessly.

Georghiu carried on in a deadpan, tour-guide voice, that imitated a computer imitating a human voice with just a touch of parody. "Many members of the international community live in the towers."

Despite himself Adawale began to recognize behind her determined face something more than an officer in a uniform. The dark intelligent eyes had the intensity of one who misses little and enjoys playing ambiguously along the boundaries of irony. Wasn't she taking a risk with him? The essence of her business was formal impersonality and yet, without knowing him at all, she was slipping in and out of the impersonal mode. Why should that be, in a world where every detail was calculated to the point of cliché?

He took time to observe the towers above and made the effort to connect with this lighter side of her character. "Such buildings are amusing in a somber way. They pretend to be friendly when they're really more forbidding than the stone mansions on the *Ringstrasse*." The reference was to the nineteenth-century baroque mansions on the ring road that followed the footprint of the ancient city walls.

She had no difficulty keeping up. "That's true. Those fortresses were part of the Kaiser's myth-making machine. Wealth and position on display. But these are the real fortresses. Made to *look* welcoming but impenetrable." Her tone suggested that she could lament and laugh at the world at the same time. "No one's admitted without 'clearance.' Odd word 'clearance,' isn't it? Systems hate things unique and unpredictable. They want everything exposed except themselves."

These momentary lapses into real discourse may have been Georghiu's way of managing Adawale, but it didn't seem like management. More like wanting to win his favor. Why? What could he be to her?

As promptly as she had emerged from it, Georghiu shrank again into the bureaucratic role. Leading the way from the lobby by another concourse, she proceeded to UN headquarters and the plethora of international agencies that fanned out around three midrise towers. In addition to commissions on the environment and trade, there was a High Commissioner for Refugees, an Office on Drugs and Crime, an International Atomic Energy Agency, and a host of bureaus less well publicized.

Apparently Adawale's business was with none of these, as Georghiu led through a door marked "Office of Security." Not only did he not know why he'd been brought so urgently to Vienna, he had no idea what the agency mentioned might be—or who might be—responsible. But he obediently presented his credentials and was immediately cleared. Now as an official VIP, he and his personal security escort retraced their steps to the lobby.

With the innocent tinkling of a bell, a transparent capsule opened before them and the machine whisked them up twenty floors into the louring Austrian sky, where Georghiu led him down a hall into a well-appointed apartment. The proportions were European, roughly half the size of his New York residence. But then there was the view, or so he was free to imagine. The glass wall looked out across the Danube toward the old city where, under dark skies and through rain, there was little to see.

The ever-helpful agent turned guide pointed in the direction of various landmarks—*the cathedral, Hofburg Palace, Karlskirche,* the *Belvedere*—though only the flèche of the cathedral were visible through the haze. Georghiu didn't appear to be the kind who would waste time on such pleasantries, and yet she rushed less than seemed consistent with a security detail.

"Your itinerary is on the table. You are expected in the Office for Outer Space Affairs as soon as is convenient. You go back into the UN building and follow the signs."

Then, resuming the more personal manner that seemed to turn on and off at will, "At five o'clock you will be met downstairs by another person, but if you have free time before the appointment, you may want to explore *Ünterstadt.* It's self-contained and totally secure. The public spaces are well-marked and unrestricted to you. None of the dangers we encounter out there," pointing across the river toward the inner city that, from this distance, looked tranquil enough. "You will see all that for yourself too, but I'm instructed to tell you that you may not leave UNO City except with security agents and, for now, that's me. Sorry about that."

On his own at last, Ope freshened up from his flight, went downstairs, and crossed the lobby once more to the administrative center, presumably to meet the unknown person responsible for this abrupt and pointless trip. Even on the way to the Lagos airport, he had fired off protests to New York arguing that it was a waste of time and money to send a theoretician into the thick of practical affairs he knew nothing about. Except for a passing reference to "planetary unrest," he received no explanation of the summons or its urgency.

It was an assignment that he would have preferred to refuse. Instead, he objected strongly enough to force an explanation, but his superiors in New York ignored his objections without a pretense of reasons. They replied only: "You are urgently needed." To refuse would have been to set his own judgment against the broader perspective of the diplomatic corps. So in the end—an end the more irritating for coming a mere two hours after the order was issued—he complied, and for twelve hours between Lagos and Vienna, gnawed on the mystery with increasing irritation.

With this bitter taste in his mouth and a hornet's nest of questions, he arrived at an office devoted to matters as far as possible from his experience. A discreet sign on the door instantly answered the question, who? and silenced the questions, why? and for how long?

UN Office for Outer Space Affairs
Dr. Boris Razumovski, Director

CHAPTER 3

THERE'S MYSTERY ENOUGH in the name on the door to scramble all Adawale's ideas without noticing the reference to "space." The name Razumovski hints at some reason behind the mystery after all. When his old friend, the physicist, completed his postdoc in New York, he returned to Europe. Since then, the two had met whenever they happened to be on the same continent but, as Adawale was so often in the Western Hemisphere, Africa, or the Far East, the meetings were infrequent.

Suddenly the office door opens and Boris rushes forward with an enthusiastic bear hug that leaves Ope breathless. Before he can utter a word, he's pushed through another door, into a chair, and a drink thrust into his hand. Slowly he collects himself and begins observing the little things that give context to the scene: Razumovski, as vigorous and gregarious as ever, is a bit wider in girth, and has advanced from vodka to whiskey but not as far as *Grüner Veltliner.*

Boris raises his glass, then pauses long enough to note the gloomy face of his grad school neighbor before pushing the pensive moment aside. "Welcome to Vienna, my friend. Sorry I had to insist. Eventually you'll understand."

Two people could hardly be more different in disposition. The Russian peasant, all jubilance and surface without depth; the Nigerian prince, melancholy enough to give subtlety a bad name. The animation of the former is matched by features that might be called average Russian—light skin, greyish-green eyes, thin lips and eyebrows, straight nose—typical except for prominent cheekbones that suggest a distant Tatar strain. Not of the boisterous kind, but of a cheerful, open temperament from which little might be expected in the way of finesse.

Ope replies in a tone intended to sound cheerful. "You're looking well, Boris." Four words before irritation slips back into his voice. "It would help to be told right off why I'm so unceremoniously summoned to Vienna."

The question is met with a sprightly riposte. "It's that book of yours, of course! On the global malaise." This verbal explosion does not entirely conceal a sigh and a momentary stare at Adawale's enduring innocence. "'The child is father of the man,' they say. It's what happens when you give birth. You become the creature of your own creation. The thing has made a stir and now you have to answer for it." Another chortle doesn't conceal a keen and inquiring eye.

"It's gratifying to have readers." Adawale replies sardonically. "But since the people you know can read, they don't need me. I've had my say." He sips his drink ponderously. "And why the secrecy? Planetary tensions are the moment-by-moment stuff of public gossip. Kindly explain."

Boris sighs again. Apparently, it's his day for deep breathing and shallow answers. "I can tell you this much. But it will only deepen the mystery. There are decisions pending that could not be more important for the future of the planet!

21

These decisions must be made covertly or they will not be made at all. Your ideas are at the center."

He peers at Ope from beneath the line of expressively shifting eyebrows. "The most important thing I can tell you is that before we meet again you will be given an extensive—and, if I know you, an irritating—initiation. Like nothing you've had before. And it won't be easy. You'll meet people who are important to our work, but they will know no more than you about why you're meeting. And they won't necessarily know one another. You'll have to trust me that all this will make sense in time."

Adawale has been around enough security operations to know better than protest. "Since I have no choice, I choose to cooperate."

At this Razumovski appears to relax as though a great deal has been at stake and some unspecified danger has safely passed. He picks up another strand of the general question—why Opeyemi for this assignment? "At this moment, you speak with authority across our loose network. Partly it's because you have your hand in both pies: theory and practice, the scholar's world and everyday diplomacy. At least that's the best answer you'll get today. On some topics of interest to us no one can speak better than you. But to put the point bluntly, your fine mind and sensibilities must first be subjected to experience that doesn't come in the library *or* in government bureaucracies. *Ergo* the initiation."

With a shake of his head Ope asks impatiently, "You expect the babblings of an intellectual to change the world by the middle of next week?"

Razumovski, perhaps dodging the time limit, makes no further response, so Ope asks, "When I meet your people, what am I supposed to add? Or am I to nod and smile and free-associate?"

"Probably." Again Boris laughs with high cheer. "You'll mainly answer questions and ask whatever *you* want to ask. There's a loose network out there representing the various global cultures you've studied. You'll meet some like-minded people who speak eloquently about the eclipse of education, a planet ruined by machinery and greed, population growth, looming pandemics, shrinking resources, a global plutocracy, the impoverished multitudes. About the stateless, the 'guest workers' without civil rights, the unemployable, the street poor, and good old-fashioned sloth—the range is limitless. Your research has deepened the perspectives of people who were trained to stop at social surfaces.

"Thanks largely to you"—he points a finger—"the conversation has been opened to deep cultural history. Many of these people will share your outlook, but some may fight you on the issues tooth and nail."

Adawale raises a skeptical brow. "The people in this international seminar sound better prepared for your work than I am."

That remark is allowed to pass. "Eventually we'll gather here to discuss foreseeable consequences and practical alternatives. What I need from you is not your knowledge but your instincts. Your touch." A guffaw punctuates this quite serious speech. "You know, I haven't forgotten those all-night conversations on the Upper West Side."

Petulantly Ope skips the reference to their school days. "So I've come all this way to preach to the choir!"

Razumovski gives him a shrewd glance and lays aside the light-hearted tone. "My friend, you have always exaggerated the power of an argument and underrated the voice of authority. It's the intellectual's foible. Take my word for it, you'll do more good than you can imagine."

What Boris does not say, what Adawale will learn only gradually, is that he is playing his last best card, gambling that the man in front of him can somehow help avoid global catastrophe. What he knows and depends on is that Opeyemi is a man of integrity with the courage to pursue a reasonable course of action at any cost.

"You're to be my guinea pig. Between one moment and the next there's an abyss that historical knowledge can't bridge. And yet we must act. I've read the book and I've reviewed the impressive diplomatic dossier you've accumulated since. You're here for your experience, your truthfulness, and your well-honed sensibilities."

He lowers his voice and becomes almost grave. "I also know you have reached the point of hopelessness. In dire times only a man at the limit, without illusions, can be trusted." His tone lightens. "So which disaster shall we choose? Noah's flood and build a boat? The fires of Sodom and Gomorrah? The fate of Atlantis? Or have we run out of precedents and must act in the dark? First, we get the well-versed scholar and push him into the void where all his knowledge counts for nothing but where decisions are made!"

That sweeping aside of experience in favor of "subjective judgment" sets off all Opeyemi's alarms, and Boris, seeing as much, tries to soften the point. "I want to know how you personally would gamble on the future of the species. I'm hoping that your cautious judgment may be a clue to what, if anything, might be done."

Then, as though he's already said more than he intended, Razumovski resorts to analysis. "You have always trusted knowledge. That's probably key to your despair. But authority doesn't come from knowing. It comes from character, and character is the accretion of the disciplined life. In the next few weeks, you'll be exposed to global reality as seen from *our* vantage point. From hot spots to the whole thing: past, present, future! People who trust your instincts more than your knowledge will be watching how the situation registers on *you*."

As though to evade the seriousness of a speech that changes everything, Adawale lays his misgivings aside for a trivial question. "If there's so much at stake, why here? Why Vienna? Every megalopolis on the planet is under siege. Why choose a smallish city in the middle of Europe, however distinguished its history?"

It's an easy question, and Boris is grateful. He mentions the proximity of the UN global agencies, then speaks of Vienna as symbol. Especially its historical resonances with culture conflicts during centuries on the frontier between Europe and Asia Minor.

"Everybody remembers The Great Siege of 1683 when the Ottoman Empire came within minutes of destroying the city. As a symbol of Western Christianity, it was hardly inferior to Rome in defending the faith against the Protestants in the north even as it resisted the Catholic Sun King's expansionist ambitions from the west."

Aside he adds, "In this I'm not defending the Hapsburgs or their Romanoff cousins. I'm pointing to what the city meant as when, much later, it, like Berlin, was divided between the allies and the Soviet Union after the Second Great War. The shards of the Habsburg empire and of Christian Europe make the old capital a symbolic site where the paths of political experience have crossed so often."

The historical topic significantly lightens Ope's mood. He lays aside his complaints and begins to look for coherence. "If Vienna is a symbol, then you must intend to go public with some plan. What's the mission of your shadowy organization?"

Boris dodges again. "No organization. More like a think-tank without walls or formal membership. Not your ordinary horse farm where old officials are put out to pasture. But there's another reason for Vienna. This city has always been Janus-faced. Symbol of rank conservatism and unrestrained imagination. Sometimes together. As when the last Emperor Franz Joseph perpetuated an empire on pure fiction and had the space of the old city walls lined with all those baroque palaces. Its glory always *was* half-mythical. What glory isn't? It's the Viennese spirit of invention, the old vitality that survives in much of the greatest music from Haydn to the present and in the Secessionist movement that dragged it from artistic parochialism to leadership in painting, architecture, and the crafts across Europe."

Adawale remains silent after this extravagant speech, sitting quietly, contemplating his friend who is, by rights, the archetypal outsider here, however great his pride in the city. He manages a faint smile and says, "You love this place, don't you? Even in the world's twilight."

"Yes, I am running on a bit. But my point is that the city with two faces is a fitting site for our clandestine efforts. It parallels our global political dilemma." Abruptly he jumps up as though the time has come for action. Looking down at his still cogitating friend, he announces, "Now it's time for your real-world orientation to begin. We want you to see the streets and visit refugee camps to get the flavor of life among the migrating multitudes and the natives who want them sent back to homes they've never had. Meanwhile, try to cut us a little slack. There's more going on in our shop than meets the eye." He chuckles. "I'm passing you along to a psychiatrist. I believe you already know Mamud Çelik?"

Adawale takes the hint and rises. "I was hoping to see him. We've been friends nearly as long as you and I. We were together at the UN in New York when he was a member of the Turkish delegation." Adawale looks at his watch. "Your security officer mentioned the meeting but not the name."

"You may depend on Officer Georghiu. Something she may not tell you is that she and Mamud's son Kemal are engaged. It's a sensitive topic with the father. All about religion and familial stuff." He pauses long enough for Ope to wonder why he's dropping that bit of information.

"Right down your street: conflict of civilizations! Kemal, the son, is an inspector with UNO Security. He often serves as mediator between the refugees and Austrian officials. Anyway, I'm handing you off to Mamud. He'll arrange for you to see whatever he thinks you need to see next. But it won't be tourism. A great deal depends on *what* you see and *how* you see it. You are to regard conditions in Vienna—above and below ground—as Everywhere, Planet Ulro."

"What does 'handing off' mean?"

"You'll be passed along from person to person. Each will decide where to send you next. I pass you on to Mamud and he'll hand you off to others, sometimes in clandestine ways. It may feel like being handled by the KGB or the CIA of yesteryear. Just keep what you learn in airtight compartments. I can't overemphasize the sensitivity of our work. If there even is a work, it's connected by random tunnels that even *I* don't have a map to."

"So," he slaps his hands together ebulliently, "With that I'll let you go."

Adawale, summarily dismissed, refuses to budge and declines the proffered hand. "Since you are the one responsible for this assignment, I'm going nowhere until I find out one more thing. I want to know that I am not being used for purposes I might not endorse."

Boris leans against the edge of his desk, chews on his upper lip a moment, then answers in a tone reassuringly free of artifice. "You are now in an intelligence zone more sensitive than you have been in before." His manner becomes quite grave. "Security is so in-secure that you and I can't even walk in the park together. You wouldn't think that this office where I shuffle papers would be so sensitive that I can't meet the people closest to me. If we were to take a walk in *Donaupark*, we would fall under surveillance from international agencies that blanket this place. When I say that there is no plan for your activities, I'm saying that even to plan would invite compromise. So the only rule around you will be spontaneity. Pure randomness. At some indeterminate point, you will be passed back to me and then we'll see what's to be done. All is contingency."

Without a word, Adawale continues to hold his gaze skeptically, waiting for an answer.

Razumovski insists. "On the honor of old times you must trust me. If this comes to anything at all, you will not have been compromised. You will have been listened to and your judgment will have been instrumental. For now, please follow orders and keep your activities to yourself. Ask lots of questions. Everyone will answer your questions. And note this: You have *one* month or a little more to perform an unspecified task. Your success or failure will determine one of the most momentous decisions in the history of life on Planet Ulro."

And on that not altogether reassuring speech the two parted. Afterward, Adawale stood in the hall, stunned by Razumovski's closing sentence and staring at the sign on the office door: Office of Outer Space Affairs. Space indeed! Boris must have been assigned to this meaningless closet of the UN bureaucracy because he'd lost his marbles.

CHAPTER 4

BLESSEDLY FREE of his official minder and with time on his hands, Adawale decides to play along with Officer Georghiu's suggestion that he explore the underground city. Razumovski has essentially said that he is to accept all suggestions as polite orders, so he will. Besides, he has eaten nothing since the overnight flight.

From the moment he steps onto the moving sidewalk, the thought of food is eclipsed by a new uneasiness. This posh urban cave is a world of endless walls, a fortress. Above, below, on every side, a polished, spacious, comfortable domain—without the human. People, of course, but an oblivion of earth and sky, of habitable space and human time. Are they, all these walls, for walling *out* or walling *in*? Neither? Both? Or is the point to separate and protect people from one another, people being inherently unpredictable?

From the foundations of the United Nations buildings, he passes the Austria Center, the European Union building, and on into a vast mall on several levels containing every commercial establishment of a modern city: food and beverage stores, clothing shops, restaurants, wine bars, and specialty shops. And not goods only but services: financial, medical, entertainment, educational, even religious. However used or unused, it's the global economy replicated and secured from contamination.

Subterranean temples to commerce providing space in over-crowded cities and comfort in extreme climates were not a twentieth-first-century invention. When "economy" still meant the ordering of hearth and home and, later, the Creator's distribution of forces in the creation—even then the underground was already associated with survival and the infinite. The Roman catacombs, the volcanic cavities like Kaymakli and Derinkuyu in Cappadocia or Gaziemir on the Silk Road were refuges from ancient enemies, burial grounds, retreats from violence, or places of worship.

But why here? A thing of wonder, of course. A marvel of engineering. The map at the entrance only hints at the proportions of the project. Yet why the expenditure in untold wealth and years of construction? Nuclear war aside, modern urban conditions were not so precarious as to justify this scale. Was it—is it—another massive over-response of collective anxiety?

Everywhere a neutral tone prevails, so perfectly adjusted to human uses that experience is superfluous: air of just the right temperature; light, perfect for seeing without having to look; anodyne music to deaden the tomb-like silence. The universal atony reminds Adawale of a brief stay in the hotel of a Las Vegas casino: a no-place where time, space, and world were suspended in service of gratifying desire.

In such spaces, sensitivity to place, direction, and duration is vestigial. Unless there are limits to the flexibility of the most flexible of species, wouldn't such faculties eventually deteriorate from lack of use? Would anyone with a satellite positioning system notice if all signs of direction were removed? No need here for the ubiquitous arrow-shaped signs that once marked the forks in country roads—this way to Paris, that way to Rome. In the *Ünterstadt* a stupefying transparency makes Adawale long for the inconvenience of the wrong turn, but how to lose the way where there are no *ways* to lose? "Ways" are excluded and along with them random encounters.

Once upon a time uncertainty was regarded as freedom and space for invention, but these pristine corridors exclude even the reference points that make up "a world." Above-ground law enforcement is an international "growth industry," but below ground it is present everywhere, visible nowhere.

In a lighter vein but still revealing, the underground reminds Adawale of twentieth-century conspiracy theories like the alleged tunnel from coast to coast of North America. It was supposed to have been constructed with atomic-powered tunneling machines called "subterrenes," intended of course for nefarious purposes. These magical devices were said to bore through mountains, reducing the debris to nuclear waste as it went. Spurious of course, but a reminder that the underground, no less than the heavens, has psychic roots deeper than memory.

Then remembering his hunger, he chooses a restaurant from several on offer where he orders his first Viennese coffee and pastry. He's enjoying a second mélange, when an attractive Chinese woman enters in a *qipao*. The traditional form-fitting dress is black silk and sleeveless, with an embroidered bamboo design that forms a gentle green s-curve down the front. The high collar enhances the appealing formality and the long slim line. Opeyemi, lacking the vocabulary of fashion, does not appreciate a style that has endured—the

Maoist era excepted—since the seventeenth century. And that's too bad, since it would appeal to the critic of a restless throwaway culture.

The woman takes a seat a bit to one side and some twenty feet away, facing him almost near enough for conversation. A spectator, if there were one, might find the choice curious where so many tables are available, might even suspect that she was deliberately observing him and willing to be seen doing so. Not being especially adept at such social dances, Ope only feels uncomfortable and takes care not to be seen noticing her.

She orders an ice café then dallies for some time with her spoon. Neither is unaware of the other's presence, though, being strangers, they say nothing, and Ope's mind wanders to the barely related fact that Austrians, so devoted to their desserts and sweetened coffees, remain shapely and fit.

Nothing more until, a few minutes later, the woman puts money on the table and walks away, leaving a shoulder bag hanging on the back of her chair.

"Madame," he calls to the receding figure. "Your bag."

She returns, retrieves the bag, and thanks him with a smile just warm enough to create a memory of herself.

CHAPTER 5

LATER IN THE AFTERNOON, when the bell rings at Opeyemi's apartment, he opens the door on his second oldest friend. Dr. Mamud Çelik greets him with a bright voice, a warm embrace, and a long-forgotten salutation: "What a delightful surprise! May the peace of Allah be upon you, my friend. I got a call just a few hours ago saying you were in town."

The two reunions of the day are of strikingly different character. The relation with Boris is like the old college friend with whom, after a lapse of years, one picks up the intellectual jousting match just where it left off. Also affectionate, but in the key of cerebral interests between colleagues who may breathe together without sharing a common universe.

With Çelik the relationship is intimate beyond even the personal, a rapport in spirit outside the measures of time. No first question like, "What have you been doing with your life meanwhile?" or "How is the family?" A bond in spirit that rejoins an interrupted conversation, begun years before, about a world of ultimate concern.

They chat for a while, looking from the sitting-room window into the dim natural light beyond, unconscious of the panorama that Officer Georghiu so carefully described earlier in this eventful day. The two make another study in contrasts: the African prince, tall, dark-skinned and solemn, and the Turk, relatively short, energetic, and joyful.

Çelik is a robust man in his late fifties with slightly unkempt grey hair and an affectionate grin. A healthy girth and comfortable folds of flesh convey physical vigor and well-being undiminished by his years. By profession he's a physician with long experience in treating the psychic maladies that afflict the modern world. Besides overflowing good humor and lovable, almost boyish charm, his authority radiates warmth.

As they renew old friendship Çelik's attention turns to the five residence towers that overlook UNO plaza below. Gesturing toward the ground, he remarks, "Twenty-first century-UNO City looks more like twentieth-century America or twenty-first century Dubai or Beijing than old Vienna, don't you think? Do you remember these buildings when they were outside the security perimeter?"

"This is my first time across the river."

"The plaza used to be living space." He points again into the chasm below them. "People lingered on the pavement: office workers out for a smoke, mothers with baby strollers, children playing, pedestrians wandering about on a sunny fall day. Now it's been 'secured,' and no one lingers. Wastepaper and fast-food trash sweep by as the wind crosses the concrete wasteland, and, seen from below, the towers thrust abruptly up from those great slabs, dwarfing human proportions." He reduces the dreariness of these dreary remarks by a hearty laugh.

In the intervening years, Ope has forgotten Mamud's instinct for seeing the extraordinary in the banal and how his conversation characteristically mixes the two.

"These buildings," he continues, "are an emblem of Western individualism, quite different from the instincts of older collective cultures. Like the masks of people, staring blindly at each other without communication. So these towers: proximity related only by the void between. From here"—he points to the building directly opposite—"those dark windows are hundreds of vacant eyes glowering across an abyss. The builders were such masters of deception that they deceived themselves."

Ope searches for, rather than asks, his meaning.

"All this glass is a lie. It promises vision. Invites us to look through and see truly. And we do, but the truth we see is the truth of deception!"

The remarks remind Ope how often in the early years of this friendship he had been fascinated by Mamud's capacity to live with a light heart in a dark world. Once he had raised the question and Mamud had remarked, "It's faith in God and the 'two kingdoms.' That comes from the Hebrew God, not from the Prophet. One who can't distinguish the profane kingdom of this world from the kingdom of God will go mad. To live in both at once requires faith."

Opeyemi, the secularist, finds nothing helpful in the remark either then or now. But it does provoke a different question: How could such a man of education and science knowingly deceive himself? Especially an analyst who devoted his life to treating incurable delusions in a psychiatric clinic.

As the two turn back from the window Ope lays a hand on Mamud's arm and remarks with a feeble smile, "I've never understood how you can see so much and be so cheerful. You say it's faith, but faith in what?"

"For you it's faith in contingency; for me, faith in Allah." Persisting in this animated mood, he adds, "I wonder if 'contingency' and 'God' may be two facets of the same thing. If so, mine conveys more information."

He punctuates the remark with a quiet laugh. "At least where all is contingency, despair is premature. We don't positively know that the world is about to end, so why not be grateful for today and being here to witness such complex times?"

They settle down together in the living room of an anonymous guest suite, and Adawale apologizes for having nothing to serve since he arrived only that morning and has yet to learn how to negotiate this strange new world.

"If the following proposal suits you, I'd like to introduce you to Aylin, my wife."

"It would be a pleasure."

"She's heard about you for years but the three of us have never been in the same place at the same time."

Ope having agreed, he continues. "In a while we'll drive to my apartment on the north side near the university. The two of you can get acquainted over a simple meal. Then the two of us can have a good talk. My son Kemal is on duty tonight—he's an inspector in UNOV Security. He would also like to meet you. He'll stop by in the evening if he can."

That settled, Çelik asks what has brought him so unexpectedly to Vienna, to which Adawale replies, "I have no idea. I'm just following orders that have no detectable rationale."

Then he adds, with a shrug and a deep sigh of resignation, "All I know is that the world is going to hell and I'm
apparently here to help it along." He continues in a tone of
nostalgia. "You and I must have been together last in Cairo,
wasn't it? We spent a long evening in the hotel discussing the
state of the world. It was bleak enough then, but just when
you think things can't get worse, they do."

"True," Mamud replies, without dropping his cheerful
mode. "You've spent a decade and a half on the frontlines of
these conflicts. I wonder how you assess the situation."

Being more interested in the personal than the geopolitical,
Çelik listens differently from others, attending to the music
of a speech as much as the bundling of ideas. What he picks
up in Ope's response is a certain disjointedness. The ideas are
perfectly ordered, but they come out as a litany of complaints
in a voice that sounds neutral to the point of indifference.

"Our cleverness has defeated us at last. We've built systems
so complex and so fast that we can't keep up, as though we
had lost all sense of the human scale of time and space.
What we call 'expertise' has eclipsed the general view of
things by breaking the world into bits of data with the result
that 'practical people' have no idea what practicality is for.
'Collateral damage' has become a cliché, but the truth is, we
know nothing of the consequences of what we do."

The analyst doesn't miss the quick transition from
personal disappointment, or that Adawale's critique extends
far beyond his old preoccupation with political decline.

"Your historical analyses of cultural contexts seem to have
deepened since we last met."

"The parallel increase in our technical power and our ignorance of ourselves is hard to ignore. We're trapped by circumstances of our own making that we don't understand. Blind change proceeds at lightning speed, while cultural maturity moves at glacial rates, if at all. We have no idea what we're doing! If we could, we'd do to the universe what we've done to the planet. All in blindness. If by some miraculous infusion of wisdom, we tried to undo what we've done, the undoing would end in a ball of fire. There are no imaginable means of stopping the race to destruction. Nothing can save us now."

None of this outburst quite fits. The music and the words seem barely to communicate with each other. So instead of responding to the hopelessness, Mamud gets up and strolls to the window with his hands behind his back, where he gazes out at the melancholy rain. Then, moving back into the room, he pauses to turn on a light before sitting down in a different chair. It's as though he were demonstrating that when nothing can be done, something unexpected, however trivial, inevitably follows.

Not to let his lament kill the conversation, Ope asks, still in the mood of despair, "Where do you think we went wrong?"

The two men know each other too well to feel compelled to fill every silence with words, and Mamud doesn't rush into this insoluble problem. He gives Ope a long, searching look and speaks in a more somber tone.

"It's hard to say just where we went wrong. Perhaps in the modern habits of thinking that we're so proud of. We had no idea where our calculative cleverness might lead. We learned how to think by connecting rational, algebraic x's and y's, thinking to secure our place in a contingent universe. Perhaps we need instead to think on a model of infinite fields of shifting relations and unknowable consequences. Once upon a time we knew that even the stars moved in proximity with all our acts. But that got swallowed up in a clockwork universe where we, practical people, thought we could know where we're going."

Another long, silent contemplative moment follows before Mamud resumes from a distant point.

"When you're free I want to take you to our clinic. I promise it will be worth your time. You'll see the global problem through a different lens. People who can no longer cope with life in any world."

Ope passes over the proposal in an oblique and disjointed reply. "I may recognize them. At moments when I'm not immersed in trying to understand, I, too, no longer belong and often don't care to go on."

"I see that. Things change too fast and generally for the worse. As the world loses coherence, so do we. We who are supposed to be able to make coherence."

Then, to relieve a mood that is not especially healthy, however realistic, he slaps his knees and announces in a quite different voice, "But first I'm going to take you home to dinner."

CHAPTER 6

THE ÇELIK FLAT IS IN an ancient neighborhood near the university. It's a small but architecturally elegant space with a contemplative atmosphere. When Ope comments on the comfort of the arrangement, contrasting his UNOV apartment, attractively designed but institutional and sterile, Mamud replies, "A house is a second skin, don't you think? It should have the shape of the life lived there. Comfortable as a suit of old clothes."

Aylin Çelik has been a name in Adawale's world for years, but when he sees her, he's startled. She is tall and straight, one might even say regal. At first glance one who didn't know Mamud's character and distinction might think them a terrible mismatch. Aylin, olive-complected with dark hair and the doe-shaped, soulful eyes of her people, is from an old Istanbul family and so cosmopolitan in appearance as to make Mamud seems folksy.

Nor does the relation between the two resemble the traditional patriarchy that outsiders often expect in a Muslim home. Aylin Çelik's manner is visibly more modest and reserved than her husband's, but as the three sit down together and plunge into a conversation more about catching up on the past than ice breaking, she is unrestrained and welcoming.

41

Mamud is clearly proud of her. He mentions that in Turkish "Aylin" means "halo of the moon." He beams with affection. "She has always loved studying languages and was a Turkish translator at the UN. Now she has all the occupation she wants as a translator."

When Ope asks about her current project, she replies, "A translation of a female Turkish novelist."

To which Mamud adds, "She's contracted to provide German and English at the same time, if you can believe it."

"The fact is," she explains, "I have one of many deadlines tomorrow, so I'll have to ask you to excuse me after dinner. You two can catch up."

During a meal consisting of a simple and excellent lamb stew served with Ekmek bread and a salad, the conversation remains general. Aylin joins in with perfect memory of the men's days at the United Nations in New York as well as their encounters during the intervening years.

They had met during a long night in Manhattan when both were stranded, awaiting the result of a protracted UN negotiation, and the conversation had been extraordinary. Mamud was an anomaly to his younger African colleague: the urbane citizen of the world who had shed none of his religious heritage. He spoke freely of his ethnic background: "You know, we Turks have only been Muslims for a thousand years. When we accepted Islam, it was much more than a warrior culture. Highly learned and not at all limited to what the twentieth-century West, conveniently forgetting its own imperialist history, called 'radical Islam.'"

In those New York days, Ope was a thorough skeptic. And the sliver of common ground between them was based on the spread of Islam to Yoruba culture in nineteenth-century Nigeria and the rise of Protestant Christianity in the twentieth. So the conversation bridged a great divide between history and experience.

Using language punctuated with the phrases of his devout tradition, Çelik spoke in their New York conversation of the great age of Islamic scholarship that had been essential to the rise of Scholasticism, the beginnings of the Western university, and the European Renaissance. "I hope Islam may contribute again to a new Renaissance. The world needs—and we need—a different kind of renewal. Without the moralism of a Western Reformation or the nihilism of the individual. The *Qur'an* isn't a book on the art of war, you know. Above all, it's a book of mercy, a sacred book. Like all books that speak of 'the highest,' it must be read as a book of praise: 'Glory to God who never changes.'"

Since those days in New York Mamud had devoted much time to encouraging mutual understanding among Islamic, Jewish, and Christian worlds, occasionally even among Muslims, Hindus, and Buddhists. Not that he had become a prophet of liberal tolerance and certainly not of the evisceration of all religion that he saw as the death of imagination. Just that he foresaw a system that reduced multiplicity to unity—a language, a person, or a city—becoming an inhuman machine. Years of experience in psychoanalysis had helped him discover the worth of differing ancestral stories and ideals passing down the generations. There the two men, and now Aylin, share broad understanding.

Since that night in New York, Adawale's certainties had been unsettled by the effects of the "enlightened" planetary system and by the posthumous influence of Yetunde's understanding of native Nigerian religions, making him sufficiently amphibious to enjoy friendships and seek exchanges across this and other cultural divides.

An hour into these recollections, Aylin offers Turkish coffee with a pastry and retires to her work, leaving the men to table talk that shifts to the present world.

"We have always observed from different angles," Ope remarks. "I wonder what basis for hope you now see for the planet."

Çelik's gaze intensifies. "That question is unworthy of you, my friend. Hope is only expectation when it hopes for foreseeable conditions. It's a fateful mistake to regard it as an end in view. Hope is a state of more-than-mind that keeps us focused on the game and at home with ourselves."

The curious remark helps clarify something Ope had detected earlier in the day. Except for the Chinese woman in the restaurant, the faces of people in the corridors of the underground all bore the marks of strain and anxiety, as if they were living on the edge of an abyss. The bodies leaned forward in a vaguely aggressive manner, forcing their way through a resistant substance with gestures that were not their own. The impression of universal paranoia inspired a question. "What does the analyst know from his talking cure that the political theorist should also learn?"

Mamud grinned. "That he can know nothing!"

Ope laughs a bit darkly. "So you wise men of ventriloquy rather than science have no answers."

An impish smile counters Ope's solemnity. "Always answering, never concluding. People are moved either by necessity or by love. All we have to work with is language, the talking cure—if there is one—for the speaking being."

As Ope waits for more, he explains, "Our task is to miss nothing. Not so much as the changing rhythms or tones of words, slips of the tongue, odd transitions between ideas, the random gesture. We must notice everything, remember everything, and accept the hard work of piecing together beings who are always unfolding in a world. We're not knowers, we're gamblers. Words are our dice, and each die has a thousand sides. We gamble on words as poets gamble on the unsayable, hoping to trigger discovery in the patient him- or herself."

"Then you and the political thinker are both embarrassed by the question of knowledge."

"For us the enemy is fixation on a thing called 'the medicalized body.'"

"Hence the term 'biologism.' But do explain."

"Suffering and death are natural enemies of the organism, but is a person solely organic? That's an axiom and, like all axioms, it's unproven. The assumption carries conviction, but so did phrenology and the virgin birth! Naturally"—he underscores the irony by repeating the word—"*naturally* we treat the biological entity as the baseline of human being. But psychic life may be more than *natural*. It also functions symbolically and suffers symbolic deficits. What's true of the body may not be true of the whole process. Sometimes when we fight the enemies of the organism, our interventions reduce the value of life by encouraging people to fixate on health."

He makes a gesture of resignation, both hands extended, palms outward. "Psychoanalysis proposes a working hypothesis—a theory, a vision, a myth if you like—of how the organic becomes something more than organic and must be treated differently. It's a matter of coping with the day that's given."

"Mind and body. The eternal dilemma."

"And with only a rough 'working idea' of what either of the terms might properly mean. The naturalists must limit their field if they're to verify anything, so the neurologist works from body toward mind, while we propose to work in both directions at once with rival procedures. Like the old Greeks learning to tunnel through a mountain from both directions until they met in the middle. The problem is to find the middle, if there is one."

Ope muses for a moment. "So the organic procedure starts with the simple and 'reconstructs' the whole."

"Yes, so long as we remember that both whole and parts are hypothetical."

At that, Ope seems almost to forget his discouragement. "The metaphor of building as a daylight operation helps, but you people seem to spend your lives mucking around underground. *Can* different metaphors meet?"

Mamud appears to take encouragement from the hint that contrary paths of research might grow from different metaphors. "Our clinic stands nearly in the shadow of the building where Freud lived. A few blocks away he sat behind the famous couch in that tiny room overlooking a tiny garden, revealing the darkest secrets of the human soul since original sin. Many developments and many revisions later, the brilliance of his insight endures. He taught himself to suspend the 'building-block' procedure of his neurological training and start with the unique speaking being in the clinic, working backward through hypothetical stages of psychic development toward primal desires. That's an 'all-at-once' procedure: archeological and teleological. It recognizes that psychic functions are on the way from somewhere toward a wholeness that never arrives."

Ope responds with a not very cheerful grin. "If you're right, it's no wonder that all ethical and political discourse sinks into a swamp of random opinions where politics dies. If that's so, then I need a clear description of what you see as the growth of psychic space."

"For anyone at all interested in ideas, it's a fascinating story. It offers a different vision of who we are that biological models alone provide. The organic story describes us as precocious animals, whereas *our* gamble is that the passage from mute desire to language is neither a part-to-whole story nor a whole-to-part story. Sometimes I wonder if that's why we often surprise ourselves by alluding to figures like the creator gods of the ancient myths."

"Your Muslim Allah is also one of those creator gods!"

"I'd say, rather, the Arabic name for the empty or inexistent One that we either face or hide from. But the story of development is a long digression that we must forego just now."

Several hours of conversation with Ope confirm Mamud's reading of an alteration in his friend's state of mind. He has always been of a contemplative disposition, pensive even. But now the muscles of his face reveal an ingrained sadness that can't be entirely concealed. Never given to rushing into conversation or action, always measured in language and tone, restrained in physical gestures. And yet something has changed. The strong, confident voice is diminished. Not the empty speech of manic depression, but in that direction. At times monotonal, even stagnant, as though he were responding from a distance or repeating a formula rather than speaking to the moment. Even the spontaneous gestures that once accompanied his discourse have become detectably wooden as though imposed by rule.

Çelik's observations having gotten this far, he steals another look and recognizes a certain listlessness in the still erect posture of the body in the chair next to him. And yet, there is a marginal benefit in all this: To friendly eyes that are older by a decade and less disillusioned, the changes suggest realism.

Ope's melancholy might have originated with Yetunde's death, but in that case fifteen years of absorption in diplomacy should have had a healing effect. Mamud risks an allusion to the loss and adds some remarks on how death can enhance and even purify love.

And in a quintessential Çelik remark, he adds, "As the shortcomings of loved ones slip away, they're added to our guiding ideals. That's more important than the facts of history." Then he concludes with the ritual Muslim formula, "May the peace of God go with you."

When his friend either can't or won't offer anything more about the tone of his life, Çelik does something every good analyst must do: He confesses himself in the same position, baffled and impotent.

"My son Kemal has fallen in love with Beverly Georghiu, may God forgive him."

The suddenness and irrelevance of the remark gets Ope's attention. "The security officer? She met me at the airport this morning. Apparently, her assignment is to 'secure me' from the coming apocalypse. She seems like a serious and intelligent young woman. I like her."

Mamud answers solemnly. "I have nothing to say against her. In fact I admire her, but we are Muslims, 'Glory be to God who never changes.' She's not like us. She's Christian. Or was. Grew up Romanian Orthodox. Then became secular. May God forgive her."

"Does that make it easier?"

"You're thinking like a European, my friend, as though secularism is somehow neutral and hence innocent. It's not neutral. It's less neutral than any of the great religions. Look at the world and measure the consequences. The secularists are individualists and relativists who find more reality in a block of wood than in a story that has inspired human history and dignity. At least the Orthodox don't live in the caverns of their own skulls. They recognize something beyond themselves. In their world there is still virtue. 'There is no other god than God and Muhammad is his prophet.'"

That outburst might have let Ope see as the analyst sees, were his own shadow not blocking his light.

At this moment Mamud's son, Kemal, enters. A tall, dark-haired man in his twenties, with the build of his mother and the disposition of his father. He is comfortable with himself as with others and accustomed to meeting his father's distinguished guests on equal ground. As the two strangers are introduced, the reason for the younger Çelik's presence becomes clear. Kemal has a proposal for Adawale:

"Tomorrow we'll take a tour of the city, if you're willing."

Ope, erect in his chair, elbows on the arms, fingertips touching in a characteristically thoughtful gesture, sees that however politely offered, this tour is no more for his own pleasure than it is optional. It's the end of day one, and already he feels the tug of Boris on his strings.

So, having no choice in the matter, he accepts graciously if a bit dryly. "It's kind of you. But don't let me interfere with your work." And with that agreement and a few other polite remarks, Kemal offers to drive him back to UNOV.

CHAPTER 7

At 7:00 A.M. OPE waits again in the downstairs atrium. Instead of feeling snug and protected in his posh refuge in the sky, he's haunted still by the image of Las Vegas in the underground: artificial worlds that render the higher faculties vestigial.

He waits to be politely whisked away under guard in another climate-controlled military vehicle, reduced to a spectator on the city where he and Yetunde had once spent their honeymoon, happy and free. No walking today in the manicured parks or moving on metro and tram through the energizing bustle of rush hour. Forbidden, the pleasure of belonging, of getting wet in the rain, of being crammed into overfull carriages and jostled by the masses of students and city workers. No chance to *be-in* the city. Condemned to *look-at* the spectacle through thick glass rectangles. This, Boris and company call "orientation"!

Soon enough Kemal Çelik shows up. Not as his friend's son this time, but as the UNO Security Inspector, armed and in uniform. Inspector Çelik promptly announces that Officer Georghiu will be driving them. He gestures. "This way to the garage. The Humvee will meet us shortly."

Adawale returns a blank look.

Çelik's formality recedes into a coy grin. "Beverly Georghiu, your security officer. My fiancée."

Once the two men are strapped into the rear seats, Officer Georghiu starts the engine that hums with the power of an airplane. As they get underway, Kemal shows more interest in personal topics than in a city tour. "My father probably didn't tell you about our engagement." The remark sounds like a slightly embarrassing afterthought. "He's not happy about it."

Without revealing any knowledge of the matter, Ope asks politely if his father's misgivings are grave.

"It's religion. At least that's never trivial. Aren't the old religions the source of many of the troubles in this world?"

Adawale, who has some sympathy with that view, notes Kemal's apparent obliviousness to the distance it opens between his and his father's worlds, as though it were only a difference of opinion.

"Beverly grew up in the Romana. Things are different in the Orthodox countries."

"I see the difficulty," Adawale remarks discreetly.

But young Kemal is not finished. "My father is a very sensible man, but he remains observant and faithful to the Prophet. He admires Beverly but our relationship hurts him." As though he wishes the topic to be less severe than it is, he giggles. "If she would convert, he could die happy."

Then a shift to the topic of their agenda. "I believe you know the layout of the city. But are you familiar with the large green areas on the perimeter? The *Augsgarten* to the north, *Prater* and the ballpark to the east, and, southwest, the grounds at *Schönbrunn* Palace? They're all refugee camps now."

And, in truth, nothing Adawale has already seen prepares him for the transformation of Vienna surveyed through bullet-proof glass for the next hour. So interested is he in the story his young guide has to tell that Kemal goes on for twenty minutes describing local conditions. A global tale: wave after wave of refugees, many of them with citizenship nowhere, threatening to overrun this and most other cities on the planet.

Kemal concludes by describing the backlash among the most compassionate citizens when faced with the blight on the city and the strain on resources. Then he ends with a riddle: "For all their compassionate efforts, even the most thoughtful obstinately refuse to see that the birthrates are against them. The refugees will eventually inherit the earth without having owned any of it."

What strikes Ope most sharply in Kemal's description is the optimism running through his tale of woe. How is it, he wonders, that the young can speak of hopelessness in a tone of confidence in the future?

The GPS suddenly sputters to life and for no apparent reason the vehicle is stopped by heavily armed soldiers at a roadblock. Adawale understands nothing of the exchange between Georghiu and the soldier except that there is trouble in the Prater camp. So the first stop on their itinerary is postponed.

"We'll get a call when it's safe to return," Kemal explains. "For now, we'll tour the inner city so you can get the feel of the streets. Then we'll try another of the camps." He gives instructions to Georghiu. "Take the Ring Road clockwise so the professor can see how things have changed since he was last here."

After that, as though thrown off his game, Kemal says little, and Beverly takes up the slack. Her relation with Adawale warms a bit as they chat about passing points of interest and he makes comparisons with the Vienna he had known in years past.

He tries to speak positively, but his tone cannot conceal shock and disappointment. What passes before his eyes is not one city but three. The first, the basis of comparison, is the sunny, cheerful Vienna he and Yetunde visited on their wedding trip. Earlier in the century the city had been known as the most livable in Europe. Famous for spotless streets, for pristine parks where families played together in quasi-pastoral tranquility, for bustling sidewalk cafés where people sat for hours talking with friends or reading the papers. That and so much more: venerable cultural institutions, a model transportation system, affordable housing for all, and generous social services for the needy.

In daylight and dark he and Yetunde had walked hand in hand through the narrow canyons and quaint neighborhoods of the historic district, enjoying the architecture of centuries past. She admired the Secessionist designs and occasionally laughed at the baroque hyperbole. Their mornings were spent in one or another of the great museums. Then lunch in a convenient *Beisl* and a leisurely afternoon in one of the sunny parks. Tired of walking, they would stop at a sidewalk café in their week-long survey of the legendary pastries and what they were assured was the best coffee in the world. Evenings were often for the opera or the concert halls. The flavor of that week would remain with him forever: the relaxed elegance and the convivial spirit of one of the planet's most civilized places.

What meets his eye now is a simulation, a mid-twenty-first century parody of its most gracious self. The objects remain, but objects don't make a city. All has turned bleak. At the edge of the parks, the landscape is marred by military vehicles and troops in battle gear. Soldiers patrol broad sidewalks formerly filled with strolling pedestrians, bicycles, and skateboards. Where has it gone, that model European city so happily composed of northern order and Mediterranean nonchalance? The carefree life has vanished, and the faces bear the marks of anxiety. Order prevails still, but the air is heavy with unease. Paradise lost. Or if not entirely lost, then suppressed or in retreat under a perpetual drizzle of chilly rain and grey clouds of more than weather.

For the historian, this second city rouses visions of a third: Vienna 1683 under the great Ottoman siege against the Hapsburg empire. From early 14 July until 12 September of that year the ancient capital at the frontier between Catholic Europe and the Turks suffered—not for the first time—a heroic and terrible siege. One day early in July, Emperor Leopold and the imperial family left, and the next day 60,000 of the most affluent citizens abandoned the city to its fate. Quickly it filled again with refugees from the countryside who lived in the path of the massive forces of Sultan Mehmed IV.

The tents of the Turks surrounded the walls and radiated outward to south and east as far as the eye could see, and by the time the crisis came all on the inside who weren't willing to fight to the death had left. After two months of brutal fighting and of unspeakable hunger, filth, and disease on both sides, the city walls came within hours of penetration and occupation by the forces of Islam.

As Georghiu navigates the traffic along the circular road in the footprint of the medieval walls, Adawale speaks of that defensive circle that had defined the old city. It had been so neglected during peaceful periods that, under threat, an outer ring of defensive bastions had been hastily thrown up in anticipation of battle.

As past and present merge in Adawale's imagination, Kemal, who knows the history reasonably well, joins the double vision of the imperial city now coinciding with itself over a distance of 350 years. As though celebrating the heroism of both sides, the two men speak of the sleepless, starving city and the gates—now only place names—where the fighting was heaviest. There the famous Turkish sappers had worked in covered trenches and deep tunnels under heavy fire for weeks to undermine the walls in the weakest places. At the very moment when the plan would have succeeded, the Polish cavalry and European reinforcements swept in from the hills to the northwest and routed the enemy. Between 6 and 10 p.m. the battle ended, Vienna was liberated, and the Turks had vanished.

If Mamud Çelik had been witness to this convergence of cities, he might have gathered other clues to Ope's melancholy, for that prolix commentary was less a description of historic events than a requiem. The analyst would have heard the music of lamentation for the miserable condition of man.

And there would have been more, because Mamud would have known that lamentation is also a song of praise that, in not saying all that needs saying, evokes love of the world *and* betrays the world.

The Humvee continues along the modern road and the ancient wall past the Hapsburg palace, parliament, city hall, and the university. Here and there graffiti mars the walls of mansions with boarded windows.

As they approach *Franz-Josefs-Kai*, army vehicles and barricades line the street where a burned-out truck has crashed into the outer wall of the U-Bahn station.

Kemal explains, "A truck bomb. This one happened last night. It ran down some pedestrians, then the driver apparently lost control before it exploded against that wall. The driver and several bystanders died, and others were wounded. We've learned in the hours since that the driver was shot while the truck was still in motion. Of course there's nothing left of him."

Just as they reach *Schwedenplatz,* Georghiu is given clearance to proceed to whatever camps they wish. There, with abandoned tour boats on the canal at one side and the entrance to the U-Bahn station on the other, they see troops checking identities and searching faces though looking for fugitives, but the sight has become routine and they move on to a nearby café for a break.

CHAPTER 8

KEMAL DECIDED THAT their next stop should be *Schön-brunn* Palace, where the vast Baroque Park with the woodland gardens had been converted into a harbor for refugees. So they headed southwest along the Vienna Row. At the entrance gate, Georghiu gained admission and they were confronted—in year 2070—by a sea of tents for the huddled masses and by the Austrian sense of impeccable order even as Kemal described more than Adawale may have wanted to hear of how the palace kitchens had been reorganized to feed the people.

Because the camp was peaceful and because he was fluent in the language, Kemal proposed a walk around the periphery. So, as Georghiu parked, he passed a UN jacket to Ope.

"Wear this and leave your security pass exposed. It will save inconvenience. For some reason the UN details are viewed as friendly, though the young often treat local security forces as the enemy."

The inmates, just emerging from their midday meal in the large central tents, wandered slowly toward their makeshift lodgings. The sight threw Adawale into another dark moment as, to his eyes, it was an unwelcome revelation of what "the free world" had come to: the modern "democratic state" revealed in the incarceration of everything its imperialism had first exposed then learned to fear.

Most people appeared disoriented as they moved aimlessly through the camp. The physical motion was languid and despondent and, almost to the person, they declined to meet the eyes of the official visitors.

Kemal, being Muslim, had been able to befriend a few, and he introduced Adawale to a middle-aged man sitting in the door of his tent. His name was Islam Quraishi, a British-trained schoolteacher from Cairo, once well-to-do, now destitute. Hardship aside, Quraishi invited them into his tent for tea, a courtesy it would have been an unforgivable slight to decline.

The cramped space was clean and neat, but the absence of hope in the air was palpable. Quraishi's wife Samira prepared tea and the father formally invited the teenage son Hassan from a dark corner of the small tent to meet their guests. Among the saddest of sad things was the demeanor of a lad who, like millions of his generation, had been "left behind"— as though the world were "moving ahead." Without home, country, education, or means of supporting themselves it was a near certainty that they would all be lost, to themselves first, and also lost to the world.

Islam Quraishi was a thoughtful man caught between fundamentalists of a religion to which he remained faithful and the vacuous life around him. Yet his dignity and authority had not been weakened by circumstances. He was that rare thing, an educated man who had not allowed bitter experience and resentment to debauch his clarity of mind or the charity of his demeanor. A few minutes' conversation was enough to see in him something of a prophetic figure, as when he explained in perfect British English:

"We didn't choose like human beings to come here. We came like animals who could only react by preserving life. This host city and country do what they can to protect us from the indignation of the populace, especially the bands of young, mainly male Austrians who understandably resent what is happening to their beautiful city and country. We are herded and fed like animals with no political status. The camp is a well-run zoo to protect us from 'them' and 'them' from us. And yet we're better off than most, thanks to the Austrian passion for order and cleanliness, to the efforts of UN officials, and to the NGOs. Elsewhere we would be refuse on a public dump. Of course we cannot be allowed to settle. We must be passed—will even be lucky to be passed on—to one of the semi-permanent camps in the countryside."

Islam Quraishi might have been one among millions who lived without hope, yet he spoke without complaining, making a gift of his bitter experience. All the while his wife Samira sat isolated, her face and eyes vacant under the limp strands of prematurely grey hair. The presence of officials in UNO jackets frightened her, and each time her husband raised his voice to make a point, her eyes widened in alarm. Then as suddenly she sank again into a pathetic stupor.

The intelligent face of the son Anwar, just seventeen, sitting obediently through his father's speech, was intermittently deformed by grimaces, and yet the features were not entirely perverted. They bore traces of both innocence and of gravity as though the cynicism that occasionally distorted them was recent. Otherwise, he maintained the polite calm instilled in him even as he held himself in reserve from the shabby clothes on his back and from the people in the room. He listened to what his father said, but in a willful, truculent mood that, to Adawale's eyes at least, foretold the world to come.

Quraishi concluded by adding, "Laws are made to protect life, but by law *we* are protected from nothing. We become outlaws by breathing. No one notices that life has been taken out of God's hands and turned over to managers and engineers. God has given up, as he did in Noah's day, as he gave up at Sodom and at Babylon. And the displaced have become Grey wolves roaming in packs, ravaging the earth, protecting our own. We have become the animals the entitled ones say we are."

PART TWO
PATHOLOGIES OF EVERYDAY LIFE

CHAPTER 1

"GET OUT! IT'S A TRAP! You're in the trap now! Your game is up! No getting out now!"

An old woman with long shocks of colorless grey hair and madness in her eyes flies at Adawale with up-raised hands as he enters the psychiatric ward with Dr. Mamud Çelik. A glance at her face is enough to show that she sees only an alien human object intruding on her space.

Forgetting the "trap," she rushes away, crosses the room, and turns off a blaring television no one's watching. Apparently calmed by having had an effect on her environment, she stands for a moment before forgetting that too. Then, remembering some other lost thing, dashes from the room in disgust muttering obscenities under her breath. Within a minute, she returns, stares at the two men, then runs at them, shaking her finger in the doctor's face.

"You don't know what I'm saying! You aren't listening!"

Another retreat to the center of the room ends in a full stop in the middle of the floor, where she wrings her hands like Lady Macbeth.

Before this interruption, Mamud had been describing the clinic. Now he resumes. "We see more and more people who have lost the will or the capacity to connect things. They live a fractured time and speak a fractured language, if it is language still."

"What can you do for such a person?" Ope asks.

But before Mamud can answer, the old woman rushes frantically back again and turns this time on Ope like a prophetess of wrath to come. "You are a generation of vipers! I told the Prince so. I said, 'At least there's the landscape.' But he didn't listen. Nobody listens!" With another involuntary swerve into a parallel universe, she grabs Mamud's hand, kisses it, and says almost tenderly, "I love you Doctor. Pardon the remark."

As that mood dissolves the shrill voice resumes. "May you choke on it! You should be killed and tortured!" Then, discontinuity on top of discontinuity, the voice—hers, if it coincides with anyone at all—becomes mournful. "'You cannot live by pearls alone,' I said. But that's only when I first knew of her. If I don't mistake myself for her."

Çelik's clinic occupies a building at one end of a city block half destroyed in the last century by an enemy's bombs, leaving the other half standing so that two eras and two wars now share a common wall. This is the ground floor of the modern concrete wing, with an entrance at the point where the dignity of old stone bumps up against cinder-block modernity.

The location of all this incoherence is a commons room. It's a large, well-lighted space flanked by a glass-partitioned nurse's station. Down the middle of the great room, perpendicular to the glass enclosure, a long activity table with chairs offers various materials for distracting the patients. Several sit quietly apart, equally oblivious of their surroundings, while others huddle together as though not wrapped in solitude. Some stand against walls or in their own warps of space. At the table one is painting with watercolors. Another assembles a jigsaw puzzle of a cathedral. Still another focuses with jealous alarm on the stranger who just entered with her doctor.

The room itself is well-ordered. The patients—most but not all Caucasian—appear clean and acceptably dressed. Yet the most cursory glance picks up the fact that all objects except for the chairs at the table bear as little relation one to another as the inmates do. An inventory of items in a warehouse would be more coherent. It's a picture of the detritus of modernity, lacking the relational "with" that makes a world. In the corner, the television again blares inanities that no one attends to. Noise without significance, unless as a consciousness-blocking device to help the patients escape their own thoughts—if any.

Among several mysteries that the inquisitive Opeyemi would like explained is why entirely uncommunicative people should spend all their waking hours in the same room. What impulse drives them out of physical isolation into the commons and holds them there like blind particles parked in orbit around an empty nucleus? But he gets no chance to ask before Mamud is called away to deal with some more urgent problem, while Ope remains in the room observing.

Once detached from "their doctor," the patients no longer see him. Another mystery: The doctor's presence had gathered the random objects into a "location," but, as soon as the reference point vanishes, location is annulled. For some it makes no difference: placidly undisturbed, staring, if anywhere, into space, with blank and clouded eyes. Others endure a gloomy, discontented torpor. One middle-aged man with his head on the table takes a siesta. Another woman, youngish and not unattractive, seems placidly "normal" until closer observation reveals no mental engagement whatever, as though she's heavily medicated.

A slightly older man attracts Adawale's attention. In part it's the incongruity of a person, meticulous in appearance and of some innate dignity, absorbed in slavishly repetitious behavior. He spends his time walking compulsively round and round the table and chairs counterclockwise, measuring each step and allotting the same number to each side of the table. In passing he touches each chair with two fingers of his left hand as though counting, each time with an identical gesture of great precision, each step and each contact exactly like the others. Unless the people sitting cause him to alter his pace by moving, he ignores their existence, but when there is disruption of the gestures, he is compelled to return to the beginning and start the series again.

In a far corner a young man in his twenties stands at a window engaged in argument with an invisible interlocutor. Unobserved, Ope moves down the room toward the corner window and takes a seat at an angle close enough to hear the "conversation." At a remove of ten feet the observer, who doesn't exist in the same universe, is free to study the gaunt cheeks and tortured brow of a man half his own age caught up in an interior clamor of revolt. The eyes blaze with aggression and hate as he rails against the world with the urgency of a battle that must be won or lost here and now for all time.

From behind the needless camouflage of a book, Ope marvels at the phenomenon of a destitute world on trial in a madhouse. But before that thought can be fully appreciated, the patient appears to awaken as from a dream. Turning around, he connects with the eyes of the man he hasn't seen before, goes quiet, then speaks in a sane, exhausted voice. "You see, I, too, carry the contagion."

The moment of clarity soon vanishes and his mood darkens. Ope disappears from his horizon as he retreats again into the solitude of his parallel world. Not raving now. Speaking person to person like a prosecutor in court, he rests his case on a single phrase: "All counterfeit; all polluted. I know because I, too, am guilty! I was born guilty."

The words seem to require a reply, but Ope, affected perhaps by the unhappiness of a person a bit like himself, finds no words. Merely lays a hand briefly on his shoulder in passing and walks away.

Later, when Mamud's emergencies have abated, the two men go to lunch in an adjacent building where Ope is free to ask for explanations. "I know it's an oversize question, but what can your art do for these people? What can you do for any of us?"

Mamud replies slowly, cautiously. "We try to help unstable people cope with life in an unstable world. Truthfully, there's little hope for most of them. But we're not only here to *heal*, whatever that difficult word may mean. We're also here to learn. If we're to understand ourselves, we mustn't neglect the exceptions. Statistical averages and norms of convention have little to teach, but the boundary cases, lost somewhere between a resourceful life and suicide, can be prophetic. It's not quite that when *they* hit the skid rails *we* learn how to stay in bounds. I don't care much for fences, but to understand ourselves we must understand what we flag as pathological. These cases are multiplied in clinics across the world and their numbers only grow. We need an account of psychic development and how forces beyond consciousness exert pressure on psychic life."

"So what about the hysteric who assaulted you, then kissed your hand?"

"Lara. Her name is Lara. She's perfectly secure here in the clinic where we can keep her from harming herself. She's a good example of the difficulty we have in passing from the unique patient to a general theory. Lara lives in fear that her world might collapse. In fact every few moments it does collapse, and the precariousness gives her no rest. She sleeps only under medication. She has no capacity for trust or hope or love. She holds herself responsible for finding her real self in the absence of any grounding in a past. So she fails moment by moment. Worse, she's doomed to succeed for a random moment now and then. Hence the logorrhea, the compulsive avalanche of words pursuing fugitive meanings."

"Then what do you treat? What does it mean to heal such a person? Is there even such a thing? I don't see what principle could support statistical evidence. Or is 'disease' a conventional dismissal of what's unintelligible?"

Any answer to all that requires more than information bits. Mamud reflects before responding, "A remarkable thing about science is how it flourishes for a while within the limits of its axioms, then hits a wall. What we call 'the century of the brain' saw magnificent technological achievements in neurology and brain chemistry, and we're much the better for it. But success came at the high price of silencing some fundamental questions."

"By 'fundamental' do you mean some kind of *explanation* of what was happening and why?"

"Approximately, yes. Lobotomies, electroconvulsive therapies, psychotic drugs, drugs for depression, historically the infamous Prozac and Zoloft. Sometimes these appeared to work as measured by commonsense norms, but practice by trial and error offered no theoretical clarity, and that's not science! No one denies that people are suffering, and some of those procedures and medications may have been better than no treatment at all. But it wasn't science."

The tone of that speech shows they have arrived at a topic Mamud is passionate about. Ope takes a grim satisfaction in further evidence that the light of modernity so often illuminates dead ends.

"Then we're essentially speaking of intuitive diseases and faith-based treatments, blind to causes and cures. If we can't see through our procedural cataracts, we're unlikely to see the symptom clearly, much less a cause or a treatment. So how are we to know which ones are the crazies?"

Mamud grins in appreciation of the point. "Historically the situation got far worse because procedures come with social consequences. Psychiatric organizations published official lists of mental illnesses that claimed to be authoritative when, at bottom, there was no basis of distinction between illness and health."

"Working hypotheses then."

"That's a nice way of putting it! You might call it naïveté. When the evidence was not forthcoming, the hypothesis was treated as verified and turned into public dogma. People trusted the doctors who trusted their training. Meanwhile bureaucracies had to decide how to distribute money to dead-end research programs based on undefinable names of imaginary diseases. A mountain of insurance claims and disclaimers piled up. Laws had to be written; lawyers had to invent arguments; judges had to make decisions. Drug companies developed and marketed products that professed to cure when, at best, they relieved symptoms, and often ended in addiction or worse. Just imagine the economic scale of it all as we congratulate ourselves on the generous funding of health care. Health aside, a whole economy rested on the flimsy hypothesis that the mind is really the body."

"I see where this is headed. You're describing an up-to-date superstition that distorts the world and the people in it, all in the name of science."

During this topic the cheerfulness of the easygoing doctor was all but eclipsed by the depth of his passion.

"The mere promise of brain science spawned a propaganda machine that had devastating social results. From science, education, government, to the social pressure of family and friends. The medical-industrial complex sends out the message that we are not responsible agents! We are machines driven by chemical balances and imbalances. Pain, anxiety, even panic—all these warning signs of defective ways of living—become physical diseases to be treated. The naturalists are compelled to write manuals listing organic 'cures' for the symptoms of 'mental diseases,' all based on the technological fact that regions of my brain 'light up' under stress or pain or the ecstatic moment of creativity. Is Archimedes' eureka moment *caused* by his brain lighting up? Or does his brain respond peripherally to *his*—not an anonymous—discovery?"

"If not mental illness," Adawale asks, "then what? If not organic causes with organic cures, then what?"

"For that, we have to be willing to start over. From a different place. I say, from language, keeping in mind that we always consider organic conditions first. In the clinic we call our hypothesis, half-whimsically, 'Prepositional Therapy,' and we *do* mean the grammatical term 'preposition.' We treat the organic being who is situated or pre-positioned in a world by language. The task is to help readjust the patient's ways of interacting with the world. Our gambit is that one suffers a linguistic, rather than—or even preliminary to—an organic 'dementia.' A person may first be an organism in the order of chronology, but what makes an organism a person is not itself organic. And the position one occupies is not a physical relation of objects alongside other objects in a container-world. We encounter the world as already 'said.' Our ways of interacting are preeminently linguistic. Prepositional Therapy is based on our modes of relating with a world."

Ope frowns. "I understand none of that! Please simplify."

Undaunted by his incomprehension, Mamud continues. "What's distorted in our patients is the ability to function in an elastic field of relations. So, therapy doesn't look around among

73

objects for origins and causes. Even the idea of a 'psyche' is a theoretical convenience. What we call a person is more like the residual traces of performances than like a 'thing.'"

Opeyemi, the diplomat, usually keeps his impatience out of sight, but at this point he insists, "But the results? What are you able to understand?"

Instead of answering, Mamud gives him another of the benign smiles reserved for people with inquiring minds. "The people you've observed in the clinic are ones that no other medical procedures have been able to help. And yet each is a functional problem familiar in the world at large. More extreme, but still a pathology of everyday life. We observe every disposition: hysteria, paranoia, compulsion, fetishism, schizophrenia, insecurity, loss of capacity to trust or to live with the unknown. From each we learn how things stand with the singular patient's ability to operate in the world."

"I suppose you're not speaking of social adaptation? Not looking for the well-adjusted person who fits in?"

"Hardly. Not in a world gone mad! Werner Brock, for instance, the one with the repetition compulsion. You saw him performing his life's work: getting the chairs in order and making them stay in order. He lives in a melancholy trance without any idea of why the order might be desirable. Did you notice that he limits himself to thirteen steps on each side of the table? In passing, he touches each chair in exactly the same way and at the same point in his stride. If the chairs are not just so, they don't match his steps, then the length of the table is likely to violate the rule of thirteen that orders his world. It's strange, unusual in its pointlessness, but absolutely mandatory for his existence. Otherwise he has to go back to the beginning and start over."

"You're saying that on an assembly line his performance would be the height of efficient rationality. He's the ideal robot we spend millions to reproduce. That comparison is not trivial."

"And yet, it's mad. Werner's relation to his world is a form without content. His sliver of an irrecoverable past exists only as a disposition without thought. Such compulsive gestures do have a relation to what is called 'normal behavior.' It's as though he's trying on his own to recover or maintain an empty past that never was. He says nothing because no words apply to an empty form. It's his duty to preserve an order that exists only in fancy. To think about it conceptually would require more courage in dealing with the fortuities of life than he can bear, so he performs like a machine programmed to rearrange an uncooperative reality."

Mamud doesn't fail to see that as this account continues Ope's own mood grows darker and the tone of his questions more earnest. Certainly not to the point of the verbal handwringing of Lara's re-enactment of Lady Macbeth, but the sensitive diplomat is visibly moved by what he has seen. His next question deliberately moves away from these dark personal details: "These cases all seem to be related to time. How are time and change related?"

"There's something in that suggestion. Werner, like Lara, leaves the impression of losing himself somewhere between contingency and necessity. Where the 'normal person'—if there is one—acts inventively, Werner lives in the rearview mirror, trying to confirm himself by repeating that empty and static form. But to be a person in a world, he would have to put himself and those chairs and tables to new uses alongside the other mad people who are, for him, either not there or in his way."

"And how does Lara keep time?"

"Each case is singular, so comparisons are misleading. But there are analogies. Lara wants to be a stable 'thing' rather than a supple function that perpetually composes, decomposes, and recomposes in transactions with a world. She lives for the moment of identity. Then in the bat of an eye the ecstasy passes into the terror of 'identity lost.' We might say that Werner *is* what Lara would be if she could succeed. Unlike him, in her moments of ecstasy, she exhibits features of the epileptic, bound to the present, without the guardrails of past and future."

"And the young man in the corner who hates the world?"

Mamud paused for a moment, wondering if there was evasion in Ope's mentioning this case last. Did he feel kinship?

"Adam. We call him Adam because, in a sense, he's everyman. He was an American student. On his own account, in saner moments, he wanted to study in a great German university because, in his words, 'Commerce has destroyed the American Mind.' If seriousness survived anywhere in the Western world, he said, it would be here. So he came to Vienna, only to find that 'the great god Mammon rules here too.' He says, 'Mind is everywhere in decay!' Unlike the other cases we've mentioned, he *wants* his world to collapse."

Ope nodded. "I listened to his railing against everything from his family to the tyranny of bourgeois culture."

"His story is interesting. He was a precocious youth until puberty, when his life became fraught with peril. Now he lives under the curse of memory without the grace of forgiving himself or others. Above all, without the capacity to forget."

"But," Ope objects, "what he says against the world isn't a private intuition. It's largely true. What can you do for a soul who is suffering from the truth? He can hardly be persuaded that he doesn't see what we all see or know what we all know."

"He doesn't need to be cured of the truth. His malaise is deeper," Mamud replies. "It invites Oedipal analysis, but it's challenging to deal with a person who understands every technique available to you and cuts you off at the pass. He responds as if he had caught you giving him poison. And in a sense, that's also true. What he hates would make a catalogue of the ills of Ulro, but—and here's the point—he loves his hatred! He protects himself from the analyst's words by listening *to* them as hostile messages, analyzing them as stratagems of the enemy. So he closes his ear to anything else that might pass *through* the words and make a claim on him. Maybe the truth all the sons of the first Adam miss is that a person who can't also love the banality of the world excludes 'the sacred,' and that, my secular friend, only means 'whatever is highest.' Such a person lives a long suicide. Adam can't, or won't, forgive the past and let it change."

"So a man can die of the truth."

"In a sense Adam is dying of hatred of his own people. Except that it's love!"

"How can hate be love?"

"His raving is a bitter love song. He goes slowly mad from the disappointment and the waste of what he most loves. So the world has put him away. But who most suffers this bitter unforgiveness? He, of course. And he ends as another dissonant voice in the universal cacophony, unable even to care for himself."

Mamud hesitates for a moment, perhaps pondering some nebulous kinship between Adam and Ope. "Occasionally he stumbles on some detail in his past life and a shadow of tenderness falls across his face. The harsh tone dissolves, he meets your eye, and for that fleeting moment you feel you're about to reach him. Then it all vanishes, and he's overwhelmed again by the tempest of resentment."

"I don't understand the part about the 'bitter love song.'"

The older and wiser of the two men gives the younger a glance of amused curiosity, as though he, Opeyemi, might be emerging from a dark place.

"Are love and hate really that different? Think of the attention Adam pours into his language. Especially the criticisms of his family. They're not only true; they're eloquent. He rails against 'the traitorous flag of the social religion'; against a 'feel-good culture' that 'anesthetizes people against thinking.' His most eloquent lines approach poetry: 'the narcosis of progress,' 'the service of mammon,' the 'tranquilized death of people whose life ended the day before it began.'

"That's not the voice of a man who has given up on the human world, as the compulsive Werner has. Still he's as mad as the prophet Ezekiel, who ate a scroll and became mute, then lay for 390 days on his left side, turned over, and repeated it on the other side—all by the command of God, no less. Isaiah, Jeremiah, and the others were just as crazy. But then there's 'truth': the most bizarre acts of the prophets became parables that have influenced us ever since. You ask, Is Adam crazy? Who exactly among us isn't?"

Ope smiles grimly. He's only half-sympathetic with that speech. "It's terrible to witness the ruin of a noble mind."

"I think it isn't ruined. Not yet. You observed Adam moment by moment idolizing an imaginary ideal and railing against a past he can't accept and won't forgive for compromising his ideal. If he could let the past go, he might begin reconfiguring the world. But his precondition is that to be reclaimed, the world must be restored to moral balance. Restoration first! When, a bit like Lara, he catches a glimpse of a life without resentment—just at that point he might learn the grace of forgetting and begin to cope. But, so far, it hasn't happened."

This line of discussion having gone on long enough, Ope chuckles dryly. "You have a radically anti-political establishment here!"

Mamud nods wearily, "Or, for you, a pre-political laboratory."

Proof at this point of Mamud's salutary influence on his friend comes in Ope's recall of words spoken long before at their meeting in Alexandria. "Do you remember that you once satirized the disease of the post-Christian West as the will to power? 'Having debunked God,' you said, 'we're on our own.' You said, 'We must save ourselves from the ineffable, and the more we try, the smaller we get. We're dying,' you said, 'of the

79

death of the gods whom we have killed!' Is Islam also going the way of Christianity?"

"Only God knows. May our Lord, the Merciful, the Compassionate, give us peace."

CHAPTER 2

AFTER ADAWALE'S VISIT to the clinic, Kemal Çelik arranged to take him on a further inspection of the city and the camps, one populated by African refugees. By schedule they were to meet early one morning in the atrium lobby of the resident towers. But instead of Kemal, Beverly Georghiu showed up. Not Officer Georghiu this time, but civilian Georghiu.

Adawale, unobserved from across the lobby, assumed that her presence had nothing to do with him this time, so he felt at liberty to study the woman who had emerged from the role and the uniform of a state functionary. Unusual qualities of mind and imagination had flashed up in the few remarks they had exchanged the day before, and he liked that. The truth was he liked women, though almost always as "symbolic forms" from a distance. Yetunde's love of a loveless world and her imaginative finesse had spoiled him, and yet he welcomed a chance to get better acquainted with Georghiu.

She spotted him in his secluded corner and approached with a cheerful apology. "Kemal was called out in the night on a security detail, so I get to be your guide today. He'll join us later when he can."

"Delighted," Adawale replied, not caring much at that moment why or even what might be on the agenda.

"Today we're going to the university. I'll show you around our shop."

"Good. I'd be glad to learn more about your project. You alluded to a student research program you're involved in."

On the way to the underground garage, she plunged enthusiastically into the topic by describing a group of graduate students who worked under the aegis of "The University Committee on Social Research." The faculty responsible for the project was a discreet group hidden away somewhere in the dark recesses of the more public Committee.

"Apparently even a secret project must have a name," she continued, "so it's called—with a nod toward Freud— 'Pathologies of Everyday Life.' Here that means almost nothing, but it's vague enough to keep the work under wraps."

Adawale, being a good head taller than she, turned to look down and fix her in a narrowed gaze. "Is everybody in Vienna paranoid? All I've seen so far might be read in the news without stirring interest. Besides, if yours is a cloak-and-dagger operation, why are you telling *me*?"

Instead of being amused, she returned his slow gaze with one of her own that said he was either being disingenuous or a slow learner. "Security measures are only explained to underlings like me when we have to enforce them. All I'm told is where to take you and—here's the paradox—I'm to tell you anything you care to ask." She added with a youthful giggle, "I don't even know who you really are."

Here was another clue to the obscure situation he had landed in, and the drive to town in Georghiu's little civilian car—no arsenal of defensive weapons this time—gave him time for another review of his circumstances. After a few minutes gazing at the people in the streets and pondering the security arrangements, he said, "Since you offer, I'd be happy to know more about your secret research."

And so she described the project beginning with her student group, who formed a kind of supplement to one of the faculty research projects. "When we're needed, we work with schools and other youth-oriented organizations under cover of the name 'Crisis Managers.'"

Then digressing, "Isn't it curious how a pretentious label can open doors for people who really know nothing except that they know they know nothing? Still, it's all quite real. We are what is called 'qualified' for this kind of intervention, but in that role, we only help keep order. Our real job is to understand disorder. We're to observe tendencies that turn up in the 'Pathologies Project.' Two jobs at once."

"And your current focus?"

"I can't speak for the faculty members, but we have seminars where they discuss our work but say little about their own. At the moment we're looking for relations among four symptoms: addiction, insecurity, escapism, and something called 'the dimming of sensation.' These may or may not be related, but this isn't a social-science project with a rigorous method. If it were empirical research, the scope would be prohibitive. Instead it's anecdotal. Like being on guard for how these topics might coincide. We're expected to be as imaginative as possible. Horribly unscientific!" The sardonic tone suggested she is not taken in by the general regard for methodology.

"The point is to observe instances of everyday life at close range. Contextually. We rely on personal encounters and interviews. Though occasionally our ideas get corroborated statistically from a sociologist on the faculty team."

"Are you free to share case studies?"

"With you, yes. Otherwise, no." She chuckled. "Not to protect the innocent, you know. To protect the guilty."

Another "Georghiu effect," as Ope had begun to call her facility for mixing irony and seriousness in a tone of disinterest. The little car was waiting at a traffic light where she used the time to consider how to describe the students' work.

The light changed and she began: "We've been studying a cluster of things under the generic term 'addiction.' The faculty claims that it's a planet-wide malady exceeding addiction to drugs. Drug addiction concerns us only incidentally. Besides, it has been studied by everybody for decades with statistical methods that have led to mountains of observations and little understanding. At least that's what we think. We're interested in addiction itself rather than this or that particular addiction."

"Then you don't think social ills result from economic or physical causes?"

"Correct. Not primarily. We're interested in addiction as a way of relating to the world—or not. Drugs and all other modes of distraction: sex, porn, food, alcohol, fashion, fantasy, video games, and all things projected on screens or listening devices that bury us in our heads and cut us off from the world. Escape from reality is rampant. What better way to hide than in the dubious sociality of other escapists? They're all ways of avoiding strenuous things like learning how to concentrate on a demanding book or follow the implications of a new idea. Makes you wonder if the thing we most want to escape isn't ourselves. Probably we can stuff all these ways of avoiding involvement with the world into the single word 'hedonism,' but that would be less enlightening."

It was a stunning speech from a person so young, a credit to her teachers and to old—and mainly lost—philosophical European education. And Ope was struck by something else unexpected. What she was saying echoed Mamud's claim that the people in the clinic were only extreme instances of universal planetary maladies. The correspondence he sensed between mental disease and the pathology of everyday life came down to adequate modes of being in the world.

A moment later Ope responded, "Interesting, isn't it, that addiction in your sense of the term is almost universal, yet everybody hates it. Condemned everywhere and omnipresent in global culture. There's a clue in that collective scorn."

She avoided the deep water by quoting an adage: "'Tell me what you hate, and I'll tell you who you are.' Apparently, we hide from the fact that we're hiding until eventually we lose the capacity to resist."

"So in hating addiction, we're denying an unrecognized inclination? Unless that's a bit too broad to be very useful."

"Early in the project we were discouraged by the feeling that we were only recording the obvious. But we *were* seeing something for the first time, and that wasn't nothing. One afternoon during a seminar a faculty member suggested we try widening our view by distinguishing the underlying dispositions from its 'target,' even objects of desire endorsed by social convention."

In the middle of this conversation Ope might have begun to wonder if they had crossed town to visit the university or just to sit in this parking lot and talk. In little more than the passage from one sentence to the next, an impression flashed across his mind for a second time: She was actively cultivating him, taking an interest beyond her duty. Why?

He recognized the genuine intellectual of the kind who rides the metro thinking of Aristotle or Goethe while everyone else reads the morning paper. But there was something more. Not strength but vulnerability, like the weakness behind every strength. Why was she attaching herself to him?

Then instantly, in less than no time at all, he saw. It was her star-crossed love for Kemal. That tangle of family and religion and his own relation to Mamud. She wasn't recommending herself to him. She was positioning herself in the field of her would-be father-in-law as a person respected by his respected friend. And all without a flicker of self-consciousness.

Adawale forced his attention back to the topic of the conversation. "If your interest is in the disposition behind desire, I suppose you find little difference between the manager fixated on wealth, the person entranced by pornography, the street junkie on meth, the valetudinarian on opioids, or the media addict. They're *all* addicts?"

"Correct. But don't ask me why. Why is out of my depth. One member of the faculty who is an analyst of some kind, calls it the dimming of desire."

Since neither knew what, if anything, that might mean, the conversation stopped long enough to realize that they had arrived somewhere, and the car had parked itself.

Adawale broke the concentration. "That gives me enough to think about for now, so show me your university."

CHAPTER 3

GEORGHIU LED ADAWALE in tour-guide mode through the assembly hall of the main university building into the quad of Arcade Court which recalled a *campo santo* or cemetery. On pedestals in the cloister, distributed along the walls and walkways and under arches, dozens of faculty members were commemorated in busts extending back to the founding of the university in 1365. Among them, more than a dozen Nobel Prize winners in a variety of fields. For a person like Adawale it was an absorbing passage through eight centuries of intellectual history, where there were so many stories to be renewed, sometimes by him, sometimes by his guide, that it took an hour to complete the circuit of the court.

Next they took the grand staircase to the reading room of the University Library and on to the Ceremonial Chamber to see copies on the ceiling of Gustav Klimt's fresco designs representing the faculties of theology, medicine, law, and philosophy—the designs all rejected then later burned by the German army. Back in the assembly hall, they paused at a niche containing the names of all the rectors of the university engraved in the red marble with gold letters. In a moving instance of historical nuance, the gold had been removed from the names of Nazi-era rectors, leaving them standing in naked infamy.

Then came a visit with Beverly's professor in a nondescript building a couple of blocks away. The university of 100,000 students had buildings all over the troubled city, and the Committee on Social Research was located in a block with no apparent relation to the school except for a modest sign at the entrance. After passing through a warren of hallways and an unprepossessing space said to be the archives of the Committee, they reached a side office belonging to Professor Gebhard Erlich.

Erlich was German rather than Austrian, husky and broad-shouldered, with a head of unruly grey hair. His clothes were well-suited to a pipe-smoking intellectual who found eating and sleeping a misuse of time. In physical appearance he might have been a raucous worker with no subtlety beyond hammer or wrench. The hands bore out the impression. Stout fingers and weathered skin more suited to the Hamburg waterfront than the library and lecture halls of an ancient university. Compared with him, Adawale was a fashionable man of the world, though neither noticed a difference that, to notice, would have been another misuse of time. Less superficially observed, Erlich was a quiet, soft-spoken man whose eyes had the depth and finesse of poetry. No wonder Georghiu was so fond of her professor.

This visit had been expected, and once the introductions were made, the three proceeded to a private room in a nearby restaurant where they could speak freely over an early lunch. Erlich was forthright and personable, but when he made no effort to open the conversation, Adawale accepted the initiative.

"I've been told, Professor, that I may freely inquire about anything that strikes me as curious. If so, may I ask why your research group is concealed behind an extravagant blanket of security? So far I've seen nothing in Vienna that would rouse public curiosity."

Erlich smiled benignly. "And we hope to keep it that way."

Adawale replied with light irony. "You must be engaged in alarming activities if you need to keep people like me from seeing what's going on!"

"Not you. You may know what you wish. I understand that's why you're here. Someone—I've no idea who—must be relying on the vigor of your inquiries to develop an independent view of something."

"Let me rephrase the question: What is being so carefully concealed from the public?"

"The public is being concealed from the public." Erlich answered wryly. "Remember Lenin's claim that the revolution would begin when factory and farm workers recognized they were in the same boat? Here too. Only the forces are different and the consequences more weighty."

"Weightier than the Bolshevik Revolution! You mean the stateless multitudes may recognize their own power?"

"As devastating to planetary order as that is, it's much worse. The multitudes aren't the most dangerous. Virtually everyone is complicit in the violence that's sweeping the planet. I know a bit about your work with the UN and your study of the clash of cultures, and I know you've seen more of the world firsthand than I have, but we're facing something that can't be learned from the macrocosmic view. The enemy of humanity on Planet Ulro isn't 'them.' It's us! A homegrown disease to which no one is immune. Everyone is an enemy to himself and to the rest."

The professor with the friendly face and the relaxed manner was certainly not reserved in his responses. More like the opening of the floodgates, so passionate was his description.

Adawale replied promptly, "Then my next question makes no sense. But I'll ask anyway: Who are all these people?"

"The briefest answer is that human life on Ulro has returned to 'the state of nature.'"

"Except that the state of nature was a myth."

"Exactly! What are we to say about the status of myth when you meet it around every corner? It's Hobbes: The mythic original situation of all against all looms up before us as the once and future reality. Or it would be if we recognized the situation. Grasp that and you grasp the whole: the security cameras on every building, underground cities, universal paranoia, the global security industry. Remember when the rabbit in the comics used to run off a cliff and stop in midair? He didn't realize there was no ground under him until he looked down. We must keep people afraid to look down."

That was not an account likely to raise Adawale's spirits. Yet from his work among the nation-states—what was left of them—he could only agree.

He didn't miss the incongruity of a mild-mannered professor so alarmed by the horrors he struggled to put in words that his hand trembled when he picked up his beer. Again he was reminded of Mamud's account of his psychiatric patients as extreme cases of afflictions present in the general populace, apparently even in the presumed models of rationality on a university faculty!

During the hour that followed the two men catalogued the symptoms of a planetary system unravelling into an atomistic struggle of all against all. People against everything.

However, such a quick meeting of minds did not guarantee a coinciding of mood. For all Erlich's sense of urgency, he was still able to grin intermittently like a man who didn't intend to let disaster steal his good humor. "It's a primeval soup where every position becomes a violent cause. Except for the forced *illusion* of order, everybody is in danger from everybody else."

Adawale replied, "And all supposed to be ameliorated by learning tolerance for differences! Instead, we get fear."

Gebhard Erlich accepted that view with a warm smile, then continued. "Your fine book exposes the cultural traditions at the root of political upheavals, as though if we could reach some syncretism of traditions, the world might be more peaceful. But perhaps those conflicts kept us conscious. Faced with a general amnesia of the past, I wonder if amalgamation might be the death of thinking. Underlying this bedlam of opinion against opinion, the worst may be the loss of cultural memory."

Within an hour these two could almost complete each other's sentences. "I see what you mean. You're saying that the decline in ideals of education as cultivating our potential for living human lives condemns us to chaos, if not a return to primitivism for generations. If we survive at all."

Adawale grew more somber, but Erlich showed no intention of letting the impending collapse of collective life steal his good humor, though the remarks that concluded the exchange were offered in a somewhat quieter tone.

"Not being a humanist," he grinned mischievously, "I don't think the disintegration of the global system would be such a bad thing—aside from being suicidal! As you suggest, the tyranny of individual interest and opinion may be the essence of our problem. But the occasional revolution can clear the decks and encourage renewal. Apart from preventing the destruction of the species, I don't see much to conserve except for a certain hard-won clarity of mind that's at risk in the best of times. By now we have organized things so well and locked them together so tightly that if we had the courage to look in the mirror, order might disintegrate. If so, what you call our elaborate security is all that stands between us and pandemonium."

When the passion of the topic had subsided, Ope asked how the Committee was responding to the intellectual pandemonium.

More calmly now, the professor replied, "There are various circles. One has developed a non-quantitative technique for estimating what ordinary people think about day after day. In fact the inspiration came from a Biblical remark that 'Where your treasure is, there will your heart be also.' The heart being a traditional metaphor for the will to act, it means what we value most, we'll think about most, and eventually act on. So we want to find where the treasures are without waiting for the act!"

Adawale sighed yet tried to keep his own tone light. "Now that wall-to-wall surveillance systems have proved inadequate, you have developed a spyglass for peering into the soul—if there still is such a thing. But I interrupt."

Erlich observed the modulation to a lighter tone. "We have groups of volunteers, classified by age, education, economic status, and other factors. They agree to keep a running diary of the time they spend occupied with various subjects: jobs, sex, social activities, family, TV, the web, social media, sports, personal finances. Also time spent reading books or in conversation with others. To make collating the data easier, the subjects are encouraged to select from a long list of likely possibilities that they may expand as they wish."

"And they keep their diaries conscientiously?"

"Surprising, isn't it? But they do. And much more carefully than anyone expected. So much so that we often speculate on why."

"And what do you learn?"

The response to this question might have occupied days, even weeks, and it did go for another hour. But the chief impression was that the Committee had found a way of tracking how people in different categories use their time, what they think about, and how rewarding their lives are. Yet none of the evidence brightened Ope's disposition.

Later in the afternoon Erlich apologized for having to leave for a meeting but suggested that Georghiu find a time when the two of them could meet again.

When the professor left, Georghiu and Adawale found Kemal waiting outside the restaurant, on foot this time, having sent his vehicle back to "base" and taken the U-Bahn from the Prater into town. Adawale requested that they make one stop before returning to Donau City. "I'd like very much to visit the Nameless Library in Judenplatz if it's convenient," he answered. "I've always wanted to see it."

And so the three of them piled into Georghiu's little car and drove to the large square, site of the medieval Jewish ghetto. In the twelfth century the square had been the center of a large neighborhood of some 70 houses facing inward on the square. Now it included the Jewish Museum and archeological site as well as the object of their visit: the Holocaust memorial known as the Nameless Library.

The monument was a severe concrete rectangle 32' long x 13' wide and tall. Its four sides are carved as library shelves filled with closed books, spines turned inward, open edges out. The generic volumes memorialize the Holocaust victims and the People of the Book. One end of the monument represents ambivalent locked double doors: either an entrance into the tomb of dark Holocaust history or into the vast world of Jewish learning. In either case, entrance denied!

Beverly and Kemal know the square well, but Adawale's slow, silent progress around and around the monument makes a different impression. Through his eyes, they *see* the memorial for the first time.

Stopped by traffic on the way back to UNO City, Georghiu turns around to look at Adawale. "May I ask what you saw that I hadn't seen?"

His reply came slowly in broken rhythm and a monotone barely audible in the front seat. "Holocaust memorials everywhere have become memorials of our planetary infamy."

CHAPTER 4

OTHER APPARENTLY random adventures followed that left Adawale feeling less able at the end of each day to find relief from the maze of dispiriting conversations. Worse were the solitary nights spent trying to take stock of his own role in the madness.

So secretive was the invisible web he had been drawn into that Mamud Çelik would not have understood. But he would have seen the risks for a man of his disposition, left flailing without purpose in Boris' dark sticky scheme. And for whatever reason, Çelik made a point of remaining in contact.

One evening he sent a message inviting Ope to a dinner with the Çelik family—Mamud, Aylin, Kemal, and Beverly!— at an ancient *Beisl* named Gmoa Keller behind the Vienna Concert House in the city. All that had passed since they met had sharpened his need for another good talk. Though the idea of the family cast a shadow over the prospect, their lunchtime discussion after the morning at the clinic had merged in Ope's mind with more recent experiences, raising new questions. So he accepted, and having accepted, began to anticipate the chance to observe the family dynamics for himself.

By this time, Officer Georghiu had gradually ceased hovering over him with her eternal security regulations, and he had learned to treat them more casually than perhaps he should.

96

So he walked out of the security zone at UNO City, across to the U-Bahn station, and took the train to City Park, alone.

At the restaurant he found Mamud and Aylin Çelik at a table in a back corner of an old cellar. The ambience was unique: an ancient building furnished with tables nearly as old, set with white tablecloths and napkins, frequented by local families with children, and featuring a traditional Austrian menu. Ope's curiosity inspired the always buoyant Mamud to recount the colorful history of the place. Then, laying his hand on his wife's wrist he added, "But mainly I come for the liver and onions that Aylin refuses to make."

"Then that's settled," Adawale replied in his best imitation of a cheerful voice. "I love that dish, especially in Germanic countries."

Since Kemal and Beverly had not arrived, Mamud asked without prologue, "So what's been happening in the grey matter since we met last?"

At that moment the beer arrived, and Ope took a sip without responding to the question. Mamud waited expectantly as Ope glanced apologetically at Aylin before remarking, "Well I *have been* preoccupied with a question since our morning at the clinic."

Aylin, noticing his reticence, "Never mind me! I'm as interested in these topics as Çelik." She often referred to him in third person by his surname. "We've lived in a perpetual analytic session for the past thirty years. We have a ritual reading of some book aloud each evening and sometimes wake up in the night and discuss it for an hour or two. So please, fire away!"

And he did. "This may just be backing and filling, but never mind. Your remarks on human development have helped me see more clearly how wrong common sense often is about who we are. Without clarification on that topic, political thinking drifts into the shallows of opinion, and that amends my convictions about cultural heritage. It seems we need more than civic tradition. The historical picture is weak unless it includes a vision of how the individual is constituted as a thinking, speaking, and acting citizen."

Mamud took satisfaction in the renewed vigor of Adawale's mind that had earlier appeared dimmed by low spirits. Sipping his beer with closed eyes, he waited for what would come next.

"In our last conversation, you mentioned two different ways of tracking the development of the political animal. One organic and naturalistic, the other linguistic." He paused. Then, "Without going into the complexities of psychic maladies and analytic practice, can you tell me, please, who we are?"

Mamud was amused by the specialist in one field, become amateur in another, leaping recklessly but deftly from one over-big idea to another. "The key," he began, "is neither inheritance nor environment. That is, both and neither. There is reason to be dissatisfied with organic and psychic accounts of development. Applied to human beings, they may end up stranded in the same shallow water, as you put it."

He searched momentarily for the best way to proceed, then suddenly asked, "Did I say before that in analysis we begin with the notion that, unlike other species, we are born prematurely?"

"You didn't. And I don't know what born prematurely means."

"It means that, by comparison with other species, the human infant is born underequipped. Even organic survival skills must be acquired slowly. And during that laborious process, it must acquire other, quite mysterious functions that are discontinuous with organic life as we know it. The idea is that we are marked from the beginning by a radical—an ineluctable—negativity. There's always an empty space, always a lack."

Ope rushed to confirm the idea. "But isn't that our essential freedom? When we conceive the human as hyper-organized sacks of protoplasm or as complicated machines, we omit—even repudiate—the primary data of lived experience: deliberation and choice. The human animal or the program-mable machine prepares the way to the anti-political Ulro disease! Goodbye ethics and goodbye politics."

"I think you're on to a very perceptive issue. Namely, that any *developmental* account of the speaking being whatever, historical or organic, leaves us very little to speak about."

At that moment Aylin spotted Kemal and Beverly just entering and Ope shifted his interest to relations among the 'family' of four, especially watching Mamud welcoming Beverly as warmly as his own child and Aylin drawing her to sit between the two of them while placing Kemal between Adawale and his father.

The asymmetry between the older and younger couples, alongside the currents of affection, offer a way for Ope to gauge the ideological tension. Whatever their intellectual reservations, they are already bound by the currents of affec-tion into a happy family. Although he, Ope, is gratified by his own reception among them even as the brief ritual causes him to feel a certain vacuum in his own life.

Kemal, true child of the family, promptly asks what they've been discussing.

"Your father," Adawale replies affably, "was about to trace the political world from the cell to the city! You must blame me. I'm the provocateur. I want to save political culture by breeding good citizens. The small problem is that I don't know how to do it."

"That's my old friend!" Mamud exclaims jovially to Georghiu, patting her affectionately on the shoulder. "It's all about where we start and what question we ask, isn't it? How culture gets 'grafted' to the organic or how the organism emerges into the open space of a world already exposed in language."

There's a pause in the general exuberance while each studies the menu and orders. For Beverly and Aylin: potato and spinach pasta with cheese and onions; for Kemal: a schnitzel and potato salad, large enough for two and, of course, the liver and onions.

Beverly unselfconsciously blossoms in intelligent company. And why not when she, like Aylin, whose father had been a university professor, had grown up in an intellectual culture. In a sense more even than Aylin, whose literary culture ran deep but lacked the old European philosophical tradition. Beverly and Mamud are also closer in disposition than the more casual Kemal and his mother. Both having entered the world though the language and sensibility of their fathers, they wear their learning more lightly, whereas Mamud and

Beverly have had to earn citizenship in the intellectual world by hard work. No wonder they respect each other and, as Ope can now see, he really loves her. Too bad, then, about the religious thing.

During dinner, the conversation becomes general, mainly about the events of the day, as though it is their habit to postpone mental exercise until after their meal.

Once the table is cleared, Beverly asks with enthusiasm, "So where are we now? How far along were you on the path from cell to city?"

Mamud replies lightly, "I'm afraid Adawale is skeptical about my way of doing things. He asks about development but wants an ideal citizen."

Aylin answers playfully. "Then give him Antigone."

He laughs. "You think she's an exemplary citizen, do you?"

Beverly takes Aylin's side, if there are any sides here. "I took a seminar in Greek tragedy last year where the professor insisted that we see 'Antigone' not as the name of a real person but a literary *figure* in the middle of a political conflict. That means that 'Antigone' and her uncle 'Creon' are names for functions in a struggle."

As he often does, Mamud asks a question with a "leading twinkle" in his eye, prompting more. "You mean there's no distance between the character and her function in the play? Not a person 'caught up' in the events of the plot?"

When she hesitates, as though the question might not be clear, he eases the strain. "It will hardly surprise you to hear that psychoanalysts have a passing acquaintance with Oedipus and family, and we also make your distinction: Oedipus' value is in being a fiction, a hypothetical figure like a paradigm. Now I think you should show us how you read the story. It might help in Adawale's search for the being who's capable of citizenship."

Aylin suggests that everyone knows the story, so why repeat it?

"First, because a good story, like a piece of great music, can't be repeated. It will be different in every performance. But also because it's a love song, even played in the key of tragedy. We need the ritual retelling of the great stories to keep us reminded of what we're capable of."

Feeling Beverly's reticence in this company, Aylin kindly offers the summary in her place. "Okay, then start with this reminder: After Oedipus' tragic career of innocently killing his father and marrying his mother, the city of Thebes is torn by civil war. Eventually his brother-in-law Creon becomes king and restores order. Now enter Antigone, Oedipus' daughter and sister! Her two brothers have managed to kill each other in a struggle for power, and that entangles the city in a familial vendetta.

"When Creon gives honorable burial to one brother and denies it to the other, Antigone defies his order and buries Polynices with her own hands. The act fulfills ancient familial obligations ordained by the gods. Then comes the struggle to the death between her and her uncle even though she is betrothed to his son."

"That," Ope recalls, "is the perpetual conflict internal to the free city-state. It always threatens to slip back into the familial domain of survival and necessity."

Kemal turns to Ope and pokes fun at his mother and Beverly, as though they're misreading the story from a gender bias. "Now they'll show you that the exemplary political role is feminine. Only the woman can resolve the conflict between blood debt and rational law."

Pretending to hit his shoulder with a fist, Beverly replies, "That wouldn't be smart, would it? Antigone doesn't end very well. Creon walls her up in a cave where she hangs herself in a heroic suicide."

"And that cave," Aylin continues, "is a figure of the deadly enclosure of law, maintained by violence all around. Creon's son, her fiancé, discovers her hanging in the cave and falls on his own sword. Then Creon's wife stabs herself with a knife. Antigone dies a public hero while King Creon destroys himself in defense of law."

"Okay," Mamud says, "now how are we to apply this happy tale?"

"The play," Beverly answers, "is mainly conversation between the two characters: Creon defending law and order; Antigone dividing law against itself. Civil law against divine law."

"From inside the city," Aylin says. "Divine law is the out-law. The 'stasis' of the state is to hold at bay—violently if necessary—the forces that law exists to exclude."

Kemal asks, "But what about Creon's ideal of civil order?"

"It's a negative ideal," Beverly answers. "It's his alternative to perpetual conflict in all these generations that we remember as the 'House of Atreus.' He stops the cycles of revenge that the gods endorse."

Aylin insists. "He suppresses—*with fear and vengeance*—any force that threatens the law against fear and vengeance! Meanwhile Antigone keeps faith with the powers of the city and with the powers in herself that the king excludes."

Kemal asks, "Why would the gods contradict civil order?"

Aylin: "Because they're accretions of contradictory traditions. So when Agamemnon, a later family member in an earlier play—when he has been murdered by his wife, Clytemnestra, his son, Orestes, *must* avenge his death. But a son *must not* kill his mother."

Mamud: "You mean that in the crisis at Thebes, Antigone is both citizen and outsider? She belongs to the city and is bound by its laws, but the law can't entirely include her because she's more."

Kemal adds, "Then this is not a personal struggle or a commonplace moral problem, as in 'What do Antigone or Creon do wrong?'"

"Right." Beverly answers. "Moral language imposes a rule and misses the point. As though Creon were right about something that she gets wrong or vice versa."

Adawale muses half-aloud. "I see where this is going. On your reading, both characters surpass an individualistic politics."

"Yes," Beverly replies. "That's why it's necessary not to see them as representations of real people. It's the situation that matters. The exemplary event. The tragic history of the House of Atreus must be jettisoned if we're to have a city governed by law. Antigone is the point where traditional familial law and Creon's civil law collide."

"And here's the crux," Aylin insists. "Both forces are present in both characters. Subjectively, 'Creon' is the name of terror in the face of uncontrollable forces. We see how his fear leads him to destroy the Antigone-force in himself by causing the death of his own wife and son. The very familial forces embodied in Antigone. 'Antigone' names the courage that demands accommodation between lawless life and lawful order. Not individuals and not morality!"

"Are you saying, then, that politics is not about people but how we arrange things justly?" Adawale's remark is made with the surprise and passion of epiphany. "And yet, if we take Antigone as a paradigm of the citizen, the citizen would *have* to be the outlaw!"

Kemal: "Or both! And she's a conflict inherent to political life. Law shows its inherent violence when it polices and punishes."

For some minutes Mamud has been absorbed by something else. Ope notices, chuckles, and commands, "Say it!"

Mamud throws a searching glance towards Beverly. "I'm thinking of gender. You two are not making a gender argument"—a gesture includes her and Aylin—"and I'm not trying to restore Antigone to the family history even if she did accompany Oedipus' nomadic wandering around Greece for years. And yet Kemal may have a point. Do you think Creon's view might, in a way, be 'masculine' and Antigone's 'feminine?'"

Beverly studies the question for a moment or two and smiles ironically. "I'm not sure." Then she teases him, "Of course a psychoanalyst might read it as a problem of the daughter's Oedipal relation to her father and the authority of the male!"

Then more seriously, "But read as a political story, gender seems ambiguous. I suppose burying her brother associates her with family loyalty and the nurturing mother, but her drama isn't about hearth and home. She's a figure in the public world of Thebes and as tragically divided as Creon himself. You remember, the chorus of citizens supports *her* against *his* law. Where he lives with terror and destroys his private life by killing his family, she endures inconsistency to the point of dying."

"Then let's add," says Ope, "that she isn't demanding the repeal of his law. Only that he make an exception in this case."

"And that's just what the chorus demands! So the city seems to be open to what you called 'the out-law' in the law. It's only the legalistic Creon who refuses."

A noisy group of musicians having entered and gathered around a large table nearby, Mamud, presuming that the young people may wish to go their own way, proposes that he, Aylin, and Ope walk two blocks up to the park where they can continue.

The security officers promptly object that the streets may not be safe after dark. Mamud waves them aside. "We'll only go to the *Kursalon*." The reference is to *Kursalon Hübner*, the elegant Italianate building with a broad terrace on the Vienna River. "There are no conferences or tourist concerts there tonight, and I know the administrator. We can sit on the veranda as long as we like."

Kemal replies, "Yes, but you have to get there and it's inside the security ring."

Beverly, seeing that objections are futile, "Then we're going with you!"

106

CHAPTER 5

THE FIVE WALK the short distance across the security perimeter without incident and settle down on the terrace that extends into the park at the rear of the grand building. It's not a clear night—romantic nights and Vienna waltzes seem to belong to a past era—but the temperature is moderate, and groves of trees shield them from the noise of the city.

With their chairs placed near the balustrade facing down the park without either the nomadic multitudes or the military in sight, it is almost possible to imagine the elegant Vienna of the distant past.

The tonal shift from a noisy restaurant to the reflective quiet of the park requires a few moments of transition at the end of which Ope has a question for Georghiu. "Beverly, you said that Sophocles' play is mainly competing speeches on rival visions of the city. If the play works as exemplary of political ideals, what strikes you about all those speeches?"

When she has no immediate response, Mamud also prods gently, "It doesn't seem very close to what analysts call the 'talking cure.' Or is it? And if so, how?"

As Georghiu is composing a response to these questions, Mamud is observing something encouraging that goes unmentioned. It is that the evening of conversation among the five appears to have relieved Ope's melancholy, temporarily at least.

Georghiu, ready to pursue the topic of speeches in the play, turns from one to the other and asks, "Are the political animal and the speaking animal the same beast?"

Adawale smiles. "Wouldn't that be explaining one mystery with a still darker mystery?"

"I suppose you mean the language itself. I've heard a lot on that subject lately. Apparently if we didn't already have language, we'd never be able to imagine it. Like having five senses and imagining a sixth. Something like that?"

Çelik laughs, gratified by her eagerness. "Something like but *patience papillon!*"

It's another moment when Ope foresees how quickly the father-in-law with the bad conscience will forgive the young people for marrying against his wishes and his principles.

The topic of language having been dropped in his lap, Mamud responds lightly, "Out of respect for present company, let's pass over both the relevant genetic and social processes of human development and take a different path to language. Aylin recently used a conundrum that may clarify the point." He gestures toward her. "Tell us about ducks."

"Imagine a child watching a duck feeding in the pond over there." She points into the shadows nearby. "Then he sees a picture of a yellow duck on a billboard, a black and white duck on TV, a toy duck in a store that goes 'quack, quack' when it's squeezed. How, in all that diversity, does he acquire the word 'duck' that gives him such joy? It seems clear that experience of the duck-object doesn't provide the word, nor does he come equipped with a prior concept of duck. He receives duck images and slowly develops the concept—but how? Is the name, perhaps, a bridge between image and idea, between sign and symbol? It's as though there is first only a flood of affects followed by a swarm of images."

Beverly interrupts, "Or it might also be the sound 'quack' that precedes, like music, provoking the visual image."

"Perhaps," Aylin responds with a cordial smile. "Either way, slowly, he acquires the objects by resuming names that have already been given by others and are 'in the air.' A joyful curiosity lures him into a world already swarming with names."

Mamud adds, "You mean that by resuming names already given he finds psychic support in the world?"

"Yes, but that's *only* the beginning. The name 'duck' moves in a diverse and unstable field of reference. His duck is neither the name itself nor the thing itself. More like a bridge between. There's a surplus potential in the word beyond both the object and concept that arrives by means of the name."

Mamud: "To that I want to add a remark that doesn't make sense at first, and I'm not going to try to explain it. So take it as a koan for further reflection. What passes in a name, in the sound of the name, is not an object or a concept but the unutterable idea of duckness."

"Oh my God!" Adawale cries. "You've all outrun me again. Even if whatever you're saying makes sense, what can it possibly have to do with the political?"

"Unless," Mamud says quietly, almost gently, "unless when Beverly discusses Antigone and Creon, she's naming rival political codes that have no name. But that, *being said*, rise up before us as possibilities."

"Ah," she says as though understanding something unintelligible, "you're saying that I'm the child waiting for the name that can evoke 'duckness' in diverse duck-images! And that I'm politically enlightened by resuming the names uttered by Sophocles!"

"Just so. The political philosopher, like the poet, baffled by the problem of action, searches for what is currently unsayable. The unspoken name for a potential consistency."

And on that idea the bewildering conversation ended in a silence as still and as dark as the landscape before them.

CHAPTER 6

ANOTHER TRIP with Kemal Çelik didn't happen as promised. Instead, Adawale spent the next two weeks meeting with UN and EU officials, listening to dire predictions without solutions by experts in global health, the planetary environment, international insecurity, threats of nuclear conflict, the deterioration of global education into utilitarian knowhow, and—this one surprised him—blind technological development as self-imposed slavery.

One morning, without notice of course, Beverly Georghiu drives him to the airport where they board a corporate jet for Geneva to join a conference of financial and corporate executives on the topic of global production and the concentration of wealth by "corporate entities."

These encounters certainly expand his store of information, but the worship of information has only dimmed understanding: trees everywhere but no forest in sight. He feels himself wandering without direction in a wilderness under the pressure of Boris Razumovski's ominous remark about time. Repeatedly the image of Werner Brock, Mamud Çelik's compulsive patient, comes to mind, struggling to keep his chairs in order. Is there kinship between Werner's repetition compulsion and Boris' scheme to make coherence of a chaotic world before the bell tolls the day of doom and all has to begin again—or not?

And yet one small mystery is becoming clearer. However random, there is a principle behind the sequence of his activities. When he shows special interest in one aspect of a topic, it seems to dictate where he is sent next. The deduction may have contribute to the sense of self-determination, but it gives little comfort. The darkness deepens as each night he returns to the apartment to contemplate the plight of the world and hear the voice of Boris' curse: a month to perform an unspecified task, then the most momentous decision in the history of life on Planet Ulro.

In this bleak state of mind, Georghiu escorts him to a second meeting with Gebhard Erlich. Arriving, as before, at the offices of the Committee on Social Research, Erlich meets them at the street door and, to Adawale's surprise, invites her to join them.

"It will be your orientation to your next research assignment." Even so, as the three sit down in his conference room, he shows little inclination to enter on the topic, so Adawale takes the lead once more by asking how Erlich's own field is related to the work of the Committee. "I don't think you mentioned which faculty you belong to."

"Philosophy," he answers, "with a research interest in language. I would like to tell you about one of the Committee projects that focuses on that subject." He smiles at Georghiu. "I remember that Beverly has already described the observations of her group on the dulling of the public mind. You also know that faculty projects focus on various aspects of the 'Pathology of Everyday Life.' My circle has whimsically christened its project 'The Tower of Babel.' The global condition of language in mid-twenty-first century.

"There are four of us: a linguist, a specialist in child development, and a psychiatrist. They let me tag along as philosopher-in-residence. Our focus is on how people understand and use words. From the point of view of skills and information the topic is pedestrian to the point of banality, yet I can assure you it's anything but. It probably gets closer to the origins of the global malaise than all the managerial chatter taken together."

This time Adawale doesn't rush ahead toward his political interests. He says instead, "It does sound a bit obvious, so I must be missing the point. An example might sensitize me to the issue."

Beverly nods in sympathy.

"Loosely put, it's about literal versus symbolic language, but that may sound more benign than it is. Here's an example from English literature, from Jonathan Swift's *Gulliver's Travels*."

He laughs with pleasure at the mention of the title as though the bare name were a musical experience. "The book belongs to the great tradition of 'learned wit.' That means, if you want to enjoy the fun, you must know something. A great deal, as it happens. That's forbidding to a world that has lost its cultural moorings, especially its stories.

"Anyway, the third section of the *Travels* is a caustic satire of the New Science, based on the actual Proceedings of the English Royal Society in the sixteen- and early seventeen-hundreds. It's amusing to contemplate how Swift and the

Committee on Social Research mark the beginning and the likely end of technological rationality."

This sounds to Adawale like the beginning of a formal lecture, but then, he came here to learn, not to listen to chatter.

"You must know," Erlich continues, "that the fictional narrator of these adventures is the gullible Lemuel Gulliver himself who, in the third part, sails as medical officer on a British ship destined to the East Indies only to get sidetracked somewhere beyond Tonkin in 'parts unknown'—as you may have been sidetracked in Vienna. He winds up alone on the imaginary island of Balnibarbi and is rescued by scientific rationalists on a flying island. Just a century after the dawn of the scientific revolution and half a century before the industrial revolution, Swift traces likely consequences of these developments over the four centuries that would follow, and all through the credulous eyes of Gulliver, the ostensible author of the account.

"I'll just mention two examples of language research projects in the most absurd university you can imagine: The Grand Academy of Lagado." He chuckles again at some unspoken irony. "It's more like what we still do at the university than we care to admit."

The last remark startles Adawale. His own academic experience had led to a similar idea and had even occurred to him in the middle of Erlich's outbursts in their first conversation.

"The first of these 'projectors'—the ones who 'throw things forward' all too hastily—this pro-jector pro-poses to cure the well-known disease of ambiguity in words. He wants words to stand still and do their proper work. That would be a one-to-one correspondence between the word and the thing it refers to. His improvement is to have speakers carry the objects they want to talk about on their backs. Then, instead of relying on slippery names, they can unpack the objects and point to them. That's to insure clarity in discourse!"

"So?" Georghiu asks, a bit impatiently.

"So, this researcher holds the same view of language as the world all around us. He wants sign systems that can 'pick out' isolated objects in the world. But the fun and the brilliance come in the projector failing to notice that the correspondence between words and objects destroys the coherence of any language and any world. And that's not the half of it. He—like his colleagues in various fields—sees his own task as manipulating reality to fit conscious ends and means. That leaves himself and his own horizon out of the process—off his own map so to speak. What about his capacity for collective tradition, for imagination, and contemplation? You see, we are firmly in the land of Ulro!"

Ope follows that, though he may feel that Erlich's interpretation is a bit exaggerated. Rather than argue the issue, he asks, "And the second experimenter?"

"You may remember that Plato says the point of science is 'to preserve the appearances,' the changing world we live in. Well, this Academy prefers research programs abstracted as far as possible from everyday life and replaced by what creatures like us can make. A new subjective 'reality'! Reducing human excrement to its original food, for example, or redistributing sunlight by extracting sunbeams from cucumbers. Plato's academy—that's where we get the word—has degenerated into dozens of similar projects for making men 'the masters and possessors of nature,' as Descartes famously proposed.

"The second language specialist has built a machine that will provide a complete system of the Arts and Sciences. It's a gigantic frame with wires crossing in both directions. Individual blocks of wood are strung across the wires and turned by cranks, so that the blocks, with words on each surface, can be rotated randomly. By producing all possible combinations of all the 'word-objects' in the language, the machine will effortlessly *produce* every possible idea without thinking. All that's needed is to be able to recognize well-formed statements."

As though the consequences are obvious, Erlich pauses to indulge his taste for satire, once again not noticing whether his audience shares his enthusiasm or even understands.

The mystified Georghiu, she who always wants examples related to the present world, erupts again: "So?"

"So," he laughs and taps his fingertips on the table in parody of her impatience, "if words were objects that we could manipulate like tools, an immortal monkey at a type-writer might eventually produce *Hamlet*! More important than the product, the *Travels*, published in the year 1726, revealed what the mind would be if it truly were the proto-type of communications theory and digital intelligence. The problem is that the projector's axioms have methodologically excluded 'intelligence' and 'communication' from the start. Concepts without thought! There is no place for a being with the imagination to invent any of these experiments however absurd they are. Worst of all, there's no place in the paradigm of a rational system of signs for the poet Jonathan Swift and his language."

Suspecting the example has more in it than he can see, Adawale asks, a bit skeptically, for more.

Overlooking the hesitancy in the request, Erlich grins with delight. He may be insensitive, even overweening at times, but he's no fool. "The point is not that parochial or isolated disciplines get the human process of speaking *wrong*. They assume that language is a skill by which we apply word-tools to communication tasks. But that formulation has already excluded the root problem. The question is, does discourse really work by applying rules, like grammar, to word-things we can find in a dictionary?"

That throws Georghiu into genuine perplexity. "If words are not signs used to make things appear before us that aren't really there, what are they? How would we get behind structure to a direct experience of a word?"

He replies without rushing to resolve the enigma. "That's the issue in both Lagado and on Ulro, isn't it? And it's a tough problem that we can't solve with quick answers that let the question die."

Beverly responds as though impatient with him for not offering a direct answer, as if she thinks he's playing games with them. "Well, that's depressing, isn't it? On your account it's a wonder that anyone ever succeeds in saying anything intelligible."

Erlich laughs at her frustration. "But it may even turn out to be a love story, though a hard love story to tell."

Meanwhile the riddle provokes a flood of energy in Adawale. "Yes, but Beverly has the right question: What is 'a direct experience of the word'?"

"The best way I know into that," Erlich answers, "is to observe a situation where the word either doesn't work as we've come to expect or where it's entirely missing when it's needed. What, for example, do the language projectors miss when they think a sign points to an object? Perhaps there's a gap of some kind they're not seeing."

Adawale responds with a slight twinkle in his eye: "That reminds me of when your train arrives in some London Tube stations where there's a space between the floor of the car and the platform. A voice from nowhere warns, 'Mind the gap.' If you're saying there is no 'word for the word,' only the gap, I suppose it's pointless to ask for an example. But is an example of the difficulty at least possible?"

"I like your example," the professor answered. "The whole business is about getting somewhere as we get to the platform by stepping over the gap. Sometimes the gap created by the word requires a long jump, a leap of faith from the sound of the voice to something quite different, like the platform. The word points a way but offers no correspondence between word and a fixed meaning. Only a fissure, a distance that's crossed mysteriously, if at all."

Adawale: "So then, an example, if you please, of our uncanny feeling when the word goes missing or doesn't work for some reason."

Erlich: "You remind me of another London experience. Once I happened to pass a shop window with a sign that said,

'Bicycles repaired here.' Then, on the same window, another: 'Clothes pressed here.' And a third: 'Apartment for let.' The unlikely collection of services in one establishment made me curious, so I peered inside. It was a sign painter's shop! In an instant, words that promised three inconsistent things didn't mean at all what they promised. They failed and left me stranded. I had to find what they didn't say. That failure reveals the difference between words as dead objects and living words that work. It's a negative experience of the word."

As both Georghiu and Adawale remain silently contemplating an example that wasn't easy to assimilate, he continues. "With that glimpse of the gap in mind between what is said and what *might be* said—if we could find the right word—we can make the point clearer by turning the experience the other way around. It's the poet's problem of supplying the missing word: He's like a broad jumper at the edge of an abyss. He leaps and, if he gets it right, a patch of earth appears in the void just where he must land. The void where no words were provided, reminding us that words conjure worlds into presence."

Georghiu looks at her watch as though she has another appointment to keep but not before taking the time to tease her professor. "Now it remains for you to show us how to use this insight. You promised it would be a love story, but you left that part out."

Erlich rubs his hands together with delight. "There's a passage in the English poet William Blake that says—not *the passage*, mind you, but *what passes in it* for one who is willing to take the leap!

Never seek to tell thy love
Love that never told can be
For the gentle wind does move
Silently invisibly.

"You can't say what love is, but in saying what can't be said, love shows itself."

CHAPTER 7

THE NEXT MORNING, waiting for Kemal once more in the lobby of the residence towers, Adawale passes the time reflecting on two events, the discussion with Professor Erlich and his peculiar vision of Vienna through the eye of a stranger. It is *his* story: the outsider everywhere, privileged or condemned to observe the follies of the world as he passes through.

Waiting in the atrium, vaguely amused with the comparison, another random thing happens. A Chinese woman—the same Chinese woman he had seen on the first day—enters and sits down on a park bench nearly but not quite opposite. Her manner is a bit too casual for business and too formal to cross distances between strangers. Again she is dressed in a *qipao*, this one a striking blue with a floral design. Out of the corner of his eye Opeyemi watches until she looks up and recognizes him with a nod and a smile to which he inclines his head in a slight bow.

That's all. Nothing really. And yet two such encounters don't quite add up to nothing. There have been enough startling events in recent days to fill his thoughts, but her reappearance moves her well up on his list of coincidences.

This time she doesn't linger, but as she leaves, she gives ever so slight a nod in his direction, making him wonder as the moment passes if she could have anything to do with his misadventures.

It all passes with the arrival of Kemal, and the two of them are soon buckled into another Humvee and heading out of town, direction Linz. All is normal between them until, distracted by chatter on his radio about trouble around the *Naschmarkt*, Kemal switches from the car speaker to an earpiece. Before they get as far as *Schönbrunn* on the route out of the city, he is summoned urgently to a site of violence. Minutes later they arrive at the market to distant sounds of gunshots. Only then does he describe the situation to Adawale.

"It's a street battle," he explains, "between young gangs of Muslims and Jews. Security people are caught between. Sorry for the inconvenience, but I have to go in there." Then he modulates to command mode: "Put on this flak jacket and helmet and stay in the back of the Humvee until I return."

As he gets out, he repeats in tones of absolute authority, "Under no circumstances are you to leave the vehicle. It's for your own safety." Then pausing only to communicate with someone on his headset, he rushes away.

PART THREE
THE READERS

CHAPTER 1

"PROFESSOR ADAWALE, PLEASE COME with us. We're moving you out of harm's way." Even locked in a Humvee in an urban battle zone, Ope knew how to pick up his bag at a moment's notice and leave without asking questions for destinations unknown. But this was different. For one who lives by conscious purposes, it's unnerving enough to be passed from person to person and from place to place without explanation. Quite another to go quietly into what had all the marks of a diplomatic kidnapping.

After being diverted to the *Naschmarkt*, Kemal had leapt from the vehicle with the command to remain locked in until he returned, no matter what might happen.

For two hours Ope was stranded there until two toughs in battle gear and armed with automatic weapons turned up to "rescue" him. Though they had keys to the vehicle and knew his name, that was little comfort. There was no way to know whether he was really being evacuated for his safety or being taken hostage.

He had time to argue the point with himself as he was ushered to an unmarked car a block away and the driver raced north, northwest toward the Vienna Woods: Who would take the trouble to kidnap a man who does nothing but read books? What possible value could he have to any criminal or

125

political group? Except that diplomats can be pawns in games that have nothing to do with them personally.

He had never been in the hills above the city, but from the map in his head he was able to recognize the sunlit peak of Kahlenberg mountain, where the Alps end at the Danube. This day, at least, that image offered relief from the greyness of the city below. They crept through the village of Grinzing and turned right at a narrow stone gate into a vineyard. Then about a kilometer along the farm road the car stopped at a house.

Not a modern concrete building like several on the paved road up from Grinzing toward the Vienna Woods, but a traditional Austrian wooden mountain house three stories tall with balconies across the front of the first and second floors. No hint here of the security precautions that might suggest a kidnapping. In fact, a wide gable with overhanging eaves gave the place an inviting alpine air. At the rear, the structure was set into the gradual rise of the hillside with rows of grapevines wrapping around both sides and behind. Nestled beneath the peak, it looked like an island of security and comfort with a rising landscape behind suggesting picturesque views of the river basin and the city.

The car stopped. One man sent a message somewhere and received an instant reply. After a brief exchange of instructions with the driver, conducted in German with Slavic accents, the second, who seemed in charge, ushered Adawale from the car to the house without explanation. Waving him inside with a firm but not unfriendly gesture, he planted himself in the open doorway and gave precise instructions in curt, efficient English. "You are to stay here. This is a safe house. You are safe here. Only one person knows where you are. That person will come soon. Do not communicate with anyone."

He gestured Ope into the entry hall, the door closed, and a moment later the car drove away.

Adawale was too experienced for panic. He had learned when in danger to bide the time until the situation clarified. "When in doubt, follow orders." Besides, in this case he was free to walk out . . . wasn't he? He retraced his steps to the door to verify the fact and was relieved to find it locked only to the outside. Nothing to be done now, so he began exploring the house from the bottom.

The ground floor consisted of two large rooms, blind in the back where the wall extended into the hillside. The first room was furnished like an office with desks in the middle and across one side, with banks of communications equipment along the back.

The second room contained desks in waist-high cubicles like a smaller version of the newsroom of the old daily papers, except that these walls were lined with books. A moment's scan of titles was sufficient to see that most were contemporary but distinguished from the popular media. Books in many languages suggested a kind of global research center. Most surprising of all were copies of his own book in three different tongues. This was no accidental development, then. The event was calculated and choreographed! But by whom? And why?

From the office he passed to the second floor—the European first floor, since in the deep past the ground level would have had no floor. This middle level was devoted to living spaces rather more like a club than a private residence or a public inn. It included a restaurant-style kitchen of modest size, a dining room with separate tables, and a large commons room or library furnished for small conversation groups, and brown leather club chairs for solitary reading. Here, too, the paneled walls were lined with books, but this time with classic titles ancient and modern.

The third floor was given over to bedrooms and baths, some private as for long-term guests and others more like comfortable dormitory quarters. On the doorpost of one of the guest rooms he found a hand-written note in English and signed by a person he'd never heard of:

Professor Adawale,

This is your room. If no one is here when you arrive, please make yourself at home. You should find every-thing you need. The kitchen pantry and fridge are well-stocked. I look forward to meeting you soon.

Wu Mai Bao

Having arrived with nothing but a small book in his pocket, he took off his coat and hung it in a closet where— mystery on top of mystery—there were pants, shirts, jacket—all one would need and all in his size! These details prompted him to think for the first time of comfort rather than the situation at large. The primary sensation being hunger, he returned to the kitchen and found a covered serving board with fresh bread, cheese, and sausage along with beer in the fridge and wine in a cooler. The spread encouraged him to take a tray to the dining room where he chose a table by the window. There was a pleasant view of the vineyard that climbed the hill at the rear of the house to the bluff where Kahlenberg perched high above, barely visible.

Slowly he ate and considered his situation. Still no hint why Razumovski had said he would be handed off clandestinely from one person to another, but given the welcome note, written recently, and the fact that he might easily walk away, he dismissed the idea of abduction. Even if he was expected, the books in multiple languages and the selection of titles in the "newsroom" posed questions enough. Security affirmed, the mystery deepened, while one idea weighed heavily. It was Boris' parting remark yet again. The one about his having one month to perform some unspecified task to prevent the end of the world! And the time was nearly up!

For the remainder of the afternoon and evening he remained alone. Having been on the run for weeks since leaving New York for Nigeria, he shouldn't have minded had it not been for the Boris curse. Ordinarily the ability to accept uncertainty was a distinguishing feature of his stoic disposition, but now, in the solitude of the strange and silent house, melancholy weighed against tranquility. He resolved to wait for the next contingency by selecting a title from the club-room shelves.

Settling down for a quiet read with a decanter of good whiskey for human company, he passed the afternoon as pleasantly as an anxiety-ridden, literate man in moral collapse realistically could. By bedtime, still no sign of the person for whom he was presumably waiting, so he made his way to his room and, in the silence of the pastoral setting, fell into a deep if restless sleep.

At an early hour, he was awakened by the sun streaming in his northeastern window. The first impulse was to listen, as one listens to an empty house. Silence. And again the compelling question: Why? Was he really at risk in the Humvee as his abductors said? He dressed and, with a single shrug at his reflection in the mirror, went downstairs, and passed though the library and into the dining room. Dazzled first by the light, he only saw the view. Then, suddenly, a woman at a table, her back to him, also looking up the vineyard toward the bluff.

She heard him and turned around.

It's she! The Chinese woman he has seen and who has seen him—twice. Once in the restaurant in *Unterstadt* and again in the lobby of the residence towers. She gets up from the table and extends a welcoming hand.

"Professor Adawale. My name is Wu Mai Bao. It's an honor." The voice is warm, pleasantly pitched in midrange, and well-matched to a manner in all respects forthright and friendly.

"Thank you for coming. My colleagues and I have read your book and admire it." There's no acknowledgment by word or gesture of their paths having crossed already or of why he might have been brought here or why she might know his book. Though her unacknowledged presence in the underground city cannot be far from the mind of either, there is no hint of connection with him, official or unofficial.

He nods, bows slightly, and, passing over the several things that go conspicuously unmentioned, replies dryly to the remark about his coming. "Did I have a choice?"

Despite the experiences of the past day and night, it's pleasant to be speaking quietly to a bright person, especially one so attractive. With what in the circumstances might pass for loquacity, he adds, "In fact I haven't had a choice since I was ordered to Vienna from Abuja. Everyone is very kind and helpful. But no one explains! Perhaps you can tell me where I am and why."

His face is habitually under control, yet she detects something around the eyes or in the tone of his voice that warns her off. "Perhaps," she answers to the questions where and why. "But let's have breakfast first."

She leads the way into the kitchen as Ope tries to harmonize his three images of this woman with her voice. The voice has the warm texture of a fine tapestry, dark in tone, lively, sensuous. English is either her native tongue or one of several, but it is spoken with such variation of tone and stress that the music alone commands interest with or without the words. And, like her physical presence, it leaves the impression of quiet strength and resourcefulness.

During breakfast Ope notices, with well-disguised irritation, how smoothly she has sidetracked his questions, but he pushes that aside and begins collecting mental notes on her character. The consummate host, deft at directing an easy flow of events by things not said. And he foresees that the better she is at the game, the longer it will take to find out anything useful. Even who she is!

So smoothly is he being managed that he silently dubs it "British charm in Hong Kong dress" and quashes a surge of resentment. Then, with a quick reflex of self-criticism, he

wonders if the resentment may have to do with being manipulated by a woman, an attractive woman, and a stranger. The
presumption of it! But then, would he care so much if she
weren't so attractive? A devious thing, consciousness! Especially diplomatic consciousness. He has much better reason to
feel manipulated by Boris, who has been pulling his strings for
weeks. So why resent this person's well-concealed patronage?

He waits attentively for her next move, using the time
to extend his speculations on her style and demeanor. Tall
and elegant, just as he had remembered from their first
encounter, and dressed still in the striking Chinese manner
that he had admired.

How does it happen that even the colors stick in the
memory of a man who has no eye for, and therefore no
interest in, fashion? At the first encounter, the dress was black
with a long bamboo design embroidered down the front. At
the second, an equally formal deep blue with a floral print.
And now a less assertive and less formal green—but floral
still—with the same cap sleeves and high collar. Disposed to
see every gesture as calculation, he reads the green as more in
keeping with the pastoral ease of the setting and encouraging
a more personal tone.

The feminine softness at close range brings his late wife
to mind with emphasis, against his will, on their differences.
Yetunde was strong but she did not have the ambiguous
authority emerging at the edges of this woman's demeanor. Wu
stands with feet firmly, if delicately, on the ground in a pose that
conveys courage and intelligence. Every gesture and expression,
however graceful, is consistent with dignity and self-possession.

She knows who she is, where she is, and what she's about, and it's not information she will soon share with him. Yet there is something paradoxical in that concentration of resolve wrapped in all that silk. A musical analogy comes to mind: an orchestra performing a hushed and tender passage even as volcanic power waits just beneath the surface for the propitious moment.

These virtually simultaneous observations take root in his imagination during the brief motion of walking into the next room. And a further impression, a pleasant inkling in the back of his own distinguished, well-shaped head: She quite likes him, and despite the calculations concealed in her lightness of spirit, he likes being liked, almost as much as he hates being used!

They take seats across the table by the window where yesterday he had sat alone, and she returns to his question. "My information is that when you were whisked away from the trouble in the *Naschmarkt*, there was a bomb followed by a gun battle between security agents and unidentified people, generically known as 'the gangs.' As your next contact, I got the call from someone I don't know. So you only arrived here a bit earlier than expected. As a result of the altered schedule, I'll be in and out over the next couple of days. I have obligations that can't be delayed. But I suspect"—she looks at him with an appraising eye—"a quiet retreat with a library at hand may not be unwelcome to a scholar."

He brushes aside an explanation that explains nothing. "It's of no consequence."

As though not to let the topic be dismissed, she reveals a small bit more. "Few know about us, but the few who do call us 'The Readers.'"

A reluctant chuckle relieves a little the gravity of his disposition toward her and the rest of the world. His reply is almost sociable. "Then you're an anachronism. Aren't we sinking into collective illiteracy? 'Words mean exactly what I choose them to mean. Neither more nor less,' said Humpty Dumpty."

She doesn't miss a ripple of passion across the flat, yet momentarily witty voice, and that inspires a touch of irony. "Don't you find people everywhere glued to their communications devices? We're submerged in an ocean of text. Hardly illiterate."

"Bombarded by pixels and decibels, passing our eyes over lines of garbled print—I don't call that reading. Reading is not a skill. We read only when we put our own world on hold and cross the threshold into one that's new and strange. Not tourists but immigrants who must earn citizenship there. Imagining and understanding before accepting or refusing."

In the pathos of that short speech, she reads his openness to seduction by an idea and replies lightheartedly without weakening the point. "Then, I'm surprised at your finding a handful of such readers! No wonder it's a solitary experience."

That repost brightens his tone, slightly. "It only appears to be solitary. In reading, we take delight in a silent conversation."

"Then you must have an unusual notion of conversation as well." And she laughs.

Apparently unaware that he might be showing more than he wants to show, given the topic and his resentment, he can't resist saying more. "Reading and conversation both take time, don't they? The world moves at a speed that leaves no time. Every road leads—roads are built to lead—to foreseeable goals. We're all for action without leisure for understanding." Realizing at last that he has said too much, he stops to see if he's said enough.

Seeing, no doubt, that she has him a bit off balance, she doesn't reply.

So, he adds, "Reading and conversation are triangular, don't you think? As we, at this moment, hold a world up between us and listen together to a choir of voices. That's thinking together."

She smiles warmly, sympathetically even, while backing slightly away. "Do you always set the bar so high?"

This time the light inflections of her voice are tinged with a fervor of their own. "You permit only the charitable response. I see I'll not be ready for conversation with you on your book until I've worked on it hard enough to paraphrase your idea."

"That might lead somewhere neither of us could have predicted."

Wu Mai Bao smiled slyly, holding his gaze by force of her own. "I often hear from one or another of our Readers"—but she interrupts herself to add, "some of them are readers even by your high standard. I've heard it said that the world as we know it has been reduced to nothing but the noise of opinions and objects that rap us on the shins."

That offers him a chance to displace his simmering resentment elsewhere. "Communication with nothing to communicate and reading as an archaic amusement." But as soon as it's uttered, he repents the bitterness of the remark, if not the idea.

Again she lets the moment pass. "Many years ago, there was a British film of a German novel called *The Reader*. Do you know it?"

"Remind me."

"I was introduced to it by one of The Readers, an elderly woman in Australia who had been a film critic. It's a Holocaust narrative about an illiterate woman in Berlin who loves to be read to by her much younger lover, a gymnasium student. Later she becomes a prison guard in the SS.

"In the decisive event, she locks a group of prisoners in a church for security. Then the church gets bombed and she lets them burn to death rather than unlock the doors, because there are no instructions for what to do if a church is bombed. It's a version of the Adolf Eichmann phenomenon, except that where he follows orders without thinking, she can't read the orders . . . or the later charges against her.

"On trial after the war the other defendants frame her, and Hannah—her name is Hannah Schmidt—is imprisoned for life for crimes she doesn't understand. Her ex-lover, Michael, observed the trial as a law student and knew she could not have been 'responsible.' Now he watches in silence as the defendants pin the blame on her and as she accepts a life sentence rather than confess the shame of illiteracy.

"During her early years in prison Michael, now her equal in shame, goes to the prison to visit her but can't bear to go through with it. Eventually he becomes a successful attorney. But here's the thing that matters: He makes recordings—spends hours and hours reading into a microphone, recording books of all kinds, and sending the tapes to her in prison."

Wu Mai Bao pauses to pour more coffee and to gauge Adawale's interest in her story. Apparently satisfied, she concludes, "Here's the connection with us. Over the years Hannah uses those recordings to learn to read, even in your sense of the word. Reading deeply, imaginatively, coming to understand who she is and what her earlier act meant. Reading makes her a human subject—let's say reading 'subjectivizes' her—and, in putting her subjectivity on trial, she becomes an ethical being, responsible for the atrocities she once committed because, like Eichmann, she had her orders. It's *she* who has become the *real* reader, while the first reader's life—Michael's life—has become a wasteland."

There Mai Bao stops, without applying the point to her own Readers. "I won't tell you what happens at the end when Hannah finally awakens to herself. That's in case you want to read it. It's a good book and a good film."

When the breakfast room begins to feel like a waiting room where two strangers linger expecting something to happen that mustn't be mentioned, Wu Mai Bao suggests they move to the library. There the topics become sufficiently casual for Adawale to ask about her work and the purpose of the house.

"Who are your Readers, collectively?" he asked.

"Collectively, we're nobody. An informal group existing only in virtual space. All amateurs, filled with passion and purpose."

Ope slightly squints at the word. "'Amateur,' from *amore*, means to love. In past ages the amateur was admired as a lover of things rather than a pleasure seeker or a specialist. Your Readers must still love the world, though it has come to ruin." This, though what he most wants to know is who Wu is and why he's alone with her in a country house.

In truth, though careful not to let it show, she is no less occupied with reading him, especially the underlying sadness that he tries and fails to conceal. She continues brightly, as though to help relieve his burden. "We 'interact'"—loading the word with irony—"on our 'communications devices.' Those whose contributions inspire discussion continue. Others drop away."

The lightness of tone mystifies him as much as the dancing eyes that play across his gaze, collecting information without pausing to acknowledge that anything serious might be going on. She seems to have no illusions about the state of the world, yet she faces it with a detachment that can laugh at what leaves him in despair.

He covers his steps by holding to the topic of The Readers. "What's your own particular interest?"

"I'm a cultural amphibian, though shallower." She waves aside a gesture of denial. "You're a scholar, but I think we may be alike in having spent our lives living across and between boundaries."

Then with a touch of deference as though it were a confession, "I was born on the borderline between Chinese folk traditions and the Confucian tradition. Later between Eastern and Western secularisms. It's a scale of differences impossible for one person to exhaust. But wouldn't you agree that if we're to know ourselves and the world, we must face what we imagine to be the whole of things however we can? In everyday interaction with the others, I spend much of my time asking the modest questions that bring out their differences."

She pauses to test whether she should stop there. As Adawale makes no reply, she adds, "When I'm not reading the posts of the others—at least scanning them to keep up—I read film. I'm always traveling, usually with a small library of films on this—she holds up her communication device—or on my workstation. Don't you agree that film is like a secret revelation of the spirit of the times? Especially art film, but even entertaining 'movies' can occasionally serve as a Momus-glass."

"What's a Momus-glass?"

"Momus was a mythical Greek figure with an infamously sharp tongue. He was expelled from Olympus for his outrageous criticisms of everyone and everything, though the only thing he could find wrong with Aphrodite was her squeaky sandals."

One sentence is enough to show how much she enjoys a good story. "Momus famously complained that the fault of mortals is that there is no way to see their hearts. Later, an English novelist compared fiction to a Momus-glass for its capacity to peer into the soul." She smiles with pleasure. "So film, my Momus-glass."

A lull in the conversation allows Ope to get up and walk about the room scanning the bookshelves as Mai Bao watches and makes casual remarks on their practical arrangements.

"While you're here, you'll meet a few active Readers. Some I know and some I've never met in person. From Colombia, a writer named Miranda Ribeiro and, from the States, one Anders Pederson. You may have run across him in New York?"

He acknowledges the remark by nodding and dismissing names that have no relation to him.

"Perhaps also a Greek named Pavlos Demetriopoulos."

He manages a smile. "I'd be interested to know why a random gathering of bookworms from around the world should require the kidnapping of another bookworm."

"Confucius says, 'The superior man abides in his room. If his words are well spoken, he meets with assent at a distance of more than a thousand miles.' It's not the bookworm in you or your ideas that persuade; it's the force of character that radiates from your book."

He has the grace not to reply to that but takes a chair once more across from her. "These people, these Readers, are they already in Vienna?"

A little grin makes a dimple on one cheek. "They're being flown in for the purpose." The dimple seems to be gently laughing at him. "You think we're children playing a game of spies, don't you?"

The topic might be as serious as you like and the moods as divergent, but a shrewd observer would see that these two, without thinking about it, are taking pleasure in bantering with one another as the conversation ambles on about arrangements in the house and his impressions of Vienna.

Eventually, like the good hostess who knows better than let her guests linger too long in one place, Mai Bao appears surprised to find that it's already early afternoon. So she invites Adawale to follow her to a balcony on the first floor at the front of the house. From there the view is through vineyards along the lane toward the village. Someone, not she, has set an outdoor table for two, with a platter of charcuterie, tomatoes, boiled eggs, bread, fruit and, of course, Austrian beer.

Silent on this bit of magic, she picks up the conversation with an inconspicuous turn toward the personal by touching once more lightly on the topic of secrecy. "I know our security regulations annoy you. It must seem overdone, not least the anonymity of The Readers. But you know from experience that what's safe in one situation can be deadly in another."

After pausing long enough to get their lunch underway, she continues. "I've never had to suffer for my ideas, but my father lived as an inside-outside official in China for years. It took a long period of high risk for him to relocate the family property without confiscation before he could flee the country. Even then he narrowly avoided arrest and certain execution. It's enough to encourage anyone who opposes the status quo and doesn't have a martyr complex to live below the radar. When 'interests' are at stake, people often flip over into their opposites in a blink of the eye."

These remarks, as bitter as a winter blast but delivered in tones as light as spring, reinforce the intriguing complexity of a character who prefers a cruel world to none at all.

As they eat together she persists with the same casual commentary. "More important for you to know is the effect of your book. It's mentioned often in the blogs. When you trace the influence of cultural traditions on political practice—from sacred books, the arts, traditional stories—you touch a nerve.

It casts suspicion on our confidence in knowing ourselves and being masters of our fate. One reader called it 'the doubtful transparency of consciousness.' Another called the book 'an introduction to the political unconscious.' You are taken to mean that there may be more to learn from reading what the tribe has forgotten than from what they think they think, or how they consciously act."

That is the longest speech Ope has yet heard from this spirited stranger, and even now it strikes him that she is listening more than speaking, but if he expects more of the same, he's to be disappointed. There's a limit to how long two strangers, mysteriously stranded in a house in the Vienna Woods, can carry on such a tête-à-tête before the atmosphere becomes strained. Mai Bao might have suggested a walk in the hills had not a quiet afternoon drizzle forced another retreat to the library.

Soon thereafter, she rises from her chair and announces, "Now you'll have to excuse me. I must go into the city. I'll leave you on your own for the afternoon, but I'll be back in time for dinner. Our meals are catered by a local *Beisl*."

Solitude restored, Ope mused on this encounter with his host, not without some residual resentment. Then, having located *The Reader* on the shelves, he settled into one of the comfortable leather chairs, put his own world on hold, and, in the company of the narrator, entered the world of Hannah Schmidt. Yet not as single-mindedly as he might have wished, for being on the same pages Wu Mai Bao admires, gives her an uninvited presence in that world. Do what he might, she's there alongside Hannah and a relation already established between them, or, if not between, then at least by Wu's one-way relation to Hannah.

For a couple, or perhaps three hours, he remained in Wu's line of sight as his vision of Hannah's experience communicated with hers. It was irresistible, this sense of gaining forbidden knowledge of his host as they lingered like accomplices on the same pages and trekked through the same countryside, discovering a new world.

Occasionally he looked up from the book or crossed the room to refresh his drink, vividly aware of Wu Mai Bao's overseeing his reading, and, more surprising, his unaccountable pleasure in her company.

CHAPTER 2

L ATER WHEN HE LAID the book aside and wandered to the window, the rain had stopped. Despite the unnecessary precaution of the officers, he was tempted to go outside. Wu having not mentioned the prohibition, he yielded to the impulse to explore the place.

There were two choices. Either walk up through the vineyard at the rear of the house or down the farm road toward the village. No one being in sight on either side of the road, he chose the latter and ambled along, admiring the density of the vines and the heavy clusters of ripening grapes, yet thinking mainly of poor Hannah Schmidt's love of the classics set against the background of Wu Mai Bao and her mysterious house.

Halfway to the paved road he heard groups of pickers among the vines in the distance. Farther on, a tractor and trailer filled with grapes emerged from the field on the right. The driver stopped at the side of the road and sat leaning on the steering wheel suspiciously watching as the noble African figure approached. It was an unusual sight, a well-dressed dignified, Black man walking down a country road on the periphery of the Austrian capital. Opeyemi stopped and raised his hand. The vintner asked in German if he was looking for something. When Ope answered in English, "From the house," pointing up the road behind, the farmer gave him a hard stare. With the sudden shift of mood and without further acknowledgment, he started the tractor and turned away. The impression was that no one knew or wanted to know what went on in the house at the end of the road.

Where the lane ended at the narrow highway up the mountain, Ope took the sidewalk down into Grinzing. Officer Georghiu had forbidden him the streets of Vienna except with a security escort, but this seemed innocent enough. There were people, but mainly in passing cars and buses, or the occasional tradesman or farmer going about his business. Some gave him a second glance, but without incident.

The "safe house" and the walk in the open lifted the oppressive sense of confinement. Passing the time in the village, he studied the menus at the doors of several wine bars, called *Heurigen*, and eventually turned in at one. A youngish Austrian server regarded him with surprise but smiled and advanced to help, when, suddenly, a patron dressed like a Bavarian mountaineer, in lederhosen, shorts, lace collar, and knee socks leapt from his seat, held up both hands with palms out as though blocking the way, and cried. "*Nein! Nein! Weg gehen!* Go away!"

Adawale, the diplomatic nomad, was not exactly a stranger to this or most other parts of the world and did not mistake the gesture as "racial" or xenophobic. Just another symptom of the general anxiety that pervaded the cities of the planet like a psychic microwave background. Instead of protesting or trying to explain himself, which, given the vintner's earlier response, would only have aggravated things, he nodded pleasantly and

145

left. After strolling a few blocks around the village, he looked in at the church, then retraced his steps to the house under the hill, musing on the term "safe house."

A safe house was once a retreat, a cleared or marked space, cut out from its surroundings and set aside for reflection. Originally "a sacred area before an altar or temple." So a space reserved for contemplation. In a secular version of that bit of philology, Wu's house beyond the city was a place where one could reflect on the condition of the world and whatever possibilities it might be open to. Security or not, considered in that light, the house was quite to his liking.

At dusk Wu Mai Bao returned, and he helped bring food in from the car. "Since it's only us two tonight, we're having a simple Austrian meal of boiled beef. Meat and vegetables with roasted potatoes and applesauce with horseradish."

He brightened at the description. "*Tafelspitz?*" She nodded. "I haven't had that in years. One of my favorite Viennese dishes!"

"Good. Let's have a drink, then you can help me serve."

After an early dinner, they retired once more to the library and relaxed into each other's company, a little closer to friends than to strangers. As she left the direction of conversation to him this time, he mentioned having begun *The Reader* and how much he had profited from her critical remarks. Then he moved on in another oblique effort to learn more about her professional history.

She answered with a dismissive laugh that contradicted the light in her eyes. "Oh, I try to leave no tracks in the snow." Then with an ironic grin, "You know we Chinese have never thought the rest of the world counts for much."

Then, slanting the conversation toward the house as though it was a safer topic, she described it as a kind of conference center or scholars' retreat where small groups of Readers came from around the world by invitation to exchange views for a few days. Then, after showing him some blogs that she judged to be typical, the conversation drifted on its own momentum a little nearer the personal.

Ope took for granted that she knew all about him, which made it curious when she gently encouraged him to tell his story as though she wanted to hear it from his own lips.

Soon it became evident that she didn't know all already. When he made a chance reference to having lost his wife, she was surprised. "How long ago? Forgive me if the subject is painful. What happened? Do you mind that I ask?"

He passed entirely over those polite questions and plunged into a topic so remote that it must have left her searching for context. He telescoped his whole life into two brief events. Not Yetunde's death nor even their first meeting and the shock of first love. It was those three folk images from Nigeria scattered on a New York sidewalk that had delivered such a shock to his cultural amnesia, especially the drawing of the diviner's tray.

The object represented was a carved wooden tray some nine inches in diameter, used by Yoruba priests for divination and consisting of three concentric circles. The outside ring enclosed birds, twenty-five or thirty of them, carved in relief and facing inward, wing to wing, waiting for whatever would take place at the empty center. The second circle contained earthy creatures with permeable boundaries, ambiguously related to different species. Amphibious crabs, a mudfish with arms growing from the nose and body but with the face of deified ancestors who retain the power to transform sacrifices into food for the gods.

Such an unprecedented digression may have deserved the imaginative skills of a Mamud Çelik when he proceeded to mention, far too briefly, the circumstances of Yetunde's death, as though in his mind nothing else had happened to him.

"The rest you know," he said, as innocently as is imaginable. "Since then, I've lived as solitary scholar and public servant, involved in everything, close to no one. So, you see, there is no surplus behind the professional dossier." His hands opened in a gesture of resignation. "*C'est tout*, end of story."

How would anyone respond to that? And Wu didn't try.

Meanwhile, she had said exactly nothing about herself. However much Ope had begun enjoying her company, he had been able to deduce little more than what he had picked up in the first hour. There was no ring, so she must not have been married—but why did that detail come to mind so readily? She had a busy life and yet seemed perfectly comfortable with the solitude of a house that was maintained for no visible purpose. Then there was the ever-present fact that he, who had an apartment inside the UNO security perimeter, was being "kept safe" on the edge of the Vienna Woods as in the set from a spy novel.

In fact, her interest in him led to her closing the information gap. She mentioned her family with a proud allusion to the generations of Confucian culture on both sides. "My grandfather and great-grandfather survived the darkest days of the twentieth century thanks to a long tradition of public service. After the Communists embraced the global market, they became industrialists in Shanghai and Hong Kong. Only when I was still a child did my father move the family and, later, much of his business interests to Vancouver, where I grew up. But I was no less rigorously trained in the Confucian classics. For that I'm immensely grateful."

She described her university years at Berkeley, then grad school at Caltech. After school, being knowledgeable in space science and by tradition a good manager, she accepted a post with NASA. Never married, though there had been a long relationship of convenience with a colleague during her working years stateside. This easy account of her life was delivered openly, with one thing conspicuously omitted—the thing Ope was waiting for: Not a word about her work here or her presumed relation to Boris Razumovski.

Once again, he was left to fill the blanks by speculation. Given her training and experience, there was nothing mysterious about her being brought to Vienna under the aegis of the Office for Outer Space Affairs, where she must have been for some time. Long enough at least to make her mark and find the work rewarding. Still, what mark? What work? And what could Readers possibly have to do with any of it? The UN and the underground city make her position and this house look more and more like a front, but a front for what? He could only imagine that she belonged to a cell concealed deep within the security apparatus, but that surmise told nothing.

The two having become comfortable in the other's company, and hence more indifferent to the passage of time, they spent the evening zigging and zagging their way across two lives, advancing and retreating in slow stages against all narrative logic. Chance acquaintance moved closer to friendship without Ope's realizing how much ground had been covered or how much the distance between them had narrowed.

Sometime during the evening, Wu took a call in another room and returned to the library with an announcement. "We have a guest arriving tomorrow whom I've never met. His name is Anders Pederson. He's flying in from Toronto to meet with us."

That set off Ope's alarms all over again. That, on top of his own peremptory summons from Lagos and the random "orientation" and kidnapping. Readers or no Readers, what could possibly be important enough to justify a person crossing half the world to meet him here? If the matter was urgent—but what matter?—Boris might have arranged for him to meet this Pederson person in New York. If Boris even knew! Someone *was* playing a game of spies, and it was very annoying.

Mai Bao continued, "I think I told you that Pederson is Swedish, now Canadian, by way of the financial district in London. As a youth, he had some small UN job in Copenhagen. After college, he left that for work in the markets in the UK. Apparently he made a lot of money, then just quit or 'retired,' as people say, and returned to the humanistic studies of his youth. Not knowing him, I know nothing of his motives, but he has become the voice of cautious optimism among us."

"He's a Reader then?"

"Yes. And keenly critical of the current state of the world, but he manages to avoid despair by hoping to restore past ideals. Listened to rather less for his ideas than for his optimism."

She gave him a teasing smile. "Between the two of you, I'm in a quandary: One of you offers truth without hope; the other offers hope by way of illusion. I find I can't live with either of you . . . or without both of you."

CHAPTER 3

THE NEXT MORNING A car arrived and a tall blond man in a crumpled business suit emerged. Ope's first glimpse reminded him of details mentioned earlier: the money, the getting bored, the "drifting" into reading books and contributing to the Readers' blogs. Definitely not promising.

The stranger entered as guest of people whom he had never met before and opened with a complaint about his flight. "On such short notice, I could only get a seat in economy!"

The briefest of introductions ensued before Pederson expressed himself again, leaving the impression that he was his own favorite topic. "I've had a miserable night. If you'll direct me to my room, I'll freshen up and catch a quick nap."

Once he had disappeared upstairs, Mai Bao opened those ironic almond-shaped eyes wide and announced to Ope: "Today I have to be somewhere else, so I'm leaving you and Pederson to get acquainted"—her tone modulated to match the eyes—"that is, *if* he catches up on his creature comforts in time."

An hour and a half later Pederson turns up again in a fashionably sporty jacket with a pocket monogram and a dress shirt open at the neck. His sandy hair, perfectly cut and freshly shampooed, has the fragrance of a man for whom the daily shower and fresh clothes are a metaphor for a clean and orderly mind. He gets coffee from the kitchen, brings it to the library, and drops into a chair across from where Ope sits reading. Sipping his coffee and casually stretching his legs in front, wide apart as though claiming his territory, he speaks in a voice that seems cultivated for the value of its charm as he announces in the loud American way, "The facilities here are nice. I was afraid I'd be put in a dormitory or something. Is the food good? Have you been here long? I'm only staying a few days then stopping off in London."

He seems to have forgotten an object in his left hand until, chancing to look down, he recognizes a copy of Adawale's book and forgets his own questions. "Since the point of this trip appears to be for us to have a good talk, I thought I might as well let you autograph your book as not." He hands the copy over and Ope obligingly signs.

"I read it during the flight. It's just the moderating voice we need when progress is being assailed on all sides."

The remark is enough to make Ope wonder what "reading" means in *his* world. Perhaps turning pages curiously, looking for useful information without bothering to join the inquiry. As for the word "progress," he gives it wide berth by conspicuously laying aside Mai Bao's copy of *The Reader* before getting up and walking to a front window as though checking on the weather.

Since the encounter has been arranged and he can hardly avoid the conversation, he seizes the opportunity of the moment to avoid being subjected to the whims of this character. "Are you a peripatetic thinker," he asks, "or do you think better from a fixed position?" Without waiting for an answer, "I'm told there's a fine prospect from the top of the vineyard. Why don't we take a turn up the hill?"

Pederson looks as if he'd much rather sit in one of the leather chairs, but as he doesn't insist, Ope either doesn't notice the hesitance, or doesn't choose to notice. Walking may be distracting, at least.

Outside, they pass through a gate at the side of the house and begin the gentle climb through rows of vines. The damp ground beneath is littered with clusters of grapes, cut and left to rot, the point apparently being to reduce the number on the vine and concentrate the sugar in those that remain. Pederson notices none of this as Ope, careful to choose the cropping rather than the sweetening side of the metaphor, thinks of conversations as grapes that, to be productive, must be expediently pruned. What neither may realize is that the pungent scent of those grapes fermenting on the ground will be remembered forever after as belonging as much to this moment as to the terroir of the local Rieslings and Pinot Blancs.

Adawale opens the conversation with a remark on Pederson's involvement in the network of Readers. "I wonder why a busy man of the world would take the time to write your blogs. Wu showed me a sample or two. I believe they're followed by other people scattered around the world whom you apparently don't know. What's the reward?"

Pederson responds with the confidence of one who is equally sure of himself and his vision. "They are an intelligent lot, these people. Well-informed about conditions but their appreciation of our modern achievements has been dulled by the problems they see on all sides."

The remark partly readjusts Ope's hasty judgment of a conventional mind. Pederson begins to seem a bit more companionable and may even prove enjoyable in conversation.

"In stressful times," he goes on, "it's easy to forget what a slow process history is. It's hardly surprising that people engaged in continuous criticism should be fixated on our collective failures. Like idealists who would trade the real world for a world that only exists in their fantasies. Don't get me wrong, their criticisms are plausible. Especially to people who haven't been responsible for getting real things done in the real world. 'The Readers,' as Wu calls them, don't *claim* to be revolutionaries, just disciplined, articulate people who mainly want to scrap it all and start over. I call that a distinction without a difference. And it's dangerous."

He ends with an indulgent chuckle that generously accepts Adawale into his own worldview. "But, so long as they sit on top of their metaphorical mountains and send words out into the void, they do little harm."

Pederson seems never at a loss for words and when Adawale offers no reply, he happily fills the gap. After all, he's doing what he was brought here do: Talk!

"Now you, for example. As a scholar, you may not exactly be in the thick of the action, but you're out there putting your views to the scrutiny of people in your field. I may not agree with some of your ideas, but I don't see you contemplating the overthrow of life as we know it. We're both trying to hold things together."

Ope stays with the personal, keeping the irony light and the questions sympathetic. "Yet you contribute regularly to the ruminations of these cloistered idealists. Isn't it a waste of your time?"

In a series of small gestures that might be mistaken for impatience with Adawale's sluggish mind, Pederson stuffs his hands in his pockets and stretches his back as though still recovering from the effects of the overnight flight. He takes another deep breath and releases it slowly. "I decided a while back that if I would write one response to these people each week, it might open some eyes to the real-world consequences of armchair philosophizing. After all, where we share the same world, there is a certain responsibility to connect, don't you think?"

Adawale continues to soften toward his companion while wondering what purpose this encounter can possibly serve. Before replying, he restrains himself with the principle that conversation begins with goodwill toward the other. "I have only just become aware of The Readers, but I'm told that your views are influential among them. Presumably that's why we're meeting. So it might be helpful if you would outline how you see the mayhem of the planet."

As they descend the hill, Ope observes Pederson not-seeing the expansive landscape, not-smelling the pungency of the grapes on the vines and on the ground, and not-feeling the proximity of the mountain over their heads or the destitution of the city in the distance. Yet he's happy to share his opinions on that unnoticed object-world.

A spectator of the scene might have found it memorable in a different way: The northern European—tall, blond, exuding Rotarian self-satisfaction, walking through the vineyard at the side of the African prince who is equal in height, superior in dignity, and far more subdued in mood.

Pederson continues the all-but-soliloquy: "My experience is in the marketplace. I made a lot of money in my day, then I gave up the rat race and moved to a city I love and resumed reading the books I loved in school. You've heard the remark, 'The old should be explorers'? I believe that. And I can say that much for The Readers. A tad reckless, but they *are* explorers. That's why I wrote my first piece. Then it sparked some interest."

He grinned affably. "Don't we all imagine in the solitude of our libraries that there is an audience for our ideas? Anyway, as my participation grew, I began taking another look at things I hadn't looked at since my school days. By now it's become a way of life. What was once called 'the contemplative life,' I believe. As I say, I largely agree with The Readers' criticisms, but they mainly wring their hands without a single practical idea. What I don't agree with is how they turn their backs on the most beneficial revolution in human history."

"Which revolution is that? There have been several."

"The Renaissance. The dawn of the Age of Man. A bold step beyond superstition and magic into the real world. The age of reason and science," he repeats, inspired by the mouth-filling roundness of the name. "Even in art. Just go to the museums and compare a painting before the discovery of perspective with the realism that follows."

Adawale, discouraged, throws in the towel on diplomacy. "I seem to remember seeing a rudimentary use of perspective in the receding horses' heads in the Chauvet cave."

Without noticing, Pederson continues. "In politics too. After the authoritarianism of aristocracy and Church, a new brighter light shines from Machiavelli to Hobbes and Locke down to us. Verifiable knowledge, mastery of nature, the industrial revolution, private property, the free market, democracy—you know the story better than I do. Machiavelli taught us to stop worrying about the rare virtues of nobility, brilliance, taste, or holiness and build a world with people as they really are. You can't make a community if you aren't realistic about people."

Ope controls a surge of impatience with the repetition of the word "real," wondering perhaps if it betrays a suspicion of some ambiguity in the term that Pederson is anxious to avoid or, failing that, to control. Then, careful not to be heard—which takes little effort in the circumstances—Ope mutters, "Community isn't *made*; it *occurs*."

Then aloud, "You may have a point. Though Machiavelli's agenda in *The Prince* is very subtle. Also I believe he may have written more than one book."

But Pederson has no time for footnotes. "We don't need an ideal state, you know. We need real-estate . . ."

"Need what?"

"Sorry. A *real state*. A state that provides order and stability so people can get on with their lives."

Adawale's mood grows darker again with this cavalier way of treating ideas that put the world at stake, already misquoting its authorities. What's intended as a refreshing stroll in the vineyard begins to feel like a freshman class. Impatiently he asks, "And how *are* people really? How do they *really* live?"

In his element by now, Pederson ignores whatever in the other's speech he may not want to hear and, stopping in his tracks, answers enthusiastically. "The simple genius of realism is that it makes sense, don't you think? Everybody can recognize it. Hobbes is obviously right: Self-interest is human nature, and survival is the basic right of that nature. It's from that 'state of nature' and the solitary struggle of all against all, that we learn to band together for survival. Hope is restored to the life that was 'nasty, brutish, and short.' Then John Locke adds the inalienable rights to 'life, liberty, and property.' Especially property! This revolution has led to democratic government and freedom from need. People rush to embrace it as soon as they understand."

Ope thinks but does not say, "And if they don't rush into this confusion of property with happiness, they're benighted and irrelevant!"

"Science flourishes in place of myth and magic. The industrial revolution has liberated men to their natural role as producers, and the financial markets have spread the good life around the globe." With a sweep of one hand over the vineyard that he has yet to see, he offers the wide world in evidence of his opinions.

Still oblivious of his audience, he waxes lyrical in praise of the Enlightenment dream: "'Give me your tired, your poor, / Your huddled masses yearning to breathe free, / The wretched refuse of your teeming shore.'

"Everybody understands these down-to-earth ideas. No postponing happiness into the sweet by and by. It's all here and now like the fruit on these vines. What everyone with his eyes on the world and his feet on the ground has always wanted." He stamps the ground with one foot, affirming an already firm understanding. "However dark the times, we must remind people of these few simple truths, and find ways to include the disinherited in the global system. What else is government about but the distribution of wealth?"

However clichéd, it's a lot to say, and, if necessary, it will be a lot to answer. But, as they reach the end of the vineyard and its vistas, the point is not followed up. Pederson stands with unshakeable faith in material progress. The two men, as different in mind as in color, stand shoulder to shoulder looking across the river delta and the hills beyond, as toward entirely different worlds. Ope draws no solace from the vineyard or the panorama of Vienna to the south, where the rain has slackened, allowing a smear of light across the city and a lesser shade of grey.

As they descend to the guesthouse, Adawale's mood is divided: depressed by the speech he has just heard but lightened by reflections on their host.

On Pederson's oration, he remarks without irony. "Very concisely put, my friend!" And the compliment is sincere. It's not easy to digest five hundred years of Anglo-American political theory into a single speech of less than two minutes. Also impressive is the caution with which some bits have been included while others were left out.

"I wonder if you find as I do that a good speech always raises new questions."

The reply is jovial. "What questions? Ask away."

"Your praise of modern rationality is irresistible. Yet I wonder if the criticism of the ages of myth and the gods might be a little overdone. If we compare two historical epochs beginning from a dogma like progress, don't we have to be especially scrupulous in our description of the earlier age? We wouldn't want to plant the idea that the case for the new depends on exaggerating the case against the old. Is there a danger of uncritically substituting a new myth for an old myth? How are we to know that we aren't blind in our own way—perhaps even more willful—than our ancestors were in theirs?"

Pederson is pleased to have a ready answer. "What's different is that we have demythologized myth. We live in the age of science and plain truth, so we know a myth when we meet one." He smiles at being the bearer of glad tidings.

Adawale is good at the diplomatic game and knows that nothing is gained by sparring with a person who has no questions. But it's easy enough to play along and—since he must—hope for a chink in the defenses of a closed mind.

"I do see the point about myth," he replies. "What I need help in seeing is how these 'plain truths' have enhanced our self-understanding or the workings of history. In, say, law and education and governance. The world gets more dangerous, people more dissatisfied, complexity more baffling, order less secure, hope less accessible. Doesn't all that make you wonder if our theory may not be quite right?"

"But that's not the *cause*, my friend. You have to understand how we got here and how we're slowly getting *there* where we want to be."

Adawale tries to hold the subject on course. "Still, isn't there a danger that anachronistic accounts of prior dark ages may be fed more by modern opinions swallowed whole and unchewed than by the historical record? It would be helpful, for example, to hear what resources the progressivist dream offers for self-correction. What if progress is itself a myth that lets us rationalize our failures until it's too late to correct our course? How would we know?"

At that moment they reach the house and Pederson is spared the trouble of answering. Wu Mai Bao has returned with food from the caterer, and after she introduces herself, the conversation becomes general and the atmosphere genial.

CHAPTER 4

LATER, AS THE THREE sit down together for a light dinner, Pederson, revived by the walk in the vineyard, renews the topic between him and Ope with a degree of vigor that threatens to last into the night.

Mai Bao, who has a keen ear for the timbre of any discourse, faces the two men with a smile that neutralizes testosterone. "It's kind of you to let me join the conversation at whatever point you've reached." Then a question that's at least as declarative as interrogative: "Where were you exactly when I interrupted?"

Pederson rushes to answer. "I believe Adawale ended by accusing me of double dealing. A mythmaker in the cloak of a rational man. Something like that."

He laughs good-naturedly in Ope's direction. "Do I get that about right, Professor?" Pederson may not turn out to be a subtle thinker, but he has a smooth and pleasant manner that is welcome where there is little agreement on things that matter.

Ope responds good-naturedly, "I believe we have the 'virtues' of calculation and self-interest on one side and poetic moralizing on the other. Though I readily admit the appeal of home-grown truths."

He waits for one of the others to let him off the hook and when neither does, he adds a trifle unwillingly, "There *is* one point where I still need help: In your excellent summary of political realism, I can't help suspecting that a modern fiction gets substituted for an ancient one. It's true that we moderns recognize myths *as myths*, sometimes, but isn't your 'bare truth' about us another myth? And there's more. When you say that the state of nature explains the world as we know it, do you mean to imply that collective life *should* be based on what we *want* even if what we want isn't good for us? Is a free and materially satisfying life better than the more strenuous life that may be *good for* us? Doesn't that substitute a new myth for an old one without regard for evidence?"

As Pederson crosses one leg over the other just slowly enough to admire a well-pressed pants leg and a fashionable, well-polished shoe, it's not clear that he has followed the question, but he's no less ready with an answer for all questions at once. "Not at all. It's not another story about what people *ought* to want. People *really* do want liberty and justice for all."

Mai Bao says nothing. Just watches where the argument will go and who the people are who are getting there. Ope adds, "If in past ages heroes, saints, poets, and philosophers *really were* aristocratic power-mongers as some say, and if those elites *really were* responsible for ordinary people living in poverty and ignorance, then the criticism would be tempting, but all that comes as a slogan, not an idea."

As an ironic sidebar, Adawale adds, "That would be equivalent to saying that artists, intellectuals and saints—the least controllable of human beings—occupy the same position as landowners and industrialists! Anachronism aside, isn't there a deficit of understanding here? We're admonished to take life as it is, not to measure it against unrealistic standards of excellence. And yet excellence is the standard carpenters, surgeons, and footballers use because it's the only sensible way to conduct life. But by now the good no longer consists in mastering ourselves. 'Evil' has now shifted to the side of nature, and we're to defend ourselves against it by acquisitive self-interest. That's the new myth of life as it *ought to be*. We can't afford to miss the moral thrust in that little modal verb 'ought.' How life *ought* to be conducted."

Pederson remains unfazed. With an open face and without taking the trouble to say what he doesn't agree with, he protests. "I don't understand. That must mean something, but I can't think what."

Instead of appearing exasperated, Ope faces the room with a friendly smile. "It's just that the mythic structure of good and evil remains unchanged."

"You mean by one interpretation of the facts?"

"I mean by two courses of desire."

"That leads me further into the dark."

Eventually Mai Bao intervenes in the debate between her guests. "Let me put your debate differently."

In a blink of an eye Pederson doffs one mood and dons another. "Oh, I know you!"

He faces Adawale, now with friendly eagerness. "Did you know, Professor, that our host is a film junkie? When she posts a response to another Reader she usually begins, 'Let me tell you a story.' Then comes the plot of an old movie she's been watching."

Mai Bao lets the remark pass with a smile directed mainly at Adawale. "I hope you'll excuse my flimsy reduction of philosophy to such a humble level, but sometimes a story can give flesh to an idea that sounds forbiddingly abstract, whether it is or not."

She straightens her back and begins her story. "Several decades ago there was a film called *Contagion*. 'Movie' is the better term since it's mainly a thriller, more entertainment than food for thought. It became famous during the subsequent global epidemic of Coronavirus. But never mind all that. The plot is based loosely on an earlier Ebola epidemic in Sub-Saharan Africa. Apparently the virus passed up the chain from fruit bats, but the story is less about biology than public responses to the viral transmission across the planet. It appears to take literally the metaphor of an unbroken chain from the bats to humans as it concentrates on the paranoid masses who threaten the work and the lives of the exceptional few who are searching for an antidote."

"Then two global diseases, one viral and one cultural!"

"Perhaps. But don't get ahead of me, Pederson," she exhorts him with a disarming smile and a raised hand as she picks up the thread again.

"The pandemic spreads exponentially, and we are treated to every sort of public and private disruption as well as to the thrill of terror. It's mainly catering for gratuitous sensation, but the description of how officials and the populace act is instructive because it rings true. While hysteria spreads globally, every means is used to forestall panic, but the pandemic has more to do with a certain understanding of human nature than with microbes.

"In fact, Anders, it's a picture of the condition you describe at the root of *your* world. Mobs in 'the state of nature' roam the streets, looting, destroying property, suspecting the researchers of withholding a magic drug that would save them. Even in scientific circles, where there are genuine heroic acts, the tale exposes few resources beyond self-interest. Once the virus' line of passage is discovered, from bats to pigs to humans, epidemiologist Ally Hextall uses an attenuated virus to produce a vaccine and tests it on herself! But here's the real point: The only people in this global jungle who don't behave like animals are a few scientists and the handful who trust them. The useful and the good people are exceptions."

Ope: "There you are. The pandemic shows more about the failure of self-interest than the bare fact of self-interest! Rarely are interests limited to ourselves." Then the social grin that he uses to camouflage his dissatisfaction with the world morphs into an expression of delight directed at Mai Bao. "So why do you say it's only a 'movie'?"

"Because of what it doesn't know. It knows there's a far more lethal disease than the one from the bats, but it's blind to—and complicit in—the forces that have made the planet into an over-crowded village and a short food chain. Those are what turn local infections into pandemics."

Adawale's interest in the topic visibly rises. "Your account sounds like the film knows very well that the myth of rational progress is willfully blind to its own consequences."

Pederson pokes fun at the sudden exuberance in the reserved scholar. "Now you're writing a sequel with a myth of your own!"

Mai Bao responds, "But look what happens to the social contract. Everyone is dependent for survival on Ally Hextall, who has the virtues of the scientist and the saint, but the masses are blinded to their own interests by fear. In *Contagion* rational agreement on collective self-interest is impossible. It shows bare human nature as self-destructive!"

Pederson dares a reply that, to his credit, seems to concede more than it defends. "Everybody knows that in the face of brutality we need heroic responders. We know it *because* the state of nature is so nasty. If we appear to set the bar too low, maybe it's so everyone can participate as citizens. The extraordinary act in extraordinary circumstances is even more necessary and more heroic."

Ope says nothing, but he stares in astonishment at the opportunism of Anders' concession to Mai Bao's argument even as she responds charitably to Pederson's idea. "I see what you're saying, Anders. Political life should be open to decent mediocrity, not just to the 'best' or to the ones who know best how to govern. Not all citizens have to be as resourceful or sacrifice themselves as Hextall does, even when their survival depends on her."

"Then," Ope adds, "we're acknowledging 'the good.' Not good people, but the good act itself—as the political standard."

"But," Pederson objects, "it's the pandemic that motivates Ally Hextall's heroism."

Mai Bao stops, trying once more to hear Pederson's point generously. "On that account wouldn't the plot show that public virtue belongs to the struggle of all against all rather than to the Hextall exception to self-interest? How can we accept a view that is suicidal of political order? Surely that won't do."

The almond-shaped eyes twinkle as she adds a coda. "A town meeting and a social contract are unthinkable in the circumstances described in *Contagion*. When the world's collapsing and people are roaming the streets like beasts in human masks then it isn't possible to organize for the common good. Either all die or a precious few transcend the hysteria."

Pederson's response is a bit off center, as though for some reason he wants to equivocate. "As I just said, nobody claims there isn't virtue, just that it shouldn't be a prerequisite for participating in the social order. Your criticism is based on the most extreme conditions, while I'm concerned with average political conditions."

Mai Bao is careful to keep her impatience out of sight even as she hears Adawale sighing deeply. "We might ask," she says to Anders, "does the situation in *Contagion* carry conviction, or doesn't it? There seem to be two ways of reading the story. First, as a reminder of how precarious the rational social contract is. On that reading it teaches us perpetual fear of relapsing into what you regard as our primitive state.

"On the second reading, it shows how improbable the idea of collective rationality really is. If we accept the myth that extreme brutality can come to its senses and make cool judgments, then we probably prefer the first reading. But I prefer the second. It requires us to examine ourselves more closely and search for new resources for self-governance. Meanwhile, I'd rather not condone a myth that authorizes us to go berserk in the face of death as though brutishness were natural or inevitable."

"It's a good point," Ope adds, with a force that sounds like discovery. "Assumptions about our origins also serve to justify our desires. As in the assumption of human equality. It encourages people to confuse the feel-good principle of *being equal* with the not-so-good feeling of being responsible for *acting unequally* well."

Pederson appeared to grasp something and responded carefully. "I take your point about the hypothetical character of the state of nature. Also that one age is not always fair to the ages that precede it, like children to parents. But what I don't understand is why anyone would want to lose the gains of security, freedom, and material progress that this myth has led to. I know conditions in the world are deplorable. That's why we're here. But my question is, what is our best last chance? What or who is to be trusted? Far from discrediting Ally Hextall, I want more citizens like her even as we hold on to progress, however limited it may be. Or should we take the path of the super-subtle and deep-thinking aristocrats who ordinary people with ordinary goals can't even understand?"

Then came the benedictory question as Adawale rose from his chair in preparation for saying goodnight: "You mean the ordinary ones who have lost their understanding and been happy to lose it?"

CHAPTER 5

AT BREAKFAST MAI BAO announced that another visitor was arriving soon. Miranda Ribeiro by name, from Argentina.

Ope responded sardonically. "Flown in especially for the occasion, no doubt,"

"True. But only from Spain," she answered with a grin. "Do you remember her, Anders?"

"The name, yes," he replied. "The feisty anti-capitalist writer, if I have the right one in mind."

"The very one. She should be here around noon."

And so it happened. Miranda Ribeiro arrived after lunch, a woman in her late seventies, sprightly as a twenty-year-old. Slim and straight, with fine weathered features and dancing eyes that suggested she might once have been a beauty. So ardent in conversation, and with such a keen mind and quick tongue that people of tender sensibility might be uneasy in her company. One disposed to indolence could be exhausted by sitting for an hour in the same room with her. Having been everywhere, done everything—and written most of it down—she tended, even in casual exchanges, to speak without ceasing of the people she had known, though never in dry moralisms and not to the point of boring the company.

171

Listening to Ribeiro was fascinating even when she sighed deeply and repeated, "All one's interesting friends are dead, you know. Present company . . . etc. They speak so well, the old ones, except for their tiresome habit of repeating themselves without listening to your response."

At that she would give a hearty warble that distantly resembled a laugh. Not laughing at her own cleverness but delighted whenever wit turned up on its own from whatever source. Then continue, "Oh, but the living 'friends,' as they call themselves! They all find the world irreparable. Nothing can change, so there's nothing to be done. With nothing to do, they wrap themselves in dullness and sink into stupidity."

Pederson raised one brow. "Then you must have a lively social life." It sounded as if these two had crossed swords before and hers had left scratches. Not that he, Pederson, was defenseless. He had acquired the facility of a British aristocrat in hurling sharp words of his own while wrapped in enough American saccharine to disguise satire as flattery.

She didn't miss the jeer at her social life. "Yes dear, I do," The sarcasm seemed to give him credit for extraordinary perception. "I rarely go out," she continued. "There's more wit in dining alone with a good book than sitting with twenty important people whose mission in life is to dumb the table down to a fetal drool."

Ope's attitude toward both these visitors was neutral. He readily acknowledged that something must be going on in the head of a man who could give Pederson's cogent summary of the liberal economic cause, and Miranda Ribeiro had yet to show her colors. Whatever ambivalence may have lingered in his attitude toward Wu, he was hardly indifferent to her, and for most of that afternoon he watched her responses to the others. He saw that she liked Pederson, though she did nothing but charmingly disagree with him, and that for some reason she remained undecided about Ribeiro. Instead of engaging her directly, she left it to the men to do the talking while missing nothing in the exchanges.

The conversation was suspended while Miranda took her usual hour-long nap, but dinner that evening promised to be anything but dull. By the time the four met again in the library, the fact was established that Ribeiro and Pederson disagreed on everything—except disagreement itself and the compulsion to keep talking. There was not a subject under heaven that they didn't divide between them, and should such a subject have turned up, the only question would have been which would change sides first.

"I read your latest blog, Pederson, advising us all to 'get real.' No more dreamers. I should have thought human affairs were disappointing enough without taking our dreams away."

"You have no doubt heard, Ma'am, that we moderns 'build on low but solid ground.'"

"Ah, yes. But how low? And how solid?"

"*I* don't set the bar, you know. I just say as I find."

"From what I've read of your posts, all you've *found* is sentimental morality. You lower us to a point where everyone can *feel* good about themselves without being put to the inconvenience of doing good things or trying to work out the consequences. You must know that the man who is preoccupied with noble feelings is the last to perform noble deeds.

That may be symptomatic of the state of Ulro, but it sheds no light."

Whether Pederson didn't listen or was only sidestepping, he skipped the connections. "Don't you prefer a bottom-up to a top-down political system?"

Then, as though the question were not a question at all, he continued, "People understand food and money and sex and power. But look at us." He made a sweeping gesture across the room. "We sit up here on the edge of the Vienna Woods, looking down like arrogant gods, judging the gloomy world below."

He pointed in the direction of the city. "I say we're sectarian abstractionists, indifferent to how real people live." He glanced toward the window and the vineyard beyond. "In this garden of contemplation, we are safely disconnected from the wretched life of the masses."

Ribeiro harrumphed, "Well Professor Adawale, isn't it illuminating to learn that you and I are not 'real people.' You've wasted all those years researching and writing your book, don't you see? It would have been far more sensible to have spent the time making money, shopping, and going to mindless dinner parties. Instead of working to overcome your ignorance, you could have 'had fun' and died with a clear conscience."

Her little bird eyes fixed her opponent like a poniard. "You've got the wrong end of the stick, Pederson. Our Readers are simple people of strong mind and character. They devote their days and nights to searching for light in dark times. The question isn't new. I quote Dostoyevsky: 'Which is more precious, Shakespeare or boots, Raphael or petroleum?'"

"Depends on who you are. You have good political instincts, Ma'am, but you suffer from the bias of the intellectual. You want to trace all the diversity of broad-minded tolerance back to a philosophical heresy you call liberalism. But there are practical differences between right-wing, free-market liberalism and left-wing liberalism of the rights of man (and woman). And you fail to notice that economics has a long history of detecting its failures and reforming itself. It knows all about greed and lawlessness in the marketplace. It knows the dangers of the plutocracy of money, of buying and selling executive power and the law, of systems strangled by legalism. The free market is our pristine example of self-reform."

She inhaled and raised a satirical hand. "Oh yes! We know what 'it knows!'"

"I know what you'll say," he interrupted passionately. "You'll say that people suffer and die before reforms can take hold. But people *do* suffer and people *do* die. The question is which ones and when. What organization of life—including the great religions—has a better record of self-correction and improving life than Enlightenment liberalism and the market economy?"

"The atom bomb makes a better example! The weapon to end all wars. And don't leave out the capacity of capital to distribute wealth efficiently—from the bottom to the top!"

Again he ignored the irony. "As I say, give it time . . ."

". . . said the fox to the chickens."

She stopped as though to force herself not to press an unwieldy agenda too far. Then continued after a moment, still in her best satiric mode. "You puzzle me, Pederson.

175

You atomize the socioeconomic order into isolated practical problems, then rearrange the incoherent pieces however suits you. Since nothing coheres, you are free to comment randomly on whatever strikes your fancy and dodge responsibility."

"And you, Ma'am, lump everything together in a single concept so we can see nothing clearly!"

"Well," she answered with a resigned chuckle, "that's a discussion for another day."

Again she stopped, as if to remind herself that when it comes to shaking people's primal convictions, the forces of satire are as limited as the resources of rational criticism. Only the hungry can be teased or reasoned into truth . . . but then, it's equally hard to renounce satire. "Of course you're right so far as you go, but you don't go far. You cleverly conceal the history of failure by purveying an illusion of selective progress and calling it success. You're like the man with the fashionable eye patch who looks at the landscape and sees it flat—you offer a counterfeit life of consumption and call it 'enhanced survival.'

"We know that liberalism tries to reform itself, but isolated reforms are surface piecework marketed as 'practical.' The same troubles keep returning. The world must go on even while we do the hard work of identifying underlying conditions. I would expect you of all people to want to know the causes—if there are causes—of our planetary disease."

He professed to be amused. "I guess I'm not as clever as other people."

"Oh, people are much smarter than we give them credit for. This isn't about knowledge. It's about sensitivity and discipline.

We have an awesome ability for protecting our complacencies against what we don't want to see. I wonder that a quiet voice in the night never whispers to a man like you that you're worshipping the coin of Mammon's realm and protecting its status quo. Do you never fear the market's traffic in human souls?"

"On your account I'm a hopeless reactionary who prefers comfortable blindness to uncomfortable vision. But what exactly am I shutting my one eye to?"

"To a marketplace that has ruined the achievements of human culture and the character of its people. To technological power that has melted the ice caps, poisoned the seas, and—for money—rendered the planet nearly unlivable. Your facts are scabs over the wounds of imagination, inflicted on rationality by grace of an imaginary you reject."

Pederson squirmed in his chair, leaned forward, and regarded her with an alarm that showed he was genuinely bewildered by the charges. When finally he replied, no trace of dismissiveness remained in his voice.

"You mystify me! The truth is the contrary of what you say!" He stopped and fidgeted restlessly before continuing. "The market isn't a negative influence on cultural institutions. It funds education and charitable societies, and the arts in all forms. It makes people freer to do what they will."

As he stopped to collect his thoughts, she held her gaze on his face, waiting, giving him time.

Eventually he resumed. "Do agrarian peasants who spend their lives grubbing for food have the education or the leisure or the money to enjoy your cultural interests, even to read one of your books? Cost-benefit analysis puts schools and universities, health care, and cultural institutions on firm financial footing. Beyond that, you must see the strides the science of economics has made in strengthening social welfare and public virtue. It makes the goods people want more widely and cheaply available and therefore more equal. It strengthens public services by rationalizing production and consumption. Economic analysis conserves energy otherwise wasted on inefficient processes and economizes the virtues you want to defend. When we increase choice, we increase benefits. I call the respect for individual autonomy and the general good of private judgment morally superior. That's individualism serving the common good."

Ribeiro was visibly appalled by his argument. The two appalled each other. The energy each devoted to these responses showed that neither took the other for stupid. Quite the contrary. She saw his faculties as having been dumbed down by generations of thoughtless dogma. There was an elephant in the room that he refused to acknowledge. Could he not—*would* he not—see how liberal globalization had concentrated wealth in a tiny oligarchy and reduced the dispossessed hordes to homelessness or serfdom? Wasn't this the very resistance in him that she had mentioned earlier? Behind his moral defense of the status quo lurked the self-defeating terror of further disrupting a world already at risk.

Having touched a nerve, she needed to take the measure of the anxiety it had roused. "I admit that your examples are well-matched to your desire. But consider: Doesn't your 'science of economics' treat all motivations as conscious preferences? And doesn't that overrate consciousness?"

When he would have answered, she held up a hand that he respectfully obeyed as she silently considered what might be worth saying. "Let's do a thought experiment," she continued. "On how commercializing a 'product' changes it." She shifted in her chair and leaned forward in his direction.

"Imagine what happens to your mother's favorite chair when you do one of the following: One, barter the chair to make space for something you need more. Two, make it a gift to a person you love. Three, offer it in generosity to a friend. Four, use it to fulfill an obligation. Five, sell it on eBay. Six, give it to Goodwill for use by the poor. Seven, give it to Goodwill *as a tax credit*."

She paused to let him count. "You see we have not one but seven chairs. Each of these acts alters the chair itself.

"Now a different example: You offer to remunerate a person for a generous deed, but he declines. How do you feel? Or he's insulted, then how do you feel? Take the time to consider these alternatives imaginatively. When you play them out, don't you find the nature of the object changed in each case? Make it psychological if you wish, though it's not just *your* psychology. It's shared, hence objective reality. Can you still say the market conditions are benign forces of exchange?"

Once again Pederson's reply is anything but careless. "I'm sure you've heard, ma'am, that 'private vice is public virtue?' It's counterintuitive, but it's true. The acquisitive desire doesn't contradict the impulse to generosity or civic responsibility or the integrity of my mother's chair. The profit motive can energize all these good things by teaching respect for our freedom to choose for ourselves. Where is the good in a society if not in the interest of people who can judge their own well-being? What you see as the corrosive effect of money, I see as a substantial moral service."

Mai Bao and Ope remained observers of this exchange as Ribeiro replied in a tone of deepening urgency.

"Let's try one more time to understand each other, Anders. Here's another thought experiment. This time not on our feelings but on how economy effects 'reality.' It's the transformation of a 'thing' into a 'product.' Imagine that you're giving a gift to the person you most love. Here's the question: In each of the following cases is the gift enhanced or degraded by market efficiency? It would be efficient to give a gift card from a favorite shop. Of course! Better still, give cash. Then your loved one can buy whatever she or he wants. Both options efficiently maximize the allocation of goods.

"But now ask yourself: Is the joy of thinking about the person and searching out just the right gift, wrapping it lovingly, presenting it ritualistically over a celebratory dinner—is all this and the gratitude following such an act of love—are these enhanced or degraded by the efficiency of the gift card or the cash? Now don't terminate this line of thought without also asking whether the idea of exchange, of reciprocation, does or does not also weaken the gift.

"Gifts aside, what's the meaning of the service freely offered to a person in need? What's the difference between giving your seat to an elderly person on the train and simply obeying the law that reserves the seat for him? Does the efficient allocation of goods and services through charitable institutions carry the same meaning as spontaneous acts *in person?* Or doesn't the marketplace subtract the human dimension? Don't these examples show the market reducing cultural practices and the organization of a human world to the caprices of desire? Soon enough the 'reality' of interpersonal space becomes the idolatry of a balance sheet."

Pederson's response to this speech showed that he had been affected by the urgency of her argument, at least. He, too, leaned forward with elbows on his knees and hands clasped under his chin.

"I follow what you're saying, Miranda, and I accept almost everything in your examples. There's truth in them. But ultimately the contrary is true. What I don't see is why those truths should cause you to turn your back on the miracle of modern economic organization. You don't seem to be a person who would recklessly destroy a planetary system that works, however imperfectly, for the elegance of an idea."

In a spontaneous gesture of frustration, she shook her hands in midair, almost wringing them. Then stopped and, inconsistently, answered in a perfectly controlled and quiet voice. "You're right. The alternative is not between accepting or destroying any abstract system. It's about concrete relations among people, with things, and with oneself. And so I continue to insist: Terrible consequences follow from the idolatry of all-powerful systems that, like machines, being inhuman, know nothing of the desires they profess to satisfy. Markets, like robots, aren't people. They have no capacity to care for the consequences of their practices. They only count beans and leave out as irrelevant whatever can't be quantified. The ethical issue arises when people pretend they bear no responsibility for how markets work. That's the moment when we lose the human world and our own souls."

Still neither of the others spoke. Ope's discussions with Gebhard Erlich at the university and with Mamud Çelik at the clinic lent additional cogency to Ribeiro's argument, but he saw that support from him at this moment would be counterproductive.

Meanwhile Mai Bao seemed to have been won over by her Argentine writer, sufficiently at least not to let the point die.

"You do see, Anders, that Miranda isn't arguing against economy. She's arguing that money isn't a neutral force for organizing the human world. It has an irresistible influence on everything it touches and becomes demonic unless it's made consistent with—and that means *subordinated to*—the demands of the good life. She's objecting to the idolatry of economy."

"The same is true for the intellectual world!" Adawale suddenly added with an unusual degree of passion. "As when generations are taught to give attention only to what is practical and useful. Perception narrows, and a vast surplus of reality ceases to register. Even experience diminishes, because sensation can only be turned into experience by being taken to heart."

Mai Bao offered a further example. "What do you think the cultural effect might be of paying a person to do a good deed? Let's say paying a child to read a book, to make the honor roll, to get into a prestigious school, or just to mow the lawn? Under the influence of money and practical success, that child is being taught that the value of all things is abstract and quantifiable. From infancy, he learns from his environment that *good* is what satisfies conscious aims. That nothing is inherently good or worth doing unless it's *good for* something. So he never develops the habit of attending to the common good of ethical and political reality."

"But you're still leaving out the force of money to bring about good results."

"No!" she answered emphatically. "Whatever good money might do is a different question. Civilized life requires an orderly distribution and the proper use of good things. Not the dominion of one! A world worth inhabiting requires cultivating good habits and practices not *only* for utility but because the good life is inherently valuable."

Miranda rejoined the exchange with a "writerly" example: "I know you, Anders, understand language as the treasure house of human experience, so you can't accept the degrading effect the public media have on it. Writers blamed for using $10 words where $2 words would seem to do, or complex sentences where simple sentences might do, or for making references to the books of the past that non-readers will find obscure and intimidating. Why should a writer let language and our cultural precedents atrophy just because people don't take the trouble to learn to read? Economize on language and love and citizenship and we squander the authority of a rich culture and diminish the quality of life in the future."

Meanwhile Adawale had begun waving a hand gently in the air as though something remained to be said. "Just as a footnote, I want to be assured that the burden of the argument doesn't come to rest on the personal. We know that gambling on insurance schemes has been debated since Lloyd's of London was an eighteenth-century coffeehouse. People met there to discuss how the risks to ships on the high seas might be shared and the costs reduced. The controversy then and now is between wagering on the early deaths versus wagering on saving lives. If we think that issue through, we can see how it sets economic efficiency, the social good *and* the social evil, in a strong light. Which way would the momentum of a 'free market' lean? What does free trade demand to be freed *from* if not goods that are beyond price?"

CHAPTER 6

THE NEXT DAY when the four met for breakfast, the same debate broke out again as though each had spent part of the night reviewing it, but in an appreciable change of tone Pederson seemed less triumphalist.

The night before, Mai Bao, ever the good hostess, had let the debate run its course until she sensed that positions had hardened and there was nothing more to be gained. For the sake of goodwill and before the discussion could reignite, she proposed that they enjoy the morning by exploring the neighborhood on foot. And so it was agreed that she and Miranda would walk into the village while Anders and Ope hiked in the foothills behind the cottage.

And so they did. Then after lunch around the table on the front balcony of the house, Mai Bao reopened the topic in a quite different key. "In the night I lay awake reviewing a story relevant to our discussion. Remember Alfred Hitchcock's classic *North by Northwest*?"

"Yes," Pederson answers with renewed enthusiasm. "Cary Grant and Eva Marie Saint. I love that movie, but I've never understood what's so 'classic' about it."

She grins at him playfully. "Then sit still and I'll tell you. Sometimes fiction can clarify ideas by measuring them against everyday reality. Remember Roger O. Thornhill? He's the protagonist, the one played by Cary Grant."

Both Ope and Miranda noticed that she names the actor because Pederson would take the actor to be real and the characters fictions, while Miranda would say "the star" is the least real of all: an image of wealth and fame who has everybody's face but his own.

"In the story," Wu continues, "the chief of a foreign spy ring calls Thornhill 'a man of many names,' though he's not a spy and has little to do with 'intelligence' in any sense of the word. He's a Madison Avenue ad man, misidentified as another man who *is* an identity but doesn't exist. By contrast, Thornhill exists *without* identity. He's the man in the grey flannel suit for whom images are real and words are empty signs.

"Anyway, no one believes anything Roger Thornhill says. Near the beginning, he says to his secretary, 'In the world of advertising there is no such thing as lying. There's only expedient exaggeration.' He's missing the important moving part: For him there is no reality principle. No wonder he's been married and divorced twice and remains tied still to his mother's apron strings. When he's in deep trouble, even she doesn't believe him. To her, he's still playing boyish games.

"That's the character for starts. Now the plot. A foreign spy named Phillip Vandamm mistakes Thornhill for an American agent named Kaplan and has him kidnapped from the New York St. Regis Hotel. But there's the problem of identity. There is no Kaplan. He's a fabrication of the U.S. intelligence services to cover for another agent who has become Vandamm's mistress."

Aside to Anders: "You'll remember her as the Eva Marie Saint character. But back to the plot: In a great comic sequence Thornhill is taken to a country house, force-fed a bottle of scotch, and put in an ostensibly stolen car, drunk, so he will kill himself. Enter the police. They arrest him, then show no interest in his pocket full of identity cards and numbers. Everybody knows—especially the officials know—that proofs of identity identify nothing. It's just a documentary umbrella to help governments to account for people.

"Proof is, number one, not a *thing*, and, number two, not conferrable. 'Identity,' like all Thornhill's words, is a cipher with no referent. But we'll come back to Roger and language.

"Once his mother posts bail for him, the advertising man sets out to find Kaplan, the person he's been mistaken for. That leads him to the UN General Assembly Hall where he is photographed, knife in hand, appearing to have just killed a man. From this point, identified or not, he's a real fugitive on the run.

"In a foreshadowing of events to come, Thornhill, now aka Kaplan, goes to the hotel room registered to that name and begins reading the forged signs of the fake identity.

"Now we can summarize the plot situation: Roger O. Thornhill can be mistaken for the nonexistent Kaplan because he has no essence and no relation to truth. Even his matchbook says so: 'ROT.' As when, later on a train, he holds the matchbook up to Eve Kendall and says, 'My trademark. The O means nothing. ROT.' The advertiser, who sells images without substance, knows he, too, has no substance, 'a decoy.' And just by the way, when Eve asks him about his marriages, he says his wives 'saw though me.' Empty. Transparent. You begin to see, Anders, this is no piece of idle entertainment."

When she stops a few moments, it's significant that, given the loquacity of this group, no one speaks.

"Yes," she resumes, "there is more. All the comic to-do about the law: the kidnapping, the court, Thornhill the fugitive, not to speak just yet of the end at Mount Rushmore where he and Eve elude their killers by climbing over the faces of four presidents before justice is meted out. The film, you see, is also about citizenship, though there's no evidence that Thornhill has ever committed a political act. Instead, speaking of speaking truly, he only sells commodities by seducing people to want things they don't need.

"But I'm ahead of myself. After Thornhill escapes arrest by catching the New York Central to Chicago, without a ticket, something happens that's not in the game of shifting images. Now, running for his life, he runs directly into the arms of Eve Kendall, the intelligence agent close to Townsend, who's under orders to arrange his murder. Eve "kindles" more than his matchbook can, and the tale becomes a love story quite beyond sentiment and sex. From here, Thornhill, the zero, begins to accrue substance and his flat world begins to expand 'vertically.'"

Ribeiro, who has been hanging on every word of the summary, laughs enthusiastically at the double entendres.

"Maybe." Mai Bao replies with a sly grin of acknowledgement. "It *is* Hitchcock."

"And a wonderful example!" Ribeiro answers eagerly. "ROT is modern man, nihilist child of Enlightenment progress. At least Thornhill knows he reduces words to meaninglessness, but the ascent from ciphers to words is a *thorny hill* to climb."

"Yes," Mai Bao replies. "At their first meeting in the dining car, just as the plot begins to turn, Eve tells him she can see he's 'clever with words.' But by now the spy ring has Thornhill encircled."

Miranda giggles.

"By means of the second Eve—the one who's falling in love with her victim—Vandamm sends Roger O by bus from Chicago to an unforgettably flat and empty farm country in Indiana where he's to meet Kaplan. The camera shoots this wasteland from above, bisected top to bottom by a perfectly straight and empty road extending from horizon to horizon. The landscape objectifies Thornhill's whole state of being. When a crop duster strafes him, he dodges, and his 'suit'—his image, his only reality—gets rubbed in the dirt and sprayed with insecticide from above.

"His situation turns hopeless—as, sooner or later, things do for mortals—and a change begins to emerge that's so slight it's invisible. It's like the intersection of two parallel worlds alike in every detail, except that in one there is no meaning and in the other there's death. So Thornhill confronts death in a cornfield and everything shifts."

Suddenly Ribeiro explodes in a eureka moment. "Oh, I see! I'd never seen that before! It's a resurrection event. Not *from* death exactly, but a resurrection *of* death. It wasn't there in any of the earlier episodes. Roger is forced out of the shelter of the maternal narcissism, and, with nothing left to conserve, he faces a limit condition. Except that limits are also thresholds of what can't be foreseen, and he—of all people—rises to the challenge! What he does from here will 'count' in incalculable ways."

Everyone in the library on the edge of the Vienna Woods—everyone but Ope—"knows" the film, but Ribeiro's point astonishes them all. Just as Mai Bao's reading of concrete life in the film gives flesh and bone to the preceding conceptual argument. For Ope, at least, Thornhill's confrontation with death in a cornfield "kindles" a spark in his own dark and empty world.

It's the middle of the story, but the conversation had wandered in so many directions during the afternoon, that they eventually broke it for drinks in the library followed by dinner. Afterward Mai Bao tested the waters and, finding them still navigable, she allowed the topic to continue.

It was Pederson who urged it on. "You said, Mai Bao, that the plot's political. But beyond the comic business about law, intelligence agencies, the UN, and the police, I don't see how politics is implicated even when the two escape by climbing down the faces on Mount Rushmore. If I remember, that's where they are ultimately saved and the spies die or are captured."

"That's the plot," she replies, "and after many turns and twists the lovers live happily ever after, as we say in folktales. And the ironic camera marks such an ending as it tracks the phallic train entering a tunnel, returning east."

"That's our Hitchcock!" Ribeiro exclaims again. And Mai Bao returns to Pederson's political question.

"I said earlier that the police aren't interested in proofs of identity. Cards and numbers don't tell us 'who.' They only help the state decide whom to include and whom to banish. That's part of the spy story."

Ope mutters obscurely, "Yes. Everyone must be ac-*count*-ed for! But there's nothing political in the state compulsion to count and control."

Mai Bao makes room for the remark but lets it pass. "I've said that Thornhill, the image of a man in a world of images, matches his language: suave, 'clever,' flat, literal, utilitarian, empty. But even the advertiser's empty language leaves a trace of things worth saying. Words aren't entirely silenced even when misapplied by automatons. The zero in his initials may say 'nothing,' but the truth he reveals is far from absolutely nothing."

Then speaking directly to Anders, "I'm *not* going to say that Thornhill finds purpose in his life by a patriotic act in destroying the spy ring. It happens, but it happens accidentally. All he's thinking about is saving his skin and, a bit later, about saving Eve, whom he has exposed to danger as, of course, she has exposed him. Love is being-exposed, isn't it? For one who's attentive to language there's much more in the name 'Eve'! But the political point is that Thornhill is no longer living randomly. Nor does his transformation have anything to do with patriotism. Citizens don't act *for* a government, nor do they have to fall in love on the New York Central. They live in view of 'a limit,' and act with others for common purposes that are often obscure to everyone."

Ope intrudes with another comment to Pederson: "That, Anders, is the element of truth in your references to Hobbes' state of nature. When we reach the limit, we get serious."

Mai Bao: "So no more games for Roger! In South Dakota, near the climax . . .

Another bawdy chuckle from Miranda: "Is that climax in or out of the tunnel?"

"Patience, Miranda! Don't shock the boys!" Wu continues. "Thornhill is persuaded by the chief of intelligence, 'The Professor,' to protect Eve by putting himself at risk. Now he's in 'civilian' clothes, as befits one who has outstripped the pinstripe image contrived for consumption. And unsuspected possibilities turn up in the fat empty zero of his middle initial."

Miranda, grinning, ". . . which *stands* for nothing and doesn't *lie*."

Mai Bao: "A cipher for anything or for nothing. It reduces 'identity' to a way of life he's now embarked on. As the Chinese Daoist might say, it's the 'way' that makes a life. And, by the way, the intelligence 'Professor' isn't concerned with Thornhill. He's concerned with doing his job in service of the country and his agent. When Thornhill looks across from the lodge at the faces on the side of Rushmore and says, 'I feel like Teddy Roosevelt is trying to tell me something,' the Professor replies, 'He's telling you to walk softly and carry a big stick.'"

"Humph!" says Miranda. Then, turning sharply in her chair and facing Anders as the adversary, "That, Pederson, in a nutshell is what your individualism gets tragically wrong!"

He returns the fire. "You want to blame Thornhill's empty-headedness on economic culture? I don't see any evidence of that in the story."

Miranda turns to Ope. "You answer him, Professor. He might listen to you."

Adawale frowns as though he prefers not to. "I'm the one who has never seen the film, so I rely on the summary. But I'd say the first task is to understand exactly what question the story is meant to shed light on."

By this time Ribeiro's irony has ruined the respectful formality of the name "Pederson," and Ope has resorted to his given name. "You may be right, Anders, in saying that the film doesn't show any *direct* economic or political influence on Thornhill's character. But if we accept the reading of the film as given, I'd have to say that the advertising executive is shifting from a hollow man to one who is acting in concert with others. That sounds political to me. At least pre-political."

Anders: "Don't falling in love and saving Eve still count as self-interest?"

At that, Miranda makes a significant advance in the argument by making a significant concession. "In a sense, you're right. Instead of condemning self-interest, maybe we should see it as an impulse we often rise above even as we serve ourselves. When Thornhill is lured from outside by the beauty he meets on the train, 'falling in love' seems a rather odd term for his self-interest. 'Falling' isn't operating under his own control, even when he agrees to fly to South Dakota to save the girl."

In an altered tone that might have been a concession on his part, Pederson observes, "By the way, if we're going in for all this close reading, then when Thornhill is mistaken for a nonexistent Townsend—'town's end'—I'd expect you to say the political order already extends as far as the 'thorn hill' but not the spy. The town ends where the spy's work begins, and Thornhill is restored to the city by love. A real citizen for the first time."

"Well observed!" Miranda replies warmly. "Not self-interest after all. It's love, transporting the self into a larger field. Eve is Vandamm's mistress, whom he intends to drop into the ocean from his plane. No love there."

"Exactly," Mai Bao says, as though resting her case. "Love and political life both belong to a person whose self-interest has been absorbed into a larger field. Roger faces mortality as the limit, then performs a political service whereby saving himself, saving Eve, and saving the country all belong to acting beyond the self."

"That's good!" Adawale responds with enthusiasm. "What we bring to the film from experience enables us to see that acting with others replaces the failure of identity with an accretion of public character."

Miranda turns to Mai Bao with a warm smile. "I agree with the Professor. Thornhill is transformed, or 'resurrected,' by facing a limit experience. There may be many kinds of such experiences, but in keeping with this story, I'll add that in recognizing that somewhere down the line I'm going to croak—the thing I may most want to hide from myself—I can discover an impulse to find a shape in life. Sometime we should discuss how the love and death themes may be related."

This is not what interests Anders, however. He's stuck on the individual. "You seem to think that the biological fact that I'm an individual before I'm a citizen is responsible for the ills of the world!"

"Thank you, Roger O!" Miranda cries. "No! It's not the fact that you start there, it's that you don't get beyond it."

Then to Mai Bao, "Please back up to the point about Thornhill's language. What does he say to his secretary about truth?"

"In the world of advertising there is no such thing as lying. There's only expedient exaggeration."

"Think about that, Anders. What would the Thornhill theory of language be if he could describe his own practice? Remember that he uses words to deceive consumers."

"'Deceive' is an exaggeration," Pederson protests. "I agree he tries to get people to want things they don't need, but he's serving an economy that lets people live well." He grins at her. "Private vice, public virtue."

Ribeiro drops her head into her hands long enough to exclaim, "Oh my God!" Then, "Why do you let your mind skip around like a jumping bean? Talking about everything at once is a way to avoid facing anything. Stay with language!"

"Just as Thornhill's 'identity' is a parody of identity, so his 'language' is a parody of language, as a 'suit' is a parody of a man. At the beginning he's on the way to the dead language of schizophrenia! But if he weren't already embedded in a linguistic world, he wouldn't even be able to compose his vacuous advertisements. There's the communal quality that guarantees the *truth* that his words are *false*. Not because he's a rogue. Because he's infantile. Mommy's boy playing word games. No response, no responsibility."

Mai Bao responds to Ribeiro admiringly. "You've become a philosopher, Miranda." She grins at Ope. "And that's what we call reading. It happens when people face reality as though it added up to a whole and accept responsibility."

Pederson looks startled as though something has hit a nerve in the depths of his complacencies. As the others go on to discuss what's to be done in a Thornhill world, he gets up and walks to the window, where he stands for a long while staring into the dark.

In an eventual lull in the conversation, he turns a sober face to his companions. "I do understand most of what you've been saying. Maybe not all that about identity and language, but I do see the argument that breaking the world up into discrete bits instead of taking it whole can be a disease. Public discourse may be destroyed along with institutions, even the family and codes of behavior. You may be right that beyond material improvements, many of the promises of the Enlightenment were misguided. Perhaps the eighteenth-century and twentieth-century revolutions are exhausted, but I refuse to believe that the half-empty glass isn't also half-full."

And, the hour growing late, on that note Mai Bao opportunely announced that it was time to adjourn for the night.

INTERMEZZO

I, YORI KASHIMOTO, am interrupting my narrative momentarily to tell you something more of the story behind the story. It took several years of work to bring my tale to the present point, where I realized I had lost my way. The unspeakable violence of the twentieth Ulro century and the unraveling of the twenty-first tempted me to see evil everywhere and good as delusion.

There seemed little point in assembling another catalogue of the failings of the mother planet or adding yet another lamentation over its fate. Ulro never lacked well-informed and well-intentioned critics or prophetic voices warning of approaching doom. But who listened and learned from those voices? The point of my years of research into the causes and the likely destiny of the planet was to help prevent the New Earth from repeating that history. But once it appeared that the flaw was in us all, I lost hope for the future of my work if not quite in the future of the species.

In this respect Adawale and I are similar. He's the historian trying to fix a broken world, seeking a means toward a practical end, while I'm trying to understand why the fixes so often fail. My progress is blocked less by ignorance of what to do next than by blindness to why we do anything at all. If, in our infinite pursuit of knowledge as power, we have lost our sense of direction, it surely has to do with having forgotten the wisdom of living well as passed down to us in the stories of the world.

Despairing of my original idea and of my competence, I eventually laid this work aside. I spent months reading like a drowning man in a stormy sea, especially Shakespeare, the very thing to be avoided by one who wishes to escape harsh reality! I read the plays straight through, one a night. Then I read and reread the ones that spoke to my condition most clearly. Sometimes I spent hours on a single scene or musing over one provocative speech. One night, in a propitious moment, a light fell across my page with the force of epiphany and I caught a glimpse of history and destiny flowing together.

The catalyst was the poet's last play, The Tempest. *You will remember the story of the magician severed from his past, facing a blank future. It's what fixed itself in my mind with the persistence of a nagging muse who won't be silenced.*

Now I am no Prospero, but I'm reminding you of his tale because there's something essential here that can't be communicated in information bits. In one boundless sentence it summarizes my enigma and perhaps yours as reader: "We are such stuff as dreams are made on."

Here's the story in brief: Prospero, the conjuror whose name means "the one who hopes," has been banished twelve years with his daughter Miranda on a solitary island in a wide and empty sea. It happened because the once-upon-a-time Duke of Milan had preferred to "better his mind" in the "secret studies" of "the liberal arts" rather than attend to the "worldly ends" of governing his dukedom. He left the administration to his venial brother

198

Antonio, who first stole the power, then sent him and the infant Miranda to a slow death at sea.

In the narrative present of the play, the marooned Prospero has only the child and his magic books just as I have only you, my imaginary reader, and Alexandros. But it's not enough. We need more. For we, like the teenage Miranda, see as history sees, "In the dark and backward . . . abyss of time." We need magic, and magic is Prospero's speciality.

By his "charms" he discovers unexpected connections on the island among people, events, and the elements of nature. He binds himself and Miranda in relation with the primal earth and water by naming the elements "Caliban" and teaching the savage Caliban "how / To name the bigger light, and how the less." The insubstantial elements of air and fire he names "Ariel," and commands "him" to exploit a sea-tempest in ways that ultimately change everything. Ariel works mainly by the power of music, for "the isle is full of music, / Sounds, and sweet airs, that give delight and hurt not." Eventually it's the music that charms the numerous participants in the tale and channels their energies differently.

A storm disrupts the harmony of the small, quiet, well-ordered island by causing a shipwreck that resurrects Prospero's past and throws his old acquaintances up on shore. "And, hark, what discord follows!"

The survivors cause a variety of essentially political disturbances. Among them is a scheme between Prospero's villainous brother, who overthrew him, and the equally guilty brother of the King of Naples, who seeks to displace the King. Also political is a comic subplot in which two of the King's servants provide a drunken summary of vices by luring Caliban into their service *with wine and declaring themselves rulers of the isle. We also hear two fanciful and contrary political visions of the island: Prospero's old friend Gonzalo imagines it as a utopia, as the earthy Caliban describes it as a dystopia. There's much more of the kind and not all bad since Prospero's "magic" transforms this topsy-turvy little world. So what does he do and how does he do it?*

He doesn't exactly do *anything! The storm isn't of his making. It's "propitious." When Miranda asks his reason "For raising this sea-storm," he denies it: "bountiful Fortune . . . hath mine enemies / Brought to this shore." The conjuror-magician is an opportunist. Though he speaks of their distant past, and though what he does in the present may have implications for possible futures, his art belongs to the present. Past and future are not his realm. He makes no effort to harmonize the past with an alternative future. He concentrates on the flow of contingent events, revealing them as they are. It's a "magic" that conceals nothing and brings nothing hidden into existence. The same world that others see, but see differently.*

For example, he commands "Ariel" to induce sleep and waking with the result that his brother, who consigned him and Miranda to death at sea, incites the murder of the King and thereby stands revealed in character.

In another instance, learning that the young Prince Ferdinand is wandering about the island grieving for his father, presumed drowned, Prospero permits him and Miranda to meet and fall in love. As nature takes its course, he gives rules that enhance their desire and induce them to bend the rules. By preventing premature intimacy, he makes "the contract grow." In many such ways he opens a space where relations shift, and does it all by giving words.

So we recognize the magician as poet whose words alter the warp and woof of a world!

Now why should such a fanciful tale inspire hope for my stalled Ulro project? Because Prospero works differently from how either Adawale or I work. Where Ope seeks to make the world better, or I pursue political understanding useful to posterity, Prospero, lost somewhere in the sea of chronology, fixes his eye solely on the moment in front of him. Which raises the question, if he's not trying to affect the future, how does his "magic" touch on the source of political association?

The answer is, he plays imaginative variations on the world as it's given, without regard to futurity and with no end in view. The new relations that emerge among beings on the island are unexpected, perhaps, but they're neither unnatural nor supernatural. No hocus-pocus. Storms do happen at sea; mariners are sometimes lost and sometimes found; young people fall in love; persons marooned on islands can be rescued. However rarely, where all is contingency, people even cross thresholds into other worlds and become new and "goodly creatures." And that brings us a step closer to the "poetic" character of human, and hence political, being.

Yet if my conjuring, and yours, does not rest on some future good—if the conjuror accomplishes nothing on his own, then what's the use? If my work and Adawale's are bound to some future good, then we're quite out of line with Prospero's experience. We may need his example.

Though he does not envisage consequences, the play itself implies several worlds beyond the island. Eventually the ship is discovered to be "magically" seaworthy, and all the characters will sail again for Italy, where Ferdinand and Miranda will become king and queen of Naples and Prospero will even be restored to his dukedom. The magician will release the villains unpunished to cope with themselves as they may, as he will liberate Ariel from his bond and leave him "free as air." All these developments lie ahead but none of them are within Prospero's ken or his care.

The one "who hopes" conjures by giving "local habitation and a name," but seers, you may know, are famously blind. It's the secret of their vision. They leave practical results and unintended consequences to managers, social engineers, or the connivance of villains on magic islands. Seers see more clearly by not searching past and future for habitable worlds. Their conjuring belongs to a peculiar time, not measured by chronometers. When spent worlds reach the limit of banality, conditions immanent to thought and language arise "magically," with the force of objective ideals in the expansive moment of vision that is (almost) outside of time. And it comes by giving names.

Prospero doesn't try to defeat contingency and secure the future by a power of his own. He gives words, and those who can hear become responsible to the bond between words and things. In this sense the island is a site of political genesis, as all are irrevocably summoned to fidelity or infidelity to the bond. Because naming alters perceptions, convictions, and affection, Prospero is the primordial legislator who originates nothing. His speaking initiates others to innocence or guilt before the tribunal of their own reflections. Except for that bond and that fidelity, we would all be Calibans, though having been introduced to language, even the figure of earth is transformed.

When the magician's work is done, he resumes his ordinary human place, breaks his staff, renounces "magic," "drowns" his "books," and says, "Now my charms are all o'erthrown, / And what strength I have's mine own, / Which is most faint."

This, my imaginary reader, is a faithful account of what intruded uninvited on my quest for the force behind political life. Mad as it may seem, it's what holds me in thrall to an eight-hundred-year-old poem, and it's what, in the middle of the adventure on which we are now embarked, I pass to you.

PART FOUR

The Citizen to Come

CHAPTER 1

A SHARP RAP on his door in the Grinzing safe house, awakening Adawale from a troubled sleep that had everything to do with Boris' assignment that he save the world within a month that had now expired.

"Professor Adawale pack your bag. We leave for Greece in an hour."

The command, masquerading as a request, came in a thick Greek accent from a stranger—another stranger!—dressed in the black tunic of an Orthodox Christian monk. The face was largely concealed by the monk's cowl, but he was short, slender, perhaps in his early twenties, and clearly a messenger. Another agent from the mysterious realm of Boris.

Startled and having not decided if or when or how to bolt, Ope obediently followed him out of the silent house and into a waiting car. Curiosity compounding with irony, he asked, "Do you mind telling me where you're taking me?"

"On a pilgrimage. You are about to become a pilgrim." The remark conveyed no interest. Just another ordinary and incontestable fact.

Seated in front where conversation should have been less awkward than silence, neither spoke. Adawale threw a sidelong glance at the little monk as they proceeded down the farm road in silence, then followed the route around the west side of the city and across to the airport on the southeast. There, instead of giving instructions and dropping him off, the monk parked the car in a long-term ramp, collected the luggage, and led the way into the terminal. He flashed one piece of identification and was handed two tickets for Thessaloniki.

During the two-hour flight, Ope struggled with another wave of resentment having little to do with the present situation but a great deal to do with feeling used. By now he harbored fewer misgivings about *what* he was being forced to do and more about *why*. His rational life had been ruled of late by insufficient reasons and the weaker the reasons, the greater the sacrifice. How dare Razumovski put him through these paces and try to make him responsible for a crumbling world order.

For sanity, he willed himself to let it all go and, as resentment waned, spent the duration of the flight reviewing his situation at Grinzing. Being peremptorily snatched from a place not at all unpleasant and where he was beginning to feel comfortable if not useful delivered another shock to his sensibility. Superficially at least, the encounter with his three companions had been enjoyable and even productive. Especially with Wu Mai Bao whose use of stories had added a new facet to his thinking. In this sudden rupture she would be acting on instructions, of course, but that only strengthened his bitterness at the condescension of his handling.

As the plane began its descent into Thessaloniki, he recognized one thing he had been blind to: The time in the safe house had not been exactly safe. That comfortable island outside the tumultuous world had allowed a little daylight to pass between himself and his somber mood, only to be torn away by this pointless trip to the Aegean, no doubt never to return.

He and the still nameless, black-clad monk stepped out into the Greek light, whose liquid radiance he saw only as a spotted runway beside a wide bay. The two men passed through the terminal and boarded a bus into a city Adawale had never visited. Over the centuries Thessaloniki had spread down the hill from the ancient acropolis to a waterfront shaped like a great amphitheater.

Climbing was not one of his favorite things, but he obediently climbed the hill on foot, and the two advanced blindly through the narrow streets of a picturesque neighborhood called *Ano Poli* or Upper Town. At the "Balcony of Thessaloniki," they paused to look down across the city where the light fell still in shafts through dark-bottomed clouds on the crescent of water below. This scene and the view of Vienna, stretched out on the plain beneath its hills, might have belonged to different planets, and the difference served to make him feel still more alienated than his sudden displacement from the Nigerian countryside to Austria a few weeks before.

As they surveyed the waterfront, the guide unexpectedly broke his silence. "My name is Markos Dimitriou. I come from Simonos Petras monastery on Mount Athos. Friar Pavlos Demetriopoulos sent me." The English was broken sufficiently to mitigate the effect of his earlier silence. "Now we go to the Monastery of the Vlatades. Then to the sacred mountain."

Markos led the way to the monastery, where Adawale faced the most outrageous demand yet. Without a word of explanation, he was wrapped in a black Greek tunic that extended from his neck to his ankles. Then a cincture or belt, also black; a black Byzantine hood; and a good pair of walking boots. He was dressed in the habit of an Orthodox Christian monk! Bodily discomfort aside, his whole being revolted against this costume. But, having been taken by surprise yet again, there was nothing for him to do but cooperate.

"You will join Brother Pavlos and other visitors. All in the habit. Not recognized on the mountain."

What Ope had been learning piecemeal only deepened his misgivings. The "kidnapping" in the Vienna Woods proved to have some relation to his work at least, but the flight to an Orthodox monastery and his present incarceration in the trappings of an ancient religion was more like a child's game of hide and seek or another chapter from a not very serious novel. But there was no pleasure in it. Wu Mai Bao's observation that no one is more at risk in an unstable world than the unclassifiable thinker came to mind and quashed his resistance. "People will make allowances for tinker, tailor, or candlestick maker," she had said, "because they know what to expect of them. But not you intellectuals. When people start dying, you die first."

"And you?" Adawale had asked lightly.

"Oh, I'm easily accounted for: I'm an official. We die second."

At that time, he accepted the remark as a witticism, but the steps being taken to conceal his identity and that of unnamed others required more serious reflection. There were historical precedents equal to Boris' subversive operation for saving the world. A particular one came to mind, perhaps because China had been on his mind of late: Over three decades in the middle of the last century, from the Hundred Flowers Movement to the Cultural Revolution, intellectuals had at first been encouraged to strengthen China by offering open criticism of the government. When that didn't work, Mao Zedong reversed his edict and ended by executing hundreds of thousands. Today's friend; tomorrow's enemy.

Such were Adawale's preoccupations as the two "monks" retraced the way through the squares of the Upper City where old Greek and Ottoman houses extend their balconies over small stone streets. In a small shop, they bought an alarming variety of supplies—bedrolls, water bottles, dried fruit, hiking boots and gloves—then boarded a bus that took them to the eastern side of the Calkidiki peninsula, destination Ouranopolis, where all proper roads ended. Ahead, the thirty-seven-mile peninsula called *Agron Oros*, the Holy Mountain, gradually rose to a height of 7000 feet before falling precipitously away into the Aegean.

Lingering at the edge of that blue, blue water was like awaiting Charon's return trip across the Styx. Not passage from the realm of the living to the realm of the shades, but from a ruined world behind into an ancient Eastern torture chamber from which no man might return.

For the journey Markos chose seats on the portside of the ferry to allow a view of the shoreline and the rising spine of a peninsula supported by buttressing ribs that descended from the center to the shore. In that austere landscape of grey rock and scraggly brush, lone monastic buildings appeared deserted, even to forbid human intrusion. But, as the elevation increased, the structures became more imposing but hardy less unwelcoming.

In the warm fall air, the boat was filled with long-bearded Orthodox brothers, tourists, and pilgrims, though here, as Ope was to learn, tourists were also called pilgrims because transformation often followed from close experience of the mountain.

As Markos was not a very articulate guide, Ope had bought a book for the purpose in Ouranoupolis and spent the trip comparing the text to the changing scene before him. The history of the sacred mountain had no beginning. The stories of the gods stretched deep into Greek prehistory, and even the deadly underwater rocks at the end of the peninsula belonged as much to maritime legend as to human time.

Christian prehistory also included all three in a legend that had never lost its force. The story was that after Jesus raised the brother of Mary and Martha from the dead, he, Lazarus, became a priest in Cyprus. In the year 49 CE the Virgin Mary made a voyage to visit him, but her ship was blown off course and she came ashore at the foot of the mountain. When she saw this beautiful place, and when its pagan statues bowed to her in submission, she asked her Son to give it to her as a garden, and so for two thousand uninterrupted years the Holy Mountain has been "the Garden of the Mother of God."

Beyond the curiosity of its endurance and a reminder that sacred places had always been cursed, that story might have made little impression on the secular historian. And yet, having been reduced to a tourist, Ope resolved to learn what he could from the stones of the mountain and ancient ways of life enclosed in its monasteries.

There were several modes of living here. One called "coenobitic" was an integrated community where monks worshiped and ate and worked together. Others lived outside the communities in little more than outcroppings of crumbling rock, but the most solitary were the wild-looking hermits who had dwelt for centuries along the cliffs beneath the crest of the mountain. These were rarely seen except by pilgrims with reason and courage to seek them out.

The curious realities Adawale now faced on this journey were altogether less distinct than the clearly defined world he was accustomed to. Well might he wonder what a monasticism buried in myth and legend for eons might have to do with him or the politics of his planet.

It was an otherworldly place without apparent relation to the real. Even light seemed to have no single source. It might rise from below or descend from above and diffuse into veils with a spectrum of colors. Even patches of sun glancing off the radiant blue water and the rocky landscape in the distance seemed to derive from within as much as from without.

These reflections were eventually interrupted as the boat made a turn toward the shoreline at an obscure place called *Megali Jovantsa*. There a few visitors disembarked on a narrow ribbon of rocky beach to hike five or six miles across to monasteries along the eastern side of the peninsula. Markos pointed to an old bus at the quay and, gathering up his few broken phrases of English, remarked sadly that the mountain was being invaded by technology. Though the purpose of pilgrimage was to get away from the world and renew one's capacity for experience, even here, the practicality of machinery threatened the life of contemplation.

As the boat moved on, the shore was tame, even monotonous in comparison with the drama of the peaks ahead. So, as they continued along an undulating coastline, Adawale returned to the history and prehistory of the mountain. Occasionally Markos aided him by identifying various monasteries that were occupied by monks from Orthodox countries.

As the elevation of the central ridge increased, the slopes became more heavily forested, the cliffs higher, and the outcroppings of rock more rugged. Except for glimpses of other monasteries or an occasional strip of hiking trail, the scene might have been mistaken for the planet before the evolution of conscious life.

Now and again the boat docked briefly to let a few passengers disembark, though most on board were headed for the central point of Daphne, port of entry to the Monastic Republic of Holy Mount Athos—*for men only*!

In the farthest distance Adawale first glimpsed the rocky cap of the mountain extending into the clouds. Even from a distance it was easy to imagine it as the point where the cosmic gods had once passed back and forth between earth and the heavens.

Then the most dramatic scene on the western coast: Simonos Petras (Simon Peter), "Simon of the rock." With that sight in view, even he could hear the echo of the words of Jesus in the name: "*On this rock [petras] I will build my church*." Having visited the scene of St. Paul's sermon on the bluff of Thessaloniki two hours before, his non-religious mind recognized an irony: Here, Peter and Paul began the conflation of Caesar with God that, theology forgotten, had gradually translated into modern bureaucratic management.

A thousand feet above the water, Simonos Petras perches like a fortress on a sheer cliff. At the edge of the stone beach, two buildings: a boathouse with a tower behind and, on the left side, a kind of bungalow with a red tile roof. Far above, two-thirds of the way up the steep cliff, covered with brush and a few trees, a complex of buildings seems to grow from a great escarpment to a height of ten stories. The immediate question: How can anyone climb that bluff from the waterfront to the monastery?

Adawale and Markos disembark and begin the climb. At long last, reaching the monastery courtyard, they are met by another monk who serves as host. He welcomes them with the jellied candy and cool water traditionally offered to hiking pilgrims at any hour of the day. Marko introduces Ope to the host and excuses himself, as Friar Alexios, in impeccable English, describes the layout of the buildings and the rules of the house. After these preliminary remarks, he leads the way to the most austere guest quarters Ope has ever seen. No furnishings except for six cots along the walls and one small stand with a water basin. Here, for the next week, he and several others will be lodged.

After depositing his bags, the two climb still higher to a room with a long balcony overlooking the bay. Many stories above the beach, the balcony extends the full width of the building, around both corners, and who knows how much farther? Anyone who dares look down may observe similar balconies on the floors below from where the natural beauty of the bay and the shore beyond is equally breathtaking. Ope, frustrated by yet another turn in this clandestine adventure, takes it all in with less eagerness than it deserves.

His host explains, "Markos has to catch the boat as it returns from the tip of the mountain to meet other members of your party at Ouranopolis. Some speak no Greek, and none speak the Slavic languages of the mountain. They will arrive tonight. Meanwhile, you may explore the monastery, but you must not wander outside the walls. This place is much wilder than you can see from the water and, the closer to land's end, the wilder it gets."

With that, Adawale, left to himself, descends to the dormitory room, freshens up as well as the primitive conditions allow, and returns to sit on the shallow balcony at the rim of the world. Through the cracks in the floorboards beneath his feet he observes the precarious angle at which the earth falls away hundreds of feet beyond the foundations even of the large building to the beach below. From here he can scan the horizon beyond the Gulf of Mount Athos, beyond Sithonia, the next peninsula, and search in vain for the peak of Olympus a hundred miles to the west.

Left alone with his thoughts, fighting resentment, he searches his memory for further connections to this part of the world. Several years before, travelling from Constantinople to Egypt, he had spent an hour with binoculars studying the opposite side of Athos from the deck of a ship in the Aegean. That evening he had read what material he could find in the ship's library, though culling a few facts from its history counted for nothing compared to being immersed in the place itself. Now he lingers for a while in this middle realm between heaven and earth, absorbing as much as a novice in his mood can absorb in an hour.

The presence of the monks, going about their silent ways, is felt rather than seen or heard, except for two tending the vegetables in the terraced gardens below the buildings, who look more like beetles than monks, keeping the slow rhythm of monastic life.

Next he descends from the top of the complex to the courtyard and wanders about observing the brothers busy with their otherworldly duties. He visits their domestic quarters, the refectory, and peers into the workshops where they have been making and preserving the famous icons for centuries.

He enters the monastery church without knowing that even Western Christians are rarely allowed there. He won't know until evening when Pavlos explains that the Protos of the Holy Brotherhood of twenty monasteries has personally approved opening the doors to people who don't belong to the Orthodox faith and may not even be Christians. Pavlos will put the reason in form of a question: "What can be more harmonious with the monastic vision than saving human life on the planet and thereby saving the soul of humanity?"

To Adawale's eye the church is more museum or warehouse for icons than a holy place. As the late afternoon sun washes the western wall of Simonos Petras and saturates the colored glass windows, it illuminates those rustic, mannered images with unexpected vitality. Unlike his confrontation with Yetunde's Nigerian drawings on a New York sidewalk, he feels no kinship with this enduring dark-age "superstition" and the artistic influence of the Greek mother-goddesses. He searches for a word that captures the spirit of the place and, finding none, reverts to the founding myth of the Mother of God to account for this counterforce to rationality.

Just before *trapeze*, the common meal in the refectory, Markos enters the courtyard with six pilgrims from Oura-noupolis, all in monk's robes and cowls. Before the evening meal, there's only time for introductions too brief to deserve the name—if anyone camouflaged in monastic robes can be "introduced" at all. First Markos presents Pavlos Demetrio-poulos, another Athonite and their official host. Then Friar Pavlos pulls back his cowl and, with only a gesture indicating which is which, mentions the names of each of the others. No more than names for the moment: Abhay Gupta, Paul Poirier, Ji-Min Choi, Burak Derviş, Brother Luke, and finally Opeyemi Adawale.

Adawale presumes that his fellow pilgrims are as alien to the place as he. Except for differences in height and girth, only the handshakes are distinctive, except for Br. Luke. His cowl obscures his face, and he neither offers his hand nor raises his head. It's an awkward moment that adds to Adawale's grumpy disposition. Just hours before he was parachuted into the Adriatic and surrounded by beetle-backed monks after being comfortably installed in the Grinzing safe house.

But the moment passes and the seven enter the refectory and take their places at the common table. The room is a plain stone gallery. A head table for the abbot, separate tables for the priests and brothers, and, farther down the room, a table for guests. World-weary cosmopolitans in a receptive frame of mind might have found the simple meal of fresh bread, fresh vegetables, olives, and fruit, served with a single glass of wine, more exotic than haute cuisine.

Afterward, Markos escorts his guests to the dormitory room, where the cots line the walls, then on to the room on the top floor where they will confer for an unspecified number of days about unspecified topics. Before the lights go out at 9:30, he explains, "You know that we are on the Julian calendar rather than the modern Gregorian. Byzantine time counts the hours from sunset each day. That makes an annual variation of up to three hours, so you may ignore your watches. We will be awakened at 3:30 a.m. by the rhythmic sound of a monk striking a resonant board called the *talanton*. Since no visitor has really been to Athos unless he has attended the 4 a.m. service, we will go there together. Service lasts through sunrise, about three hours."

This may not have been welcome news to Adawale, but it had a positive effect. In those few sentences he recognized a man of some mind and a good host who would prevent this from being a totally lost week of his life.

"After breakfast, we will begin two days hiking the Holy Mountain in pairs. That," Pavlos continues, as though anticipating a great number of things, "that's because 'the Great Yes' precedes 'the Great "Why'! To catch the spirit of the place you should travel in silence. There are truths and there are truths. We are searching for something the Holy Mountain may have kept alive for millennia, and it will begin to appear during your *pilgrimage*. This can't be explained. It must be experienced. So, I leave the experience between you and the mountain."

The unexpected announcement causes a visible wave of apprehension across the room. Judging from what can be observed by heads and hands, none present seems especially youthful, the invisible Br. Mark excepted. The whole affair is strange. Adawale may not be displeased to realize that he's quite vigorous enough for the challenge, but he can see that Poirier, Ji-Min, and Derviş may be in their late fifties and Gupta well beyond that.

Pavlos is neither insensitive nor slow. He certainly registers the general response but ignores it and proceeds to practical arrangements without acknowledgment. "The monasteries will welcome you for rest and refreshment, for meals if you happen there at mealtime, or accommodations for tomorrow night. We will meet back here at the end of the second day and begin our deliberations on the third. Meanwhile, we will travel in pairs, each pair taking a different direction. Paul Poirier will walk with Ji-Min Choi, and Burak Derviş with Abhay Gupta. You, Br. Luke, will travel with Professor Adawale since he has Russian and some Greek and can interpret. But be advised, Adawale, Luke is traveling under a vow of silence. You may speak to him, but he may not reply."

Arbitrary. Presumptive. And mad! That's Adawale's internal response, barely controlled by a lifetime of diplomacy. Two days of mountain climbing, against one's will and in the no-company of a person, no matter what kind, who may not even speak? But what's to be done? Stage a futile protest, or take the long swim to Egypt!

Breaking off the instructions, Pavlos prepares to leave the room, though the company is too shocked to notice. Suddenly remembering something omitted, he adds over his shoulder, "Be sure to take a hiking stick and gloves." He points into a corner where rustic pieces of tree branches of various sizes and lengths lean against the wall in a corner. "Believe me, you'll be glad to have one."

Seven hours later the pilgrims attend a service that lasts until sunlight begins to illumine the church through the stained glass. Even for pagans it's far from monotonous. The scene is always in motion: veneration and kissing of icons as the monks enter, a cantor's chants answered by the communal hymns and prayers, the golden censer swinging from above by three chains and filling the air with the sweet smell of frankincense. The monks move about constantly, lighting candles or ringing bells, but what is most exotic and puzzling to Western outsiders is the veneration of the icons. Not worshiping the objects but honoring the ideal beyond the object. Contemplation of whatever the name "divine" evokes.

Ope, in the best of times, might have a kind of academic curiosity without feeling a need to understand men who have spent thirty years—or ten minutes!—kissing icons and repeating "the Jesus prayer" in their caves. But he has learned one intriguing fact: Pavlos Demetriopoulos is a trained academic philosopher turned monk who seems equally at home in the daylight debates of the agora as in the predawn superstitions of an Orthodox Christian service. Perhaps because a few hours earlier he and Markos had stood on the spot in Thessaloniki where St. Paul delivered a famous sermon, he might be capable now of finding a relation between Pavlos' veneration of icons and his worldly efforts to save Planet Ulro, but only if he weren't faced with still more vivid apprehensions of the day ahead.

CHAPTER 2

SOON AFTER BREAKFAST, Ope and Br. Luke begin their two-day pilgrimage to the summit of the mountain, the direction Pavlos has assigned them! As they begin the steep descent along the wall of the gardens, still high above the sea, Ope observes the young monk's limited agility with a sinking heart. For a while he attributes it to the ungainliness of the robe that closes him in and seals him off from the exterior world. The path itself aside, navigating with arms and legs impeded and vision limited to a few degrees straight ahead is reason enough for stumbling.

The path winding downward toward the water is often scattered with loose rocks, and it's clear enough from a glance at their maps that the whole trip will be at least this difficult. Along routes cut into the rock wall on one side and dropping precipitately away into emptiness on the other, they inch forward carefully until the first climb along the coast south. Direction Grigoriou, the next monastery along the path up.

Neither of them is an experienced climber, and on the first sharp rise, Luke's hiking boots that look too large for his feet slip on the path and he goes down on all fours. The slide ends at Ope's feet with his black robe covered in chalky dust. Only the gloves prevent serious abrasions to his hands. But he climbs to his feet again and pushes stubbornly ahead.

So absorbed are they in the task before them, they have no leisure to think about themselves or why they're here, but plenty of time to appreciate what the next two days will demand. As, slowly, they learn to read the paths more accurately, as their sense of balance adjusts and the reflexes are reprogramed, another issue arises that aggravates Ope's residual list of grievances. It's the matter of Luke's silence. It's inconvenient to say the least, and it expands Ope's discontentment.

Two cannot walk together on the narrow path, so, from a sense of responsibility, he deliberately walks behind to keep an eye on his less steady companion. He recognizes a degree of fragility as when, slipping on a rock or crossing a stream, Luke instinctively reaches for the helping hand. But help is awkward from behind, and gestures of caution are useless to a companion who can see nothing from beneath his cowl but the path under his feet. Occasionally Ope offers a verbal warning, but since Luke can't reciprocate, he begins to feel like a condescending nag.

However, under the necessity of the climb, experience accumulates rapidly, and in segments where the path has been worn smooth by centuries of pilgrim feet, the first hints of camaraderie emerge. By the end of the morning, they are sharing, unconsciously at least, a different and richer communication than might have occurred in a whole day filled with chatter about the beauties of the land- and seascapes or the difficulties of the trek.

The ever-changing surfaces make them breathe to the same rhythm on the climbs, and they pause simultaneously to catch a breath at the top of each a rise. A language of gesture develops to warn of obstacles, to halt for a drink of water, to retie a bootlace, or admire a view. Especially the last, when they're stopped in their tracks by an unexpected window on the blueness of the sea or, from the top of a ridge, by the prospect on a tall stand of distant pine or leathery Spanish Chestnut trees.

The first resting point along their way south is Grigoriou in a setting that is less vertical and less dramatic than the soaring fortified walls of Simonos Petras but no less sublime, both being built into the craggy side of the mountain. What they cannot see at ground level and will not see because they have a schedule to keep is that Grigoriou sits on rock formations that jut sharply into the sea so that the water crashes against the rocks on three sides. But the sound is there, and it registers on them unaware.

At the monastery, a monk greets them with refreshing spring water and the candies that restore energy. The hikers carry water bottles, of course, and there are springs enough along the way, but it's also necessary to conserve energy by keeping the backpacks light. Their rest is luxurious, but the way to the top is long and their plan is fixed.

The next segment of the trek south takes them farther up, along an ancient cobblestone surface, then a steep descent into a deep gorge, and up another of the ridges that radiate from the central spine of the peninsula, and down again to the sea. In one of the gorges, the path is lined with silvery grey-green shrubs and feathery brush spiked with thorns. When Ope's robe gets caught and holds him fast, in trying to free himself he gets a gash across one wrist. For some time thereafter he holds the wound closed with his other hand to stop the bleeding. Luke sees and offers to carry his hiking stick, as it's the only help he can offer under the circumstances.

The next rest stop, named Dionysiou, is embedded theatrically in the mountainside above the increasingly wild and inaccessible coastline. It's a felicitous place where they might gladly linger for the remainder of the day if discussion were allowed and if, as aim-directed travelers, still counting time by worldly clocks, they weren't determined to reach the peak for sunrise tomorrow. It's here that Ope finally gets his wound dressed.

They allow just half an hour for this break before plunging again into the wild. Though Ope might speak as much as he likes along the way, there's little incentive when he can expect no reply from his companion other than a nod or a wave of a hand. So he speaks rarely. Once when, involuntarily, he says, "We should stop again at Dionysiou when we return," the sound of his own voice seems to surprise even the landscape and startle him into his own presence. To this longest remark in three hours, the only response is a nod of Luke's deep cowl as they move on.

Ahead the way is blocked by an amber-colored cliff glittering in the midday sun. On the face of the rock, a marker directs downward toward another pebble beach along the shoreline. Then up again to an intersection of paths, one leading still higher to their left where monastery St. Pavlou (St. Paul) nestles in a grove of chestnut trees—secured in centuries past from pirates and other marauders. It's another place for food and a night's lodging but reluctantly, in obedience to clocks and calendars, they pass it by.

The instinct for schedules is one of the habitual reference points that the rhythm of the pilgrimage quietly changes. In the afternoon the hikers' inner rhythms slow and the pace moderates. Something begins to intrude on Ope that's too close for words. Not just the rubbing of feet inside the boots and the aching muscles in the legs, more severe going down than going up, but something more. He has come to recognize Luke's keen sensibility to the environment and his good judgment, though something else is not quite right with him.

The youthful exuberance of such a young man has worn thin too early, much earlier than his own, despite the difference in age. From the beginning, he had been more inclined than Ope to slip and skid and bark his shins on the rocks, though he appeared to be as much as twenty years younger. By now the deficiency is evident in the way he moves, in his lack of agility climbing over rocks or crossing the brooks that lie in their path. For him the rising sense of responsibility diminishes consciousness of his own aches and pains.

Beyond the path to St. Pavlou, they plunge into a different world. After hours of exposure on sun-drenched paths and ridges, after the thud of their boots against rocky paths and the dry clatter of rocks dislodged by their feet and sent tumbling downhill, they step into a dark primeval forest like a womb. The soft leaf and pine-needle floor and the cooler moist air draw them into the intimacy they had not felt before of walking side by side.

After the forest come still more treacherous ascents and sudden plunges into the defiles between the hills. There along one stretch of relatively level ground, they encounter people:

two men and a mule train conveying goods to destinations still more remote. Two monks leading the animals and the loaded cart lift their hands in friendly salutation, but the unlikely sight in such a difficult wilderness landscape is no less startling.

Soon after they arrive at St. Annis, situated a thousand feet above the port, and enjoy once again the gift of spring water and candy, though a problem has emerged, or rather two. One is timing and endurance. The second is negotiating the first where conversation is precluded. By now both are worn to a point beyond exhaustion, and St. Annis has a guesthouse where they might stay the night. But if they're to be at the mountain peak for sunrise tomorrow, they must get much farther along today. So the daunting problem of negotiating a critical decision without speech.

Ope's eventual solution to both is to read aloud the descriptions from the map and suggest alternatives to which Luke can respond with a gesture. So he passes the map to Luke and says, "It's now early afternoon and the summit is another five hours of even more difficult climbing. If we overreach ourselves, we may be stranded in the forest for the night."

When Luke offers no response, he continues, "Physical stamina aside, when we reach the top, there will be water but no food and no shelter. However, there is a point called Panagia just above the tree line." He shows the point on the map. "It's a grassy saddle with a chapel, water, and an empty building for sleeping. But there are no conveniences. Panagia would put us little more than an hour from the summit, which we could easily reach before dawn."

With his head bowed attentively over the map, Luke follows his words without response, and once again Ope feels the frustration of speaking to another who can't reply. However irrational, it feels insulting to one so tired, but he suppresses the frustration and explains, "Either we continue the climb three hours more to Panagia and risk a night in the wild or we remain at St. Annis and miss the dawn."

He waits for the decisive nod that will decide the question, and when it comes, they move promptly on.

From St. Annis up the mountain, the way is even more primitive. At any moment they are likely to emerge from deep cool woods onto the face of bald rock into clear midafternoon light and warmer air, confronted occasionally by a vision of a sublimity that strikes even the mute into deeper silence. The coastline extends from St. Annis and the bay below their feet all the way back to Simonos Petras. But that is nothing to the view straight ahead. Across the water and the two other great fingers of land that form Athos' sister peninsulas of Sithonia and Kassandra, their eyes travel on across the Thermaic Gulf west of the peninsulas to the Greek mainland where, for the first time, they detect the snow-covered peak of Olympus against the western sky.

During the afternoon there are stops in the ever-changing landscape to contemplate stands of virgin forest, or waves of silvery-green olive groves along distant hills, or crystal-bright peaks where the earth seems to be its own source of light. More and more frequently gestures pass between the two, gradually becoming a language for expressions of surprise and delight.

Fatigue causes the instinct for schedules to subside, and the rhythm of the pilgrimage imperceptibly relaxes. This loosening is something the mountain does to pilgrims or does *for* them. Occasionally they stop just to listen to the silence of the earth or the wind rustling through shrubbery and trees. By now, thanks to Luke's vow, the din of ordinary life has grown quiet and given a place for whatever the moment offers.

This is the point where Ope begins to catch Pavlos' idea of the pilgrimage as something other than an arcane religious ritual. It dawns on him, first in feeling and more slowly in idea, that their host, caught between two worlds, has a different kind of knowledge. What he knows is that when the resources of energy are depleted, there is wisdom in those aching muscles and joints and feet, that as desire fades and the clamor of the will is silenced, one is opened to contemplative adventures that habit precludes.

As Pavlos' intention becomes clearer, Ope can see that the mountain creates an envelope of silence around Luke and him, and that the splendor of the journey comes in being turned away from themselves and attuned instead to the mountain. Even as the steep path ahead is made easier by a sense of movement toward light, the darkness conveys a different sense, like a promising inner emptiness after the falling away of personal interests and anxieties. He has no way of confirming his feeling by comparison with Luke's except when he turns, more and more often, to look behind as though to connect with something familiar. At such moments, Ope offers a smile of encouragement.

The route to the summit connects the east and west sides of the mountain, and the smoother paths are evidence of more traffic than before. Yet the going is slower and the environment still more alien. The land rises on their left, getting ever wilder in proportion to the narrowing of the way, and occasionally they must stop to clear forest debris from the path.

Two more hours restore a sense of a human world at the convergence of five roads marked with consoling names and arrows that lead off to other monasteries. Here Br. Luke immediately drops into the shade of a tree while Ope, concerned for his welfare, brings him a drink from a cool spring a few paces away.

Luke accepts the water with shaking hands as Ope, alarmed by his exhaustion and their circumstances, waits for him to drink, though he delays to give time for Ope to turn away. Taking the hint, Ope busies himself with his pack then returns to the stream bank to quench his own thirst.

There he finds an ancient monk like an apparition with unkempt yellow beard standing by the water. He dips his canteen again into the stream and, in a few awkward words of demotic Greek, offers the old man a drink that is accepted with a nod. When Greek doesn't work, he tries English, but the monk pays no attention to the words. Just continues muttering under his breath: "Lord Jesus Christ, Son of God, have mercy on me, a sinner."

With that simple prayer, all of Ope's resistance to the Athos cult returns in a wave, but since the time remaining till darkness is precious, he stifles the response and prepares to move on. Where the old monk takes one path, they take another, moving, despite their sense of urgency, ever more slowly toward the summit.

In place of forests, stunted trees with bark like driftwood and the acrid air full of the menthol scent of rosemary. The forest quiet becomes audible in the songs of birds and insects and bees only to be replaced with the different silence of a barren surface and empty skies that offer no points of reference such as the ancients might have understood.

Ope wills to suppress a sense of disorientation before it can even reach the intensity of panic. The coastline that had been a reference point is now concealed by the forests below, and in the thinner air of these heights he is dulled by fatigue and a weakening sense of direction. Even the colors have modulated from the greens and browns of nature to the unfamiliar pallor of emptiness. Nearer the peak still, the shrinking mountain becomes a moonscape under a Greek sky, once god-infested for people of agile imagination. But for him, empty and abandoned.

They have passed the timberline onto an arid, rocky desert. At one point, as the terrain gets wilder and the paths narrower, he catches a glimpse, across waves of green forest, of the tip of the peninsula far below. According to the map it's *Karoulia,* named for the "pulleys" used by the ascetics for centuries to hoist their food from boats below to the cliffs above.

At last they arrive at Panagia. It offers little but water and a covered space for sleep, but in a small chapel lamps are kept burning before an icon of the Virgin, who has haunted his way since the service at Simonos Petras.

The two enjoy a fresh drink from the spring and, while the sun sinks in the west, they stretch their legs on a bare rock to rest their travel-worn feet. As twilight slowly creeps across the Aegean, they watch a lone ship in the distance bearing southwest toward the Peloponnese. Ope, still quietly concerned for Br. Luke's welfare, considers several moments in the day that had puzzled him.

When he had been tripped up by thorn bushes, Luke had come to his aid as hikers do in difficult terrains. Off balance at that moment, he had blindly accepted a gloved hand that felt delicate in his rough grasp. Even the arm seemed to have insufficient force for the task. Then he connects the odd fact that at their rest stops Luke never removed his gloves. Not even now at the end of the day. And two other details quickly follow: the care with which the young monk conceals his face and the clunky hiking boots that he never takes off. Staring at the boots awkwardly extended now on the rock, Ope can tell that the feet inside are too small for them.

A momentary fantasy of angels assuming human bodies leads to a realism hardly more probable: Luke might be ill, or gay, or not a monk after all. Not even a man. As neither man nor beast has been what it appeared since he was ordered to Vienna, perhaps Luke is a woman in disguise? He dismisses the thought. Not only are women not allowed on the peninsula but, by an astonishing monkish scrupulosity, even female cows and sheep are forbidden! Besides, Br. Luke is well known to their host Pavlos, the Athonite, who has invited them all with the blessing of monastic authority.

With that, his speculations drop away, and he's restored to the present moment, where Luke has turned away to remove his gloves and untie his boots. Then as though gathering up all his remaining energy, he turns and looks Ope full in the face with eyes intensely open yet serene as a Zen garden.

Wu Mai Bao! Her whole being in the face! Simply, miraculously *there*.

He catches his breath and a smile envelops his face in a moment when the singular human, striped even of her identity with herself, reveals its essential role. When she turns to face him, he doesn't notice the gawky monastic robes or a world transformed edge to edge, earth to sky, past to future. A flood of affect alters even the world relations. A warm and radiant light in a sky, empty an instant before, dances with life and with love.

"You!" He stares.

"The mountain!" she whispers.

"What's the mountain?" He asks, laughing.

"This! What's happening." She slips her hands into his as all their senses reach for the essential other while seeing only the eyes. More like falling through them, falling as from the top of a mountain truly named for the mother of the god of love, into a borderless and bottomless sea.

She reaches for his arm, clasps it in both hands, and pulls them close. Presently he lays a hand on the back of her head and draws it down to his shoulder as, in another expansive moment outside the measure of time, before thought or desire can catch up, both are recreated to a new life in a new world.

Seconds or eons later, thinking restored, he holds her hands in his, turning them over, examining the bruised palms, the battered fingers, and the scratched wrists. He feels purged of all the compromising Vienna experience, eclipsing even the melancholy years of failed diplomacy.

She adds, "They say the mountain has been working miracles for three thousand years. It apparently hasn't lost its power."

Astonished again, he studies the face that now absurdly appears as a Chinese Madonna. Then, the weariness of bodies forgotten, he climbs to his feet and raises her by an elbow concealed somewhere in folds of a monk's black habit and takes her in his arms.

They had stopped at Panagia to sleep, but part of the miracle that follows is that, weariness eclipsed, they don't sleep on this island at the top of the world named "most holy." Instead, they decline the cover of the shelter and spend the hours lying side by side under the panoply of stars that shine for them alone. Not speaking, but transformed as dancers are transformed, lost in the dance. It's no less a night of passion than those between Dido and Aeneas or Héloïse and Abélard or Tristan and Isolde. A night spent searching to find names for what lies too deep for words.

Sometime in the night Mai Bao sits up, fascinated by an electrical storm in the distant southeast. It was impossible not to feel the proximity of the gods, as jagged fissures split the sky from the heavens to the sea long before the audible grumbling of the immortals reached Athos. The lovers feel as in an ancient theater on a Greek hillside watching the rival Olympian passions arrive from a distance and take possession of the actors then pass into the audience.

An hour before dawn, the two get up, fill their canteens and begin the ascent to the peak. If yesterday's ascent had been a descent into exhaustion and an emptying of the self, the morning climb is an ascent toward the glory of the same world now appearing under the aspect of love.

Hand in hand, without gloves or cowls, but with Mai Bao's hair tied still in a tight knot atop her head, they follow a zigzag path in the dark until, eventually emerging from a defile between sharp boulders, they step out onto bare rock before the Chapel of the Transfiguration and the great iron cross, on the same promontory where good news arrived from Troy a millennium BCE.

There is nothing to hear but the whisper of waves six thousand feet below warning sailors of man-eating rocks, and the surprise is how many stories are borne on a single shaft of light falling on a rusty piece of iron thrusting up from earth to sky.

Wrapped again in anonymity, the two monks begin the long descent to Simonos Petras. They bypass St. Annis, intending to break the journey at St. Pavlou. The "vow of silence" having been rescinded, they celebrate the wonders of the mountain with cheerful voices. The woods reverberate with the songs of birds, the chatter of cicadas, and the music of two voices walking together in the Garden of the Mother of God.

But one topic has been postponed too long. Ope had not asked, but Mai Bao needs to acknowledge a debt owed the God in whom she doesn't believe.

Reading her mood, Ope says, "I've been wanting to ask how you happen to be on the mountain incognito and in violation of a prohibition so old and venerable as never to have been written down."

"It's not a protest, you know. I understand why monastic life must be lived apart from the distractions of the world. Gender is one distraction. Women and men both find a certain freedom among their own kind."

"A violation still," Ope observes gently.

She hangs fire a moment. "Pavlos had the idea first. Who but a monk would have imagined a connection between the Holy Mountain and a destitute world? I objected to the subterfuge, but not because of the rule. My objection had to do with the irrelevance of this detached sanctuary to our all-too-worldly project. Only an insider could have seen the promise and managed the deception. Finally, he convinced me to trust him, though I still had no appetite for the subterfuge or the hardship."

Ope insists gently, "We all, we six, agreed to a subterfuge of our own"—he pointed to their Byzantine habits—"though I still don't see the point of any of it."

"I can see this much," she answers. "Pavlov thinks that the meanderings of history have thrown up the possibility that the efforts of a handful of arch-conservative monks to preserve their two-thousand-year heritage may now be converging with a handful of intellectuals who are trying to save humanity from itself."

Ope shrugs. "When all cures fail, we may as well gamble on whatever offers." Then, momentarily, his habitual melancholy reasserts itself. "So the week ahead is to be spent building very long bridges." But the seriousness of the remark is undercut by the smile he can't keep off his face as they talk.

"It may be easier than you think. Athos has always been a storehouse of forgotten ideas, as when, centuries ago, it encouraged the restoration of classic learning. Conservation may be futile in our case, but there's a family resemblance between our project and theirs. In violating the gender rule, Pavlov is covertly disregarding tradition and fulfilling what he calls 'the rule of love.'"

"What, pray, is 'the rule of love?'" he asks, grinning. "It's a contradiction!"

His face continues to glow with a light Mai Bao has often searched for in vain. "Does falling in love . . ." It's the first time the idea has been invoked, and it requires a break in his sentence to be fully heard. "Does falling in love require us to go soft in the head or take up theology?"

She passes over the irony with a smile of her own. "If 'rule' is an obstacle, call it the 'way' of love."

"And that means what exactly?"

She replies with irony of her own. "Every true lover knows!"

They continue the descent as occasionally the canopy of the forest gives way to open vistas where they stand for long minutes, hand in hand, studying the land and the sea. At one such moment they spot a band of darkness approaching across the water. A thunderhead, seen whole, bisecting a sun-washed sea. Eventually alternating waves of water and light reach the shore. Heavy, flat-bottomed clouds envelop the peaks and creep down the valleys between distant ridges. Occasionally sunlight pierces the darkness, making it easy to imagine the negligent gods just overhead playing their eternal games with the mortals below.

The drama of the fast-moving system holds them spell-bound until the darkness is upon them. Just as the drops of rain begin to pelt their robes, a splinter of lightning strikes somewhere above the path, and Ope begins searching frantically for shelter.

Finding none, they hurry on as fast as is possible along a way that rises and falls between stone bluffs and the blind abyss. They laugh at their predicament, stumbling along the wall on the right in robes now soaked with rainwater and clinging so closely to their legs as to impede forward motion. Then the great sheets of water obscure their path.

Eventually, Mai Bao spots what appears to be a cave in the rock just ahead and above. They reach the spot, too wet to care about the rain, and fight their way through the underbrush to the cave. Hardly a cave, more like an indentation in the face of the mountain, but sufficient for two to huddle together out of the torrents. Wordless again, looking out from a narrow harbor, captivated by the storm.

When she shivers, Ope puts an arm about her shoulders and pulls her against him. Until that moment, even in the night lying side by side, there has been no physical contact except the touch of wounded hands and the gentle embrace of exhausted bodies. But this is different. After a few moments, Ope touches her on the chin and turns her head toward him. But before he can kiss her, she lays the tips of two fingers on his lips. "Not now. Not here."

"Why?" Neither plea nor protest, just smiling, curious. "What we said at the summit was a vow. It's like taking ourselves in the palms of our hands and making a gift to the other. Athos is a place for timeless vows."

"Yes, but a vow is also worldly, and we're between worlds."

She pauses for a moment before adding, "I have a different reason."

"What's your different reason?"

She chuckles. "To respect the monastic rule in letter even as I violate it in spirit."

With a shake of his head, Ope ponders the remark. "You are a surprising person, but I do see what you mean. And yet what compromise can there be between us here in the wilderness? It affects no one else."

She openly laughs at him. "You're still an individualist, Adawale! Our vow isn't about consequences, and it's not just between us. If it were us only, it would be empty. We can't live without a world, and having a world requires fidelity between it and us."

That remark, aided by a cold rain, is enough to postpone passion, so after the calming of the storm, they resume the hike and spend much of the rest of the day laughing and exchanging histories as though being alone on top of the world or, alone earlier in a house in the Vienna Woods, has nothing to do with impending planetary disaster.

CHAPTER 3

THE THIRD EVENING ON Athos all six "monks" climb the stairs to the common room on the "first floor" of the monastery fortress, the stories being counted here from top down. It's a place where the privacy of their deliberations can be assured. And it's the place where Adawale first observed the bay and a strip of stony beach a thousand feet down. Standing on the narrow balcony in daylight was one thing, but in the dark it is like being suspended weightlessly between the star-studded arc of heaven and its reflection in the now dark water below.

When the members of the little group are assembled, and before any words are spoken, there is a detectable change of mood in the little group. Not just in Mai Bao and Ope, whose new relation remains concealed under the identity of Br. Luke. But the general tone is entirely different owing no doubt to the mountain and its transformation of six hikers.

For starts Pavlos repeats the brief introductions of two days before. Then adds, "I surmise from the mood of the room that this has been a genuine pilgrimage. It was essential that a forbiddingly difficult inquiry with no agenda begin with clearing the mind and sensibility. Pilgrimage is a mode of initiation. So it's right that the welcome should be renewed for people who have been renewed."

241

Pavlos was trained as a philosopher and he taught in university for a while, until the ancient idea of rational contemplation drew him to the quietude of Orthodox monasticism. He had lived for some years on Athos, withdrawn from the world without turning his back on it. Exactly how this conference had come about, even his connection with Wu Mai Bao, remained obscure, except that Adawale had heard his name at Grinzing and surmises that he's one of The Readers.

"We'll get underway early tomorrow," he continues. "However, before the proceedings open, I have three things for you. First, a confession. Second, a glass of wine. And third, a bedtime story.

"The confession is that Br. Luke and I have imposed on you. We have a secret. It's that as a monk he is an imposter. But then," he says, grinning, "so are you all. But there's more. In the outside world, Br. Luke is a UN official from Vienna named Wu Mai Bao."

On cue Wu drops her cowl and lets her hair fall. Immediately it's clear from the surprise on their faces that Abhay Gupta and Paul Poirier know her from the past, but that Ji-Min Choi and Burak Derviş do not.

Before questions can take shape, Pavlos explains. "The deceit, like the deceit of subjecting you to these disguises"—he tugs at the edge of his own sleeve in illustration—"is all my doing. All reasons given are true, but this was the only way to bring a woman to Athos.

"In her defense, I must add that Mai Bao resisted coming because, detected or not, it would violate the monastic spirit. She even defended the rule of exclusion on grounds that monastic life, like all single-minded pursuits, must forego distractions. I argued in turn—leaving theological controversies aside—that forbidding distractions for the sake of contemplation, however valuable, might also deprive the world of an essential source of light. You know that here the feminine is restricted to the icons of the Mother of God. But in desperate times like civil war all refugees, including women, have been welcomed.

"My point is that the state of our world is direr by far than the political conflicts of the past. In the end, the rule was waived for us, privately but officially, in the belief that our work, conducted in the appropriate spirit, required a discreet exception. Nonetheless, I apologize for making you parties to deception. You will please be silent on this matter. If this became common knowledge, Mai Bao could be subject to imprisonment for a year, and it might cause unpleasantness between Athos and Greece, the European Union, and the United Nations."

Then Pavlos produces the wine and fills seven glasses as people begin to talk informally among themselves. Since all are here for the first time and each pair has travelled a different path for two days, all have unique stories that initiate friendship and deepen experience.

Abhay Gupta, the Indian philosopher, who happens to be standing next to Adawale, asks with a twinkle in his eye, "And which direction did you and 'Br. Luke' take?" Coming from another, the question might have been mischievous, but Gupta belonged to the only surviving original school of Buddhism, the Theravada school, whose name means "Teachings of the Elders," and he fit the name in every respect.

Adawale answers with a straight face and an uncommon lightness of spirit. "We went to the top of the mountain. That's not easy for a man of my sedentary habits. Nor was it made easier by a companion who was bound to silence for the duration!"

Tactfully, Gupta changes the topic. "I have been amused by the reviews of your book. From the historicists, mainly. They're always ready to discredit any account that doesn't serialize historical events as a chain of causes and epochs."

Ope smiles. That point of criticism from the scholarly community had disappointed him at the time, even as he remained a historicist himself without realizing it. At present he feels a world away from all that, as though it had happened to someone else in another life. "If I were writing it now, the criticism would be even harsher."

"That's curious. May I ask why?"

"In those days I still assumed that if we examined the roots of our misunderstandings, we could boil our conflicts down to a consistency and make the world more hospitable. This trip—several weeks ago I was summonsed blindly to Vienna—has convinced me that troubles can be useful things. Now I would say that unanimity, planetary harmony, even if it were possible, would not be desirable."

Gupta grins broadly. "I see what you mean. The wish for a perfect system is a death wish. University conservatives wouldn't care much for that view."

He was a much older and compassionate man who did not miss the urgency, even the repressed passion, in Adawale's words. He looked him keenly in the eye as he spoke, taking the measure

244

of his disappointment. "What I heard in your book was a voice striving for a fictional hope while living without hope."

Ope sighs, then chuckles. "You're a keen reader. I think I didn't know that until today."

"Today? What happened today?"

"This morning Mai Bao and I stood on the summit of the mountain watching the sun rise. You know how spectacular it is, but it's not about one spectacle more or less. The world didn't change, but I may have. We may be damned, but in a contingent universe how would we tell the difference between destruction and new beginnings? Either way there's the question, what's to be done?"

Gupta did not answer. He only looked up into the eyes of the tall African so acquainted with trouble and laid an affectionate hand on his shoulder. "You remember the ending of sonnet 73? *'To love that well which thou must leave ere long.'*"

Shortly thereafter Pavlos taps on his wine glass again, calling the company to attention. "For this retreat without an agenda I am only your titular host. Wu Mai Bao is the one we must thank. At one point in the negotiations with the presiding Athos authority, we were asked what we were going to consult about. Off the top of her head Mai Bao answered, 'The coming citizen.'

"I repeat that inspired phrase because in passing over the destitute state of the world in silence, her spontaneous answer implied hope where there seems little to hope for. And here's a parallel question: Where do we start when we have no idea where we're going? Perhaps with a name, for, like hope, naming neither starts nor stops with an object. A name is a channel for desire. Even the name of a cat."

He gives a Cheshire-cat grin. "Indulge me, please, in a few lines from T.S. Eliot.

> When you notice a cat in profound meditation
> The reason, I tell you, is always the same:
> His mind is engaged in a rapt contemplation
> Of the thought, of the thought, of the thought of
>   his name:
> His ineffable, effable,
> Effanineffable,
> Deep and inscrutable singular Name.

"We, gathered here with the barest trace of an idea to discuss—we might do worse than begin with the name Ulro. It's the name the poet William Blake gave to a delusional world preoccupied with the selfhood, the senses, forgetfulness, mechanism, rationality: 'single vision.' The name, the less-than-a-name, conveys the bare scent of historical catastrophe, of imagination sacrificed to rational self-interest. Ulro has had many names: Hindu 'Kali Yuga,' Buddhist 'Samsara,' Hebrew 'Gehenna,' Christian 'Hell.'

"Since our business here is to name the unnameable, set all this against one other name: Athos. It's *more* than an idea. It's an age-old beacon in a troubled world. We might do worse than follow these two names as paths toward hope."

Then Pavlos changes keys entirely. "But I promised you a bedtime story. It's an ancient story of the mountain. A love story really. A story of love and war among the gods. Millennia ago, the cosmic gods were eclipsed by the Olympian gods and dropped from sight. To us they're characters in a fairy tale. The story goes like this:

"Once upon a time—which means a time before times—Uranus, Father Sky, and Gaea, Mother Earth, begot many children. But Uranus refused to let them be born. Eventually, in frustration, Gaea gave a sickle to one of the unborn, named Cronos. When Uranus next came to make love, Cronos castrated him and threw his genitals into the sea. From his sperm was born Aphrodite, goddess of love. And from his blood, falling to the earth, sprang the giants, the *Gigantes*. Cronos succeeded his father, Uranus, and ruled over the mythological golden age but, being jealous of *his* sons in turn, he swallowed each at birth. Gaea, Mother Earth—why the incest taboo is unnecessary for the immortals is another story—anyway, by trickery, Gaea preserved the child named Zeus. The result was rival generations: cosmic gods and Olympian gods.

"Eventually the two, the children of the giants and the Olympians, came to war. It was called the *gigantomachia*. In the end the giants lost, and it is said that Poseidon, Olympian ruler of the sea, had them buried on Athos. Athos himself was one of the giants, and this mountain is the stone he had thrown at Poseidon into the Aegean. So Poseidon used the mountain to bury the defeated enemy.

"But here's the point. If we assume that our species has a future, as we must to get up in the morning, and if we are here as forerunners of Mai Bao's 'citizen to come,' then we should take note of these old dreams. The ancients have left us innumerable versions of the struggles of the gods of earth and sky. The Holy Mountain, reaching across the millennia, may inspire a different perspective on this troubled planet. It has been touched by the prehistoric loves and the wars of rival gods and remains much as it always was, a place where the real and the imaginary, time and eternity intersect. Where all else has failed, I hope we will take the time to explore 'the Athos option.'"

This speech meets with respectful silence. And with the topic of love and war firmly on the agenda, the brief opening session ends. It's about 9:30 as counted on whatever clock orders life in a monastery, and Mai Bao retires to Pavlos' cell as he goes to the dormitory with the men.

CHAPTER 4

ON THE MORNING of the third day, after the service that lasted till dawn and after the communal breakfast, the six "monks" climbed once more to the conference room far above. Mai Bao, being tacitly acknowledged for some unstated reason as moderator, opened with a famous line from the French poet Valéry: "'*The age of the world's end is beginning.*' We're not here to pass judgment on that prophecy but to look for a beginning in this ending—if it is an end. If even *that* intention proves to be immodest, then we may ask what follows when something must be done where nothing can be done."

At that moment there was a knock on the door, and she pulled the hood over her head and around her face. When the innocent intruder proved to be the novice who regularly cleaned the room, conversation was suspended as Pavlos reminded him gently that no one had access to the first floor for the duration of their meetings.

He left, and Wu resumed. "Some of you know that I'm associated with certain UN offices in Vienna that take an interest in the informal consultations among a network of people called The Readers. They are freelancing inquirers scattered around the world who keep tabs on events and the attitudes of local populations.

"You may also know Professor Adawale as a scholar of the cultural and political partitions that threaten global peace. He's a veteran member of the UN diplomatic corps based in New York, where he helps respond to planetary crises of various kinds. However, you will *not* know about his current work, since not even he knows why he was sent to Vienna on an open-ended assignment concerning the impending disaster. His assignment has been to go wherever he was taken, talk with whomever he met, and ask whatever he wanted to know—all with no defined topic or end in view. That has led him here. His one restriction and ours at this officially 'inexistent' conference is to keep his activities under the public and bureaucratic radar. Now I'm going to ask him to get us underway."

Like most things in this segment of Ope's life, no warning preceded this moment. So he spoke briefly and informally from his chair facing the balcony door to the west. "Since arriving in Vienna, my experience has been more useful for being random. I have listened to the views of many people on the state of the planet, including exchanges over the past week with some of Wu Mai Bao's sleuths. Many of these people love the world enough to look the worst in the face and act as caretakers.

"A common theme among them is what one thinker a half century ago called 'democratic materialism.' The essential reference is to an atomizing historical vision in which all things—people, governments, economies, even the objects in isolated worlds—are considered unrelated particles. The theme is individualism, perhaps not exactly beginning with the Protestant Christian Reformation, but certainly crystallized in its secular transformation as the world economy.

"That issue aside, the prevailing mood is that our better cultural legacies have fallen away and that no effective political discourse is now imaginable. Many inside and outside official channels suspect that we're spiraling downward into chaos on multiple fronts at once, not least because of a rationality that does not know its own blindness. We could spend weeks discussing the likely causes of an infinite list of ills—universal social unrest, plutocracy, systems too complex to be understood, the impending death of the environment . . . but"—he paused like a fly looking for a way out of a spider's web—"it's pointless to wring our hands and repeat the obvious.

"If we are here, as Wu Mai Bao suggests, to think the unthinkable, then I must confess that I, for one, don't know how. The darkness is so deep it's blinding. But I have received the impression of late that when we can see no way forward, the best way may be to think ahead by thinking backward, not to repeat the past, but searching for inspiration. But back where? How do we find our way back?" He raised his hands in a gesture of emptiness before continuing.

"I wonder if that's what Pavlos Demetriopoulos has already addressed in casting this conference as a pilgrimage. An invitation to step as far as possible back from the world as we know it into a place as far from the ordinary as possible, where our most unconscious habits are disrupted. For two days we have sacrificed comfort for intense exertion, emptying our minds of practical aims, 'cleansing our powers of perception,' so that, refreshed, we may consider the pre-political conditions of any collective order even if it should demand a better account of what or who we are."

251

Ope may have been repeating truisms, but it is interesting that the usual disjointedness in his speech had diminished. Where in conversation with Mamud he had spoken in a lexicon and syntax that belonged to rationality but in a voice that dropped off into the monotones of abjection, now he spoke with a singularity of mind and voice. Still, given the subject, this speech didn't invite ready responses. The outlook being acknowledged as bleak, anyone present might have asked, why come all this distance—not to speak of having to climb a mountain!—for a conference with no agenda?

Ji-Min Choi, the Oxford-trained Korean diplomat and polymath who knew Adawale's work and had a passing acquaintance with the man, tried the minimalist approach of asking for clarification. "You use the term pre-political. Since the pre-political might offer a clue to the political itself, where we seem to have run aground, I'll ask what you understand in the term."

Adawale didn't respond immediately, but that mattered little in a company where there was no constraint of time, so no impatience. Presently Mai Bao, as though preventing an awkward silence, replied. "If I understand correctly, Choi, the question is about the condition of a being who is ready for political life. And to that I might respond with an example. You must know that I'm not a philosopher. I only catch such large issues on the fly. But if you'll indulge me in a brief story . . ."

"Aha!" Pavlos cried, further lessening the dark mood. "You may not know that Wu Mai Bao is notorious among The Readers. Her motto is 'When you don't understand an idea, put it in a story.'"

Wu Mai Bao's proposal to begin a conference by telling a story brings smiles to several faces. As Ji-Min Choi nods his head in agreement to her proposal, she begins:

"I'd like to mention a film, from nearly a century ago. It belongs to a trilogy named *Three Colors [Trois Couleurs]* for the tricolors of the French flag. The story presumes that the colors represent the political virtues of liberty, equality, and fraternity. All three films were written and directed by Polish director Krzysztof Kieslowski with the French Revolution and the Enlightenment tradition in mind. But one thing is different. Here, being alive isn't enough to qualify one for participating in collective life. Political action is only possible among beings who are already engaged deeply with others far beyond the boundaries of consciousness. Having measurable alpha waves and a body temperature of 98⁰ F isn't enough. Animals don't make the cut, and some people wonder if all homo sapiens are capable. So the question is, what kind of historical experience must one have to participate fully in the social contract?"

Ji-Min wonders aloud if education for citizenship, might be the answer and if so, what kind? "But I interrupt. What's the story?"

She smiles and begins. "In Geneva, an attractive student and model named Valentine hits a dog in the street with her car. She drives it to the address on its collar and meets a misanthropic retired judge named Joseph Kern. Please notice now how prominently law figures in this plot.

"Valentine is an innocent who 'instinctively' accepts responsibility for the people and the world around her. Even for a judge's runaway dog. The result is a series of encounters, all initiated by her, between two people who are so different that of all relationships that might be imagined between them, fraternity or brotherhood may be the least likely. Especially since neither of them much likes the other. Valentine is as disgusted by Kern's electronic spying on his neighbors' private lives as he is disdainful of her sentimental innocence. And yet each repeatedly goes out of the way to understand and challenge the other."

Mai Bao pauses as though sifting through the story for the essential points, then resumes. "The interest for us is in the relation between these two characters, who come endowed already with strengths and dispositions rooted in personal history. Antagonism between them will change into something entirely different that foreshadows relations between political adversaries.

"Here's a single example that gives the flavor and the subtlety of the plot. Judge Kern is a seasoned student of human nature. He says of his career as a judge that by profession he's a lifelong 'spy.' But his experience is tainted by cynical understanding. An early betrayal by the only woman he ever loved has left him cold and hard and resentful. When Valentine first enters his house, she discovers him intercepting his neighbors' telephone conversations. Those exchanges show a social fabric so damaged that conversation has shrunk to monologue and community to self-absorption.

"For example, there's a heroin importer, an old woman who makes her daughter's life miserable demanding attention, a telephone love affair between a young attorney and a weather girl who is so abstracted from meteorological conditions that her predictions are usually wrong. All are instances of failed kinship and broken social bonds. In response to Valentine's disgust at Kern's eavesdropping, he retorts, 'At least I know where the truth is.' In fact he knows too much to understand.

"The provocative encounters between this political realist and the sentimental innocent survive various temptations to more commonplace relationships. Valentine learns *because* she holds sensations, pleasant or unpleasant, up for examination, works on them, takes them to heart, and turns them into experience. No passivity in her. And the result is that she discovers a world quite different from the place she imagines.

"Kern gives her an education in realism, but reciprocally, something in her works subterraneously on him. She fascinates him, and he learns. But what he learns isn't a softer, kindlier disposition. He learns that getting the evidence right and knowing 'the truth' about guilt and innocence never tell the human story. Under her influence he stops spying, confesses to his neighbors, and hands himself over to the law. He even comes to love his dog, all thanks to a new orientation that has no common name.

"Both characters learn through strife, because both care too much not to learn. It's what enables him to guess the story of her dysfunctional family and addict brother as it enables her to guess the betrayal that ruined his life and tainted his conception of 'justice.' Here it's called *fraternité*, a bit like friendship, a bit like familial affection, a bit like love. In these two, fraternity as care-among-friends gets reinvented as face-to-face exchanges become another name for political discourse.

"This is not Enlightenment self-interest modified or softened by a new idea or a new 'personal skill.' It's not a 'value-added' experience or a fuzzy compromise. It's a transformation by events. And it discovers that they are not now—and never were—autonomous individuals. There was already a 'we' in each of these two 'I's.' They are figures related as truly to each other as Valentine is related to her troubled brother by the kinship of body and blood.

"The exact political quality of this *fraternité* is visible at the end when Kern learns about a ferryboat accident on the English Channel. No words, just his face as he watches on television as Valentine is rescued at sea. It's the historical disaster of 1987 when a ferry named The Herald sank in the English Channel. Valentine is one of the six protagonists in these three films who are rescued from the shipwreck and who *herald* a different mode of being. Their faces and Kern's convey the transformation and summarize the trilogy.

"Of the other two films in the series, I will only say that each exemplifies a social relation necessary in the ideal citizen: *Blue* interprets freedom *[liberté]*, *White* interprets equality *[egalité]*, as *Red* interprets brotherhood *[fraternité]*. Each of the three pairs of protagonists, thrown together by an accident into the sea—water as the maternal element of birth and rebirth—incarnate one of the virtues celebrated by the French Revolution. The difference is that here they are rendered as *preconditions* rather than results of political life, especially as the rescue in the Channel prefigures the historical unification of Europe.

"In summary, the characters Julie and Olivier in *Blue*, both French, become responsible for acting freely in the world; Dominique [French] and Karol [Polish] in *White* experience a hard-won equality both in love and law by gaining a common language; as Valentine and Joseph Kern *[Rouge]* learn to live between the certainties of law and the deceptions of blind affection. The point is that the citizen is not a natural formation. She or he is already constituted in mind and sensibility, and capable of acting with others in an already constituted open space where life can flourish."

When Wu finishes, Choi, who appears to have no prior acquaintance with her, responds softly and indirectly to the assembled company without concealing a certain critical edge. "In relying on stories, Wu doesn't *prove* anything. She's doing what Professor Adawale imagined: searching for inspiration, listening for ideas. At least that helps us keep a stiff upper lip in dark times."

Adawale, careful not to seem partisan, replies a bit more concretely. "The story seems to conceive of the political animal as more than an animal with a built-in calculator of his own interests. Perhaps there's an older logic by which politics is not about freeing people from bondage or redistributing wealth. That might be helpful to us."

Paul Poirier, who knows the film, has been raptly attentive to Mai Bao's reading. He's a tall, dapper cosmopolitan who somehow manages to look French even wrapped in a monk's robe. Widely respected as essayist, literary editor, and culture critic in his own land, he knows everyone of intellectual importance in Europe and has held frequent visiting appointments as lecturer in the Anglo-American academic world though, for whatever mysterious reason, they have always been temporary, never permanent. Not only does Poirier know *Three Colors*, he sees something in Mai Bao's use of the story that Choi, his partner on yesterday's hike, seems to miss.

With an enthusiasm for film as typically French as his metropolitan accent, he suggests that the characters' belonging to a social world is a necessary but insufficient predisposition for political life. "I wonder," he muses, "whether when we invoke the phrase 'the citizen to come,' we are searching for traits of character we're disposed to favor or describing a certain capacity for action. As Adawale says, neither conservation nor management. If we've lost our way, it must be that we've lost ourselves. But what, then, would we be losing?" He shrugs his shoulders. "Do we expect to find the ideal citizen or just keep the question open? Perhaps we can only agree to live with an enigma that arises moment by moment."

So far, the old philosopher, Abhay Gupta, had been sitting with his eyes closed, so still that it was hard to tell whether he was working on the idea or sleeping. Now the eyes slowly open, and he remarks very quietly, "There's already a hint in the air that somewhere down the line we'll have to distinguish between the biological and the political animal. Wu's characters start with conflict, *polemos*, not harmony. We may discover that we don't need to redefine ourselves so much as clarify the political as perpetual invention in situations of stress. At least the range of our search might narrow if we didn't need to worry about definitions or alternative systems. Just imagine ways of responding moment by moment to unsettled situations."

Gupta's speech fell like a stone into an empty landscape and lay there in silence. Until someone innocently renewed the question: "So if not *what*, then *who* are we?" and Gupta closed his eyes again.

The question "What are we?" seems clear enough until Gupta's four—or was it five?—sentences show how Mai Bao's film had complicated the matter. When no one responded two or three stood up and wandered to the room for a drink from the large pitcher of cool spring water. Others remained quietly in place musing on a discussion that seemed to have ended before it began.

Burak Derviş, sitting beside Ope facing the balcony door, gazed from his angle into the bright southwestern sky toward one of the cradles of civilization. Derviş was an Egyptian Muslim scholar from the al-Azhar Mosque in Cairo and a champion of what, in the world outside Islam, was sometimes called the "Muslim Reformation."

It was he who eventually offered a suggestion. "Without trying to resolve Gupta's riddle—since it's the question itself— I want to go back to the initial condition of the characters in Wu's narrative. Even in a plot summary we respond to the characters' predispositions because they are ours. That lends support to Poirier's remark that if we've lost our political way, it may be because we first lost our relation to ourselves, hence to others. In political thought the character of the citizen is often taken for granted or comes too late."

While they puzzled over the topic that Gupta had casually dropped on the table, Paul Poirier noted their proximity to the claims of Adawale's book on the unconscious origins of political theory and practice, and Mai Bao added the example of filial piety and responsibility to ancestors in Confucian tradition:

"Those social roots grow by being passed on, cultivated by memorizing authoritative texts, and held in mind by repetition. Modernity seems impoverished by the absence of voices that witness to how things are done. I don't understand Gupta's reference to perpetual invention, but perhaps our dilemma is that we're perpetually starting over as though from nothing. At least *Red* seems to suggest that the ideas and ideals that work have a history that must be developed or discovered afresh in every citizen."

Adawale brooded a tad impatiently. "Yet the world and its people are all fragmented. Those with complex and stable histories are as threatened as those who live one moment at a time without memory." He sighed deeply. "I can't see where we go from here. I take Abhay Gupta's point about politics as belonging to conflict rather than harmony, but when recently I heard an account of the struggles between Antigone and her uncle Creon in Sophocles' play, I found little hope in it. As though in two and a half millennia we had learned very little."

Then, in response to several questions, he summarized Aylin Çelik's discussion of the play, emphasizing the debate between Antigone and King Creon on the law.

CHAPTER 5

THE MORNING CONVERSATION is suspended by the bell summoning them to the refectory for lunch. So with Antigone fresh in mind, the six descend to the courtyard. Pavlos might have arranged for them to take the simple mid-day meal in their private room, but, applying another principle of contemplative monasticism—that silence clears the mind and makes it more imaginative—he insists that they shut the door on their topic and resume their anonymity. So they take the stairs down the five stories to the courtyard and proceed in silence to the refectory for the communal meal of bread and fruit and a glass of wine.

Lunch each day will be followed by a brief rest period to be used as one wishes, though the rule of silence will remain in force and be respected by the pilgrims. On this fifth day on Athos, Mai Bao and Pavlos have administrative arrangements to attend to, so when Poirier, Derviş, and Ji-min wander off in various directions, Adawale and Gupta climb once more to the first story and linger on the porch outside the conference room. A lively mind could hardly tire of the view from this hub of the world, where the history of human beings and their gods impinge from every direction of time and space.

No pair among the seven could better appreciate the blessings of silence than these two. From their perch on the balcony, cooled by the breezes from across the bay, they have a vision of the rows of greenery in the monastery gardens below, highlighted by the yellow of gorse and the purple of heather blooming among the rocks. To the side, the hilltops gleam in the early afternoon sun, except where intermittently girded by low-flying clouds, and the bay modulates from blues to greens according to the coruscations of the light. No sound except for quiet lapping of distant water against rocks in dialogue with the songs of birds and the humming of honeybees from somewhere beyond sight.

After the quiet hour, all reassemble and the communal search resumes with signs that the interim has been well spent. This time Poirier supplies the direction.

"Adawale's pertinent account of Antigone as citizen outlaw seems to have moved us beyond the person of the citizen and nearer the function of citizenship exemplified by Wu's film. All this inspires me to mention another Greek tragedy: Aeschylus' *Oresteia*. As you will remember, these three plays are chronologically earlier than the Oedipus family myth, but they form a thematic sequel. Let me just summarize the relevant details in Orestes' story."

"Feel free." Gupta remarks aloud, amused. "This is becoming a storytellers' convention rather like the old Panhellenic competition of rhapsodes where the best reciters of Homer competed for the prize. If this, too, is politics, then it's the politics of play!"

And Burak Derviş adds, "And what else can we do but tell stories in a world where, as the Qoheleth says in *Ecclesiastes*, 'there is no remembrance of former things'?"

Ji-Min proves the point by cautiously pleading for time. "Before we leave Antigone, I'm still trying to see what's positive in her. When she violates Creon's law, buries her brother, and dies for family tradition, is that a new social configuration that might replace Creon's, or does she remain a captive of the familial vendettas? As the play remains a tragedy, doesn't the city remain a tragic institution? Instead of a cure, isn't that a fair pathology of Planet Ulro strangling in its own legalistic systems?"

"Good, Choi." Poirier counters with a smile. "That's just the question Aeschylus may answer. He may help us imagine a step beyond where law is not 'discipline and punish,' but essentially pedagogical."

"Then give us a bit more of the family history," says Ji-Min. "I remember it's the same family, crowded with generations of violent protagonists."

Poirier: "And the story of Orestes overlaps *Antigone* at just the point where the conflict between familial and divine forces destroys public order. When Agamemnon returns from the Trojan War and is murdered by Clytemnestra his wife, the dark forces that Creon can't control may lead to a different political result.

"But first, the reminder: Agamemnon's brother's wife, Helen, has been abducted by—or absconded with, who knows?—the Trojan prince Paris, and Agamemnon is off to Troy to get her back." As he speaks, he points through the door south toward the Peloponnese and marks a line in the air from Mycenae east to Troy.

"As Gupta has implied, we're still stuck in the history of the family. Except that Artemis won't release the winds so

Agamemnon can get to his little war. He has to bribe the goddess by sacrificing his daughter Iphigeneia.

"Now skip ten years: After his Greeks win the war, he returns to Mycenae, where Clytemnestra is still enraged at him for murdering their daughter. In revenge, she kills him. Then comes the event that stirs the political imagination: Clytemnestra banishes Orestes, their son, to Athens for seven years because he's obliged by family piety and by Delphic Apollo to avenge his father. *But* he is also obliged *not* to kill his mother. No exit."

Ji-Min chuckles. "That's what Greek tragedy means."

"So, Orestes kills Clytemnestra and his uncle, her lover. Then he wanders around Greece pursued by ancient chthonic deities called the Furies or the Erinyes. Females, by the way!" He winks mischievously at Mai Bao. "Their task in the tragic universe—it's Antigone again—is to punish family impiety and continue the cycle of blood debt. Just the thing Creon wants to exclude by law.

"But this time the plot takes a different turn. Athena gives Orestes sanctuary in the Parthenon. Her act comes with a warning that if we read the play as a moral psychodrama of modern individuals, we miss the political entirely. The crux comes when the goddess of wisdom—*and warfare*—responds to all these conflicting forces by inventing something new.

"She convenes a court to hear Orestes' case. The court is composed of twelve Athenian citizens with her presiding. There are three issues . . . " He holds up one finger at a time. "One, the demands of blood vengeance. Two, the respect owed to the Furies for maintaining the familial system. Three, the rival honors due to mother and father.

"When the trial ends in a tie, Athena casts her vote for Orestes, and with that we have a new legal order. Except that it doesn't harmonize the inconsistent forces. The goddess is wiser than Creon, or she's in a different place. She knows that repressed forces don't go away. They return with a vengeance. So when the defeated Furies threaten to take their revenge by ruining the peace of Athens and its countryside, Athena forces them to redirect their energies away from vengeance and toward protecting justice.

"In exchange, the city will honor them. But, knowing how repression works, she reminds them of the thunderbolts Zeus had used to defeat the cosmic deities in the *gigantomachia* that Pavlos told us about the other night. Zeus' weapons are kept in a storeroom to which she holds the keys. And with that warning she sends the Furies back, placated, to the ancient caverns of the earth."

Derviş takes satisfaction in Poirier's example, and remarks to Ji-Min, "Now that moves us a step ahead. It opens a space between the bonds to the hearth and to the city, without either going away. The difference is rendered inoperative. Not banished but hybridized."

What especially interests Mai Bao is the recognition of perpetual strife. "I don't want to drag gender into the discussion, but it is a conspicuous element in the conflict between private hearth and public city. A kind of double bind between Antigone and Creon repeated between Agamemnon and Clytemnestra. The female Furies are weapons or protagonists in that struggle."

Pavlov sees her point: "Which brings us to Athena. Maybe we should consider her more closely."

"Exactly," she answers. "Because in her, gender as well as public and private are neutralized. She opens a space between Orestes and the vengeance of the Furies that has nothing to do with compromise. We can see as much if we don't mistake her for a bourgeois individual, born prematurely from her mother's womb and having to learn to negotiate ambiguous relations. She doesn't even have a mother. She springs from the head of Father Zeus, full-grown and armed for battle. Barely female at all. She's a neutral political figure, a figure 'other than' familial or civic law. As if, in Aeschylus, natural gender has been deactivated."

Choi is skeptical. "Perhaps, but is it enough? We now have two private and two public obscenities: instinctive hysteria that devours the child and authoritarian tyranny that threatens both family and city. Does Athena offer an insufficient compromise or a compelling third way?"

A puzzled Adawale asks, "But what does it really mean to say that Athena may open a third political alternative?"

Paul Poirier's perception appears to expand on the spot. "Ah, of course! Mai Bao has exposed the personalist fallacy!"

"What's 'the personalist fallacy'?" Choi demands in a voice filled with irony. These two men had come to know each other fairly well on their two-day hike.

"Approximately," Poirier replies, "it's the commonsense dogma that a human being is a definable organism with an interior psychology. As when we search like the anthropologists for definable things with determinate natures. But when with Mai Bao we read Athena as an androgynous idea rather than a person, doesn't the goddess supersede the gap of natural gender? Neither male *and/or* female, nor a synthesis of public *and* private. Perhaps that is an exception that cuts the Gordian knot."

"Well then there's hope!" Ji-min says. "Now all you have to do is explain what that means!"

Ope ponders the possibility aloud. "It might mean an alternative account of law. If the only thing the Athena-function has accomplished is to make a new law, excluding different outlaws from the city, then little has been gained. That's our stake in the Orestes-Athena story and the Antigone-Creon story. If these stories are psychodramas—Poirier's 'personalist fallacy'—then nothing's changed. But if Athena even temporarily neutralizes contrary forces, that reconfigures the opposition between law and outlaw. We'd have to think the law differently."

"I repeat," Choi says, "what does that mean?"

The conversation appears to stop there, except for one thing: Gupta is wide awake. He has been silently but attentively following the speakers, as though it is not the role of the wise man to provide answers.

When Gupta keeps his silence, Pavlos makes another effort. "If Athena is not offering a political compromise or a new consistency for Athens, perhaps she represents a new dynamic, a new channeling of energies. She might be altering the path of time and change by neutralizing construction and destruction. Or hybridizing them, as Derviş says. In place of a struggle to the death between two legal systems, a living city."

Choi is growing still more insistent on clear answers. "When Athena imposes a new solution on the Furies, doesn't she perpetuate Creon's rational law, making civic tranquility the new order? To prevent chaos, she buries the Furies with a violent compromise. There's no other word for it. Isn't that Creon all over again? She covers over the traumatic history of humanity as though we could live without the police and punishment. From Oedipus to Athena to global Ulro, we're still caught in the tragic city of the antique Greeks. The nation-state still lives off the vitality of its enemies. And that won't do!"

At last, Gupta shifts the ground ever so slightly. "But is Athena's judgment based on a principle of practical reason? It's true that she doesn't describe either a defensible plan or an ideal goal. But back up one step in the narrative: The trial ends in a hung jury, and she takes sides *without offering juridical reasons*. So far Ji-Min seems to be right."

He pauses, as though letting the point sink in. "The more useful question might be, how are we to see the Furies at the end? Are they suppressed by a new law? Or are they 'reassigned'? The first would be Creon's violent solution, but there's another way of seeing it that might be new even in the twenty-first century. Perhaps the goddess—unless it's Aeschylus—has detected a radical inconsistency in law itself and doesn't try to settle scores. She forgives both sides. Forgiveness as changing the subject, passing on, doing something else. Such an unselfconscious forgiveness, without the sentimental claptrap of one person blaming another and seeking or foregoing redress—that may seem like a small thing, or it might be an astonishing discovery."

These remarks rekindle Mai Bao's enthusiasm. She must realize that he's saying exactly what she's doing in respect of the law against women on Athos. "Then essentially," she muses, "Athena deactivates the conflict by walking away from it because she knows that in the Furies, and in Athens, when drives and interests are domesticated by force, they're only strengthened. Legalized punishment would let crime recoup its strength and return to fight another day!"

Gupta adds cryptically, "As law begets violation of law."

When no one speaks to that, Pavlov continues Mai Bao's effort to heighten the effect of Gupta's cryptic point by para-phrasing it. "The Furies are the out-lawed forces that required the civil law in the first place. So if we're looking for a Greek synthesis or a final solution, we're still making law. But, if the citizens-to-come don't act from a penal code, but act imaginatively, cognizant of analogous historical possibilities as in these ancient stories—then we're in a different landscape. We don't retreat into repeating the past or try to create some new thing. Collectively we look around, see what needs doing, and do it with the ideas and materials available. For conventional thinking it's an unsettling possibility, because we're afraid that, without the guarantees of law, anarchy will come again. Gupta's idea—unless it's Aeschylus'—is neither to follow rules because they're rules nor to sweep them aside without thinking them through. Athena may embody some such an idea."

Ji-Min meets that, or perhaps all three of those extraor-dinary speeches, with equal proportions of energy and perplexity. "That, Pavlos, is unthinkable. It's the antithesis of the concept of governance itself! A ship without a pilot would break up on the rocks. Ergo: no ship. You may as well say that when people violate the law, the law's at fault and should be abolished. That's the kind of incoherence we're here to prevent."

Pavlos smiles at him affectionately. "Or we may have to retrain our captains!" Then, as though the thing most needed at that moment was to save the day, "I think we're headed into another swamp. So let's do something else for a while to clear our heads and gain new inspiration: Let's adjourn for the day. And tomorrow morning I propose that we take a break and walk the mountain again for a few hours. Let the silence and physical strain of hiking refresh our vision."

He laughs. "The world outside would think we were crazy—or worse, that we were a group of mystics. Certainly we seem to be overstepping the ethics of ends and means just as we do when we climb over rocks to get no place so long as it's not the no-place where we began. So let's go our solitary ways, listening *uselessly* to birdsongs and the chatter of the cicadas, emptying the mind, restoring inner stillness."

PART FIVE

THE BEYONDNESS OF THINGS

CHAPTER 1

ON RETURNING TO the monastery after the solitary morning trek on this fifth day, the seven gathered for lunch. Then during the quiet hour, Wu Mai Bao returned early to the conference room and found Pavlos there.

Through the silence she heard a chant resonating from the church five stories below:

"*Agni Parthene*, 'O Pure Virgin.'" Pavlos broke the rule of silence long enough to identify the famous monastery choir and the Orthodox hymn. He explained that the hymn is often used as a concert piece but rarely performed in the monastery.

He picks up a folder from the table and passes her an English translation. The words may make little impression on her secular mind, but the modal harmonies of the a capella male voices punctuating the midday hush exert a magnetic effect like what Opeyemi has come to feel in the company of the icons.

When the others assemble, the mood is uncharacteristically jovial. Without resolving anything, they have apparently left the marginally rancorous spirit of yesterday behind.

Burak Derviş catches the tone. "My second walk in the Athos garden was to the top of the ridge. Less for the exercise than to soak in the milieu. This trek was like returning home, only to a home I've never had. I paid attention to the little things, like the textures of the earth and the diversity of the flora. The mountain shifted my sober mood over the state of the world to hope. That may solve nothing, but it set me back in tune and happy to resume our discussions."

Burak's speech inspires Abhay Gupta to ruminate on having taken the shuttle to Dionysiou and climbing the stony path to St. Paul's. He teases Pavlos gently for having misled him:

"My zigzag route did not lead to the inner peace you promised. It was like our discussions. Apparently going nowhere until, unexpectedly, it opened on a view of the coastline below, of the monastery above, and the glittering light off the summit of the mountain that I, for one, will never reach. But that path taught me to look back with an open mind and press on in hope for no particular end. Now it encourages me to add a different kind of tale to our pursuit of 'the citizen to come.'"

Poirier: "Another story! Good. We must prove the Qoheleth wrong about our not remembering the past, and wrong in adding, 'neither shall there be any remembrance of things that are to come after.'"

So Gupta began. "This is an ancient story about a garden. You know it already, but I'm asking you to set aside what you know and listen in a new way that will require patience and imagination. Not a Greek garden this time. A Hebrew garden, also from the Torah.

"Once upon a time, we are told, before distinctions had been made among the creatures of the earth, all roamed about doing whatever appetitive creatures do who lack language. Then one day . . . but stop! *We* can say 'one day' because *we* can mark the time of before and after. But at the opening of this story *no one* and no thing is *there*, or so we're to imagine. No language. No objects or subjects. No delimited place or event. *We* can say all that because we are already 'placed' in a full language. But this story is about an imaginary non-place where 'place' first emerged."

In what follows, Gupta avoids the conceptual knots of the philosopher while taking delight in the intricate game of words: "One day in this mythic scene a creature heard a noise."

"A creature who was not *there*!" The skeptical Ji-Min intruded satirically.

Gupta: "Vibrations in the air were not new of course. They might have been heard at any time if suitable organs of perception had coincided with whatever it is that finds significance in bare sensations. Trees fell in the forest and thunder roared, but they went unheard because there was no one to hold one sound in mind and distinguish it from the next. No one to take account of the gap between the first sound and the second.

"But now we're to imagine that on a singular occasion—the first 'occasion' there ever was—someone *heard*. One—before there were two—but I'm running ahead of myself! We're speaking of the first primate to be seduced by a name. The mythical first animal capable of being singled out by a word, split apart and made human. 'Singled out' by hearing itself spoken to. A voice calls, 'Adam!' What this singular creature could not know, because it didn't yet know how to know, was that the voice of 'God,' walking in

275

the garden, had called him Adam, 'the man.' *That*, we're to imagine—no facts here, mind you—that was the first voice and the first word that the first 'he' ever heard."

Mai Bao's eyes glint with the delight of speculatively reaching into the unknown as she had done this morning on her solitary walk in the "Garden of the Mother of God." She had felt herself in the presence of "the sacred" which meant to her whatever most deserved revering, as the ancients had revered Athos. There were stories of the Greek gods on the Holy Mountain long before the Christians claimed it, even before Zeus and company moved west to Olympus. Time out of mind, it had been a sacred place with a temple and an oracle of Apollo and pagan hermits living on the cliffs at the tip of the peninsula overlooking the "man-eating rocks." As dangerous and cursed and exciting a place as the garden Gupta was describing.

Burak Derviş usually said little, though his intensity of listening often catalyzed the room. As a Muslim, the book of *Genesis* remained a sacred text for him, and he now rises in defense of its literal truth:

"But it wasn't the first word! In both versions of the story, *Genesis* 1 and *Genesis* 2, there had already been words. Not only creative words, 'Let there be earth' and everything in it, including the man and the woman, but when the call comes, Adam has already named the beasts and the woman Eve. Still more important, he has already received—and violated—the prohibition against eating fruit from the tree of knowledge. All this *before* the voice in the garden addresses him as 'Adam.' So, not the first word after all!"

For some reason Gupta enjoys this rehearsal of how poorly he's telling the story, enjoys it nearly as much as he enjoys the language games. Giving Derviş an affectionate paternal smile, he replies, "Good for you, Burak. True on every point . . . but one: The 'let there be' is a gesture without words, a herald of worlds in the making. Nonetheless, I *am* blatantly misreading the text, and you're right to ask why. Try this: The text is a record of a distant oral tradition like the creation stories from the Babylonians, the Hindus, the Egyptians, the Greeks, and many others. In oral traditions stories grow and change with the circumstances of their recitation, like living organisms. We, now, are reading the elements of one ancient story in a different context."

Derviş persists. "But when you switch the beginning of a story around to make it the middle and put the middle in front, it's not the same story."

"Quite right. And if you'll bear with me, I'll come back to all that. Meanwhile, I'm reading the text all-at-once, as though whatever happens, happens in the same moment, as a single creative event."

Paul Poirier has also been tightlipped so far, but Gupta's description makes him uncomfortable too. Yet when Derviş appears inclined to continue his protest, Poirier intervenes, "I'm sympathetic with your view, Burak, but let's wait until we see where the story goes."

Gupta gives a gruff Gupta chuckle and tries to set the issue in a broader perspective. "Stories, especially mythic ones, can condense complex sequences into simultaneous events the way the blueprint of a building represents space.

So when we speak of a world before 'world' had a name or of a moment before there was an 'is,' we speak mythically of what never happened. Yet it's what—for the world to be as we know it—must have happened. That or something like it. We're not trying to make the myth consistent with historical accounts. Each retelling is a reordering in response to a different question. As a meteor might collide with a planet and add new chemical elements. The meteor of this heterodox reading of the Adam myth contains a new truth-element that alters the whole reality."

Waving his own wordplay aside with the back of his hand, he continues. "My reading of the myth puts the address to Adam first because our concern is not with the details of creation—'the facts'—but, by means of a single word, establishing a being who is open to himself and to a world. An unknown voice and two syllables—or however many syllables it took in that ur-language to say 'Adam'—was sufficient to distinguish the one creature who can hear."

A degree of skepticism in at least half of the participants inspires Adawale to ask, "Are you implying that even God, or the voice of God, is a figure in the myth? Not a being entering from outside?"

"Yes. Here 'God' is undecidable. Both figures function as the phrase 'morning and evening of the first day' functions where there are no days or night—no time—outside the story. But back to the naming of Adam:

"Note that to address someone is to name, to call him out, to set him on his way, into his own presence. Poirier has anticipated me when he speaks of naming as setting us in the presence of other things, in this case things already created in the garden that Adam will bring to light by continuing the naming process.

"We may imagine the primeval voice hollowing out a place 'inside' him where the sound can resonate long enough for him to 'listen back' from the second to the first. The inside illuminates a place 'outside,' where he encounters a world that concerns him. His hearing is already a response, and his rank changes. All at once! 'The first man Adam.'"

Adawale was not the only person present who found these distinctions as blinding as the afternoon sun reflected into the room by the glass of a balcony door. For a few moments the sound of chairs and shoes shuffling on the wooden floor punctuates Gupta's story as Adawale and two or three others move out of the light.

At that point the discussion seems to lapse without having mentioned the rest of the tale and without having illuminated anything whatever. In that moment they all do something rather unusual for such verbal people. They keep still for a length of time that might feel awkward in a place less given to the leisure and discipline of the contemplative life. For more minutes than anyone bothered to count, they sat on, facing one another quietly, comfortably, neglecting the creation story itself, considering Gupta's strange way of telling it.

Eventually Pavlov broke the silence. "Let's get a drink. I need to think about this strange man Adam."

Several got up and went to the table at the back where the usual platter of bread and fruit had been placed beside the usual urn of cool water. Others stepped outside to look again from the balcony to the beach far below and from their "garden" toward the finger of land across the bay.

No one hurried, but when eventually they reassembled, Pavlos captured Gupta's gaze with a mischievous smile. "One thing you mentioned without explanation is that this creature, this man, having heard and responded to the creative call 'Let there be Adam' and there was—that the new man can now go on with the language game by naming the animals himself."

Derviş renews his former objection. "But the animals already had names!"

Poirier takes the remark as resistance. "No Burak! The story is simultaneous, a non-chronological category. From that perspective, every detail is coexistent with every other detail like the plan of a building. 'Before' and 'after' are collapsed into the moment."

Derviş persists. "You may say, if you like, that it all happens in an Eternal Moment, but then you put the name 'Adam' first! On Gupta's account, as soon as there's speech, there's a first and a second. Are the elements of the story sequential or are they simultaneous? You can't have it both ways!"

Gupta ponders the objection for a long moment before replying with a broad smile. "You want me to tell the truth. But I'm not trying to tell the truth. You're the truth-teller. You're reporting the 'true' sequences of an ancient record of an already ancient oral tradition, where that standard of truth could never have applied. A myth corresponds to nothing. It isn't repeated correctly or incorrectly. It's performed and considered for what passes in and what passes through the performance. At best it throws light on a present situation. The Adam-event, or something like it, opens the possibility of our sitting here discussing the potentiality of a citizen yet to come."

If Adawale has any significant thoughts on this way of reading the myth, he has so far kept them to himself. But he hasn't lost sight of the ostensible aim. "Then your Adam prefigures our elusive citizen?"

In his characteristic tone of generosity, Gupta skips a step: "And so we add the tree. Adam is told that he . . . "

"—and she . . . the woman," Mai Bao interjects.

". . . now they, a community of two, unless it's three . . ."

". . . or maybe four," says Poirier roguishly. "Mythic gardens tend to be serpent-infested . . ."

"Yes," Gupta answers. "They—two, four," he waves his hand, "or an infinite number, since all the mythic sons and daughters of Adam and Eve are implicated in the scene—they may eat of every tree in the garden but one."

The corners of Adawale's eyes squint with intensity as though he has found a missing link. He proclaims on cue: "Let there be law! Adam doesn't already naturally obey the law, because to obey he would have to be capable of disobeying and nothing corresponds yet to either."

Derviş with ironic exuberance: "Wrong! It all happens at once. Whatever was created is already what it will become!"

Opeyemi dodges the criticism. "Still, there's no obvious reason for law to come into the situation unless the prohibition not to eat the fruit makes him subject to law and whatever it prohibits."

Directing his question to Gupta, "Yesterday you spoke of the 'outside of the law.' Is there an inside and outside of the law in the garden or just a retrospective 'lawlessness'?"

Gupta continues the thought with a new twinkle in his eye. "Receiving the first law, the first man occupies the unique place of freedom. A rule establishes his capacity to obey or not obey, to do or not to do. Free to choose well or badly. Free even to take exception to there being a rule in the first place. But the freedom to get *himself* wrong, opens the capacity to get himself right."

Derviş says darkly, "That would mean that the fall—falling—is not a *quasi*-historical event but something inherent to Adam's way of being. But then his creation would have been a punitive act from the start. You seem to be denying what the story says: that the two are dismissed from the garden as punishment. Surely their act requires penitence."

To which Pavlos replies, "What he's saying is that the transgression and fall prepared Adam and Eve to enter a world beyond innocence where they choose and bear the responsibility. The fortunate fall doesn't result from some relatively trivial act that entails blame and repentance."

Poirier tries for the historical dimension. "The imputation of guilt and punishment in this story goes back many centuries. But the story doesn't necessarily mean that their Creator leads them into temptation, knowing they will fail the test. After all, He's the one who created two trees and forbade them to eat the fruit of one. Wouldn't you think that, knowing all, He would know that in singling out the one tree as forbidden, He provides the incentive for transgression? He shouldn't have to wait for St. Paul to explain it to Him."

"No. No!" Derviş cries. "They choose to yield to temptation. Eve, when she's tempted by the serpent; Adam, when he's tempted by Eve. It's straightforward transgression, and expulsion from Eden is the punishment."

Gupta only smiles. "Then all posterity is painted with their brush. Think how much ink has flowed over the centuries trying to make sense of how *we* can be guilty of *their* acts. How would that interpretation throw any light on the condition of Planet Ulro?"

"So how," Poirier demands, "do you explain this act of a devious God? If, as you say, the story does what myth is supposed to do, how does the fall clarify *us*?"

"The point is that fall and expulsion are not *moral*, they're *ethical*. Reading requires that we try to see a consistency in the act of Adam's Creator. If He's a cheap trickster, then the story's worthless to us. Would a God who set such a complicated creature at the apex of His creation be so frivolous as to care about one tree or another? And why give a command that He knows will be violated at the first opportunity? Does He need to set up a test of His little man's obedience when He already knows he will take the first opportunity to fail?"

Then aside with a mischievous smile, "I'm remembering that Dante, reading the myth as literally as Burak, estimated the total time in Eden at about six hours! That doesn't strengthen a literal reading."

Derviş: "But this is not a generic tree. It's the Tree of the Knowledge of Good and Evil!"

"True," Gupta answers. "And if they hadn't eaten the fruit, the story wouldn't clarify us. It's about their capacity for independent action—or non-action. Like us, they're preoccupied with the forbidden, and they incorporate its fruit into themselves by eating it. 'Preoccupied,' in that they forget the other tree, the forward-looking Tree of Life. The fall is not a loss; it's the advent of their potentiality for acting responsibly."

But Derviş wants it both ways. "Why not a moral lapse as well?"

"Because moral lapses are backward-looking. If the fall were punishment for a past infraction, *our* guilt would make no sense. But if it's ethical rather than moral, it reveals the character of a being who has things to do and who is already in debt to his potential for doing them well. Not in debt for past transgressions against a rule-governed world—not even if the rules are divine. Ethics is not about obedience to rules. It's about *ethos,* Greek for 'habit' or 'custom.' So the character of one who dwells in possibility."

Pavlos, delighted, remarks aside to the others, "That's as clear an account of original sin as you're likely ever to hear and, read as a parable rather than history, it's completely naturalistic. Even if you think the appearance of homo sapiens happened over millions of years of evolution, you'd still need some such event for us to be who we are. And—just so we don't lose our way here—it resembles what Mai Bao called a pre-political condition in the film *Rouge* and even more closely to our foray into Greek tragedy."

Ji-Min, still suspicious of the whole theological game and wishing to depose it, demands one more time what all this subtlety has to do with the future of Planet Ulro.

As no one takes that up instantly, Poirier asks in a voice shaded with high French skepticism, "But what of the penalty? Aren't Adam and his progeny condemned to earn their bread by the sweat of their brows? That must mean something. It sounds like punishment to me! How does the 'curse' relate to all the rest, to the call, the creation of Eve, the naming, the temptation, and the banishment from the garden? Isn't your theory of synchronous narration in danger?"

Gupta: "Meanwhile we mustn't forget that we're still looking for the citizen of the future. The Adam-event continues the search for the being who can act rationally, with others, beyond his own self-interest. In having speech, he is no longer 'innocent' as a child is innocent in responding to its organic desires. Adam—now the name of the citizen-to-come—is capable of investing his desires in ideals. So we call his fall fortunate! Now he can take responsibility for himself, for Eve, for his habitat, his children, his city. Once again we catch a glimpse of the political life. It's there if we can read it. The Adam of the future might be the custodian of all things but master of none. As archetype of the citizen, he would not be an anthropological entity with a definable nature; he would be a project underway, whose being is his mode of being in language moment by moment."

Pavlos moves to respond but defers to Mai Bao, who has contributed little to this segment of the discussion. She raises a different question, in the shadow perhaps, of the old Chinese yin-yang. "I know this is a man's story, told by men, mainly for the consumption of men, but I'd like to hear more about the primal mother. No one here has said so, but Eve seems to be dropped into the story to let Adam off the hook. Yet if the tale is universal, whatever it says must apply to both. Meanwhile, we're here in the garden of the Mother of that creator God. I wonder what the myth has to do with her."

Opeyemi: "Aren't you the one who showed us a way beyond identity, gender or otherwise, in Athena's act?"

Pavlos, the closest thing to a theologian in the room, suspends whatever he had wanted to say and replies to Mai Bao. "I don't see that the myth is about sexual gender, either man or woman. When the Creator says, 'It is not good for man to dwell alone,' the emphasis may be on 'company' rather than gender, though if descendants weren't prefigured, the story would never have been told. We remember that language requires at least two. A community of speakers. The religions of the Middle East were profoundly patriarchal and exposed to the perils of the Oedipal challenge. But those may be historical, not 'natural' or 'mythical' circumstances. Gupta would probably say"—he threw a glance in his direction without getting confirmation—"the myth clarifies Eve's mode of being just as it does Adam's. Both are present, because when an organism appears as human, that new dimension is inherently a figure of more than one, as animals are not. Under the combined regime of mother-father and child, it's a figure of three, and three opens on infinity."

Mai Bao appears to accept this answer, but she wants more. "And what about the Virgin?"

Pavlos smiles at her and sighs. "That question may eventually also bear on our political agenda, but if Eve is not initially about gender, the question of the Virgin must wait for ideas as yet unexplored."

Ji-Min explodes: "Oh my God!" Then, correcting himself, casts an ironic eye heavenward. "Do forgive the irreverence!"

Then, turning to the opposite side of the circle from Pavlos, he continues. "How is the Virgin Mary an improvement on the Greek virgin and her new regime which may or may not have accomplished anything?" He has now reached his best satirical mode. "Gupta hinted that Athos might inspire a political model but now we're wandering off into darkness and mystery. We've often heard that *only a god can save us now,* but apparently, in the absence of god or goddess, an icon of the Mother of God will do!"

But he isn't finished. He addresses Pavlos directly: "That will lead nowhere, you know. Athos is only a *community.* It exists by exclusion. Women excluded, children excluded, probably Muslims like Derviş, secularists like Adawale and Poirier, and pagans like me, all excluded. There's no political solution down that road. We'd be better off with Athena's tragic Band-Aid. Communal ghettos are symptoms of a world disintegrating. You won't cure a sick world by hanging an icon of the Virgin on the wall of every city hall on Ulro!"

Gupta enjoys the fun *and* takes him up firmly. "Nobody's doing theology here, Choi! In fact, Ulro is strangling on theology, sacred and secular! But that's a story for another time. Yet we mustn't pass over whatever has mattered to many through the ages. Especially what has offered even an illusion of benefit to humanity. And, before you say it, one thing more: This is not cultural relativism. The path we're on requires the utmost discrimination. There is one thing blinder than imagination without reason; it is reason without imagination."

Pavlos meets this exchange with a benign smile. "I agree. No one here wants to reinstate theology. In the present state of the world, theology isn't even a viable possibility. Scientific rationalism has taken its place and given us a new fundamentalism. For millennia the Holy Mountain has gone about its daily business while the outside world has been torn by the wars of gods and men. Athos has witnessed it all without losing its tranquility. *In* the world, responsible *for* the world, but not *of* the world. Our gamble is that there *may be* something in this heritage that speaks to our planetary dilemma. But that's rushing ahead. First let's ask Mai Bao, who has a way with a phrase, to renew her word 'the beyondness of things.'"

CHAPTER 2

A WARM AFTERNOON FOLLOWED THE exertion of the morning hike, and the participants took another break before Mai Bao could reply to Pavlos' request for more on "beyondness." During those few minutes she walked out to the balcony, where she was joined a moment later by Ope. The two stood side by side gazing into the distance without communication, other than the discreet pressure of two arms touching. That touch was much more than two bodies meeting in relation. It was relation itself, dissolving the separation of two.

When the next moment Gupta wandered outside and saw them, he went tactfully to the far end rather than interrupt. No more than five minutes later, as all three returned to the conference room together, his eye met theirs with the casual smile that contained no hint of having felt a charge in the air that no sensitive person could have missed.

It was Mai Bao's turn to speak, and she picked up Pavlos' earlier suggestion. "The word 'beyondness' is intended to say that there is more in earth and in heaven than definable objects in a container world. The issue is something like this: 'Reality' is larger than the set of things present to our senses and to our systems of knowledge. When we consider the limit of what we know, it's obvious that we live toward the dark unknown. As industrial processes leave 'waste materials' behind, so the axioms of positive knowledge necessarily leave everyday experience behind.

"I like to imagine a beam of light that enables us to see the back wall of a cave. In following the spot of light, we ignore what is swallowed up by the surrounding dark. That's especially true of the one holding the light. The point of light *is* the blind spot. It both reveals and conceals. Just so, the pursuit of verifiable knowledge leaves blank places. Infinite ones."

The skeptical Choi asks her to please explain her example.

She who loves detecting traces of the sublime in ordinary things, whether fiction or fact, is prolific in examples. "There is blindness of several kinds. Let's take any object. Say an apple. There's the red, sweet, juicy apple as seen by a hungry child; the apple as seen by the fruit picker as part of the day's work; or for the supermarket purchasing agent, one of thousands of consumer items with a cost base and a profit margin; for the legislator, an abstract situation requiring rules for production, transport, sale, and safe nutrition. For practical reasons, all these pass over the unique object. Botany and chemistry and physics also subtract the 'appleness' of the apple in order to take it as an appropriate experimental subject.

"Then there's the historical weight, factual or fictive, of Adam's apple. Every light is also a 'blind spot.' And so far, we've only mentioned a human subject interpreting an object!

"More to the point, consider the painter or poet who 'resides' with things themselves. The apple is given to the artist as a singularity in a limitless field to which she also belongs.

It is like the artist's window opening on infinite relations beyond. Contrary to representations, art works like Adam's giving names: It resounds with the boundless and gives us over to wonder. And, isn't that what happens at Athos when tourists become pilgrims?"

Pavlos: "So your beam of light lets what was in darkness 'ex-ist' in the original sense of what 'stands forth' within our range of access. Neither the apple nor the poet 'stops' on an identity or definition. The event leads infinitely off in both directions so to speak."

"Now we're imagining worlds beyond the world." That's Ji-Min, who adds sarcastically, "So, otherworldliness after all! This is my day for theological jitters!"

"No one is suggesting anything supernatural, Choi," Pavlos adds gently. "Isn't it obvious that infinite reality exceeds our imagination—in cosmology, for example? And doesn't that fact endlessly intrigue us?"

Mai Bao: "Good. Now, since we don't all share it to the same extent, I need help understanding our bond with dimensions remote even to imagining. The artist can't be indifferent. She must observe closely and distinguish because, like Adam in giving the names, she cares. Is that a practical disposition, or does it somehow belong to our being's way of being?"

Poirier objects: "Perhaps the difference is psychological. An occupational hazard. Artists are just different!"

But Derviş disagrees. "No, no! The point of her analogy is that we have access to different ways of being, and that affects who we are. Adam, naming the beasts, doesn't face them like a spy or a consultant from outside. He's the participant in the scene with the ability to respond to things as *they* require, not as *he* requires."

Ope: "Then we've stumbled on the root of ethics and politics! Reading his tale synchronically—the moment that extends back to first creation and forward to the expulsion— he faces, and will always face, a choice! Beyond the gates of Eden where, for him, for the artist, and for the rest of us, freedom persists."

Poirier: "What does that mean?"

"I don't know yet."

Pavlos intervenes. "I suspect there is a clue in the moralistic reading of the Adam myth. It stresses the curse of labor, the curse of death, even the curse of sexual reproduction. That heritage would destroy the artist too."

Derviş: "You're saying that if Adam judged his fate as punishment and lived in resentment of having been banished, he would hate his place and turn away from things, and that fate would easily pass on to posterity. *Does* pass on, in fact, as it accounts for the choices each of us perpetually makes. We, too, may face the world with resentment of our fate or with open mind and heart. The same world seen differently."

Ji-Min: "So, I suppose, if he hates his condition, he'll call things by the wrong names?"

Gupta, who for some reason never sits in the same chair twice, murmurs *sotto voce* from a different side of the room. "Hum. The decadence of language. That's an Ulro we've ignored."

Pavlos tries again to gather up the strands of a scattered exchange. "Our fascination with the unknown suggests two dispositions toward the boundless. We may fear, reject, and hate whatever lies beyond our range of receptivity and call it natural evil. Or, remembering that love thrives on contingency, we who are committed for life to what is given may respond with an amorous disposition toward the boundless, rejoicing in the adventure."

This rambling conversation was somehow improving Adawale's mood. The company had grown accustomed to seeing him on the edge of his seat, waiting for them to fill the hole in the political. Now he leans forward in Derviş' direction with an urgent question. "So is our ideal citizen to face the disintegration of the planet by learning to love the bomb or, like a poet, by finding the right name for doomsday?"

"Exactly the question!" Ji-Min again erupts in sarcasm. "If the icon of the Virgin doesn't work, we must learn to love one another. Mandatory love counseling for everyone on the planet. After five hundred years spreading this gospel, we won't feel so bad anymore. We can hold hands as the last tsunami rolls over the last beach and sweeps us away. Then all will be well!"

Pavlos appears oddly sympathetic with the periodic resurgences of melancholy or irony, as though even they might be heralds of hope. He replies, undaunted by all these symptoms of dissatisfaction. "Your objections are entirely correct within limited frames of reference. At the very least we'd need to understand love differently. The word has been ruined. We can use it only if we speak it differently. The old Greeks took it up in the form of disruptive Eros, which required integrating the just person or the just city. The Christians preferred

293

another Greek word, *agape*, which eventually degenerated into psychology, sentiment, and the gospel of the sex shop."

"So what's left?" Poirier asks whimsically, grinning.

Pavlos: "What's left is the great 'Yes!' that precedes the great 'Why?' or the "No!" that leads to defiance and the death wish. One way or the other we are disposed affectively toward the magnetic tug of the boundless. Being immersed in it, we, like Adam and the artist, can celebrate as though the All—or the Nothing—added up to a whole to which, for convenience, we assign a name."

It's an extraordinary moment. Ope sees only a blur, Mai Bao also seems to have lost the thread, Gupta has shut his eyes again, while Poirier and Ji-Min remain at cross-purposes with Pavlos. Derviş alone seems still in tune. The rest look up or down or beyond, even at the back wall that's blank except for a provocative icon. They have never been more disconnected or more at odds in mood than at this moment. Discord seems to have reached a peak that requires a full stop.

Then the bell rings in the courtyard below and they rise silently, one by one, and descend the several flights of steps to the refectory for *trapeze*, the evening meal, as solitary as six planets in alien galaxies.

CHAPTER 3

DAY FIVE BEGAN with Gupta picking up the pieces of the wandering discussions of the day before by recurring to Mai Bao's "beyondness" that for some reason he called "the boundless." As usual, he offered no hint in advance of where he was headed or why.

Gesturing toward the open balcony door, he began, "In the year 415 BCE, about 150 miles to the south, there was a famous meeting of a distinguished group of Athenians—'men only'!—who discussed the topic of Eros. We have already associated Greek Eros with a rational disposition, but hold the criticism in abeyance for a bit if you please.

"At the time of this dialogue, as Plato records it in the *Symposium*, Athens was at war with Sparta and, among those present, were some who knew that Greek civilization was at risk. It was a tantalizing juxtaposition of political crisis and the theme of love in a darkening world. Perhaps Pavlos had reason to begin our dialogues with a story of love and war among the gods and men."

Then Gupta smiled in Mai Bao's direction. "At the Symposium all the participants were male except for one, in disguise, who was there and not there. It took those men all night to get to the heart of the issue, but when the climax came it came in two voices. The most profound speech on

Eros came in Socrates' voice but quoting his female teacher, the Arcadian priestess named Diotima of Mantinea. So in an androgynous speech, if you will, the case is made for philosophy, 'the love of wisdom,' as the final rung in a ladder of love that begins in physical passion and ends in wisdom."

"I like that!" said Mai Bao, yielding to an impulse of the moment. "The combined mother-father figure at the heart of the ideal of love."

But Gupta, lost perhaps in his own thoughts, did not pick up her remark. He was staring into space as though he had forgotten what was passing in the room. Patiently, everyone waited for him to return, and when he did, he was still in the company of Plato.

"I must ask you to be patient now. As patient as you were with the legend of the Adam event. Hold the political question at bay for a time and, with our discussions in mind, just listen to the topics of these ancient speeches. They form a cumulative and corrective exploration of Eros. There are six, or seven, depending on how you designate the last one.

"First, Phaedrus offers a totally conventional praise of love. Second, Pausanias distinguishes between base love and noble love. Third, the physician Eryximachus extends the concept of love to an amorous mechanical principle, like gravity, that holds the cosmos together. Fourth, the comic dramatist Aristophanes follows with a fantasy of a spherical male-female human, cut in two and perpetually seeking its lost matching half. Love, he says, is desire of a divided being in pursuit of the whole. Fifth, the tragic poet Agathon adds only the essential connection of love to beauty.

"Then comes Socrates, for whom love means need, lack, or absence: the nullity of a missing good. But the heart of his speech and the nucleus of the symposium isn't his. It's his reiteration of Diotima's account of love as a ladder. The ladder that begins in lust for a beautiful person ends in desire and pursuit of the inexistent whole of things. It's named 'love of wisdom.'

"And yet, the speeches don't quite end there. A last one is given to the deceitful politician and general named Alcibiades. It's a peevish but admiring account of his efforts sometime in the past to seduce Socrates, who declined physical love because he loves wisdom more than objects of physical gratification: Love as distance, postponement, ideal."

Poirier threw both hands up and cried, "Unbelievable! With only a vague idea of where we were going, we have been retracing the path of that conversation all along. Maybe not from unfulfilled desire up to wisdom, but we seem to be in the neighborhood. We've followed that Greek path and ended up someplace entirely un-Greek!"

Burak Derviş, scratching his chin, wanted to know more. "I didn't know we've gotten anywhere. What place have we ended up, unless you mean that our end was in our beginning?"

Gupta offered a summary speculation. "We have criticized Athena's law as excluding the Furies' instinctual drives from Athens. Something similar may happen when desire follows beauty. Love for what is well-proportioned, orderly, and gratifying is an easy love. The love of the boundless—the dangerous and terrifying—is a different love much closer to the strife of political life. It's easy to love intelligible consistency, but the sublime threatens order and security."

Mai Bao found a question in his synopsis. "What would change in our story if we read it as a love story?"

"One thing would change," Ji-Min replied. "If you're going to speak of loving the beyondness of a limitless and indifferent universe, even of a void beyond knowing and not-knowing . . . well, then you'll have to love human suffering and death and the destruction of Ulro! If I'm to believe my ears, our 'progress' seems to be that trying to perpetuate anything at all is an uncreative moralism!"

During Ji-Min's protest, Poirier, who often expressed his indifference to an idea by not looking at the speaker, spent the time tracing with his eyes the lines of the timbers on the back wall as he waited for an opening to get back to Diotima's ladder.

When the opening came, he protested, "At this moment I don't see a difference between Athena's legalism and our political horizons. We're also trying to put the Erinyes of desire back in their bottle! We want to bind the law and the outside of the law together in a new law that would then exist to repress its own 'out-law.' We went to lunch on the notion that our project depends on finding a way beyond that point."

"Exactly!" Pavlos added, leaning forward in his chair as the quietism of his usual manner approached fervor. "You have heard the accusation that the antique Greeks were all children? The Greek philosopher begins in sensuality, then he or she—there's Diotima!—embarks on an erotic path toward wisdom."

Derviş, apparently arrested by the notion of loving the sublime, ignored the political and went off diagonally in a different direction. "Does anyone happen to remember the name Khidr?"

Gupta would have remembered but he didn't speak, so Burak continued. "Once a group of Islamic soldiers were caught between an enemy city and the desert. Faced with death, they spoke of nothing but the impossibility of finding water.

"All but one. As the others talked, Khidr jumped to his feet, ran into the desert at the risk of his life, and found water! When he returned and his companions had drunk, they realized that he had brought more than ordinary water. He had found the Water of Life for which everyone is always searching."

At that point in the story, someone in the room—probably Ji-Min—asked by what magic H_2O became a miraculous water that everyone wants but no one can find.

"The Water of Life," Derviş replied, "is just ordinary water *seen differently*. The reality we've been speaking of here is the imaginative reality that gives context to experience.

"All the men but Khidr had been in despair, and what happens in despair is that we see no way out. Paralysis follows. Action sinks into passivity and misery. The warrior becomes a coward. His strength turns to weakness. His eyes go blind and heroic virtue vanishes.

"Adawale has asked the question, what we do when something must be done but nothing can be done? No hope of water. Either we despair, which is suicidal, or we respond to the limit condition. To the impossible! One courageous soldier's act in the face of death turns H_2O into The Water of Life, because The Water of Life is love even in the face of death.

"When Islam says that every act ends either in victory or in martyrdom, it contemplates the situation of one who is born to die. It's not morbid to hold that certainty in view. It's the springboard of care!"

For some reason Pavlos looked dissatisfied with the last point, but as he said nothing, Burak concluded that Khidr's act and the paralysis of the others demonstrate dispositions toward mortality. Faced with certain death—either now or later!—they choose not to act where he chooses *not* to not-act. The result is that the gift the other warriors couldn't find, because they thought it had to *be found*, was there all along."

CHAPTER 4

THE ATHOS CONFERENCE had begun with a hike on the mountain and Opeyemi's renewal of Lenin's question "What is to be done?" and ended with Mai Bao asking him for a closing response, as though the whole event had been for his benefit.

Less startled than before, he began in a confessional mode something like this: "I can only repeat the question we began with: What is the responsible thing to do for a world where every act ends in unexpected consequences, as often as not making deplorable conditions worse? Even if the human condition were a disease to be cured, how long would it take to heal the hearts and minds of billions, one person at a time?

"Put the matter this way: If we take the gods as names for the unknown that exceeds our ken, have we perhaps neglected the most important set of stories of all? Haven't the gods always taken revenge on mortals who ruin their birthright? Ours may be one of the moments when only a flood, universal war and pestilence, or a collision of galaxies can prepare a place to start over, even in some unimaginable way. In myth, renewal seems to follow destruction as though we were toys of the gods. Small wonder if we live without hope!

"Or perhaps all my efforts have been in service of the wrong question. Gupta called this a convention of storytellers.

Digging around in the fossils of neglected memory under the inspiration of our Athos muse, I have come to think that the search might be the thing itself and that we may have been enacting the very citizenship we were looking for. In putting ourselves in the way of whatever parables collective memory could throw up, we may have discovered that the citizen-to-come and the polity-to-come never arrive because they shouldn't arrive. If they did, wouldn't they be 'untimely' static conditions that would block the way rather than open a free space for invention of new ways and conditions of being?

"Though I will leave Athos still asking what if anything is to be done, the slant of the question has changed. Back in Vienna, Wu Mai Bao inspired me to read *The Analytics* of Confucius. The coincidence of that book with these discussions suggests a disposition that may have been staring us in the face for five thousand years. Perhaps in unpropitious times, all lovers of wisdom can do is what we have done here: stand aside, compose ourselves, cultivate our own understanding, and wait. . . even if it means waiting a hundred years. As another poet says, 'They also serve who only stand and wait.'"

When the last session of the Athos conference adjourned and the seven had said their farewells, Ope and Mai Bao collected their few belongings and made their way down the cliff to the dock below. The four others, on different schedules, were staying the night before going their separate ways. Pavlos proposed to accompany Ope and Mai Bao on the ferry to Ouranoupolis.

As the two waited for the third on the dock by the bay, an ancient chant, performed by the monastery choir, drifted down from far above like an unsought blessing on the departing pilgrims, and the coincidence brought smiles to their faces.

When Pavlos arrived, there were few people on board so they could lounge comfortably on the forward deck and talk without interruption. Early in the week Ope's trip down the bay may have felt like leaving the known world behind and passing into a dark Asiatic unknown, but as the boat pulls away from the dock and they watch Simonos Petros recede into the distance, both he and Mai Bao have a sense of leaving behind their proper place and emerging once more into a ruined world.

So once the boat slips from the dock at Dafni, their first stop, the three friends gravitate once more to the topic of love that had, among the seven, opened the floodgates on a plethora of new perspectives. Having confirmed Pavlos' intuition of the altered relationship between her and Ope, Mai Bao speaks in a more intimate key as she recurs to the topic of love in the context of Burak Derviş' heroic warrior Khidr.

"Would it be right to say that in risking himself to save his companions, he lives his mortality 'as if' he weren't mortal by risking what's at risk anyway? Is that an act of love and, if so, what does he love?"

Ope suggests, "Maybe it's the story of Socrates the philosopher living and dying for Athens."

Instead of speaking to the question directly, Pavlos smiles and says, "I have a parting gift for the two of you. It's the plot of an opera called *L'Amour de loin*, 'love from afar.' It's from the turn of the present century by a composer named Kaija Saariaho.

"On a trip to Paris a few years ago a friend took me to see it. It addresses your question, and I hope you'll find a copy of a recorded performance if you can't find a live performance. Its global significance lies in the music, especially the subtle orchestration, but the story alone is thought-provoking and, in my opinion, climactic to all our conversations."

As Pavlos gets up to move closer and be heard over the noise of the boat engine, Ope responds almost aside. "It's striking that we retreated to the mountain from a world that has lost its memory and spent several whole days retrieving bits of that lost heritage. Like rediscovering ourselves as creatures we didn't know we were. Before Athos I wouldn't have understood what a valuable gift a story can be!"

At that moment the boat swerves sharply to avoid something in the water, and Pavlos gets splashed by a wave over the bow. After shaking the water off his robe, he shifts his seat and resumes.

"The opera is based on a legend of the twelfth-century troubadour named Jaufré Rudel, who falls in love with an ideal rather than a real woman. The libretto doesn't repeat a true story about persons in love. Historical or not, they are fictions, and the plot is a laboratory for exploring love itself!

"Presumably Jaufré first wrote love songs to avoid his political duties, but in the fiction a pilgrim arrives from across the Mediterranean with news that the ideal lady of his poems really exists. She's the beautiful Clémence, also originally

Provençal, now Countess of Tripoli, living as an alien on the north coast of Africa. The pilgrim who mediates between the two might be little more than an androgenous procurer crossing and re-crossing the sea, except that eroticism here is more ideal than sensual, and in the milieu of courtly love the Pilgrim is an intercessor for souls rather than bodies.

"You can see that the real 'story' of the opera will be in the experience of the characters, and so it is. But for their affects, we need the music more than the action. Yet a bare plot can show why it is so important to our topic."

Ope intervenes facetiously, "This isn't going to end with everybody dead on the stage, I hope! This isn't the time for a Liebestod. No stories of love and death, if you please!"

"We'll just have to wait and see, won't we?" Pavlos grins and proceeds. "In one encounter with the Pilgrim, Jaufré is distressed to learn that the messenger has already revealed his name to the Countess and even recited his poems to her. That untimely exposure of the ideal to the real encourages him to cross the void of the sea—his first and only voyage—to meet this lover in the flesh, as though that were possible!

"In turn, Clémence is told that the poet is coming to meet her, and she suffers an attack of anxiety. She knows she isn't up to his ideal: not as beautiful, not as noble, not as pious as the woman in the poems."

Mai Bao, listening with the anticipation prompted by a good detective story, remarks obscurely, "Life and art imitating each other!"

Pavlos: "It's important that both Jaufré and Clémence want this meeting, though both fear the gap between realism and the ideal. The poet's voyage is stormy, and his apprehension induces a serious illness—unless the voyage is the illness itself. He compares himself to Adam suffering the loss of Eden, remembering the tree, lamenting its fruit. Meanwhile, the Countess debates her own worthiness, while the simple women of Tripoli express impatience with this idealized love-at-a-distance stuff.

"In another instance of the noncoinciding of the ideal and the real, Jaufré arrives, dying. Imminent death now holds the lovers at a distance as they confirm their love and he dies in Clémence's arms."

Ope, in vigorous mock protest: "Is this conjunction of the ideal and death going to take a theological turn as well? Die now and be happy in the sweet by-and-by?"

Pavlos laughs. "That depends partly on the facts of the fiction and partly on you. If you find it unpersuasive, keep in mind that you're not hearing what matters most. You're hearing only 'the facts.' But love isn't composed of facts."

He raises his eyebrows at the two of them as though insisting that new love recognize itself in the story. He, Pavlos, would know that only two people enthralled by first love—and isn't genuine love always first love?—only they can supply the music without benefit of musicians. So he had saved the story of the opera for them alone and decided to accompany them back to Ouranoupolis.

He breaks off the account for a few moments and risks another slow gaze at his two friends, silently blessing them in lines misremembered from Jane Austen: "Never two hearts so open, never feelings so in unison."

Ope muses, "So this love, like Greek love, ends in frustration and lack?"

"That would be rushing things. There's still a third act to the opera, and it belongs to the lady." He nods at Mai Bao.

"At first, she rails against an unloving God who has cruelly taken her poet from her. All the while the chorus mitigates her sacrilege by an interlude that foreshadows transformation. In her mind her absent poet and her distant God coalesce into a single figure of love, and she begs forgiveness for making an idol of the real and blinding herself to both ideal and real."

"You seem to be saying," Mai Bao speculates wistfully, "that to love any 'real' thing genuinely, we must be lovingly attuned to the beyondness of things."

He smiles. "Otherwise, trying to possess the object, to master it by knowledge and preserve it from change, we would kill it. Without the loss Clémence suffers, without the coinciding of the ideal and the real as distinct *and* inseparable, she would have missed love itself."

"Then what does she do at the climax?" Ope asks.

"She decides to become a nun who will devote the rest of her life to love-from-afar."

While Ope groans in disbelief, Mai Bao responds from a different place.

"I feel the truth of what you're describing, Pavlos, but I need to see how the ideal works. What's the relation, for example, between love at a distance and Athena or the Virgin?"

"Did you have time to read the essay I gave you on the evolution of painted images from the Byzantine icons to Florentine humanism?"

"I did, and thank you for it. The account of how in art history the Virgin entered Orthodox Christianity as a mutation of the Greek virgin goddess also helped me see how Florentine humanism turned an impersonal image into a real woman and a mother, even equipped at times with a psychology. Whereas Athena as a political ideal has no psychic history."

Ope quips, "Then at least she won't be needing psycho-analysis!"

Pavlos ponders Mai Bao's complex question for a moment. "Perhaps Athena overlaps with Gupta's suggestion of an increasingly impersonal love in the *Symposium*. When, in all her cool, androgynous glory, she subordinates sensuality to a new political idea, we were tempted to interpret it as a detached redistribution of power. After all, she's no one's mother. Among other things, she's a political function. And yet when she gives the victory to Orestes and sequesters the passionate Erinyes, she may anticipate a politics *not* based on power. At that point we may detect a resemblance between the goddess and the Virgin."

Mai Bao catches the point. "So in the world before the opera, Jaufré neglected his political duties for the pleasure of writing his songs. Much like the early speeches of the *Symposium* speak of love as desire for objects of gratification. Then, captivated by inspiration of an ideal love beyond himself, he becomes a true poet. But when the Countess enters by the mediation of the Pilgrim, his real seems to coincide with his ideal . . ."

Ope uncharacteristically interrupts her in midsentence. "I follow what you two are saying, but why the death theme?

308

I don't care for this being-toward-death thing. As though the point of life and love—even the polity—were to make a beautiful corpse. Why is it as much about dying as about love and poetry?"

Pavlos: "Because the issue isn't life or death. It's presence or absence. As in the ambivalence of the historical troubadour: Was he real or wasn't he? He's an ideal that condenses a way of life. No less 'real' after his 'death' than before. People die, but ideals don't, even if they drop out of sight for centuries."

Mai Bao: "Then the poet's being *is his singing*. He doesn't re-present his lady. He sings, and in the celebration he—and ultimately, she—is assimilated to the song. Momentarily both figures violate the ideal by trying to hold it in their hands. With him in her arms she clings to a corpse and falls into despair."

Pavlos again, as though he and Mai Bao shared the same thought: "As love at a distance remains inaccessible, drawing us in advance beyond ourselves in an 'embrace' of the boundless."

Ope finally catches the spirit as well as the idea. "That would mean that to be lovers, we must accept an endless pursuit of what, if grasped, would be a corpse."

Pavlos reaches for the hands of the two and clasps them together in his: "As you two must always seek to cross the uncrossable distance between you and find joy in the oscillation between. Never forget what happens when Jaufré and Clémence try, each in turn, to grasp the ideal in the real! You are binding yourselves to the joy of an eternal search."

Without removing his hand from the others, Ope's eyes open like two lights in his handsome face. "If you've got this right, then the citizen also exists in the pursuit of potentialities rather than a political real and does so without ceasing.

"Pavlos' reply is benedictory: Taken as a means toward ends to be achieved, political action becomes idolatry. But taken as iconic—like the Madonna on the wall—it leads us into unforeseeable paths. Like first love, unattainable as a star in the heavens, but attainable as a path. And, if I dared to be theological, I'd give the name 'God' to the void between and beyond the interplay of all reals and all ideals—but I decline to be theological!"

PART SIX

ESCAPE TO THE STARS

CHAPTER 1

IN THE LOBBY of the five towers, the two pagans who had found love on a sacred mountain parted ways. Opeyemi to his twentieth-floor guest suite, Mai Bao to the UNOV Office for Outer Space Affairs.

"If my orders allow," she said, "I'll come up after I've reported to Boris."

Within the hour, she knocked lightly on the door and rushed into his arms, alone for the first time since the dawn of their new world. The rest of that day and the night that followed need not be related here. Those fortunate enough to know from experience don't have to be told, and those who don't know—their numbers are sadly large—would be voyeurs incapable of knowing.

Late in the afternoon of the next day, the two sat in their observation post over the old city with glasses of wine as Mai Bao filled in several gaps in their story. "You have been kept in the dark by Boris' order, but now I'm free to explain more. You know him well, but among the things you don't know is that he is much more than a Space Agency bureaucrat.

"For five hundred years the decline of the planetary order was foreseen by thoughtful people who with prophetic acumen often identified the seeds of decline. But such messages go unheard until they're fulfilled in material reality. Then they're on everyone's lips and turn into the clichés we call 'the news.' But in recent years those voices have escaped the numbing effects of publicity and inspired far-reaching projects.

"Specifically, a secret international plan for building a self-sustaining generational starship to search for places in the galaxy where a remnant of the humanity might be transplanted and saved."

Instantly Ope saw where she was headed and sprang from his chair in alarm. As the scope of the project unfolded before his imagination, his stoic demeanor fell away and the drama in the room shifted from her account to his reception. With a face blank as death, he paced with increasing vigor back and forth before the window, his upright posture bowing under the weight of the revelation. The immensity of the project and its universal consequences, pleasant and not so pleasant, emerged before his eyes.

Without missing a gesture, Mai Bao calmly continued. "At a time when masses of people are homeless, without citizenship, and lacking the necessities of nutrition, health care, and education, the challenge has been to conceal the costliest and most perilous venture in history from public awareness. Global economic participation being essential, your ingenious friend devised a plausible cover story. The story was that a ship, a prototype, was under construction for exploiting the natural resources of other planets in the solar system, thereby enriching Ulro."

As she smiled at the pacing figure framed by the window across the room, Ope's astonishment was complex. He could only admire the boldness of the scheme while being alarmed by its political significance and repulsed at having been drawn blindly into the thing.

When his reactions were sufficiently under control to speak calmly, he exclaimed, "Extraordinary! Other issues aside, it's ingenious in idea and execution. Announce the construction to everyone while hiding the purpose. Never underrate our proclivity not to imagine. If those of us in public service had known what was happening, we would have been first in line to protest. In fact, we *did* protest the plan to exploit the neighboring planets, but we never suspected it as a ruse for a one-way trip to oblivion. And at such a price! Save a smidgen of humanity by bankrupting the rest!"

Ope sat down again and lapsed into silence, busily rearranging his world to fit a new reality. Mai Bao's short speech had converted a centuries-old destiny into an unexpected chance for humanity to save itself, however long the odds, however obscure the consequences. Then he returned to Boris' immense presumption. He, Opeyemi, had been assured that, once he knew all, he would support whatever cause he was being compelled to serve! Well, he didn't support eschatological fantasies, and he deeply deplored the hubris of the thing.

When he was sufficiently restored to himself, Mai Bao reached over and took his free hand in hers.

"You must appreciate how little I have known. How little I know even now. I don't know how all this evolved. I don't know how large Boris' circle of confidants is. And only now do I know why they exist. I know least of all what role he may have in mind for you or for me. I learned the true purpose of the ship under construction just before the trip to Athos."

"Did he recruit you after the plan was underway?"

"I don't even know that, but it's what I suspect."

"Now your NASA experience makes more sense. You were an obvious recruit. But for what? What were you told that persuaded you to accept the position?"

Without an answer to that question, a new dimension dawned on him and he rushed ahead. "What do The Readers have to do with an engineering project? And why send seven people on retreat to the Holy Mountain? How do I get mixed up in all this? I've been out of my element all along. Now it seems you are too. Yet you're apparently one of Boris' trusted insiders. It's not rational."

"Then it's time to tell you that I'm not what I seem."

Ope had recovered sufficiently to laugh with a semblance of relief. "Let me guess. You're going to shave your head and become a monastic." Had it been necessary, the happy intensity of her gaze would have assured him that knowing more would not compromise their new relationship—would have, if assurance had been needed.

"My closest technical experience was at NASA with the old international space stations. We had learned a lot in those years, and that may have had something to do with being recruited here. But I've never been so much as asked a question about all that. I came on board for quite different, even opposite reasons." Her attention suddenly wandered to a new strand in the tapestry: "Unless I've been biding time, waiting for my true assignment!"

He stared. "As a double agent, you mean! To do what?"

Not for the first time, she was pleased by his quick grasp of the situation. More playful, too, since Athos had brightened his somber outlook. Yet her answer was cautiously indirect. "You've been wondering long enough why you're here. Boris didn't bring you. I did. He got the officials in New York to order you to come, but it was my idea."

"You? You did it?"

He stared at her, astonished. "But why? Why introduce a bookworm into a space drama, and with such high stakes?"

"First, someone stumbled onto a global underground of intellectuals whose purpose in life is to keep tabs on their world and exchange ideas with one another. We discussed before how dangerous intellectuals are even when they agree with you."

She grinned. "You can't even tell from the books they write what they'll say tomorrow."

"Thinking abhors the state of the state."

"Maybe my real job was to placate or at least to keep an eye out for dissident opinion. Even as I took my orders to mean the opposite. To join in and build bridges crisscrossing the distances among readers. Like a *salonnière* in eighteenth-century France, except that my salon is in virtual time-space. When your name began turning up among The Readers, what caught my eye was your effect on others. 'Professor Adawale' was the name of a new energy and new lines of discussion. Soon I discovered the moral authority in your voice even where your ideas seemed dubious. You were speaking to forces below the radar, and ordinary intelligent people were paying attention."

Ope raised an eyebrow. "To my *dubious* ideas! That's nice to hear."

She acknowledged the satire with an eyebrow and replied, "I'm not *that* simple! Not *your* ideas. I didn't find your ideas at all. An author, like a father, is only one who comes before and prepares the way. He can't know where his path is tending. You begin by making connections that nobody else thinks to make. Eventually I got a copy just to see for myself what the chatter was about."

"The dubiousness, you mean!"

"Don't be disingenuous, Adawale! This is not about you. Anyway, the only cogent criticism against the book is the one you mentioned at Simonos Petras. The assumption that culture conflicts are evils that can and should be corrected."

He had resumed his seat at her side and sat looking down at the floor as she added gently, "It's the disappointment behind your melancholy. The same engine that drives Boris' heroic efforts to save the world from itself. You both want peace at any price."

"While you're in love with war and suffering?" Adawale had faced controversy and answered criticism of his research for years. But just the hint of criticism coming from *her* was different. It made him feel exposed.

"This is easier for me, she continued. "You were bred to the idea that suffering and death are evils. I was bred to the creativity of Yin and Yang. Both opinions have been around for centuries. I wonder if that makes them any less flimsy. And how would we judge?"

He relented. "Lately my understanding of complicated psychic processes has been deepened. You aside—us aside— this trip to Vienna has been good for my education. But

318

having glimpsed the virtue of inaction, I am more than ever irrelevant to Boris' heroic effort to save the world."

Mai Bao shifted in her seat, squared her handsome jaw, and took his protest head on. "The point of your summons to Vienna was not so arbitrary as you think. I partially know and partially guess that Boris, as a brilliant physicist and manager, is isolated at the top of this pyramid. Yet he has sense enough to distrust himself. Whatever he may have expected, I was not sufficient for the role. He needed someone with intellectual and political authority who also had human qualities that would command respect and inspire others. When he recognized the need—that was my contribution—*you* were his choice. He trusts you as your audience does. You have become a kind of political muse. Of course the situation isn't just political. My few hundred Readers are not a global political force, but do you remember what Pavlos said about the cenobites in their caves praying for the world?"

His satirical eyebrow arched and she reminded him of something he had found absurd at the time. Pavlos said. 'It's enough to know that there are people in the world who love it that much.' As Boris anticipates the task of staffing the ship, choosing the ancestors of eventual colonists, and still more the moment when he must give the order to launch the Galatea—the prospect of such decisions would give a good shake to the confidence of any serious person. All I saw was that he needed someone to confirm that he is doing the right thing. Someone he could trust to retrace his path and arrive at the same place. I learned only by a chance reference that you and he had been friends, then later how much his ideals had been shaped by your friendship at Columbia. Only then did I broach the subject."

"So what does he want from me?"

"I can't answer that, and I'm not sure he could. But he'll get the confirmation he needs. Or he won't, and that will be confirmation too. Either way, you will have made the difference. Otherwise, I have no idea what role he may have in mind for either of us, but his speculative mind never stops at simple ideas. He sees possibilities like a world-class chess player and changes directions as deftly. Occasionally you can see him inventing on the spot. My guess is that the heart of his clandestine plan is to subvert the subversion."

He stared. "An underground beneath the underground?"

"Boris began initiating me to the starship plan as though waiting for me to discover that this wasn't his real game. He's an old intelligence operative, you know. He runs whatever he runs like the Cold War CIA and KGB, creating discrete compartments within the circle of spies to hide the most sensitive work and protect it from ossification in systems. He seals small teams of operatives in their own spaces. Only a few people would have any idea what's happening, and I don't know who they are. But you can be sure they don't know much. Even he will have grasped the whole game only in retrospect."

"There is an ingenious coherence in that at least."

"Only after reporting on the Athos meeting was I told to speak openly to you."

Ope lifts the eyebrow again. "Then Boris knows about us. And if he hadn't approved, we would never have met."

"He knows. But let's go slowly here." She paused as though dipping a toe into dangerous water. "Where trust is great, it's possible for people to be circumspect and transparent at the same time, but it takes imagination as well as trust."

After another of the frequent pauses that helped hold the conversation to a casual pace, she went on. "Boris knew us both and our circumstances before you and I met. He may have foreseen, or hoped at least, that we would fall in love. It is also true that if he had not accepted the situation this afternoon, I would not have found the time to come up here."

"You would have sacrificed your own happiness even in ignorance of what exactly you were sacrificing it for?"

A full minute passed before she replied, but that, for him, was reply enough. Eventually she added a barely audible whisper: "Yes."

Another few moments, then: "All along we have been on the edge of life and death. I don't think my personal happiness counts for much weighed against the survival of the species."

Then she let him decide the direction. "The worst didn't happen, but we both need to know exactly how things stand."

She emptied her glass and held it up. "Shall I open another?" She meant, another of the half dozen she had brought up with her earlier.

She replenished both glasses and gave her story an unexpected turn. More than unexpected. She broke through one of the impenetrable security barriers that set people on new ground. "We're close now to the recruiting stage. We'll be looking for young people who are willing to spend the rest of their lives in space. It's a stunning thought, isn't it, that people may choose to go on a one-way mission without any reasonable hope they will ever get off that ship."

"You actually believe in the conspiracy within Boris' conspiracy!"

"And you don't?"

"What I believe is that I'm helping spread the human stain through the galaxy. In a few billion years, if we're lucky, we will have infested the whole cosmos with Ulro locusts."

She looked earnestly at him, set her glass down on the table before them, and took both his hands in hers as she had on the mountain. "At any rate, my love, it's why you're here: not to implement an impossible syncretism between hostile cultures. You lost that struggle. Now you're to give us another chance."

He passed over her point to continue building the opposite case. "Even now we know practically nothing about this mission or its chances of success. And the recruits will be told very little of what we know now. Especially—if my guess is right—of the cold civil war built into the flight plan! Doesn't that make us con artists exploiting other people's lives on the basis of a fantastic theory?"

"When the world is on the brink, there is no time to count uncountable odds." Mai Bao let that cryptic remark sink in only to discover that in putting the point to him like that, she spread his vertigo to herself.

"At least now you know what you've been doing here, and I've just reported to Boris that you're ready for action. Next comes another set of meetings with people whom neither of us knows. Then you and I are off to the moon, literally, for a tour of the starship."

Ope was thunderstruck. He stared, wide-eyed and open-mouthed, barely attending to her actual words. He erupted, "Oh, No! . . . No, no. No, no, no! You've got the wrong man." Then, as she didn't reply, he stared as though she had gone suddenly mad.

She replied gently. "You know, my dear, Boris was also throwing you a lifeline. He must have recognized that Yetunde's death destroyed your happiness and that your work thereafter had slowly defeated you. Where you found only reason to despair, he threw you into the path of wild contingency. Modesty risks itself on the beyondness of things. As we went blindly to Athos!"

CHAPTER 2

SOMEWHERE IN THE UNDERGROUND maze beneath UNOV, a small group of some twenty people assembled to confer on urgent topics "to be announced." They arrived one by one under unusually stringent security restrictions. The best informed among them might have been able to account for the summons, but since Razumovski alone knew the extent and the ramifications of his far-flung project, all would have been surprised by the people who turned up.

They arrived one by one, presumably to conceal relationships that might have compromised the project. There were surprises for everyone and second glances as they tried irresistibly to connect the dots among "cells" that knew nothing whatever of one another. Mai Bao detected, of all people, Abhay Gupta and Pavlos Demetriopoulos in the room. Opeyemi acknowledged Beverly Georghiu with a nod as she entered. Then he discovered Mamud Çelik and witnessed his astonishment as he saw his future daughter-in-law who was equally astonished to see him.

And yet Adawale could hardly have missed the fact that none of these people were surprised to find him in the company. There were also people from several nation-states whom he had known through the UN. Mai Bao identified a man named Ortiz Rodriquez as manager of an obscure construction project somehow associated with the Office for Space Affairs. The whole scene was a tribute to Razumovski's skill in keeping his people in airtight compartments.

Boris entered last and greeted each person briefly before inviting them to take seats around the large conference table. With a few direct and undramatic words, he opened the assembly that Adawale had ostensibly been summoned so urgently to attend:

"Since there is no one here but us," he said with his usual exuberance, "I'll begin by congratulating you on being part of, conceivably, the most momentous project of the Anthropocene era. Unparalleled even by the Manhattan Project. Each of you has only known a fragment of what we've accomplished together: Together we have been building a generational starship! That ship is now in moon orbit and could be launched within the year."

The stir around the table was not great, but there was surely not a single body that did not stir involuntarily at the almost casual announcement that followed.

"The bad news," he continued, "is that we have a small window of time—a few months at best—before conspiracy theorists set off planetary alarms." And preserving his good humor in the face of such odds, he added, "We can get it done, but we haven't a minute to lose! So we're here to consolidate our knowledge and begin the countdown."

What followed was a description of the one-way exploratory mission deeper into the Milky Way, searching for habitable planets to colonize. Then questions, arguments, reviews of alternatives were considered and rejected, and consequences anticipated. The state of general understanding was such that all this took only the remainder of a single day.

In this group cloistered somewhere under the Danube—who knows where?—there were no amateurs, and all had accepted their assignments on trust, knowing little more than that the stakes could not be higher. Judging by the consternation of his audience, it was another Boris masterstroke to reveal the purpose of their work to them, all at once, then to slow down and spend whatever time might be needed to bring them all into his vision. Those who needed to know had accepted the camouflaged project as a vehicle for scientific research that would exploit the local planets for industrial materials and expel industrial contaminants, both nuclear and other waste, from the atmosphere and the seas.

On day two, they went on to the business of the moment: coordinating the diverse activities of the various teams and combining their talents to prepare for the Ulro escape.

A key question came early: Was Boris certain that there was no less extreme expedient?

He responded, "Colonizing space was an old and not particularly appetizing idea in the last century. Meanwhile declining conditions combined with technological progress in the space sciences added pressure that something be done. However, the security question that made it necessary to atomize the project created a high risk of self-deception."

For the first time, Boris showed physical symptoms of the stress he had been under for several years. Not that his will flagged, but his face seemed almost to wilt from its unflappable joviality into a careworn mask that had known intense anxiety in the solitude of sleepless nights. As he raised his right hand and ran his fingers through the hair at his temple, the hand even trembled before an indomitable will commanding its body into submission.

"I lived with that question day and night for years. And then I had an idea: If I had a single person of intellectual courage and integrity who was politically astute but well outside my own scientific competence, and if this last, just person in Sodom could be innocently exposed, so to speak, to all I knew, he or she might provide a fresh critical response to the situation. I had known such a person years ago in New York. We had been neighbors and spent many long nights debating the state of the world together.

"Later this man established himself in academic circles and beyond as a distinguished political scholar and a wise UN diplomat. So not long ago I arranged for Nigerian-American Professor Opeyemi Adawale to come to Vienna and study the situation in the most innocent and random way possible. He was told nothing about why he was summoned. The deliberate lack of method was intended to let his views take shape with the randomness of ordinary experience."

During those remarks many eyes in the room well-trained not to divulge curiosity or self-interest drifted across Adawale's face as he sat gazing with unfocussed eyes so as not to see.

Razumovski continued. "There's madness as well as genius in that method, so I decided to let him piece together his own view of the situation bit by bit. He has been doing that for weeks in conversations with people of all sorts. I know very little about where he's been or who he's talked with. Even now he has been given no chance to report his views to me, since he had no idea where all this was leading. So now I'm going to ask Professor Opeyemi Adawale from UN New York to report to all of us."

Ope, though startled, stood and spoke from his place in a quietly resolute voice. "There is an adage to the effect that a man on his deathbed can be trusted to speak truth. I don't know how that may be, but the odds should be still better when he's speaking to his neighbors in a ward for plague victims."

A somber chuckle rumbled across the audience as he continued. "I came to Vienna believing that the imploding planetary systems might be saved by a new political consensus or social contract. That was an intellectualist dream. Contract and consensus only spell out consistencies already reached. The proximate cause of our condition is a centuries-old process of shortsightedness, forgetfulness, and decay. That means there have been moments in history when we were less foolish. But I am now convinced that no power present or conceivable can bind up what has been unbound. Global security, if it were possible, would only bind us on a wheel of repetition.

"Once I thought that education was the only rational solution. If we knew the good and had people enough to teach it, we might restore the will to perform the good. This was another rational dream on the scale of dark-age superstition." He seemed to shudder at the memory of his own folly.

"How long would that take, do you think? Change would have to begin in one human heart at a time, under the influence of absolute authority. But no such authority is imaginable and change on such a scale is fantasy. An absolute ruler wouldn't live long enough to make a difference in billions of human hearts. And such a message would dwindle into clichés faster than the words could be spoken.

"So here we are in the underworld, having come to ruin by the waste of our own potential. The spirit of our noble institutions has withered into legalism, and we are the rabbit in the comics who has overrun his cliff. When we look down, we'll fall into the abyss. This briefly is why I believe that the only chance to preserve the species is to colonize space."

He paused and looked down at the table as though loath to let his remarks end there. When he lifted his head, his face conveyed the stony resolve of a Roman general. "Even so, let's not deceive ourselves: Whatever the blemish is, we are sure to export it with the starship. What we can hope is that the time we buy will be used in the pursuit of the wisdom we now lack."

Despite all the centuries of discipline and experience gathered in that room, those words turned the air to stone. Each breath was broken off in a quiet gasp and each body went rigid with resistance. Then, in a single moment, the faces modulated from horror to resignation and conviction.

On that note, Opeyemi ended his testimony and Razumovski, without comment on the instant of high drama, moved on to the practical business at hand:

"Earlier I said that the Galatea is essentially ready for launch now, and that the crew who will fly it are in active training. That confronts us with the human question: How are we to select and recruit a pool of potential colonists whose great-grandchildren may not live to see a colony established?

"I'm asking three people to head groups who will attend to the personnel issues: Professor Dr. Adawale, Dr. Mamud Çelik, and Wu Mai Bao. As the work of these groups will impinge on all our specialties, we must all be ready to share whatever advice they need. Between us and them there are no security walls. To get this underway, I have prepared a distribution of all persons present today into three discussion groups for airing preliminary questions and establishing the lines of communication. Each group will be moderated by one of these persons.

"Adawale's group will deal with the broad question of education on the ship for establishing and preserving indefinitely a politically active culture.

"Çelik's group will focus on long-term psychic health in space and the psychic profile of recruits.

"Wu's group will be responsible for recruitment and security.

"The boundaries between groups are to remain permeable, and each of us may be invited to consult on any of these topics at any time. This is no practice run. Recruitment and training begins as soon as possible. Then the countdown for launch."

With that, the uniform tension in the room broke and individuals who had been isolated for months and lived for years in guarded silence were free to relax into the solemn joy of a shared project. Visibly, security barriers began to dissolve as people got up and began milling. As they sorted themselves into their groups, guarded whispers rose to a chorus of unrestrained voices and eager conversation.

CHAPTER 3

"I AM SENDING YOU TWO to the moon." A few days after the meeting of Boris' inner circle, Wu and Adawale were summoned to the Office for Outer Space Affairs, where the opening remark was accompanied by a boisterous Russian guffaw:

"Call it a honeymoon, or a crash course in life in space. It's all preparation for selecting the personnel for the mission. When you arrive, the project leader will give you a survey of the base first, then you'll be ferried out to the ship, where you'll have an apartment in the actual living quarters for as long as it takes to explore the environment and imagine the shape of everyday life.

"The chief of construction will take you over the ship top to bottom and explain every aspect that will bear on the lives of the civilians on board. Material conditions first. To facilitate construction, many of the social parameters have been anticipated, but you're the ones who must imaginatively flesh it all out. Keep in mind that once the ship is launched, passengers and crew will belong to a single social body, rather like a terrestrial military base surrounded by a civilian town.

"When you return, you and your teams will design initial forms of civilian life in space: how people will choose to spend their time, what social supports they'll need, the psychic consequences of surplus leisure. Most of all how the children will be cared for and educated, since successful colonies, like all political groups, wholly depend on transmitting the heritage of civilized life to future generations." Then Boris looked pensively at the floor and added in one of his rare lapses from joviality, "if there ever is a colony!"

They knew him too well, these two, to mistake that for a tremor of doubt, and the moment was allowed to pass.

"I've said that the various decks, the means for moving people, systems for providing essential goods and services, office spaces, medical care, leisure activities, schools, exercise facilities have been designated in advance, but you're not to take them for granted. Most interior structures are flexible, so don't hesitate to propose alterations where they're needed. Your agenda is the preservation of a good life in perpetuity."

Ope moved to make some response, but Boris raised a hand to stop him. "Not now. There'll be plenty of time to discuss all that."

Finally, their schedule. "After three days in the safe house to recuperate from the trip to Athos, you will be flown directly to Kourou, French Guiana, under the cover of my office. From the Guiana Spaceport you will take the shuttle to the space station and on to Moon Base. After the indeterminate period on the starship, you'll return to the base for debriefing with engineers responsible for the civilian facilities. Then back to Guiana and Vienna."

❖

All happened as Razumovski described. On the flight to the moon station, they got a first glimpse of the Galatea. From a great distance, it might have been a small, cigar-shaped asteroid or, a bit later, a monstrously outsized ocean liner as seen along the line of the horizon. As the distance closed, even Mai Bao's experience at NASA was insufficient preparation for an object of such size, built by human hands in empty space.

A few days passed getting familiar with the moon station that would serve as "Ground Control" for the first years of flight. Then they were dispatched to the ship itself. As the shuttle approached the open docking bay at its stern, the massive machine blocked out the sky. Having experienced varying degrees of weightlessness at the base and on the shuttle, they felt the artificial gravitation system as a return to terrestrial conditions.

The honeymooners were shown to a small apartment on one of the residential decks that would serve as "home" for the duration of their stay. During the late stages of construction, some workers and crew members remained in residence on the ship, but the residential decks themselves remained unfinished, awaiting the results of more detailed planning.

Even after adapting to the living conditions in the moon base, one thing came as a shock and an amusement to Mai Bao and Ope. It was the design of their quarters. The cubicle footprint of the private spaces, called "bio-units" by the engineers, were designed as two equal rectangles. The first included a living room or parlor just large enough for two, with an efficiency kitchen on one side. The second, connected rectangle was called the "bio-kit," as though insisting on the animal-human nexus. This space consisted of two squares. A bedroom nearly fifteen feet wall to wall was divided in half again for a bed, built in on three sides with storage drawers beneath. The remaining portion of the square had a small desk and a dressing table with storage beneath. The wall at the foot of the bed was the reverse side of the media screen in the living room, fully functional on both sides.

The most curious feature of the apartment, however, was the actual "bio-kit," matching the square of the "bed-room" with a pocket door between. On the left inside of the door, the shower was a floor-to-ceiling glass cylinder with sliding sides opening in opposite directions. To use the device one stood on a disk at the center and asked by voice for water that eventually drained away below. Opposite the shower was a sink flanked by a pole that turned for the use of a full-length mirror on one side and, on the other, an electronic control panel above with a cabinet below. Deeper into the room was closet space on one side and opposite, another glass cylinder enclosing a toilet.

Having surveyed their bio-unit, they passed on to the residential deck itself and the larger apartments for families of three or four. In all, every function of life was supported by voice-controlled robotics: food preparation, cleaning, temperature, lighting, and a device that reminded residents what to do next, should there, indeed, be anything left for humans to do. Like the creator-God of old, one had only to command, "Let there be . . ." and instantly worlds materialized across the side of the room courtesy of a screen connected to the ship's universal memory system.

High on Mai Bao and Opeyemi's list of duties was estimating how quickly and how well people would adapt to life on board, and how they would respond to being urged—or drawn—outward into public spaces by the confinement of the private units. The "bio-unit" was a central hub for estimating how people would move and how they would spend their time on board.

Having settled in, the two spent several days touring everything from the bridge to crew's living quarters, from production systems in the bowels of the vessel to an observation deck at the top. Thereafter, the ship was theirs to explore, a process that absorbed two active weeks interspersed with discussions with the designers and construction engineers.

Their work done, the two returned to Kourou with sheaves of photographs and blueprints in hand, whereupon Mai Bao received a message from Razumovski with instructions that, after landing in Vienna, they were to proceed immediately to the safe house in Grinzing.

They arrived in the middle of the night and slept until late the next morning. On waking, the first rush of sensation was the comforting familiarity of home! The commodious proportions of the rooms, the music of silence, the light from the window, and the corporeal sympathy with nature in the vineyard and the Woods above.

They descended the stairs to the breakfast room and kitchen, filled with the joy of being in their own habitat after the sterile environment of a mammoth machine. All was as it should be, but for one thing:

No sooner were they seated than Razumovski entered from the library, where he had been catching up with his daily global briefing. From the spring in his step no one would have guessed that he had the future of humanity in his hands. But then, Boris was of the rare type whose firm faith in the unpredictability of events enabled him to keep his balance in a seriously out-of-balance world.

He began, "I trust the starship meets with your approval."

However glad they were to be home, how could they not be enthusiastic at having had one of the grandest technological wonders in human history at their disposal for weeks? So both expressed once more the astonishment they had shared for many days.

Pressed for time, Boris cut the exchange short. "Today we three are here alone to discuss your relation to the mission in the light of all you have now seen. Building that mammoth ship and recruiting technicians who may fly it has been the hard part, but now comes the impossible part. It's your part, and it comes in three phases.

"Phase One: Inventing the patterns of everyday life for several hundred prospective colonists—or the colonists' ancestors! Though you two bear responsibility for the whole project and answer only to me, during this first phase you will be aided by Mamud Çelik." This came as another surprise, since no immediate associates had been mentioned by name before.

"How you distribute responsibility," he continued, "is your business, but since the team must speak with one voice, Mai Bao will report to me. Unless security gets compromised, this house will be your headquarters, with Officer Georghiu in charge of security. One of her virtues is that she neither snoops nor asks questions. She will be at your disposal full-time and provide your connection with the world beyond your team. She's privy to everything except what you're actually doing. So, with her and with all your aides and advisors, the strict operative rule is 'need-to-know.' The resources of the Office for Outer Space Affairs are at your disposal, and Georghiu is your facilitator. This project, you see, doesn't exist, *and* it's the only game in town."

He scrolled through his communications device before resuming. "In this first phase, we're not playing Moses delivering commandments, but you will be selecting the right people and transplanting a mode of political life to the ship. Those selected must bear that culture already and must have the imagination to adapt quickly and be skilled in passing it on.

"Phase Two: Recruiting may sound easy, but it won't be. And it will entangle you in maze of security risks. Ope, your orientation has been so covert that even the people included in the sequence have not known who you were or even what they were part of. Now recruiting will be even more secretive. If you thought you were inside a spy ring before, I assure you it was nothing to what you're entering now."

Ope raised one eyebrow but said nothing.

"The two of you—but primarily Mai Bao and Mamud— will draw up a profile of the starship populace and proceed with selecting appropriate recruits. Mamud's professional skills will be invaluable in making psychosocial evaluations, and he is the only person beyond us three who may know about this process."

All the while Mai Bao's enthusiasm had been visibly growing. "For all that, we'll need to draw on a broad spectrum of educational specialties, high achievements, and diverse backgrounds for the initial pool. How can that possibly be done in a timely manner or done at all under these restraints?"

Boris held her question in abeyance and gave Ope a chance to get a word in. "Unless you intend to draw the people from ones we actually know—which would be far too narrow—how do we even begin to find candidates under the necessary security rules?"

Boris rubbed his hands together with vigor and Mai Bao smiled at this expression of private delight that often preceded his producing a surprise from his sleeve.

"You're right. That does seem insurmountable, but I have made a start. It's only a partial answer, but some months before you were summoned to Vienna, I began an educational program for young people who might be recruited for the global diplomatic corps. That, at least, was the ostensible purpose."

The other two exchanged grins, knowing very well by now what to expect when Boris started a story this way. He really enjoyed clandestine games in which he could deceive everyone else for worthy causes.

"My first line of contact has been the embassies around the world, but it has expanded beyond that. The effort was received with such enthusiasm that it's no longer just a front for starship recruiting. Most of the target group are youngsters we may want to interest in careers in diplomacy. To that end, a group of our best young professionals are already on board a ship in the Indian Ocean to lead the recruiting effort. With the profiles of the starship population in hand, you two and Çelik are to join that cruise. Who knows? You may even steal some of our recruits! The diplomatic service will be losing some but gaining others."

Mai Bao erupted, "Brilliant! Simply brilliant!" and continued thinking aloud. "Publicity will be the security cover for recruiting a few adventuresome souls who want their lives to make a real difference. Then what comes after the ship? It's a long way to the moon!"

"Oh, that's not difficult," Ope replied, joining Boris' game with an eagerness almost equal to hers. "We bring them to Vienna in small, fairly homogeneous groups and fill in what we haven't already learned about career ambitions, familial connections, romantic interests—whatever might be advantageous or a hindrance. There's also Boris' well-advertised ruse of exploring the other planets for industrial uses. That could be added to the smorgasbord of jobs on offer. This part would even work on the cruise ship. Not just diplomacy in the usual sense, but involvement in the new space venture. The advantage would be to get them used to the idea of space travel, while we observe which ones pick it up quickly. The world is full of young people who, in the absence of authoritative cultural patterns, are waiting for someone else to imagine their lives for them."

Boris grinned and indulged once more the telltale rubbing of his hands together. "While you're reinventing civilization as we once knew it, I'll work my contacts and see how much they can do for us. When your profile of the populous is ready, we'll fictionalize it enough to draw out what we're looking for. I'm betting that there aren't many college students who will turn down a posh cruise on the open seas under the aegis of the UN. Especially when they hear we're looking for a few bright and adventurous people."

He stopped a few seconds and sat gazing up at the brow of the mountain. "Of course, when you solve one problem, you create others and have to cover your tracks. Both kinds of recruiting must be successful, else we raise suspicions. When we get there, even the launch of the starship must be behind the security veil. Otherwise, the political fallout will be terrible. Certainly it would mean my head on a platter, and it might discredit the UN itself."

But that idea didn't delay him long. "Okay, Phase Three has two parts. Abhay Gupta and Pavlos Demetriopoulos will be working with you, Adawale, to draft a system of education and civil governance."

"But a system for whom?" Ope objected. "Won't it take a generation to have a pool of citizens or students sufficient for a system? Unless by 'system' we mean an advance description of how life may be best lived in such unusual circumstances. It would remain open to confirmation and revision by the living itself. Certainly we must anticipate what people will need to know to live a good life in space. That ground must be prepared now."

Boris found something amusing in that. "I think we may depend on life in space insuring a swift expansion of the population. We're counting on it, and we must plan now for a full population and full preparation for citizenship. Never forget—by the time of any landing, everyone on the ship will have been born into your world and be a graduate of your school. We have no choice but start with a vision from the top. And there's another reason for that. On a one-way, generational voyage, learning isn't just about teaching the young. All modes of knowledge and development must be preserved for everyone's participation. Sanity may depend on it!"

To that vision Adawale objected energetically. "Why is that not a continuation of the social engineering that has dramatically failed us here? Are we transplanting human life or a university? At full size, the ship will have no more people than a small town, and they won't all be Nobel laureates!"

"In a general way, you're right, Adawale. But you're not being asked to spin a rational plan out of your consciousness as spiders spin webs. That's the difference between managing present affairs and understanding people as historical creatures. One shows us how to live; the other gives a vision of a consistent world. We're consulting the collective achievements of human experience. You'll see that in the people selected for your circle.

"On your second point, we're not trying to reproduce the specializations of a research university. But we are acknowledging that the humblest performance is measured by the highest ideals. Even teaching a child to boil water is done in the light of comprehensive principles."

However startled Opeyemi may have been by the practical difficulties of the task as described, he saw Boris' point. "I do understand the difference between preservation of past achievements as a baseline for future re-vision and the practical aims for the starship Academy."

Boris pressed ahead with the agenda. "On another topic. Comprehensive records of Ulro life, including complete research libraries, are now being loaded into the ship's memory systems. So 'preservation' may be ignored for now. But as you're reinventing education, you may as well start with all available models and do the job well. For that, Mamud may be invaluable since he has access to a small army of researchers who can help you mine our collective educational experience. All this will inform your discussions of what, ultimately, is to be taught, by whom, and when."

This time Adawale did more than raise an eyebrow. "And all of this in a few weeks less than no time at all! And once these miracles have been performed, how are they to be preserved? Some will not even be relevant for generations."

"Like most of human history!" But instead of answering his arguments promptly, Razumovski stopped to consider as though the topic had just taken some delicate turn and the essential point was still to come. When he continued, it was in a quiet different tone of voice. More subdued. More pensive. Almost in soliloquy.

"I know we're playing god here, but it's what happens when people abandon—or are abandoned by—their gods. We kill the gods, but sometimes we don't learn what difference it has made until centuries later, in retrospect. When we've destroyed our habitat and sold our birthright, the god-position doesn't go away. It gets usurped by substitute gods."

He stopped as though to make a fresh start, rubbed his hands together as though what came next mattered most. "Now here's the thing that dwarfs all the rest. You've been feeling it in the room, but no one has mentioned it. You know the *secret plan* is to escape Ulro, to live in space, and eventually to establish human life elsewhere, but then comes the *top-secret plan*! It's a brazen subversion of the culture of hyper-technology on the ship itself!"

He let that sink in a bit before clarifying. "After your weeks in Vienna, your time on Mount Athos, and your stay on the starship, you know that managerial culture worships its own rationality, and that that is both antithetical to our aspirations *and* essential to saving humanity. The people who run that ship will be trained to do things but not to see what makes things worth doing."

Mai Bao had long suspected that Boris was inviting her to guess at some plan beyond anything he had hinted at, and here it was at last!

She was flummoxed by the scope of his imagination and his daring, but she said nothing. Only stared at him with incredulity, watching him watching her.

"So, Adawale, here's the second part of your educational plan. With the help of Gupta and Pavlos you are to invent a small council of civilians with the authority to preserve our vision even when the orientation of the ship overruns its practical ends as, sooner or later, practical aims always are overrun."

Then back to Mai Bao, but refusing to acknowledge the astonishment written across her face: "Somehow your group must manage to recruit a few people capable of serving on Adawale's council. They must have character that will command respect among the people and the strength to resist

Starship Command, should it—or rather *when it*—becomes necessary. The crew will be under orders from Ground Control not to tamper with the independence of whatever civilian authority we establish, and vice versa.

"Never mind the inevitable rivalry of the two groups. That's just what we want. Survival will depend on technicians, their machines, and their discipline, but the aims of the mission will depend on civilian political understanding of the life good in and for itself. During the flight, while the destiny of the ship is the destiny of all, no one will let these differences threaten survival, but keep your eye on the principal relation. In fact the relation between the technocrats and the council will evolve over the years in unforeseeable ways."

Finding himself on familiar turf, Ope picked up the theme. "If there ever is a self-sustaining colony, the starship will have to move on. What else is such a machine good for?"

"Can't a starship be beaten into a pruning hook?" Mai Bao offered.

Ope chuckled. "Still, two grave dangers remain: First, any efficient command structure will conscientiously reproduce its own authoritarianism in the colonial governance. And second, where technology has replaced necessity, the habits of political culture may gradually be forgotten."

Razumovski grinned. "So all you have to do is to arrange for your political culture to survive in an unfavorable environment among unforeseeable people for a thousand years. At the end, if there is such a thing, they must have the will to win, if necessary, over technological dominance, whatever the price.

"Now when all that's done, you five should probably visit the ship together to test your ideas with your hands on the controls so to speak."

With that, and without pausing for other remarks, he picked up his phone and said, "Bring them in!"

He got up went to the front door as Officer Georghiu entered with three others in tow: Mamud Çelik from the university, Pavlos Demetriopoulos from Macedonia, and Abhay Gupta from Delhi.

CHAPTER 4

WHAT ACTUALLY HAPPENED between this point and the launch of Starship Galatea is less important than the two people at the center. The Grinzing safe house became ground zero for all aspects of the "Grinzing Project," except those Boris reserved to himself. Though Mai Bao and Opeyemi were the only persons in residence, Mamud, Gupta, and Pavlos came and went at all hours, always accompanied by the faithful Georghiu whose personal access, however, was limited to the first floor.

Only these five were admitted to the basement planning center where countless photographs, blueprints, and other documents revealing every dimension of the project were plastered in every available space. This inner circle may not have been armed with a clear ideal of the good polity or a distinct portrait of the citizen of the future, but it may be possible to detect from a distance just such a polity being enacted among them.

One achievement illustrates how things went. The fulcrum of Mai Bao's contradictory task of inventing modes of life in space and Ope's inventing an academy proved to be the governing Council that was to function as civil authority for the duration of a flight that might never end. (And yet, through the lens of Ishmael Kahn's accounts of life two and a half centuries later on the starship, it is possible to see that this innovation was the greatest achievement of the Grinzing Project.)

The Council was to bridge, if not resolve, the deep-state inconsistency between the technological ideal of control, order, and security and the political ideal of collective life perpetually reinventing and renewing itself. The key factor—as Boris had foretold—was education, for all who were born on the ship would be educated and live in the ethos of the Council. So while a substantial number of people would perform essential technological functions, all were to be grounded in the same ideals of life.

Though in the first generation the scale of collective life would be miniature, the responsibilities of the Council would inevitably expand with the population to include whatever legislative and judicial functions might be needed. But the key function after education would be to monitor the partition of the ship's command system and the civil systems, especially on Alexandros so that neither was compromised by the other.

As the role of this hypothetical Council expanded in the minds of the planners, it was quickly dubbed "The Council of Elders" after a remark Adawale made one morning to Pavlos and Gupta on the topic of suitable people for the council:

"I have an image of Diogenes the cynic wandering around Athens in the daylight, looking for a just man! Now all we have to do is select five or, say, seven wise rulers from a pool of adolescents whom we've never met!" Subsequently the remark led to reconsidering the age restriction on recruits.

And so while intense planning for the conservation of the species went on below stairs, in off hours the art of living-well flourished upstairs between the two lovers, not least because imagining ways of life is much like what they were performing together: theory and practice reunited.

Ope's first glimpse of Mai Bao's apartment revealed new dimensions of her character. The rooms were at once commodious and spare. Nothing too precious for serious living. No depending on stuffing to suggest substance where substance is lacking. No pretentious furnishings that line walls like mute servants waiting for orders that never come. Order, but the order of use. Witness the book lying open and unfinished on a table, or the flowerpot on the window seat wilting for water, or the chair that could be pulled closer to the window for light. These rooms invited one to resume the book or stretch the mind in conversation or just gaze contemplatively at vineyard and bluff.

Yet the room had to expand for two stacks of books where there had been one, two chairs by the window, twice as many clothes, and more open space for the exponential growth in ideas between two in dialogue with the cosmos.

One night in that increasingly hospitable parlor as Mai Bao and Ope turned the problem of social stability on the ship over and over, looking for a way to divide authority and guarantee stability, he suddenly asked, "If we want the wisest people as governors and the most knowledgeable to run the schools, why not recruit people who can do both and put the

Academy under the supervision of the Council? They will be needed as teachers in any event."

Mai Bao hesitated. "But, as you have said, we're limited to the young and biologically fit. I don't see how we're to find governors at all. Besides, 'recruit' is a military term for reproducing something like infantry *soldiers.*"

"Meaning we can produce and recruit technicians, even a ship's commander, but not wisdom."

"Where do we get *recruits* who can inspire the arts and sciences in the quickly expanding population that Boris imagines?"

She leapt ahead. "If not wisdom, then what's to prevent abuses and eventual paranoia? What's to even protect against a corrupt commander? Though some of this will be the responsibility of Mission Control for a while."

"With what means of enforcement across such distances?"

"The authority of cultural habits will serve."

Ope was genuinely alarmed by the problem of political threats internal to the mission. "It works two ways. The commander must be insulated from pressure from both crew and civilians, and the same goes for the Council. I mentioned the possibility of a malevolent commander to Boris and he offered an expedient that seems to be our only hope in such cases."

"What's his solution?"

"If a commander becomes corrupt or incompetent—even senility is possible on a generational ship—then the crew must be able to act legally rather than mutiny. Mutiny in space would be suicidal for everyone. In this single case, he says, the crew should be able to appeal to the intervention of the Council as a voice of communal sanction. In the event of confrontation, even violence between crew and commander, it wouldn't be nice but neither would it be anarchic."

Mai Bao added, "Every aspect of life will inevitably grow more complex: the schools larger, more grounds for disagreement and conflict over physical spaces as the population expands, greater need for teachers, and on and on. If we have the right Council members to begin with—if we can work that miracle—they would provide checks on each other and be free to expand the Council as new responsibilities require."

These examples of how the work proceeded tell little about the personal situation between the Nigerian Oyo prince and his Chinese handler, unless, taken all together, that's exactly what they do tell: love thriving on indirection, distance, postponement. Daily life was tuned less by the idea of being in love than by absorption in the shared project, punctuated by the chance touch of a hand in passing, the secret intimacy of feeling the other in the next room, or the unexpected joy of sharing an idea. Taken all together and viewed in retrospect, this love, when declared on the mountain, was already tougher in substance and higher in intensity than the grasping love of objects.

Two weeks after the discussion with Boris, they were on the cruise ship somewhere in the Indian Ocean, facing the formidable task of getting to know so many people well enough to match criteria and make selections.

It would be curious to know how several hundred-young people responded when asked to imagine their lives either in the diplomatic corps of a failing planet or as part of an international fleet of industrial starships, not knowing, of course, that they were really being vetted for a one-way voyage in an incubator or a coffin. And yet that scheme must have hovered like shadow or halo over the luxurious cruise. In any case, those who matched the unpublished criteria were taken up by the inner circle and observed as closely and quietly as could be arranged.

It's a curiosity, to say the least, that a full year after Athos, during all the time spent imagining the details of life in space, Wu and Adawale had never seriously considered joining the mission themselves. The leisure they had for one another was so scarce that their private time was rarely devoted to considering their own future. However that may be, sooner or later the possibility would have to be faced, and when that moment came, it would come in the most extraordinary of ways, because that's how Razumovski operated.

It is a likely possibility that early one morning somewhere in the middle of the ocean on the recruiting ship, Boris met the two of them by appointment, ostensibly to discuss interim recommendations of the Grinzing circle. Alone together on an upper deck with a panoramic view of the sea, some time passed working back through the plan. When that was done, he pushed the papers aside, got up, and paced in front of the great windows several times as though to stretch his legs. Seen in that environment as though for the first time, he remained the animated Russian with the straight nose and the Tatar cheekbones. However energetic and commanding, neither his posture nor his mood expressed satisfaction with a difficult job well done. The sense was of some more urgent problem hanging in the air.

When the pacing stopped, he planted himself just in front of them with his back to the windows. The man who had appeared unruffled by the prospect of the world coming to an end was stymied by something greater. "Well done," he said with finality, "and yet . . ." He fidgeted uneasily for a moment before continuing. "The most important issue is still to be resolved."

"There are so many. Which issue do you mean?" Opeyemi asked, puzzled.

"I'm been trying to see how the wealth of experience that has gone into all this work is to be transferred without loss to the denizens of the starship. A static plan, however rational and thorough, is one thing. Executive experience is another."

He rubbed his hands together as though molding a new idea from base clay, but no laugh accompanied the gesture this time. A long solemn gaze rested on each of them in turn, then he spoke cautiously, even sadly. "Beyond the engineers, you two deserve most credit for organizing this project. Meanwhile, we can be happy that it has given you each other."

He stopped, resumed his seat, and sat fidgeting aimlessly with his fingers on the arms of his chair. It was such a long un-Boris moment that the two, who probably knew him better than anyone else in the world, wondered if he might be seriously ill or if he had bad news.

He didn't drag the suspense out. "I want you two to consider joining the mission."

They were stunned. Twice stunned. Stunned once by the scope of the proposal. Stunned again as the idea struck each simultaneously as exactly the right thing to do. Quietly, between heartbeats, the herald of a new life in a new zone of existence. The idea even provoked hesitation about turning over what now appeared to be the achievement of their lives to the inexperienced young.

Boris continued, "Mamud has convinced us that the ship should be populated from the beginning with people of all ages and conditions. Healthy development needs flesh and blood reference points to show the young what lies ahead for better and for worse."

Mai Bao responded with amusement. "How Confucian! Practical acts are performed in relation to the ancestral past and prepare the way for posterity. The function of the ideal is as real as . . . "

"Exactly!" He broke in. "And you two would provide the moorings for the Council of Elders. It would give the recruits time to grow into a new culture that is your native habitat. You have the authority and the instincts. The character and the collective bond toward a single purpose." He grinned as coyly as the forthright Russian face allowed and passed over the matter of age as just a detail. "If you plan it well, you might even be the parents of the first human born in space and of the first child to pass through your school system. We're already planning for well-matched couples who will provide the second generation. Fortunately, we don't have to recruit fertile breeders. We can leave that work to the glands."

He didn't ask for a response, probably because he saw what he needed to know in the glance that passed between Mai Bao and Ope. The proposal was left hanging in the air unresolved as they passed to another, no-less-surprising topic.

"I have another proposal. Unless you counter with substantial objections, I propose to ask Abhay Gupta and," looking at Mai Bao, "your Miranda Ribeiro to join the mission. If they can pass the physical screening, of course. Then the Council would actually have some elders who are old and wise! That's not trivial. They would have authority with civilians and crew while offering counterforces to each other."

Astonishment on the heels of astonishment. Once again Ope and Mai Bao were speechless as Boris filled the gap somewhat defensively. "Gupta is old. We've discussed the advantages of that. You've worked closely with him for months, as you would on the Council. The same might be said for Miranda, but she would balance the abstraction of the philosopher with the concreteness of the writer. You know what a hardheaded realist she is, in the best sense of the word. And you'd have an authoritative woman of years to match Gupta. Both would be models who'd meet the mark and show the way."

By this time Ope had recovered enough to reply, "Well, it's a forceful argument. No one equals to these two unless you could get Pavlos Demetriopoulos to hang up his monk's habit." He chuckled. "I suppose the Athonites are already too close to heaven to risk one of their own on such a venture. Besides, there won't be any virgins to venerate. Or not for long."

A mischievous expression spread over Boris' face. It hinted of pleasure, even relief that all his plans had been so readily accepted. "Since you mention it: You may not know that Pavlos is leaving the monastery."

He took a moment to reflect on something that bewildered him before continuing. "Philosophers do things for the strangest reasons! Then when they try to explain themselves, they only make it more obscure. In a recent brief exchange about how the plans were developing, he said the queerest thing.

"'As much as I love Athos,' he said, 'I've come to see the Orthodox position on the Trinity as leading to a monarchial political theology. That's exactly what your celestial sardine tin will be—a parody of the supreme theological One. The power of the machine will dominate the imagination and turn people into calculators. Just like on Ulro,' he said. 'Then the mission will be defeated by its success, as Christianity has been defeated by the Church's ambition to manage the City of Man. That must not be allowed to happen.'"

Boris continued in amazement. "What a peculiar way of grasping our most secret fear! Then he offered his services on the mission if I could find a place for him. So, I'm consulting you."

Mai Bao replied promptly as though she detected nothing at all strange in the idea. "There are also peripheral advantages. With those three anchoring the Council, much that we're trying to fix for the future could be left to develop along the way. And, while the Academy gradually takes shape in their real world, they would give the Council immediate authority."

Then an idea struck her that she found amusing. She gave Boris a brief account of Gupta's Adam myth. "It's almost as though the gods had amended the story of expulsion from the garden, providing three guides to lead the way into a new world. I can't think of three wiser people or three with such different experiences to help invent new modes of life."

Ope continued her line of thought. "On the Galatea it will take all the wisdom available to reimagine everyday life. Where there are no present goals to strive for, people will have to be shown how to find purpose in the day. Otherwise, they will go slowly mad or become catatonic. They will need real—not false—aspirations.

"And in the absence of economic and social competition and of hedonist culture, it will take years to develop alternative habits like intellectual, artistic, and scientific interests. Meanwhile more casual pursuits will be needed. Boredom may be one of the temptations that reveals our humanity, as Gupta argues, but someone has to put that idea in words and exemplify alternatives."

"And all that," Mai Bao picked up the idea, "will put the Council and the Academy at the center of daily life. That's a good thing, and those three will miss no opportunity to encourage education as the highway to new and more satisfying lives."

Ope then had a question for Boris. "About Pavlos: You're already embedding a surreptitious rival to the military-technological discipline of the mission. I wonder if the inclusion of an ex-monk and a highly articulate theological voice might be a third and disruptive component. If the religious impulse should catch on in the populace, as it often has when people are needy, is it possible Pavlos' influence might weaken the Council's political purpose?"

"Absolutely not!" Mai Bao took the point up with passion. "If anything is in short supply in small communities, it's diversity of ideals. Where there are too few ideals, the future strangles on repetition and political life withers. I know the history of the species is preserved in the memory systems, but that's all static information and artifacts. The explorers will need exemplary figures with imagination whatever the content of their fictions. And since there won't be many, the examples should be as diverse as possible. Pavlos understands that, and he's not hidebound. On the mountain he showed independent judgment in bending the rules by concealing a woman in the monastery. That's just the kind of vision a farsighted Council needs."

Adawale studied her point for a moment before replying, "Let me flip the question over. The Greeks aside, we all know from experience that education is often a sufficient sanction to encourage people to do what they know is best. A little religious appeal might not be a bad thing in the mix we're considering."

Boris listened closely to this discussion. He may have grown up Russian Orthodox, but he was really a child of science who supported the argument for diversity on the grounds of a literal-minded materialism. Opeyemi having reversed himself and conceded Mai Bao's point, it was agreed that Pavlos, Gupta, and Ribeiro would all be checks on the others, catalysts of imagination, and effective mentors.

So much having been decided, Boris got up from his chair. "Now that we have some real elders, is our five-member Council in place?" And waving the rhetorical question aside with a chuckle, he walked away down the observation deck before either could answer.

At the next convenient port, he left the ship and rejoined it farther along, bringing Ribeiro, Pavlos, and Gupta with him so they "could be visible in the recruiting process."

At the end of the cruise, the students were duly classified into three groups: those for whom none of the opportunities were appropriate, those who would be passed on to UN recruiters for diplomatic service, and those whom Mamud would meet in Vienna for further evaluation.

There is one other curious and rather romantic detail that turned up centuries later in researching this story: Beverly Georghiu and Kemal Çelik appear in the cruise ship log as recruiters and among the ones ultimately selected for the mission itself.

CHAPTER 5

WHAT OCCURRED thereafter remains a mystery. We know positively from the ship's logs that Wu Mai Bao and Opeyemi Adawale were *not* on board at launch. Whatever intervened to alter Boris' expectation must have come on quietly since it made no detectable stir among the inner circle who would have taken it for granted that they would all spend the rest of their lives together in space.

So much for what we don't know, but what *may* have happened is too instructive to pass over just because the historical record is thin. So once more, imagination to the rescue of possibility.

Thanks to the decisions of Abhay Gupta, Pavlos Demetriopoulos, and Miranda Ribeiro, many things that were to have been decided before the launch were now deferred. Perhaps that bit of good fortune gave Mai Bao and Opeyemi leisure to attend to a nameless apprehension that had gradually claimed them. If the event had been observed, it might have appeared in something like the following manner:

The combined sensations of new love and exhaustion from the labors of the day guaranteed that falling into bed each night was a sweet experience for both. And yet in the small hours of one morning Mai Bao roused with an uneasy feeling, as though she—or they—had missed something essential. She could point to nothing amiss, but when the anxiety grew, she mentioned it, and for several nights thereafter, as the two lay together in the dark, beating about a bush that neither could see, the idea began to take shape that the whole enterprise was somehow flawed.

Eventually Opeyemi gathered their apprehensions into a question: "What if Boris has got it all wrong? Not wrong about Ulro, but wrong about the solution. Maybe we're taking a short-sighted practical view of conditions that can't be 'managed.'"

His intuition gathered steam as he spoke. "It may be counter-productive to resist evil—as though it were an objective thing—by transplanting it elsewhere. Better sometimes to push destructive forces ahead to their point of exhaustion."

"Then you're having doubts?" Mai Bao asked, astonished.

"Something has been nagging at me since Athos. Not the means but the end. Yet here we are, like social engineers, constructing a mission as if we could penetrate the mystery of iniquity, read our destiny, and match people with a solution. When a machine doesn't work, we consult the technical manuals—which, by the way, don't agree!—and begin making adjustments. Fix broken humanity by situating it differently. Isn't that the paradigm that has brought us all to grief?"

Mai Bao studied the question until Opeyemi decided she was asleep. Just as he lay back and closed his eyes, she sat up and replied, "On your account, the disease is us, and Boris' efforts amount to putting it in hibernation and spreading it through the cosmos."

Under the force of her new insight, he plumped up his pillow in preparation for examining an idea half repressed until that moment. In the same instant she lay down again.

"I don't go quite that far," he protested, "but I begin to think the greatest technical project in history may accomplish nothing. Boris knows the risk, but what he cannot know—because to know would require scuttling the whole idea—is that gambling on a utopian fantasy just substitutes one anthropology, one picture of the human, for another. If the projection of an ideal 'end' were to succeed, it would leave us just where we are, with nowhere to go. As Gupta would say, 'We, who don't believe in God, have appointed ourselves to His office!'"

Mai Bao stared into the dark in his direction. "Is that what you think?"

When he didn't answer, she added, "If you think *that* at this late date, what will you do? You were brought to Vienna as Boris' conscience, to judge his idea. You've never been asked to say yes or no, but in effect you've endorsed the scheme. So what will you do?"

"Nothing. I don't *know* he's wrong. Where all is contingent, it may turn out well. The Ulro crisis and the starship project may be a new permutation as important as the Neolithic Revolution. At least Boris has done something where others have done nothing. It's just that in all our busyness, I don't see a real idea. The same mindset that ruined one planet can go on to ruin others. That's not a solution."

"Yet you allow Boris to assume your approval. Even that you'll be on the ship, at the center of the Council and the Academy. Ready to help make the experimental polity work!"

"More like a caretaker of a flying museum. We're not inventing. We're mechanics, and the mill keeps turning."

He stopped for a moment and shifted gears. "You know, I'm not saying I won't go. If we go together, why not go? At least we'll be acting. I've spent my life going in circles like the rat in a maze. I just don't see much difference between going and staying put."

There was a long pause as if Mai Bao was looking for a pertinent reply. Finally, she said, "We can't know what will happen either way! All we *know* is that conditions will change. As Miranda likes to say, quoting somebody—she's always quoting somebody!—'the readiness is all!'"

This discussion or something like it would have gone on night after night until the fog began to lift, for these two didn't miss the bus by accident, and their names, as I've said, aren't in the records.

It must have been Mai Bao who eventually moved them toward a decision after Opeyemi's conjecture that they might as well go as not. "Let's say the planet is doomed, since we think it is. That shifts the issue from aims in view to ways of living and dying. Everybody's always dying, in any case, so either we spend the rest of our lives keeping faith with Boris' intention, searching for a suitable planet, or we stay here and keep faith with terrestrial contingencies by bearing witness to the past and an obscure future. We aren't likely to see an outcome, but it clarifies one thing: Where the future is blind, living *well* must be something other than living *toward* a specific condition."

Opeyemi connected those dots quickly. "True. Practicality is the most impractical of things. It has no way of justifying itself."

He thought for a moment. "You're saying that in either case we should sit still and wait, until a course of action turns up."

"Not *should* wait." She avoided the moral implication. "We *might* wait. Without trying to force events or ourselves into some blindly desirable channel."

"Waiting is the hard part."

"It's your idea. Since Boris is inventing nothing, we may as well stay here and nurture our own powers. That's not doing nothing!"

"It would differ from the adventurers in space. At least we would have to stay alert, while they . . . they'll be going essentially nowhere, burdened with passing whatever time remains to them. Sloth is a danger we can only underestimate."

Mai Bao broke the tension with a somber laugh. "Pavlos, Gupta, and I, with the occasional help of Boris, have been studying the burden of unrelieved boredom on the ship. One afternoon not long ago—I think you must have been in town—the question took a new turn: What might prevent their degenerating into passivity or hedonism or simply going mad?"

Opeyemi remained skeptical of Pavlos' religious language, but he trusted Gupta and wanted to know what he had said on the subject.

"He said the boredom of the mission might not be a bad thing, that it might clarify something essential about us that has been either passed over in modern life or treated as a medical condition. On the ship the unreality of past and future will be inescapable. People will live in the sensation of the moment on the dimensionless razor edge of presence, *or* they will learn to invent new—or perhaps very old!—modes of living in eternity."

The idea frustrated Opeyemi. "Gupta may imagine there's something positive in that, but all I hear is a recipe for madness."

"Not at all. Imagine us living together in this house, absorbed in exploring the universe together. Remember the armchair traveler almost always sees more than the tourist. Unlike the people on our starship who will never get anywhere at all—I mean in their own lives—we can go to the stars without leaving home, grateful for every day as it arrives. As for the surrounding world, that's the easy part: cut our investment in what we have no faith in anyway. Keep our eyes on the ideal and treat banality as distraction or as so many bad examples."

He chuckled and yawned. "By going to sleep, you mean?"

"No. By waking up!"

She stopped and sat gazing toward the window as if searching for more light than another grey dawn was likely to bring. "It's true, we'll no longer be cogs in a machine of our own making. People may think idleness is a ghostly state between life and death, but contemplation isn't passive. It's more active than action. Sometimes contemplatives don't sleep because they're too inspired by the ideas that keep them company."

Opeyemi, patiently waiting for light that didn't come, revolved the idea of their living a cloistered existence, holding the real up between them, weighing its worth. That, he thought, might be paradise enough. Then he saw: like Athos! If that passivity constituted citizenship in a destitute world, then they might be good citizens either here or in Boris' great incubator in the sky.

After all the secret bustle of the launch had subsided, attention at the house in Grinzing must have concentrated on how best to live in a world that was going the way of all empires. Or put their question this way: Is it possible for beings to live as included but not belonging? The question is not about being physically present. It's about in-habiting as though one didn't. Not turning one's back on the only world there is, and certainly not mistaking it as the standard of the good, dimming oneself down in anxiety and impotence. Is it possible to live in a world as though not living in it?

This was the challenge Mai Bao and Opeyemi woke to one tranquil morning soon after the time of their life was restored to them. They lingered a while in bed, enjoying the fragrance of vineyard and earth, attending to stillness punctuated by the croak of an occasional boat on the distant Danube, not thinking about a world they were powerless to mend.

It was one of several ritual moments in the day when they reflected on the path they had travelled and the path that lay ahead. Everything encouraged deliberation, even the cottage. The very walls and furnishings stood in living witness to the singular events that had occurred there and to what hadn't occurred just yet.

Soon enough, according to the order of the day, the two performed their morning ablutions and went downstairs dressed for breakfast.

Over coffee at the table by the window, Mai Bao asked, "So what shall we do today?"

Opeyemi, startled, as though the question were unique, gazed at the limestone bluff above. "Suppose we climb the hill and hike in the Vienna Woods."

Surprised by the improvisation, she grinned, "It would be fun, wouldn't it? In remembrance of Athos!"

"We can take a picnic."

And so a bit later, shod in the hiking boots from Thessaloniki, they set out hand-in-hand northeast across the vineyards and into the forest beyond. The eastern end of the great European massif was nothing like the wrinkled, rocky landscapes of Greece that made muscles and joints burn with the climb. As they passed easily over the carpeted floor of old stands of oak and beech, the incline was often steep but rarely enough to require a helping hand. They walked joyfully in the long shadow of their pursuit of a distant sunrise over the Aegean.

As they reached one of the bald terraces at the top of the hill, they encountered another historic hermitage, this one associated with the twelfth-century Augustinian monastery of Klosterneuburg below the north slope. Deciding to make a day of the hike, they passed Kahlenberg by and found a resting place in the woods near Leopoldsberg where the perspectives opened out in all directions.

Accustomed by now to contemplating wide expanses of time and space, they studied the panorama before them, relating it to the vista from Athos, comparing the present with the past, history with myth, finitude with infinition. Though the Aegean pilgrimage had occurred months earlier, it remained—and might forever after remain—as vivid as yesterday and, in some indefinite sense, functioned as compass.

They spread out their lunch with their thoughts open to the unavoidable topic that would make this day equally memorable. It is a well-known fact that language, if it says anything, says more than it's meant to say, as Mai Bao's question over breakfast had asked more than she meant to ask. Its renewal at lunchtime took a new form: "What shall we do with ourselves in whatever time we're given?"

Both their lives had been ordered by global politics and outer space affairs, but having declined to trade the pandemic of Ulro for a trip to the stars, they now confronted a dilemma that is mostly avoided: "How shall we live and what shall we live for?"

The idea would have seemed preposterous to people who, taking themselves as a starting point, lived randomly, one moment to the next, each pleasure or pain displacing the one before. Instead, these two preferred to shape themselves in shaping their life rather than fritter away the opportunities of the day.

Some obligations were already in place. Boris, for reasons unknown, wanted the Grinzing planning and communication center to remain open for business, at least so long as the Galatea could communicate profitably in "real time." So the Grinzing house was to remain in the information loop with the ship, probably to help Boris feel secure and in control. It *was* about security and control, wasn't it? Knowing that the two of them were like members *in absentia* of the ship's civilian Council.

On her own, Mai Bao was disposed to remain in contact with The Readers, less to rehearse the planetary ills than to offer anecdotes of the human spirit rising to the challenge in history's darkest times. Whereas Opeyemi, having suspended his diplomatic appointment months before, resolved not to detach himself entirely from the UN post, but to accept ad hoc assignments where and when, in his judgment, his presence might matter. The world was still with them and not to be avoided.

When lunch was finished on the green knoll at the top of Kahlenberg mountain, Mai Bao emptied her wine glass and, instead of packing up to move on, sank back into the grass, resting on an elbow as she studied Ope's face with a curiously earnest gaze. She considered him from a distance as one at a turning point between two lives, trying once again as they both sometimes did—and inevitably failed—to take the other whole like a natural object with determinate boundaries.

Falling in love was part of their transformation, not as being overwhelmed by passion but as two people differently configured, coinciding on a point of supreme importance and being altered by the event. Like two star clusters, drawn by gravity toward one another, until eventually they form a larger galaxy or, as also happens, pass through and beyond without joining. Such was the path of their love.

Presently she roused from this deep study. "You know, from the sound of your voice and the expression of your face, one might think you had just been released from prison. In the restaurant in Ünterstadt where I first saw you, you were a contradiction. Handsome, dignified, reserved, but, around the eyes and mouth, the marks of care and discipline held together by heroic resolve."

He tossed it all off. "And what I saw across the room was a woman so beautiful, she terrified me."

"Terrified you, did she! Well, that's not very complimentary."

He chuckled. "Anticipatory disappointment is closer. A silly conviction that no one could be that attractive on the outside without being less on the inside."

"But" she corrected him, "we're discussing you. How do you imagine spending time?"

Having no ready answer, he invented as he spoke. "I would especially like to read more deeply in the classics that have shaped the civilizations. The epics, myths, folktales. Especially the sacred books."

The spontaneity of the idea was obvious, and she watched its development without comment.

"It's all your fault, you know. You've spoiled me with your yarns. Before you, I knew all kinds of important things. Then I started listening to old myths and reading old books, watching films, learning from the inside how people have lived and what they have lived for. I can see that empirical observation doesn't get us far, because it works backward as though forms were natural things requiring nothing from us. That's where the story is. Now I need to understand how we come to care enough to ask questions."

She accepted it with a smile. "To what end?"

"To no end. Just that I begin to see how blind we are to the predispositions embedded in history and language. These things choose us before we choose them. Rousseau said that if you want to think, you must start by putting the facts aside."

Mai Bao repacked their basket and handed it to him. "Well then," she said as they began the descent, "homeward bound. We have a life to begin."

Rather than backtrack, they chose an unfamiliar path toward the river and around the base of the hill toward the cottage. Somewhere along the way, she returned to the perpetual reciprocity of forming and being-formed. Not bringing a law down the mountain for regulating the future but refining the earlier question of living-how and for-what. The same question she had been endlessly contemplating for the space wanderers, and the gist of her idea was that by living the day "deliberately," the form would unfold on its own. Exactly the opposite of her assignment for the mission.

Back home, they caught up on the planetary "news:" Two new environmental disasters, one off the coast of Kamchatka and one in Antarctica. Famine spreading across Africa and India; violence against the migratory multitudes and politicians who supported them; a virus passed from bats to humans, promising a new global pandemic. The world unchanged.

For Adawale it was another temptation into pre-Athos despair. "All is lost," he said. "If philosophers can't suffer tooth-ache patiently, how do we to live with gratitude in such a world?"

"All is not lost so long as contingency reigns and we remain faithful."

"Yetunde used to say to me, 'You're an ethicist trying to correct the world,' she would say. 'But ethicists live in despair.'

Boris and I both wanted to 'fix things,' to bend reality to the shape of desire instead of accommodating desire to the real as in the religions of old. My disease was feeling responsible for the success or failure of the world. As though if I took a nap, the world might collapse."

"And now?"

"When we're too far gone to save, it's madness to think we can stop it. So I must learn that, without turning my back on things, I can respond where it can make a difference. Otherwise, I must trade the burden of the *old task* for the joy of *no task*. It feels like weightlessness. Instead of living in a deficit, all time seems to be gathered into the moment in our safe house."

But that night Ope lay awake gnawing on an earlier objection. Mai Bao had a new habit of suddenly speaking into the dark. "I can hear the wheels turning. What are you thinking?"

"I'm still thinking that we've just renounced Boris' millenarian scheme of a new habitat and are now doing the same thing by planning how we will live. Isn't that a projection of how things *should be*? How do you conjure with the *might be* rather than the *should*? Possibilities rather than moralism?"

Mai Bao, seeing the cogency of his point, replied slowly. "Maybe the fixed schedule and the projected goal create the problem, whether we legislate it for ourselves or someone legislates for us. But aren't we just recognizing that the contemplative life must have *some* form? Without form there's nothing, but the forming isn't toward a fixed goal. When living and forming are indistinguishable, we live without means and ends."

He chuckled. "I see this is going to be a Chinese dictatorship but then I do approve of real cultural revolutions. At least there's a certain rhythm to them. But what about coherence?"

"Even a ramble through a new city has coherence—when viewed in retrospect." She held up a finger. "Just a minute." She got up and retrieved a book from the shelf under the window.

"I want you to read aloud a few lines of a poem. Pavlos mentioned them to me. He refused to quote them because 'Hearing them won't be enough,' he said. 'You must look them up for yourself.'"

Opeyemi took the book and here is what he read:

> I said to my soul, be still, and wait without hope,
> For hope would be hope for the wrong thing; wait
> without love,
> For love would be love of the wrong thing; there
> is yet faith.
> But the faith, and the love, and the hope are all in
> the waiting.
> Wait without thought, for you are not ready for
> thought:
> So the darkness shall be the light, and the stillness
> the dancing.
> T. S. Eliot, *East Coker*